# SOULLESS

C. K. HART

Content Warning

This book includes:

Abuse of minors and women

Sex

Violence

Death

Foul language

# CONTENTS

For fearless, cussing women with scratches on their knees and grass stains on their dresses.

# Middle World

Canaan

Palen

Navar

Philistine

N
E
S

# PROLOGUE

Jez sat in the kitchen every morning with a cup of coffee in her hand. Her legs were always crossed on the stool that sat near the window. How she contorted them like that, I will never know. Her hair was set in rags she strategically spun through her golden locks the night before so it would be in perfect curls the following day.

That's how I always see my sister, Jezebel, when I close my eyes.

When I close my eyes again, I see Dad. He is in his usual catatonic state before death. His words were few, and then one day, none at all. He was the shell of a person who d out the window as music played nearby—the same old radio Jez uses in the morning to wake me. Only the songs are much happier when Jez listens to them.

Jez cried when the men in blue took him out of the house. I had never seen her cry before. All her perfection, ruined.

I thought I was broken when I pushed my hand out to wipe the tears that had fallen down my sister's cheeks. She was so sad, and I... I was relieved—no tears. Broken, I was not like Jez at all, who was always so put together with all her pieces in the right place.

All I knew was after she cried and cried and cried, things got better. She didn't have to wake up in the middle of the night to take care of Dad or cover my ears when he had his fits. There were no more double shifts at the pawnshop or counting coins for his medication.

Jez told me with Dad gone, she was finally able to take her boss up on his offer to work at his club. Dad never wanted her to work that job, the one that made us money, the one that made us comfortable. He was selfish.

Her job was easy. That's what she told me. All she had to do was look pretty and pose for men, and they would pay her.

Jez worked late into the night. I could never stay up long enough to see her return home, but sometimes, I would feel the weight of the bed as she slipped in quietly. When I woke up, she was there, her makeup still on and her hair spread across her face.

Then things changed. Slowly at first. A bruise on her chin or a cut on her lip she covered with makeup. Jez made sure she was absolutely perfect, which wasn't hard. She was perfect, always.

Sometimes, the yellow and purple bruises would snake down her legs or arms. I never said anything. She was happy. It had been so long since I had seen her smile—and not the smile she would fake to make me feel better—it was real.

Jez sang in the shower and danced in the living room. She made enough money for us to move out of the old studio and into a two-bedroom apartment. It was still on the east side of Harmony. There were still bars on the windows and roaches in the sink, but it was better.

She decorated it with curtains made of Dad's old clothes. He never wore them anyway, as he sat in his chair with the radio on, rocking back and forth.

From then on, no matter how bruised and battered or how many nights she was gone, she only smiled and smiled.

# PART 1

NAIVE

# CHAPTER 1

*Dear Emerson,*

*We have arrived at a town called Warshaw. The middle ring is much nicer than the outer. Harmony has nothing on this place! Except for our secret spot, Emerson, nothing will ever compare to that.*

*B says this is where they fly us into Jericho.*

*I hope this letter finds you well. B doesn't like me buying stamps, but I thought you would like to know where we are since you will make the journey yourself soon. I can't wait for you to meet B. I will send money when we arrive in Jericho.*

*Only one more day, Emerson. I will see everything we have ever dreamed of. B says you will live with us, get your own room, and go to the school near his villa. (He calls his house a villa, Emerson!)*

*Things are finally looking up for us!*

*-Jez*

This letter was sent three weeks ago. I reread it every day. She sounds so happy. I can't wait to tell her about what Riley gave me for my 18th Birthday, but it will have to wait until I see my sister in person.

Riley is nothing like his brother Corey. Even though they have the same brown hair and honey eyes, they couldn't be more opposite. If I had to describe Corey in one word, it would be *creepy.*

4

Not Riley Bronze. He is thoughtful and always has been. He shares his lunch and makes sure I never walk home alone at night. Corey thinks I should get used to doing things on my own. That I should learn about what the real world is like. He says I won't always have someone around to "*play bodyguard.*" And maybe he is right, but I will have this. I look down at the silver piece in my hand. The gun Riley definitely stole from the shop, from right under Corey's nose.

These are the kinds of things they are not supposed to have, but I don't ask questions. Corey and Riley are always getting their hands on contraband. It's part of their gig, the one Riley makes sure I know nothing about.

"Hold it like this," Riley says from the safety of Jez's apartment living room, with the colorful curtains drawn. It's *her* apartment because everything here smells, feels, and *is* hers. None of it is my own, right down to the clothes on my back. "Only take the safety off if you're about to use it," Riley instructs while he flips the lever on the side to show me. I nod at him as he squares my shoulders with a gentleness only Riley possesses. He looks mean, but he is soft.

He tucks a strand of blonde from my face that was covering my right eye. "Look down the barrel. See those lines? That's where you put their heads." He says.

I roll my eyes. "Riley, that's morbid."

"No, it's reality. Never give them a second chance, Emerson. They will take that chance and run." *Emerson*, he never calls me by my full name. That means he is serious. He has been more and more that way recently. Not at all the fun-loving Riley I used to know.

5

I see the pain behind those dark eyes. The truth. The one Riley has never told anyone, not right out anyway. That he knows a thing or two about second chances. And third, fourth, and fifth chances.

Riley will soon be gone as well, and there goes my last friend in Harmony.

He leans in to see where I aim. His dark hair is buzzed, making his ears stick out, reminding me of when we were kids.

When Riley was drafted into the Palen Army, not even his brother could stop it. He already has an outpost to report to after graduation. It is outside the wall. They never give the Inner Ring to people like us, people like Riley. If you were born in the Outer Ring, there is nowhere to go but down.

Jez really showed them.

"Any news from Jez?" Riley asks as if he knew I was thinking of her. He is still hunched over, looking down the barrel of my pistol with me.

His cheek grazes my shoulder. The stubble on his jaw catches on the fabric of my school uniform. An ugly white collared shirt paired with a navy skirt. "No, not after the first letter. She will write again soon. I'm sure she is just busy with wedding planning. And you know how B is." I lie.

Riley's face falls as he turns his head to look at me. "No, I don't, and neither do *you*. You have never met him." He states.

Jez told me all about B, how he is a gentleman, and how he wants to get us out of Harmony and into Jericho, where he lives. But it is true, I do not know B at all.

I turn my head slightly, looking into Riley's right eye—the one with a gold fleck in it. Jez told me men like when you look at them *past* their flesh and bone. *Look at them like you're searching for their soul,* she would tell me.

It is hard to look for Riley's soul because when he straightens and clears his throat, he stands a whole foot taller than me, putting me at his chest. He also hardly looks me in the eye long enough for me to see anything at all, let alone the deepest part of him.

When I first met Riley while Jez was working at the pawnshop, I thought he hated me. He avoided me like the plague, always slipping to the back to be as far away from me as possible.

Jez told me to follow him one day, but before I could reach the door he was always disappearing behind, his father had stepped in the way. He smelled like gasoline and always talked too close to my face. All the Bronze boys have the same square jaw and dark features, which makes them terrifying creatures, yet beautiful.

He grabbed my shirt and pulled me close to his chest that day. "You should come work for me, kid," he told me before planting a wet kiss on my forehead. Riley stood behind him, hardly even 12. I'll never forget the look on Riley Bronze's face before he grabbed me by the wrist and pulled me to a room in the back.

I thought I was in trouble with how tightly he had squeezed my hand. "Don't ever talk to my Da again, understand?" he told me, but I wasn't listening. The room had some discarded toys and a TV. We could never afford a TV. I was instantly hooked.

After that day, Riley never let me out of his sight again. Every shift Jez had after school, I was there, and so was Riley. We watched reruns of a show about cowboys with guns. The shootouts had pistols that looked much like the one Riley has gifted me. We laughed at their strange way of talking, and cried when our favorite characters died. During the time we spent together, I guess I convinced him to like me somehow.

Years later, when Riley's father was shot and left in that very room, the police chalked it up to some pissed-off gang member his father had owed money to. It wasn't uncommon in Harmony for that to happen. It also wasn't uncommon for the police to give less than two shits about its people. They don't care if we live or die, not in Harmony.

Riley turned up at my place that night. Jez was still at work. There was a knock at our door I planned on ignoring, like Jez taught me. When Riley called out to me, I broke our rule and let someone in, not just anyone, Riley.

He didn't tell me what was wrong, but I knew something wasn't right. He was all jittery. His eyes were sunken in like he hadn't gotten sleep in a long time. His face was swollen from a fight, which wasn't unusual. What *was* unusual was he was *here*, and he was scared. I just didn't know *what* he was scared of at the time.

Riley clears his throat a second time, and I am forced to the present once more. "Can you stay?" I ask him as I slowly put the gun back in its holster.

A little too slowly because as Riley watches me, he says, "It's not going to hurt you." He laughs as he continues to watch me struggle. Then, "No, I have a shift." He answers my question. Riley works at the pawnshop, the one his father owned. Now, it belongs to Corey.

"But it's my birthday," I plead jokingly. He rolls his eyes and glances at the door. I know he doesn't want to go. I also know he doesn't have a choice. Nevertheless, it's fun to tease him.

"Come see me. After Corey leaves at 11 like he always does." Riley says coolly.

"Fine" I push my bottom lip out and pout as he passes me and reaches for the knob.

He looks down at me on his way, "Come on, don't do that." He spins around quickly and brushes his finger across my bottom lip so it makes a small slapping sound. We both laugh. I used to get mad when he would do that, but now, when I get the old Riley back, even for a second, I take it.

"Don't tell anyone about the gun, Emerson." He warns me, all serious again.

I step closer and look up at him, pretending to be appalled. "Why Riley Curtis!" I exclaim. His lip twitches at his middle name. I ignore it. "Did you *steal* my birthday present?" My words drip with sarcasm. Now, he is full-on suppressing a smile. Every now and then, I can get him out of that stiff personality he sometimes takes on.

Riley leans over and places a kiss on my cheek. "Anything for you, Em." He says near my ear. My face burns for reasons I cannot explain. Riley has kissed my cheek many times. We know more about each other than anyone else. Many of Riley's wounds from fighting have been mended by my own hands, not all of which were so easily accessible. I know every scar on his body.

Lately, something has changed. It's not a bad change, just... different. His words have become less playful, his actions more thought out, calculated. Still, he always finds a way to see me during the day, even with his job and school, and now with the Palen Army creeping its long fingers around his neck.

Maybe he feels bad for me because my sister has left. Maybe he thinks I need someone around now, especially since the apartment is empty. I still go to school, have barely passing grades. I still cook, clean, and take care of the bills with the money Jez left me. I have been doing everything by myself since I was a child, he knows that. Riley has always been overprotective of me, even when I don't want him to be.

I can't help it when the little girl I used to be screams at me from the far recess of my mind. The one who thought I would marry Riley, who thought he was mine and mine alone. Of course, he is not.

In fact, he has a girl who comes into the pawnshop and stares at him. He flirts with her, and she flirts right back. Her dark hair falls in perfect curls, and she is closer to his age, or at least she looks it, although I have never seen her at school. Her full lips are always coated in a thin layer of neutral lipstick, and she wears skirts that lie nicely on her hips and expose her legs. She is exactly the opposite of me, with my pale blue eyes and white hair to match my sisters. My stubby legs and curves could not even compare to the gazelle Cherry is. She could be on one of those posters on the trains, the ones with the ads for useless, expensive shit that is *not* meant for the people of Harmony.

I see how he looks at her. He has never even glanced at me that way. When he does things like that, I shrug it off. I am not the one he wants. No matter how hard my heart pounds against my chest when he is near.

"See you at 11," I assure him, and he is out the door.

# CHAPTER 2

It's the end of the month, which means everyone needs to pawn their things to make ends meet. It's fun to listen to them fight Riley over the price of their items from under the desk on the other side of the counter. "Come on, this is the price Corey gave me last time," a familiar voice begs. They all say that. I all but roll my eyes.

*Well, I'm not Corey.* I guess the words that are going to come out of Riley's mouth next. "Well, I'm not Corey." He says right on cue. I can hardly contain my laugh. Riley puts a hand down on my head. It's his way of telling me to shut up. "Try 5th and Main." He tells the person I cannot see.

The man sighs. "No, no, I will just take it. I need the money by tomorrow." I have never seen the man, but I recognize his voice. He is a regular. I look up in time to see Riley nod his head as he takes the watch from the man's hands. He dangles it in front of my face, I take it, inspecting it the same as the last watch, the last bracelet, the ring, the broach. It's clean. The diamonds aren't cloudy, one is missing, but it's as good as it gets here in Harmony. I tap Riley's leg with it. He reaches down, grabs it from me again, and sets it to the side before shelling out the money to the man.

When the door dings, I know it's safe to speak. "Shitty watch, good customer," I tell Riley. It's true. He always comes back for his things, and as much as he protests, he knows he will never get a better deal in all of Harmony.

Riley leans against the wall behind us and crosses his arms. "What did you see?" He tests me. Riley is teaching me how to spot real from fake. In people and in deals.

I glance at my own watch and then back up to him. "Real diamonds, but one is missing. The battery needs changing. It's running a bit slow."

"Very good." He praises me, and I can't help but smile. Riley takes his seat on a milk crate in the corner. We continue our game of cards we started when I first arrived. It keeps getting interrupted by customers. I use that time to peek at Riley's hand. He caught on after the hundredth time, but he hasn't said anything. It's a whole separate game all on its own.

Riley knows if he puts up a fight, I will leave. Riley doesn't like being alone at the shop, and I don't like being alone at home with nothing but the same songs playing on repeat over the radio station here in Middle World. So, I cheat, and Riley lets me.

The door dings again. Riley's eyes go wide before he shoves me with a hand on my shoulder back under the desk with a warning to stay put.

With my knees to my chest and my heart thumping, I wait. "Riley, Ri." A raspy voice calls out from the door. Riley straightens his shoulders uncomfortably. His father called him Ri. He hated it.

"What can I do for you, Briggs?" Riley says in his fake voice, the one he uses to shmooze customers into buying fake furs. Women always want what Riley has to offer, and men always want to make their women happy.

I listen carefully. There is more than one set of footsteps on the broken wood flooring. One of them is a woman. Her high heels clack on the surface as she nears the front desk. "What you can do is pay up," Briggs tells him. Riley almost laughs but changes his mind. I can read him like a book.

"Yeah? That so?" He says instead. Briggs laughs, and another deeper laugh joins in, another man near the counter. One of the goons from the club that is always with Briggs, I forget his name.

Then the woman speaks. Her voice is quiet as if she is afraid of her own words. "It's not like that," she tells them, rather unconvincingly. I recognize that voice. It's *her*.

"Come on now, Cherry, you know the rules. No one spends time with you girls without pay." Briggs tells her. "Not even Corey. And we know how you *love* to keep Corey company, isn't that right, Cherry?" he says so obviously to Riley and not to her. If it gets under his skin, he doesn't show it. He's always been cool under pressure. I wish I was like that.

Cherry takes her time before answering. "Right." She agrees, and I know it's to spare herself a beating.

Riley sighs and backs up. He heads for the safe and pulls out a few bills I can't see. He doesn't so much as look at me, keeping my presence a secret. "Whatever, man, just take it and leave," he tells them nonchalantly as he throws the money down on the counter. It's not enough. The cash is the correct amount, but they clearly came in here looking for a fight and not the kind where they haggle down the prices or make a trade.

Briggs snorts. "You don't need Cherry anyway, not when you have that blonde slut." Yeah, yeah, I heard it all before. It's no skin off my back. I get called worse on the way to school. "You sure have her wrapped around your finger." Briggs clicks his tongue. "You know, when you leave, there will be no one here to stop me." Briggs spits. Riley huffs out a laugh, but what Briggs says is not funny.

I look up at him to see him staring straight ahead. It doesn't look like his eyes latch onto anything. Just the void, whatever is past the men and Cherry, which is nothing. "I wonder if she will taste as good as her sister." The other one chimes in.

Riley's jaw clenches, and his hands follow suit. They bunch up into fists, turning his knuckles white. I want to grab him, reach out, and push my fingers through his so he doesn't hurt himself. The room grows unbearably quiet, so much so I am afraid my own breathing will be heard.

*Ding.* The door swings open and crashes against the shelf beside it. "Big night, boys, big, big nigh—Oh, hey, Riley." Corey's voice echoes through the deadly silent room. I never thought I would be happy to see or rather hear Corey.

Riley blinks, his eyes shift to his brother. "Come on, boys, they will be there any minute." Corey's words are drawn out, like he has to concentrate on each syllable. He's drunk or high, probably both. "Unless you're offering *Riley* to the boys of Jericho, I suggest you and Cherry head on down to the club." Corey slurs.

*Offering?* I figured out what my sister's *real* job was long ago. I know she did not just stand on a stage. I also never held it against her. She did what she had to do to survive. She made sure we had food, which is more than Dad ever did. I never asked questions, and when she told me one of the men wanted to take her to Jericho and make her his wife, I didn't think much of it.

Jez told me she and B were in love. That he had been to the club many times and was a good man who just wanted to help someone like her get out of the Outer Ring. Jez is so easy to love. It wasn't hard to think someone would want to help her like that. I guess I shouldn't be surprised they offer their best women to the richest people in the world. The 1%. Jericho is unattainable if you're not already a part of the families that live there or marry into it.

Briggs still doesn't let it go. "Maybe we should wait for the blonde. She has a habit of showing up here, walking around in those skirts, just asking for it," he says. Riley is still fuming. I place a hand over my mouth to avoid getting him in trouble. These guys just don't know when to quit.

Briggs huffs at the idea. "Right. You wouldn't want someone to whisk her away to Jericho like her sister, would you, Riley?" He asks.

Riley blinks. This time I have no idea what he is going to say next. "They wouldn't want her," Riley says plainly. My mouth falls open.

Of course, I shouldn't *want* to be wanted by these men *or* the club. Still, hearing those words from Riley pulls at my heart. "She's not right," Riley continues. He points up to his temple and taps the skin there three times. *Crazy,* he is suggesting I am not right in the head. I can't believe this. It takes everything in me not to reach up and hit him where I know it will hurt.

"They might not mind that, if you know what I mean," Briggs counters. The crazy ones are the most fun." I can't see his face, but his words are so arrogant I know there is a smile on his face.

Riley has a dangerous air surrounding him. He thinks he has won with whatever strategy this is. "They will care when she doesn't pass a blood test," Riley is quick to say. Her father did a real number on her." He tells them a lie. My father was a lot of things, but he never laid a hand on me or Jez. Not that he could have, even if he tried due to his illness.

Now, I am bright red and furious beyond belief. The whole of fucking Harmony will think I have STDs. I suppose that's one way to get the club off my trail. They only hire clean women, no drugs, no pesky viral infections, certainly not the incurable kind Riley is making it seem I have.

Word spreads fast in Harmony, school will be an absolute nightmare on Monday, I guess I will call in sick... forever.

Finally, Corey speaks up again. "Fuck heads, let's gooo." He sounds out of breath at the end of his sentence.

The sound of flesh on wood above me has me flinching. Briggs leans on the counter. I pull myself into a ball, so he doesn't see my boots.

"I know what you are doing. She doesn't need to be clean *or* sane," he whispers, something meant only for Riley's ears. "You can't protect her forever. The club will come for her. They already have their eyes on her," he warns.

Riley lets out another huff of laughter. "See you around, Briggs." He says smoothly, dismissing them. Then, the shuffling of boots followed by the clicking of heels. The door opens and shuts. I hadn't realized I was holding my breath for so long until my vision starts to darken.

Riley is still staring out the window when I look up at him. I wait to unfurl myself until I hear the car leave the lot, but before I can make my way out from beneath the desk, Riley kicks the milk crate. Cards flutter to the ground around us. "Fuck!" is all he says into the silence. Followed by a deep breath before he balls his right hand into a fist and punches the wall.

The building is old, crumbling like the rest of the city. The sheetrock falls to the ground in pieces. When he takes his hand away, there is a hole where his fist used to be. His shoulders move up and down heavily.

I have only seen him like this one time. I'm not sticking around for the next part. I silently peel myself off the floor. My legs are nearly asleep from holding them close for so long.

Riley still faces the wall. I make sure to be as quiet as possible as I reach the door. If he hears me leave, he doesn't say anything.

I flip the sign to closed so whoever has the misfortune of needing to pawn something doesn't have to deal with Riley in one of his moods, the kind that has given him a reputation for violence.

The last person he exploded on ended up in the hospital, and the person before that... well, he's dead. Most people are scared of Riley for that reason. They know the truth as well as I do. It wasn't hard to put the pieces together. Now, he has a permanent look on his face, as if he has seen something he cannot unsee.

Jez told me I often ignored the bad and saw only the good. The part of Riley that is under the terrifying shell. But I have a suspicion the anger I see now is much further than that. So deep that when it comes to the surface, he has a hard time putting it back under.

Still, half turned towards Riley, I hold my breath as I pull the door. It dings when I open it. Riley flinches at the noise but doesn't turn around. It's dark now, and if I don't get back soon, I will be paying a hefty fine for breaking curfew. One I cannot afford.

I slip through the door quickly, and without looking back, I begin to run. Until I am three blocks away and five stories up. Until my heart threatens to thump out of my chest and my legs throb.

Only when the door is locked, and I am safe under all the quilts Jez made. When I am listening to the stupid broken radio to drown out the city noise do I let myself relax.

Monday can't come soon enough. There will be a letter from Jez. I just know it. Then, I won't have to worry about the club or those men Riley was talking to. I will be in Jericho, and everything will be the way it's supposed to.

I reach a hand out and turn the knob on the radio even more so I don't have to hear my own thoughts. My eyes grow heavy, and soon, I don't hear my own thoughts *or* the same old songs on the radio.

My dreams are filled with Riley.

# CHAPTER 3

When I am pulled from sleep, the room is cold and dark. I have the blankets up to my ears, but a breeze comes in through the window, sending shivers down to my toes.

The radio still plays. It's on a commercial, the same commercial that plays every time. I know every word of it, just like I know the loop of songs the station placed before they shut down.

I sit up and look over at the nightstand. The gun Riley gave me sits under the lamp. My mind slowly clears the fog of slumber. I think back to when I got home. I didn't leave the window open, did I?

That's when I start to become increasingly aware of all the things that are so *so* wrong.

My bedroom door is open. The hallway light is off. The curtains are parted. The window is cracked. This window is the only one in the apartment without bars. Because it's on the 5th floor, the fire escape doesn't come up to this side of the building, making it impossible for people to get to.

That's when I grab the gun and flip the lamp on. My eyes adjust. In the corner of the room with a cup of what smells like coffee, Jez's fancy shit, in his hand, is Riley. Not the Riley that was occupying the space behind my eyes only seconds ago. The real Riley.

I hadn't realized I had the gun stuck out in front of me, my finger on the trigger, until he speaks. "Put the gun down, Em." His voice is hoarse, low, like when he first wakes up in the morning.

My hands shake as I lower my arms. The air around him is thick. The same as when I ran from the pawnshop, the air I was too afraid to breathe is now all around me. *It's just Riley. He won't hurt you*, I remind myself, but I still feel violated. "I could have shot you." I finally get out.

Riley shakes his head. "No. You wouldn't have." He points his cup towards the gun. "Safety's on." He says, almost bored. I lower the gun and basically toss it back onto the nightstand, glad for it to be out of my hands. My fingers instinctively run through my hair.

Then I watch as Riley moves for the bed, coming around until he is next to me. He stops at the nightstand and blinks down at the gun before he bends down and exchanges his mug for the silver piece. It looks smaller when he holds it than when I do. Riley flips the bar on its side so the safety is off. This has the hairs on the back of my neck standing up. I try not to be afraid of the man before me, and for the most part, I am not. He doesn't seem to notice my discomfort as he sets it back down again gently.

He takes a seat at my side, making the bed dip. My body rolls towards him as he sits there, staring out the open window he must have scaled the brick to reach. I shake my head in disbelief. "You broke into my house." I laugh at the absurdity of it.

Riley relaxes just a little at that. His back isn't as straight, his head even sinks a little as he looks down at his hands that are clasped in front of him tightly. He even lets the corner of his mouth turn up in a smirk I would have missed if I blinked.

The air slowly returns back to normal. "I just had to make sure you made it home." Riley's jaw clenches. "I knocked." He says plainly as he sinks into the bed even more. "Radio was blaring." He says as if it's the radio's fault he had to break into my home.

I ignore him. Instead, I pick up his coffee and take a swig. The whole house smells like it, *like her.* I smile into the white mug as I think about my sister. "Thought you didn't like coffee," Riley says over his shoulder at me.

I hadn't even noticed he was watching me. "I don't," I say, handing it back to him. He just stares at the brown liquid sloshing back and forth in his hands. We sit there for a moment longer. Silences with Riley are not uncomfortable. Sometimes, he needs time to think. Riley runs a hand over his short hair as if he has forgotten it's buzzed and not the long brown that almost reached his bushy brows. His hand falls to the stubble on his chin.

Finally, he turns his head in my direction. "They gave me my shipment date." He says through gritted teeth. "Day after graduation." He tells the window because he has used his allotted two seconds of looking at me.

Today is Saturday. "That's only a week away," I tell him what he already knows. "When did you get the news?" I ask.

"Yesterday." He braces himself. He thinks I'm going to be upset he didn't tell me because it was my birthday. When I don't react or say anything at all, he finally takes another look at me. He *really* looks at me.

Finally, there in the light of the lamp is that gold fleck in his right eye, the color of the sun. I wait patiently, afraid if I say anything, he will look away. Finally, after what feels like so long and yet not long enough. "Tell me something good." He whispers.

A game we used to play when things were hard. When Jez didn't come home for days, or his brother kicked him out again. *Tell me something good.* "I don't have STDs." I try and fail to stop a smile from devouring my face.

Riley shakes his head. "No, no you do not," he agrees. Then, "I'm sorry. Shit. I'm so fucking sorry, Em." Then there is that air again, the one that suffocates him, blinds him with rage.

I reach my hand out and pull at his shirt sleeve. "Don't be," I assure him. "I'm going to be in Jericho soon. None of this matters." I don't know who I am trying to convince, me or him. I haven't heard from Jez since her first letter. There was never a guarantee I would get to go.

It was our plan, my sister and I. We would watch the sunset on the roof, looking over the edge to Harmony, and tell each other everything we would do together if we got to Jericho.

"I hope that's true," he says.

Riley grabs the coffee again and takes a long drink. "Tell me something good," I say with a yawn. I lay back down and let my head fall into the pillow with one of Dad's orange T-shirts as the pillowcase.

My eyes begin to feel heavy. "You," he whispers, which has me smiling from ear to ear as I watch him down the rest of the coffee and set the mug on the nightstand. I slide to the other side of the bed and pat the blanket next to him.

Riley kicks his shoes off and crawls under the comforter. He is still in his jeans and a torn black shirt that is too tight.

Just like when we were small, we curl into each other for warmth. It's nearly morning by now, and the birds have started their songs. The room glows as light filters in through the window. Riley wraps a hand around my waist and pulls me into him. Soon he is fast asleep. He must have needed it, too, because he sleeps well into the morning and no matter how many times I try to peel his arm away, he only holds on tighter.

# CHAPTER 4

*Dear Emerson,*

*Jericho is beautiful. It's always warm here. There are palm trees and fresh water falls every day. It's kind of like the terrarium we made when you were 12. I don't ask how they do it. All I know is this is paradise, Emerson.*

*Redacted* *Redacted* *Redacted* *Redacted*

*Redacted* *Redacted* *Redacted* *Redacted*

*Redacted*

*There will come a day when we are together again. Just be patient.*

*Lots of love,*

*-Jezebel*

That's it? That's all I get? Most of it was redacted. I hold the paper up to the lamp's light, trying to see if there is something I missed. Nothing. This wasn't how it was supposed to be. "None of this is how it's supposed to be," I say to the empty apartment. I throw the paper down on the coffee table and turn the radio up.

*Jezebel.* Is that what she is calling herself now? New city, new name. I can't imagine calling her by her full name, not when I have only known her as Jez my whole life. I pick up the letter again and turn it over to write on the back. Jez didn't leave much money, not money I can use anyway.

Apparently, her plan to send some from Jericho has backfired as well. I have been writing my replies on the back of her letters to give to her in person.

I don't blame her. I am not her responsibility. I knew if things didn't work out, I would have to find a job. With Riley leaving, I'm sure Corey would give me a job in the pawnshop. All that talk about the club is nothing short of frightening, but I try to push it aside. I tell myself I will stand my ground and make sure they don't get what they so desperately want.

I push away my anger as I write.

*Jez,*

*Jezebel,*

*As you can see, most of your letter was redacted. You will have to tell me what you said when we see each other again. Don't tell me they don't let you swear in Jericho?! I could never live there if that were the case.*

*Riley got his shipment date—the day after graduation. I'm starting to get nervous. Soon, there will be no one in Harmony I trust.*

*I miss you terribly. Every time I wake up, I forget you're not here for a minute. I sometimes think you will come bursting into my room in the morning to tell me I'm late for school.*

*By the way, I am skipping school.*

*Maybe indefinitely.*

*There might be a rumor going around that I have STDs. Don't worry, I don't! Obviously.*

*I wish you were here to set the record straight. They wouldn't say any-thing if you were still here, I know it. You have this way about you that makes you so... believable. I like that about you. I know I will always get the truth, even if I don't ask for it.*

*Anyway, I know this letter will not reach you until I do, but I hope you can feel how much I love you through the walls of this goddamned city, through the Inner Ring, all the way in Jericho.*

*Em*

*Emerson (since we use our full names now.)*

There is a knock on the door as I stare at my response, wishing I could afford to send it to her now. Quickly, I fold the paper and place it back into the envelope for safekeeping. *I will make it to her.* I make a promise to myself before walking to the door, where the knocking persists. Brown, angry eyes will be waiting for me on the other side—Riley. I skipped school, and he is probably pissed. Especially since it's the last week. For a second, I think of ignoring him. The last thing I need right now is a scolding. With a shake of my head, I push the idea out. Ignoring him will only get me in more trouble.

When the door swings open, I see Riley's eyes, but it is not Riley who stands there. It's Corey. I should have grabbed the gun. He smiles down at me, his eyes widen slightly. When I follow his eyes down, I realize I am still in my shorts and an oversized T-shirt that hardly covers my ass. I am not wearing a bra, and I'm becoming increasingly uncomfortable the longer Corey stares.

Corey runs a hand through his dark hair as he makes his way back up to meet my eyes. Pretending I don't notice his not-so-subtle look, "What do you want?" I ask as confidently as possible. I keep my hand on the knob in case I need to close the door.

He takes a step back and leans back, looking down the hallway. Checking to see if anyone is there. This has my throat closing and my pulse jumping. He wants us to be alone. "I need a favor." Corey licks his lips.

"No."

Corey's eyes darken, and a smile plays on his lips, "You didn't even let me tell you what it is," he coos as he runs his hands over his long brown hair—the same as Riley's used to be before he decided to cut it all off for the Palen Army.

"I don't want to do you any favors." I start to close the door. Trying my best to look at him like he has completely lost his mind. Because he has.

He puts a boot on the door to stop it. I *really* should have grabbed the gun. "I will pay you." He rubs his hands together. I still try to close the door to no avail. "I know how much your sister made. I know it isn't enough to pay for this fucking apartment." He tries to peek behind me.

That's where he is wrong. That's the *only* thing that is paid for. Jez paid the whole year so I wouldn't have to move, just in case it was a little longer before I could get to Jericho. Good thing, too, because she hasn't told me *when* exactly I will be moving there.

Food is a little harder to come by. I have been living on a bag of rice and whatever Riley will share with me during lunch. "500," he barks when I do not answer.

I look at my sad kitchen, bare shelves, and I know what I will find if I open the refrigerator, *nothing*. "What's the favor?" I ask timidly. My body floods with immediate regret when I see the smug look of satisfaction on Corey's face.

He holds his hands up as if in surrender. "All you have to do is sit there."

"At the club?" I ask.

Corey hums his response as he nods.

*Do not take any jobs the club offers you.* I remind myself of Jez's words. "No, I'm not doing that." I try to shut the door again, but Corey's large hand catches it this time.

"1000." My mouth falls open at his offer. That would get me more than just food. I could finally fix the heater, maybe even patch my school uniform with a new sewing kit. Jez was so adamant about not doing *anything* for the club, no matter how well they pay. But even now, my stomach growls, and I can't ask Riley for money I know he does not have. How bad could it be?

Corey sees my answer before I say it. "Okay, but if you say I just have to sit there, *that* is what I am going to do," I say firmly. He nods his head slowly. "If you ask me to do *anything* else, I'm out. Got it?" I wait for his answer. I get another nod from him, another low vibration from his chest.

For a fraction of a second, I can tell why so many women fawn over the man before me. Muscular build and clear, tanned skin. His teeth are straight and sparkling white. But he is evil, just like his father was.

"You will need to change," he tells me, finally placing his hands in his pocket and moving away from the door. Wear a dress." He looks me over once more. "Maybe some makeup?" His mouth curls into a devious smile.

I will agree to anything if he leaves. "Right. When do I need to be there?" I ask, trying not to sound annoyed by his presence.

He looks at the expensive-looking Rolex on his wrist and contemplates his answer. "Meet me at nine. Don't go in through the front. The girls enter through the back." I try not to cringe at the thought. I am now one of the *girls*.

Before I can talk myself out of it, "Okay," I agree as I begin to shut the door slowly so he doesn't think I'm slamming it in his face, even though I want to.

With my body behind the wood, I watch to make sure he leaves. Instead, he steps back, and our eyes meet. Corey watches me like a predator watches prey. Like he can't wait to sink his teeth into me. I've seen that look before. It was for my sister. The door closes, but I don't relax until his footsteps fade.

Now, I have about five hours to panic about what *exactly* this job includes while also avoiding Riley. Corey wouldn't offer so much if it wasn't important. I remember Jez saying something vague about a once-a-year event the club would host around graduation. She would always wear her hair up and her shortest dress.

A steady beat comes from the club's heart, from a stage I have never seen. The back is full of girls getting ready in front of shared mirrors. They slide black around their eyes and apply pink to their cheeks and noses the way Jez used to. They know I do not belong here. I can feel their eyes on the back of my head as I approach Corey's office.

I have only been here once before. Jez had a doctor's appointment in Alliance. It's mandatory for all the girls to go once a year for a checkup. She needed an advance on her paycheck to cover the expense. I had to retrieve it for her. It was just as bad last time. With all the music and chatter, the room reeks of cheap perfume and cigarettes.

When I knock on the door, I hear the shuffling of feet before it clicks open. Cherry scurries out, adjusting her hair and straightening her dress. How does she still look perfect? Corey, on the other hand, sports messy hair and a half-tucked shirt. It's not hard to figure out what those two were doing in here. She lifts her nose into the air and gives me a sideways glance as she passes. I make sure to look straight ahead to Corey.

He clears his throat and pushes his hands through his hair. A nervous habit of his. "Emerson. Glad you could make it. Just sit here." He looks around me, trying to find Cherry again. I follow his finger to a black leather chair. When I sit, he closes the door and comes around to the other side of a desk in the corner. There are papers piled high on the shelves and a large safe behind him that goes into the wall. "All you have to do is walk out onto the stage and find a seat," he explains. "Do not pay attention to those around you. Just sit and say nothing." He tells me with a wave of his hands. "Don't move, don't talk." He reiterates as he taps a finger on the desk. What has him nervous, I wonder?

I nod my head, trying to avoid his eyes, or I might be reminded of Riley, who is going to be more than pissed. I really need the money, though. After this, I am done with the club, and I will be well on my way to Jericho to find Jez. *Just this one time,* I promise myself. I seem to be making a lot of those promises lately.

My attention remains on those tapping fingers. "If anyone asks how old you are, tell them you are 21." He continues, all I can do is look at the desk and nod. The tapping stops. "Tell me you understand." He lowers his voice to a threatening level.

The less fight I put up, the sooner this will all be over. "I understand." I give him what he wants.

Corey takes a drink from a silver flask he had tucked into one of the drawers. Of course, he's drunk. He sees me staring and promptly holds out the flask in an offer. I take it and prepare myself for the bitter taste of vodka. I tip my head back and let the liquid pour into my mouth. I need courage, so I take another for good measure. All the while, Corey is busy staring at my chest.

I regret wearing one of Jez's dresses, but the only dress *I* own is about three times too small. Jez made it for me when I was twelve before I hit my growth spurt. Jez doesn't think I am done growing, either. She predicts in a few years, I will be taller than she is. *You will grow into yourself, Em, baby, don't worry,* she would tell me as we stood in front of the bathroom mirror.

Corey laughs as I pull my jacket around myself and try to hand him back his flask. He pushes it back towards me like he knows I will need more than two measly swigs to get me through tonight. I try not to make a face at the burn in my throat. Then, he is out the door with another reminder to stay put until he comes to get me. So, I do. I sip on the vodka and wait for what feels like hours, but the clock in the corner says otherwise.

Finally, the door clicks open. I stand so Corey can escort me down a long hallway behind the stage. I recognize Cherry and a few other girls from the pawnshop. One man with a wire to his ear and all-black clothing leans into Corey to speak to him. "You're fucking crazy." He whispers, but it's so loud that everyone can hear. "If she gets chosen, you better be prepared to make an offer. She's not old enough, man, you know the rules." My heart jumps into my throat. *Chosen? For what?*

Corey looks like he wants to scream. "She won't get chosen. I know my audience." He basically spits at the man. "Besides, who are *you* to

31

question me?" He raises his voice a little before looking around. He has drawn the attention of every woman and security guard. Corey looks around anxiously before he lowers his voice again. "We just need to look like we have the variety, even when we don't," he assures the man.

Then he turns towards me again and puts his mouth too close to my ear. "No one wants you, Squirt." Maybe the vodka is kicking in, or maybe I am well past the days Corey's nickname, paired with his blatant hate for me, has any effect.

"All right, ladies." The older woman, Karla, I heard Jez call her once, claps her hands together twice. "Go on in and sit down. You know the drill." She eyes me specifically to make sure I am not going to fuck up...whatever *this* is.

I take my coat off and leave it on a nearby chair. I don't miss the eyes of the other girls when they spot the dress Jez had to have worn over a dozen times to this very club. Of course, it barely fits over my ass, and Jez was lacking in the cleavage department, so I fill it out more than she ever did. Which I hate, but I didn't have many choices, not ones that wouldn't leave me practically naked with all her other options. So, the low-cut black dress with lace detail and missing pieces from each side of my torso is what I am stuck with.

The music stops, and the room grows quiet as we shuffle our way out onto the stage. I follow what the others do. Which is easy because all they do is find a chair and sit, just as Corey said. The stage has white spotlights that shine down onto each of the chairs. It's blinding and hot, but I do as I was told. The lights make it impossible to see what is beyond. It's all dark aside from an exit sign that looks far away, because it is.

There are murmurs in the distance, in front and beside me. Soon, out of the shadows comes a hand, followed by an arm, all attached to a man in a black suit. My spine straightens as other men come from the same dark abyss beyond us. The girl in front of me doesn't move, so neither do I.

I let my eyes wonder, watching the men make their way onto the stage when they find what they are looking for. Two point at a girl with black hair and deep skin. One even runs a hand up her arm as he inspects her. He pushes her hair from her neck, checking the skin where it was resting on her shoulder. Then he holds up her hands and looks under her arms, the same with her legs. Corey didn't say anything about people touching us.

*Just sit and say nothing.* I try to look past the men to the red glowing sign. *Exit*, I wish I could exit this building right now. From the corner of my eye, I see one of them near me. *Just keep looking ahead,* I tell myself, *don't move.* He passes between me and the girl ahead of me. Blonde hair and blue eyes, just like Jez, just like me. He disappears somewhere behind me. His shoes slide across the floor, stop, then continue.

Suddenly, he is in front of me again, this time with a devilish smirk. I grip the bottom of the chair tightly in an attempt to stop shaking. He leans over so our faces are mere inches apart. I can smell his cologne—floral with a mix of spice.

Locking onto the spot between his perfectly manicured brows, I slow my breathing to keep the panic from taking over, praying he doesn't hear my heartbeat against its cage. *It will be over soon*, I tell myself over and over again. He lifts my chin with his finger. Then, he pushes my hair behind my ears with both hands. His movements are so quick I have to stop myself from flinching. I become as still as a statue, focusing on anything but him. But it doesn't matter. "Look at me," he whispers. I do. I have to, right?

He drinks me in. Left eye, right, nose, down to my lips. "I'll be back for you." He promises. His hands still cup the sides of my face.

Unfortunately for him, I will not be here next time. In fact, I will never step foot into this club again. *That* is a promise that will be kept.

He takes a step back and shakes his head. The blonde man calls out to someone I can't see. "You were right. You do have quite the variety." He smirks down at me and licks his lips. Then to the girl he inspected first. Finally, back to me with that same smile that has my chest pounding. "We have strict orders, as you know." He says to the darkness. "But let me make a few calls. We might want her too." He tells the person.

I want to scream. I want to run. I can't be here. I wasn't supposed to be here. Goddammit, why didn't I listen to Jez? The club doesn't bring anything good. My feet unfold from the prim and proper sitting position. The blonde stands there, rubbing his hands together in front of him like he is begging me to run so he can chase me.

Just before I can talk myself into *actually* moving, "Why don't we let the girls get ready for tonight's performance." Corey's voice comes closer as he speaks. "You call your boss and let us know," he says coolly.

The girls all stand, but it seems I am frozen. Corey places a heavy hand on my shoulder. How did he reach me so fast? Then he pulls me up with the others. On wobbly legs, I follow the girls out and back to the dressing room. Corey walks behind me in a terrifyingly calm manner. When we are out of eyesight, he leads me into the office with a vice-like grip on my wrist. When he pushes me in and closes the door, the fog of fear is gone. Things go quiet. I breathe in and out deeply, trying to contain my anger with Corey, with Jez, with Harmony.

*Fucking liar,* I fume to myself as I watch the man in front of me act like nothing is happening, like it's just another day. Like I am not about to be shipped off somewhere with a strange man. "You told me I wouldn't have to do anything. You said they wouldn't want me!" I shout at Corey.

He paces back and forth in the small room but doesn't say anything. "Give me my money," I demand. I'm taking it, and I'm getting out of here. I'm getting out of Harmony. I will just find Jez when I get there.

"Just calm the fuck down," Corey says as he runs his hands through his hair. "Let them make their calls. They don't want you. They can't," he tries to convince himself.

I hardly stop myself from shouting again. "What do you mean they *can't*?" I ask. How the hell would he know what they can and can't do?

Corey rolls his eyes like I should already know the answer. "Their boss, he has a preference, he isn't going to take you." He assures me, but even he looks like he doesn't believe it. "Trust me." He shrugs as he sits in his chair and searches the top drawer for something.

Corey's fake confidence pisses me off. "Give. Me. The. Money." I say through clenched teeth. "Give it to me!" I yell when he doesn't so much as look at me. He has found what he is looking for in the desk drawer, a blunt. He lights it, looks up at me through his dark lashes, then holds it out for me to take. My attention goes to the burning rolled paper, then back up to Corey. My vision goes red. I keep his eyes when I spit the words, "Fuck you." at him.

Corey laughs through his nose before his jaw tightens "Listen, Squirt, you made a bargain. In order to get paid, you have to hold up your end of the deal." He takes a puff of the blunt and blows the smoke into my face.

"Sit there and do nothing. Done." I tell him. "That's what you told me to do, *that's* what I did." My words are monotone as I remind Corey of the deal we made.

A quiet, annoyed laugh escapes the man across from me. "I said sit there and do nothing, and you basically eye fucked the guy right in front of me." He states like it's a fact.

My blood boils, but when I open my mouth to let Corey Steven Bronze know exactly how I feel about his little deal, he speaks over me. "Riley saw it too, you know." He laughs louder this time. "Had to step out of the room, he was so angry. It looks like he couldn't protect you after all." Corey pauses to take another drag. "You and your sister are whores." My eyes widen, the whole room is red now. He peeks up at me with satisfaction, he wanted under my skin, and that's exactly what he got. "That's not a bad thing." He shrugs again. "Everyone has a place in the world, even whores, like *you*." Corey stands and walks past me to the door. Just then, there is a knock, like he knew there would be.

I don't turn around to look at who is on the other side as he opens it. "CJ says the boss won't take her." The same security guard as earlier. Relief floods me. When I finally turn for the door, for Corey, I see him shifting through a wad of cash. He dangles the money out in front of him like it's a game. When I reach for it, he pulls it into his chest and takes a step in my direction. "Told you." He gloats. "No one wants you." He shakes his head. Tears threaten to fall, but it's his earlier words that do it. He was right. What I did tonight might not have been outright prostitution, but I did sell a part of me to the club. I let him use my body, and now I am taking his money. I have no idea how Jez did it all these years.

Then, when I thought things couldn't get any worse, past the cash he still dangles in my face, past the women as they fix their hair and adjust their shoes, I see Riley.

He is standing at the end of the long hallway near the door. He's angry. You can see it, feel it, even from all the way over here. I want to explain this all to him, tell him Jez hasn't sent money and I haven't eaten real food in over a week. But those are all just excuses. He knows it, I know it. I prepare myself for his wrath, the kind that takes him over and turns him into someone I do not recognize. I ignore the next words Corey spits in my direction as I take the money and shove it into my dress.

By the time I reach Riley, he is opening the back door for me. The frigid night air tickles my exposed skin. I don't even bother trying to go back to find my coat. I deserve it, the cold. Walking right past Riley through the door, I accept my fate. The metal door clicks back into its hinges, I turn to Riley and force myself to look up at him. The neon sign nearby casts a glow of pink over his features. He looks down at me with those brown, all-knowing eyes. Then he places a hand on the small of my back and guides me away from the club. "Not now." He speaks over his shoulder at the building as we walk towards the apartment.

It's deadly silent. Riley doesn't say a word as he takes his jacket off and places it around my shoulders. A kindness I do not deserve. We walk the entire way without so much as a glance in each other's direction. I take my heels off to walk up the five flights of stairs. Riley follows, keeping my pace. I think my body is trying to postpone the scolding I am about to get because I walk extra slow on the last flight. No amount of procrastination will help I am afraid.

When we finally reach the door, 52 B, he takes the key I gave him, Jez's old key, and unlocks it. I thought it would be better than him scaling the building. I curse at myself for making that decision.

We don't say anything to each other. After the click of the lock, he steps inside and flips the lamp to the right. He is being too quiet. It's not like him. I can't take it anymore. I push my hair from my face before following him inside. Riley reaches around me to close the door calmly. His nearness causes a shiver to run down my spine. "Aren't you going to say something?" I bite my lip after, regret flooding my bloodstream.

His only response is taking the heels from my hand. Riley places them on the ground neatly, next to the messily discarded shoes. The only indication of his anger is the clenching of his jaw. He wants to say something but is restraining himself.

Next, he pulls the jacket from my shoulders and hangs it on the hook behind me. He is so close I can smell him. The scent that was left in my bed just two nights ago. I lean into him sightly, maybe for comfort.

Whatever comfort I could have received from it is short-lived because he takes me by the hip and forces me to turn away from him. My face is now against the wall. All the air leaves my body. When he takes the distance between us away, when I can feel his body against my own, he finally speaks. "Do you want to work at the club?" he says into my hair. His words are so calm I can't help but swallow as fear takes over my senses entirely.

This is a different kind of anger, the kind that comes from betrayal. Riley has never put his hands on me, and even still, with a tightening grip around my hip and his shoulder in my back to force me against the wall, it feels more like punishment than abuse. I shake my head in response to his question. Riley is not satisfied with my answer. "You have to say it, Emerson. I need to hear you say it."

"No." it comes out more as a plea than anything. It's true. It was a one-time thing. I don't want to work there.

Riley pushes me further. "Do you know what they do to girls like you?" This time, a hand snakes its way around to my middle, laying softly on my lower stomach. I don't have time to think of how nice his skin feels on mine, where the dress lacks fabric.

I know what this is about. It's to make sure I know how dangerous the club is. Words didn't do the trick the first time, so now he is using force. It's a scare tactic. Little does he know I am past scared of the club *without* his punishment. For some reason, I do not stop him, do not explain. "They don't care if you want it or not. They just take." He places a boot between my feet and uses it to push my legs apart one by one until they are spread to his liking. "Is that what you want, Emerson?" He isn't done proving his point.

My body is doing things I don't want it to. I can't think. I don't even know if I am registering what he says. Wait, do I want what? This? *Yes,* I almost say out loud. What the club has to offer? No.

Riley shoves me harder into the wall when I do not answer, all that comes out is, "I don't know." It's breathy, needy. I hate myself for it.

My legs instinctively try to close, but Riley keeps them apart. This shouldn't be happening. Riley doesn't want me. My panties should not be soaked, and my brain should not be wondering if he is hard under those jeans.

As far as I can tell, Riley is entirely unaware of the fact that I am unraveling right before his eyes. "You don't know what?" He now has my wrist in his hand and is pulling it to my lower back. Then he takes the other and follows suit until they are firm in his grip at the base of my spine.

My head clears long enough for me to say, "I didn't have a choice. Jez hasn't sent money."

It's still not good enough for him. "You always have a choice on whether you share your body with someone or not." He is getting more aggressive, using the leverage of my hands in his to push me further until my breasts are up against the cold wall. Jez's stupid dress bunches around my waist. Exposing my black panties to him.

*A choice,* I laugh to myself. "Like right now?" I ask, turning the question around on him. "Do *I* have a choice?"

I can feel his breath against the back of my neck. I can't tell if it's anger or need I feel radiating off of him. "Tell me to stop." He says plainly. At first I think it's some kind of test. But that's what he was doing the other night as well, I realize. When he broke into my apartment and placed the gun down without its safety on, he was telling me I had a choice. That I didn't have to say yes to his presence.

I don't want him to stop. I have dreamt of his body against my own like this many times. But I would be an idiot not to see what is really going on. Whatever *this* is was brought on by what he saw at the club. Only interested after seeing that someone else might *actually* want me, no matter what his brother says. "You don't want me." I try to call his bluff.

Riley laughs. It's low, vibrating through my body where we touch. I continue, driving home my point. "You saw the way that man looked at me-" I am cut off when he pulls at my wrists, bound by his hand. I am being held up only by him as he forces me to lean against his body instead of the wall. His cock pushes into my ass. I suck in a breath hoping he doesn't hear the moan I let out when I release the air trapped inside of me. Is that his answer? To a question I didn't mean to ask? His way of telling me that he *does* in fact want me.

"I *said*, tell me to stop," Riley growls.

I bite my lip hard to stop myself from saying *anything* at all. What will come out will only be begging and pleading for him to *never* stop. That is more embarrassing. So, I only shake my head.

His lips fall to my shoulder, a gentle kiss before, "It's going to take more than that," he tells me as he releases my hands and spins me once more so I am against his chest. My palms press against his chest as I instinctually attempt to stop myself from falling.

Then his hand is on my chin, and he is forcing me to look up at him. Just like the man at the club, but this is so much...more. "I know your answer, Em." He looks down at the lack of distance between us, to my exposed legs. "I can smell it." I lean into his hand as it remains on my chin. I'm suddenly too warm. I need this dress off. It's like sandpaper on my skin.

I squirm under his gaze, following his eyes down, knowing exactly what he means. He licks his lips, and I watch him do it. Mesmerized. That's when I make my move, the one we both knew would happen. I take that lip into my mouth and suck. It doesn't take long for our mouths to collide as we drink each other in. It's exactly how I thought it would be. It's better, actually. He is perfect. So perfect. Always has been.

Soon he will be gone, and I will have wasted all these fucking years *not* kissing these lips. What was I thinking?

"You gave me no choice, Emerson." He talks as he moves to my throat, trailing my collarbone before moving lower. "You thought you could do that shit and get away with it." he breathes. I don't even care how or why we ended up here. All I can think about is the sensation between my legs as the stubble of his chin scrapes against my skin. How many times have I wished for him to be this close to me? Dreamt of his touch?

Soon Riley is wrapping his arms around my middle before he lifts me from the ground. He carries me to my room with ease. When he tosses me onto the bed, he leaves me for a second, and reality comes crashing in. What we are about to do.

When he comes back with the gun I go still as a statue. He takes the safety off and places it on the nightstand beside us.

Giving me a choice.

# CHAPTER 5

Riley's intensity is nothing new. He has always been able to make women swoon, and men shit their pants with just one look.

At school, he is a loner both by choice and because no one crosses the Bronze men. It is best to just stay out of their way entirely. It didn't take long for rumors to fly. Riley's name was in the mouths of every student and parent in Harmony, with different versions of what happened the night they found Riley's father in the pawnshop.

I have never asked and never will. If he wanted to share with me, he would have. That night, he showed up with a faraway look in those brown eyes, which has never left his face since. I made a promise never to speak of what we both know. What *everyone* knows.

Tonight, I look into those same eyes as he scans my body, from my blonde hair down to my toes, as if he is trying to memorize the image. I swear it's like daggers slicing trails as evidence he had been the one to travel these roads first, see me, *all* of me. Those honey irises that once were compared to a wolf's by Jez. Jez who was so obviously a sheep, prey, and she was okay with that. Just like Corey said, she knew her place in this world. Do I?

Before me, I do not see a predator. I do not see bloodlust or danger. I see a survivor. We all knew his father had a darkness to him. One he passed on to his children. Riley wouldn't have done what he did if he didn't think it necessary. It's not a game, life, not to him, not to any of us. We didn't get a choice in the matter. It's always been kill or be killed. Riley made a choice, one that doesn't need any further explanation than that.

I search Riley's face, giving him permission to touch. His brows push together. "I don't know if I will be able to stop myself once I start." He stands over me by the lamp as I lay on the bed. The black dress covers almost nothing. It may even be torn from our encounter at the door. "You have to stop me if I go too far." He moves his attention to the gun again.

Without thought, I sit up, reach for his face, and turn it away from the weapon and back to me. I swallow hard as I nod my understanding of his words. Riley goes somewhere else. Just like at the pawnshop when his eyes did not latch onto anything in particular, as if he is reliving something awful. "Riley." His name falls from my mouth with ease. However, I have never said it quite like that. Desperate.

He blinks away whatever was at the front of his mind. Finally, I have all of him again. "Come back to me." I tap the sheets of the bed that were not made this morning. I've done this exact motion before many times in our lives. Inviting Riley into my bed, but tonight it's different.

Riley obeys, crawling over the top of me and pinning me beneath him, his legs straddling me on each side. His hands grip desperately at my arms, he pushes them up until they are over my head. He leaves them there as he moves down to my waist and pulls at my dress until it's past my legs. His hands somehow never leave me until the dress is gone completely and he is on his knees at the bottom of the bed. Riley dangles the black, definitely torn dress on one finger as he looks at me. I am bare, aside from the thin fabric of my panties.

Before I can be embarrassed or think of all the imperfections that stare at me in the mirror every morning, Riley drops the dress and moves over the top of me again, kissing the spot over my heart. Taking my breath away along with all my racing thoughts. He kisses lower, taking a nipple into his mouth. A deep noise vibrates the sensitive nub. I suck my bottom lip into my mouth to stop myself from squealing at the new feeling.

It's *all* new, yet I have played this out in my head hundreds of times. I run my hands over the top of his head, feeling the softness of his hair on my fingertips. I miss when it was long.

Riley runs a hand down my side, over my ribs, and under my hip until his palm is firm on my bottom, pulling me upwards to meet him. With my hands free, I quickly pull at the fabric of his shirt. He throws it over his head without missing a beat and is back on me in a second.

Then everything speeds up. My fingers wrap around Riley's belt. Finally, I tug the leather out of its loops and start on the brass button of his Levi's. They are off just as quickly as the rest of our clothes. When it's just us in our underwear, I take the time to look up at him. Only to find him frowning down at me. His jaw clenched tightly. I reach up and trace the muscle that looks like it hasn't relaxed in years. It's what gives him that chiseled jawline.

"Don't do that." I paw at his lip like he often does mine. "Just be with me." Words I have wanted to say for so long but never had the courage to.

His brows come together, confused. "You don't see it, do you?" he asks, and I can't for the life of me figure out what he means.

My head cocks slightly to the side as I try to find the answer on his face. "See what?" I ask when I do not find what I am looking for.

"What everyone else sees when they look at me." He lifts me into him once more, sending spikes of ecstasy up my spine now that there is basically nothing between the two of us. I moan into his mouth, and he seems pleased, but he still has that look on his face.

I lick my lips, which has his mouth twitching. "You don't scare me, Riley Bronze." I tell him.

"You might change your mind." His hand comes to my middle before sliding down past the elastic of my thong. "You *will* change your mind." He whispers as he parts me with his middle finger. His words sound distant.

He takes his time, and it kills me. Building me up, letting me come to the edge of climax before slowing his pace. My clit throbs. As if he knows, he runs a finger over it in slow, circular motions. "I will take what I can get before you do." Then he is down onto his stomach between my legs, his frown replaced with hunger.

Riley furiously licks the spot between my legs, dipping in his fingers along with his tongue. He holds me flat against the bed with the other. He doesn't know his own strength. It's heavy, possessive. It makes me feel like I couldn't run away even if I wanted to. I don't. In fact, at this moment, I want Riley to be a permanent fixture of my body, with his head between my legs.

I grab at the pillows behind me as another wave of pleasure makes my toes curl in on themselves. This time, he doesn't stop. My legs fall open further. He pushes them so they are flat against the bed. Another possessive gesture. The pain of how far he spreads me adds to the pleasure.

He tentatively licks and pokes and bites until I can't hold back anymore. I am screaming his name as I climax.

I'm still recovering as he slides back up to me. "Taste yourself." He demands in a soft whisper. Riley holds his pointer and middle fingers up to my mouth, asking me to open. When I do, he slides them past my teeth, settling onto my tongue. Salty and sweet. Sweat and lavender. I suck him into my mouth further as I glance up at him. "I knew it would be good," he seems to say to himself.

Those two fingers remain. Riley locks his eyes on mine as he shoves his fingers further until they touch the back of my throat. I gag on them at first, then relax with him inside me.

"Turn around." He doesn't move from my mouth. I would do anything he asked if he always said it like that. With his eyes narrowed in on me and his voice low and sultry. I turn slowly. He keeps his fingers firmly pushed up against the back of my throat. They twist as I twist. Riley uses the position as a sort of leash because wherever his fingers go, I go, too.

When he lifts me into a kneeling position, I stay there. Then he settles behind me on his knees as well. He uses them to spread me apart. Now choked and unable to move, he runs his length over the sensitive spot at the base of my spine before lowering himself perfectly beneath me. He reaches between us, positioning himself at my center. At this point, I am drooling and nearing another climax from this action alone.

As he pulls me down onto him, I let out an involuntary moan of pleasure. It's not gentle, in any way, as he plunges inside of me. He fills me completely and then more. I close my eyes as pain takes over, followed by a rush of extreme pleasure I have never felt before. My legs begin to shake, and I know it won't be long until I'm coming on top of him. The noises leaving my body feel foreign. Probably because I have never made them before, not even when I would think of Riley while my own fingers filled the space he now occupies.

Whatever he is doing to me is both agony and delight. Punishment and pleasure. He pulls me down further and further, over and over. It's nothing short of ecstasy. I am lightheaded, enjoying each breath of Riley's that slides down my back. Something about him filling two of my spaces at once has the rest of me igniting.

"I will never get enough, Emerson." The sound of his voice has my eyes rolling back. I flood him with my orgasm, which only makes him shove his fingers into me deeper.

My ears ring, and my chest heaves in heavy ups and downs. We stay like that, our bodies moving against each other, as I relish the feeling of climax. When I relax, he removes himself from my mouth, using both his hands to push me further into the bed. My wrists go back firmly in place at the base of my spine. Riley keeps going, holding me there as he drives into me.

I don't think I could ever get enough, either.

With one final growl that will forever be etched into my brain, he collapses on top of me, his seed leaking from between my legs. We catch our breath together, our chests moving in and out at the same tempo before he falls beside me. I stay on my stomach, looking over at him in awe. My eyes feel heavy, and my body is definitely going to be sore tomorrow. He leans over and places a kiss on my shoulder before standing and slipping back into his boxers.

His footsteps make their way to the bathroom, where the faucet turns on. Cold water, like always. When he returns, he places a cloth over my head and then slides it down my back. Which ignites me again even though I don't think I could take any more. Riley reaches the spot between my legs, where he gently dabs the cloth over the mess. Then he pulls the covers over my body, pushes my hair behind my ear, and pulls the string on the lamp so we are in complete darkness aside from the sliver of light from a part in the curtains.

When my eyes adjust, I see Riley staring up at nothing, his hands behind his head, his face pinched. "What now?" I ask him and myself. I really don't know. He will leave. I will wait for Jez for God knows how long. The club will breathe down my throat, and the money I make anywhere else will never be enough unless I sell myself to them.

He takes a moment to answer. Like he is having one of those internal debates with himself. Riley pulls me into him with one arm and uses the other to stroke circles on my bare skin. "Go to Jericho." He whispers. "Find your sister." His fingers stop their sweet circles. "Then *I* will find *you*." He promises.

# PART 1

---

Naive

# PART 2

---

FEARLESS

# CHAPTER 6

Chapter 6

My alarm blares. When I reach over to turn it off, my hand touches paper instead of metal—Riley's handwriting. Last night plays in my head on a loop. Even my dreams were replays of Riley's body against my own.

I slam my finger down on the alarm to stop its buzzing. Then, I open the note Riley left for me. *You snore.* That is all it says, and I can't help but smile as I crumple up the paper and toss it in the nearby bin. I don't know what I expected.

I make my way to the kitchen, where it is evident Riley has made himself at home. There's leftover coffee in the pot, and he checked the mail. It's in a neat pile on the otherwise messy countertop. He put a letter with perfect script on top. Jez.

My hands can hardly work fast enough as I peel the letter from its envelope, ignoring the rest of the pile. Her perfect penmanship on the front of the envelope now has a tear down its middle.

*Em,*

*B and I have decided you should finish school in the Outer Ring. You wouldn't like the schools here anyway. \*Redacted\* \*Redacted\* \*Redacted\* You have friends there, a life, I can't up and move you to a new place with a new school.*

*Ask Corey for a job at the pawnshop, and don't let anyone talk you into taking a gig at the club.*

*Remember that day in October, \*Redacted\* \*Redacted\* \*Redacted\* \*Redacted\* \*Redacted\* I won't ever forget and you shouldn't either.*

*Sorry, this letter is so short. I don't have a lot of time.*

*Save yourself the money, do not try to write back.*

*Lots of love,*

*-Jezebel*

My heart sinks. So much for Riley's plan of going to Jericho, especially now that I am clearly unwanted. I don't need to know the words that were redacted to understand what this means. She doesn't want me.

All our talks about Jericho, all the plans we made. Jez wasn't talking about *us*. She was talking about *herself.*

I shove the letter in my school bag, uncaring if the paper crumples.

It's a little sister's destiny to be unwanted by her older sister.

When I get to school, I don't have time to look for Riley through the crowd of people before the broken bell rings. Its unsettling tune cuts out at the end. So far, I have been laughed at a total of four times. It will only get worse. I know it. I was supposed to be gone, not here enduring what can only be described as torture.

It's not the teasing that gets to me. It's the fact that my hopes were up. I had a whole life planned in my head for my sister and me. Now, that will never happen, and I have to live *this* life instead.

Lunch comes around and I haven't wanted to spend the money I got from Corey on much. I'm certainly not wasting it on what the school considers a healthy meal. It's all slop with warm milk on the side.

I search for Riley at the tables, but he isn't there. Sometimes, he works lunch at the shop so Corey can check on the girls at the club. I sit on the bench outside and soak up as much of the sun on this weirdly warm day in December. It's always warm like this before it snows.

As I read Jez's letter for the hundredth time today, I force myself to keep it in one piece instead of tearing it into little pieces and scattering it to the wind.

I'm stuck here in Harmony with everyone else who can't escape. What's worse is I was stupid enough to believe I wasn't like them. That I was different, determined enough to get out.

Riley doesn't come back, I know, because I was late to class waiting for him. Maybe even Riley doesn't want me. I push the thought from my head. *Sulking gives you wrinkles.* Jez's voice fills my thoughts. It always does, especially when I do not want it to.

After school, I walk to the pawnshop first, determined to find Riley. The streets are busy as usual. Jez taught me the right streets to travel on. Avoiding men with ill intentions and women who offer their services to anyone who passes by.

When I get to the storefront, I look through the window first. It's an instinct. I would avoid the place altogether when Jez wasn't working and still do not go in when it's just Corey. Today it is, but I have no choice. Not if I want to find what I am looking for.

Corey is talking to a tall gentleman in a uniform—the same tan the military wears, one that will soon be on the back of Riley with his last name on the tag. Right next to a pin with golden wings. Jez says the ones with the fewest pins on their chests are easiest. Easiest for what? I never asked. Of course, I know the answer now.

The military man talks with his hands, accentuating each word with a raise of his arms. He pushes them out to Corey as if trying to explain something.

Today, I do not get to avoid Corey because there is nowhere else Riley could be. If he isn't here, I can't help but think he has taken on another job again—one he promised to avoid if he had any other choice.

Something about Harmony has it craving the taboo. Corey's business caters to most men in the Outer Ring, but some have *other* preferences.

When I slip in the door, I can feel Corey's daggering eyes on me first, even with my back turned as I pretend to be interested in a very ugly coat. Their conversation becomes quiet, but I can still make out some of what the man says to Corey. "I'm counting on your discretion." He says so calmly the hair on my neck is standing on end. Then the man in tan heads for the door. I peek around the side of the rack. Pins line the left side of his chest—not an easy one at all. He takes one look at me from the corner of his eye with one hand on the door, half open, before leaving.

I follow him with my eyes until he is around the corner. "Eavesdropping, Squirt?" Corey hums. His face is red like a child who just received a scolding. Unlike his brother, Corey doesn't hide his anger well. Riley keeps it in until he cannot anymore. Corey does quite the opposite, letting it drift slowly out of him and onto the people around him. No matter how calm or collected he may seem. If you look close enough you will see the twitch of his eye, the repetitive tapping of his fingers.

I shake my head as I muster the courage to look him in the eye. "Where is Riley?" I ask straight to the point.

Corey's features contort into a disgustingly smug smile. It's obvious he knows something I do not. "Well, I *could* tell you." He almost purrs as he swings his legs over the desk and hops down to the other side. I don't move. Jez warned me of men's primal need to chase. *If you don't run, they don't have a reason to catch you.*

I make sure to straighten my back and look him in the eye. "He wasn't at school."

He breaks for just a second, but long enough for me to see the confusion underneath his cocky mask. "What will you give me if I tell you?" he leans in close enough I can smell the cologne on his skin. It's not enough to hide the booze on his breath.

I wouldn't give him anything. Ever. But maybe to get what I need, I could pretend. "I don't have much to give Corey, you know that." I make sure to dip my words in honey before I say them.

Corey's eyes drop to my middle before snaking their way back up to my face. "You have more than you think." My bottom lip might catch fire if he doesn't quit staring at it.

"Tell me where he is, and maybe I will find something to give you." I can't believe Jez's lessons are kicking in. I even lean in a little as I speak. I can see his gears turning as he thinks of his answer.

Then, as if realization hits, his brows scrunch together. Corey looks down at me in surprise. "He didn't tell you?" He shakes his head slightly.

Then it's my turn to be confused. "Tell me what?" I ask.

"You are with him all the time. I just assumed-"He takes a pack of cigarettes out of his pocket and pounds them on the palm of his hand. He shakes his head in disbelief, with a hint of smugness. "Fuck, he *really* didn't tell you." Corey huffs.

"Tell me what?" I repeat louder this time.

Corey laughs. Then he checks each of my eyes like he is looking for something. When he doesn't find what he is searching for, he shakes his head again. "He is gone, kid." He holds an unlit cigarette between his lips. *Gone.* The word just doesn't make sense.

I look up at Corey for answers like he did to me moments ago. Right eye, left, but I find nothing. For a second, it almost seems like Corey cares, his features soften, but when I blink, asshole Corey is back. "Did you hear me, Squirt?" He heads for the door. I follow. "Gone. The Army shipped him to the wall." I follow him outside, where he lights a cigarette. Corey holds it out in my direction. Why does he do that?

I shake my head, both at my disbelief and his offer. "What do you mean?" I demand. "He told me he wasn't supposed to leave until after graduation," I tell him.

Corey leans against the wall of the pawnshop. "Well, then, he's a liar." He turns his head to me before he blows the smoke into my face. Riley is many things, but not a liar. He wouldn't do that, especially after the night we shared together. He wouldn't just leave me. He—but I am out of excuses.

"Go home." Corey's words pull me from my near spiral. Tears sting at my eyes, and Corey can tell. "Don't fucking cry. Go home." His words grow louder at the end, and this time, it comes with a shove to my shoulder that has me tripping over myself.

Embarrassed and now crying, I run home, just like he told me.

The home everyone has left me in. Jez and now Riley. Now I have no one and nowhere to go. How could they do this to me, leave me here?

I go to the bedroom and rip the sheets off the bed. I should burn them for what he has done to me. I want no reminders of last night.

I want back what I cannot have.

Gathering the blankets in my arms I head for the window, the one Riley climbed through. Then I throw them out of it, not caring who may be below. "What the fuck!" I shout at the walls.

Next, I pull Jez's letter out of my bag and hold it in my hand. I read it one more time before I pull at its corners, splitting it in half with a scream. Then I take those halves and tear them again and again until it's nothing but tiny bits of white on the stained carpet.

# CHAPTER 7

When I step out of the club, illuminated by the pink neon sign, it is well past midnight. In the silence, it emits a low hum I find oddly peaceful. The air is crisp with the chill of winter, sending plumes of clouds out as I breathe. Soon, the season will change, which I welcome. Winter has never brought anything good to me.

The air was frozen, just like this, the night Riley decided I was not worth an explanation. It was snowing when Jez started working at this exact club. As if the universe was showing me my cruel fate to end up like my sister, it was snowing on the day Corey asked me if I would like a job at the club. To which I said yes.

I was twenty-one, the bills started coming in, and the pawnshop wasn't paying enough to keep up with everything. Now it's been nearly five years since I got sucked in. Seven since I was left behind.

Twenty-five is not a bad age. Jez will be thirty-five this year. I smile at the thought. She would have made a big deal out of it. She probably would have bought a cake with money she didn't have and made us celebrate the coincidence.

The screech of the back door closing pulls me from thought. Corey hands me a blunt after taking a long drag for himself. I take it, pulling the smoke into my lungs, holding it there to reap its benefits. It's been a long night. The men were more than generous.

Turns out, I'm not too bad at this. The music makes it easier, mixed with weed and booze. Not just for myself. If you feed enough of it to the men, they become docile. The next day, you make them think they got their hands on you when, really, they could hardly even stand. You would think they'd catch on, but they never do.

Corey has been strangely more than understanding. He makes sure I am never on the other side of a fight, and he never asks me to do anything I am uncomfortable with. I mostly dance. I like it, too. It's something I am good at.

The other girls make their complaints about my work, how I do not share the same responsibility they do. Corey never brings it up. He even calls me by my stage name, and not the not-so-endearing name that was more fitting for a little sister.

"See you tomorrow, Babe?" Corey asks as I hand him back his blunt. *Babe,* it sounds better within the walls of the club. It's better than a flower or fruit, I suppose.

I wrap my jacket around myself and look down the street towards my apartment, trying not to think about all those years ago when I took this walk with Riley on a night as cold as this one.

Lies, all of them. Working for the club has not only taught me how to catch the lies but tell them, too.

Almost, I *almost* let myself forgive him when I think of all the shit we go through just to get through the day. Just to make it in Harmony without getting swallowed by the concrete itself. Lying makes it easier. You lie to yourself, mostly. "Yeah, I guess." I shrug up at Corey. It's not like I have any other plans. I might as well make some easy cash.

Corey turns for the metal door but only opens it halfway before turning back to me. Warm air rushes out of the club. "Do you want to sit in again?" He looks like he instantly regrets the offer but continues anyway. "For the Jericho boys, they like to see the blondes, but they never take." He assures me. Just like he did that day. I have to laugh to myself because my sister, my near twin only with much softer features, was chosen by one of those men.

"How much?" I counter.

Corey grins. "500." It's the same offer he gave me the first time. I know this game, so I start to walk away, flipping my hair behind me as I go. "1000," he calls out to me.

I laugh up at the sky so he can hear me. "I'll be there," I say.

The door slams behind me as Corey goes back to the warmth of the club. I hurry home. Walking right past the mailboxes outside our door. I used to check it every day, hoping to see a letter with perfect script. After a couple of years I gave up.

Instead, I head straight to the cupboard and make myself a cup of coffee. It's going to be light out soon. I think I will just stay up, maybe go to the roof to see the sunrise. The way Jez and I would often do.

The bitter taste of the coffee makes me cringe, but I'm glad I have it when I climb my way up the fire escape. It warms me from the inside out. I can't help but be reminded of Jez as the scent wafts into my nose. Jez lied the most of all. She would take me up here and make promises she could never keep. I know why now. It was fun to dream, and it kept both of us going.

The sun is warm but not nearly enough. My arms fill with goose-bumps as I wait for the city to start moving. Lights turn on. People crawl out of their homes. Women giggle on their way back from a one-night stand.

The silence right before makes it seem like the world is suspended in time. There is no debt to pay or hunger in your belly. No one has wronged you yet or ever will because you will be here with a cold mug in your hand, looking up at the sky forever.

It never lasts. When it gets too noisy, I grab my things and head back down the stairs. When I unlock the barred window and climb through, I hear the clicking of a small brass door. The mailbox outside the apartment. With a huff of annoyance, I head for the door. I *should* check it, even though it's most likely full of credit card offers and debt relief programs with Jez's name on them—Jezebel M. Knight. I hate looking at that name.

Still, I make my way out to the hall, peeking around the corner for nosey neighbors before opening the lockbox labeled 52 B. The small door falls open from the force of its contents. Paper falls like snow to the floor around my feet. Cursing, I scramble to pick them up.

Jez's name is nowhere in sight as I look at the scattered envelopes. No, they are all addressed to me. Emerson D. Knight. There it is, as I wished it would be all those years ago. I would recognize this handwriting anywhere, Jez.

For a moment, I am frozen. Then, I gather them all in my arms. There must be at least fifty letters here. My heart sinks when I see the postage date. They all came today, every single one of them.

Shoving them into the bottom of my shirt so I can carry them all, I return to the apartment. I scatter them onto the table and carefully peel the envelopes open one by one.

They are all the same.

*Dear Emerson.* Followed by... nothing. *Redacted,* I am tired of seeing that word. They all end with: *Lots of love, Jezebel.* I can't believe this. I got my hopes up, and I can't even see what she wrote.

The anger I felt that day, when the weight of being left behind threatened to crush me, wells up in my heart all over again. I can't stop the tears from falling onto the useless letters, leaving smudges on the black ink. My face warms, and I want to scream at the top of my lungs. Instead, I push the letters off the table until they are spread across the kitchen floor before going to the radio and turning it up. My fingers tangle in my hair as I think of what this means.

Someone in Jericho must be playing a sick joke. Jez was done with me. She said so. Quickly, I head to my room, ripping open the desk drawer where there are discarded school assignments I never turned in and old bills, but at the very bottom is the first letter she sent me from Warshaw. I don't know why I kept it all these years.

She only started getting censored in Jericho.

Originally, I thought it was just a formality. Jericho has always been a secret. The only thing we are told about it is that it's a paradise. The top of our mountain, yet free of snow and ice. I knew they were strict. Their rules for who can enter and who can leave. It didn't seem too far-fetched for them to be careful of what information they shared as well.

Jez would not send me letters knowing I can't read them, would she? *Unless* she sent all the letters at once to tell me she, in fact, cannot say *anything* at all. That her life in Jericho is not what it was supposed to be. All the pieces come together, excruciatingly painful because I didn't see it before, how dumb and naïve I was, *am.*

*Nothing will beat our secret spot. The terrarium. Remember that day in October. Jezebel.* Not Jez.

Our secret spot was where we made our plans, and the terrarium housed a spider, a *trapped* spider that later died. Goddamnit, it's all a plea for help.

Finally, I think of her biggest warning. The day in October, when she stood on the roof and overlooked the city below. She stepped up on the ledge without fear and held her arms out to balance herself against the wind. "What if?" She asked to the sky. "What if when we get to Jericho, it's not at all what we expect?" The image of her peeking over her shoulder at me sticks to the back of my eyelids.

*What if,* that's a phrase you just don't say in Harmony. *What if's* get you in trouble. "It will be everything and more," I told her, mostly to get her off the ledge. It's not uncommon for women in her position to take their own lives. It's easier than facing reality.

"Would you stay with me?" She asked, "Even if it was miserable?" I remember inching towards her as she spoke. I needed to get to her, to save her.

*What a weird question,* I thought to myself that day, not knowing the truth. "I would never leave you. You know that." I assured her.

When she turned back to face Harmony, I took one large step in her direction, putting us within arm's distance. Her robe blew in the wind. Then, "Would you leave me?" It wasn't a question about Jericho or if the grand city would live up to our expectations. It was about right then and there. She was going to leave me. I felt it in my bones and even though she didn't jump that day, she *still* left me.

"Even if it's miserable," I say to myself. The same as I did that day.

# CHAPTER 8

"What the fuck?" Corey holds up his arms in annoyance. "You didn't," he says in disbelief as I approach him. His jaw is already twitching, and anger radiates from his direction as he watches me sit in front of a mirror.

The same as I do every day, I use Jez's red lipstick to line my lips. "I did," I say back to his reflection, bored. He can't tell me what I can and cannot do. No matter how many contracts I sign for this damned place, he doesn't own me, not like this.

When he steps towards me, he lowers his voice so the other girls cannot hear. I watch his every move carefully. "My office, now." I roll my eyes but stand to follow—past the shocked faces and prying eyes, past the mirrors I can't help but look into as we go. I look so different. I hardly recognize myself.

I know what this is about. I also know we don't have much time before we sit for our guest from Jericho. "What the fuck," he says more to himself than me.

I roll my eyes again. It's hard not to. "You already said that." I remind him. He places his hands on his hips and looks up at me through his lashes. For a second, I see *him*—Riley. Suddenly, it's not Corey's disappointment, it is his brothers. The kind of disappointment that makes your stomach turn. I hate being reminded of what that feels like. I also hate the fact that I still feel like I am wronging Riley in some way when *he* is the one who wronged *me*.

Corey clenches his jaw before checking his watch for the time. He crosses his arms in front of his large chest before slowly, too slowly, coming back around to my side of the desk and leaning against it. Far too close for my comfort.

Corey is a lot of things, malicious, quick to anger, his eyes linger a little too long, and he doesn't give a damn about personal space. But he's not stupid.

He keeps his face neutral, but I can see him fuming beneath the surface. "You sure you want to do that, Squirt?" he finally says, his nostrils flared.

I laugh at his attempt to get under my skin with the nickname. "They like to see the blondes, but they never take." I remind him of his own words. I reach up to tuck the strands of brown out of my face.

My quick dye session this morning left my bathroom stained, but my hair is now the perfect chestnut color, just like the box described. Paired with one of Jez's faux leather skirts and a top that leaves little to the imagination with its thin white fabric, I know I will be the picture of perfect for purchase.

Corey smiles, not the kind he uses to seduce women or the fake kind that doesn't quite make it to his eyes. "You're crazy," he says with a light shake of his head. Under the anger lies curiosity, and beyond that, I do not want to know. "Alright." He agrees to let me sit. It's certainly not what I thought was going to happen. I prepared myself for fire, for rage, a storm that would end in injury. Corey has never hit me. I never gave him a reason to, but I never left my guard down around him, either. Cherry and the others are filled with bumps and bruises, some of which are from the customers. Some are not.

Three quick knocks have me jumping out of my skin. I look at Corey, who still stares in that strange way, and then at the door. When Corey makes no effort to move, I turn the handle, opening it for him. Cherry stands on the other side. There is the rage, not who I thought it would come from, but there all the same. "You can't let her go out there," she looks through me to Corey.

I hold my tongue. I'm not one to add fuel to the fire. Cherry's large eyes land on mine. They are hot with anger. "There are girls who have been waiting years for this." Cherry tries. "You have no idea what you're getting yourself into." She continues as tears well up in her eyes.

"And what is that?" I ask her because I am genuinely curious. Do they know what Jez is going through right now? Did Jez know what she was getting herself into? Of course, Cherry would not tell me.

Cherry looks me up and down. I feel Corey's gaze burning a hole into the back of my head. "Let's just say you can't dance your way out of this one. They want more than you're willing to offer." Cherry spits.

*Whatever it takes.* Jez did the same for me. After Dad died, she took care of me. She did the unspeakable. She put on a happy face. She pretended everything was fine for years. I can, too.

Cherry looks over her shoulder at the other girls impatiently as she waits for my answer. Thankfully, I don't have to provide one. Corey comes up behind me, places a hand on my bare shoulder, and answers for me. "She will sit. Time to go." is all he says before security gathers us and walks us behind the stage.

Straightening my shoulders, I prepare myself for what is to come. To be chosen would mean a free trip to Jericho, *to save her*. I breathe in and out slowly. *For Jez*, I tell myself over and over again.

The lights dim. *For Jez*. Karla whistles through her teeth as she gives us the go-ahead. *For Jez*. I push away my fear and take my strides without hesitation. *For Jez*. I look out beyond the lights, hoping to latch eyes with one of those men in their tailored suits.

Just like before, they emerge from the darkness and begin to assess the women on stage. Even though I don't have to do anything but sit here and look pretty, it's hard. I think of all the things that could go wrong, all the ways in which my plan could fail. My heart is pounding, and sweat is accumulating on my brow.

The men seek out their desired woman. Cherry sits beside me. A few are very interested in her. If what the other girls say is true, they always are. I wonder why they haven't made a deal for her.

A couple of men walk by, whispering into each other's ears as they pass Cherry and the men who ogle her. One laughs. His teeth are too white, his hair is perfectly slicked back, and he has three watches on his left wrist. He walks over to the men who stand between Cherry and me. "He'll never let you take that one. Trust me, I've tried." He says in a low whisper. I note the way he refers to Cherry as not a woman but an object. It's not surprising.

I can't help but look over, watching as realization dawns on her. Her eyebrows quirk upwards before her shoulders sag. Then her eyes close for a second too long. Now she, along with every woman who sits in the spotlight, knows. Cherry's chances of getting out of her are zero for no other reason than Corey's selfishness.

They continue their search, leaving Cherry behind. Her shoulders move up and down as she whimpers.

The men walk out of my peripheral. I track them by the sounds of their footsteps. A certain man's steps come up behind me, then retreat before he circles around again. He passes so closely in front of me I can't even see his face, only the black suit with the top buttons undone, a undone tie lies draped around his neck.

"Mm," he hums to himself, low and terrifying. Then he leaves again—or at least I thought he had left—until I feel my own hair being lifted from my shoulder. I keep as still as possible until the man, with my hair still in his hand, comes into view. "What's this, little blue?" he asks me. *Blue*, like my eyes, like his. My eyes go to the brown strand between his fingertips.

All thoughts leave my head. I swallow so hard you can hear it. He seems to like this reaction because he cocks his head to the side with a curious grin and drops my hair. He bends down onto one knee. Then, he wraps a hand around my neck. His flesh is soft, cold against my own burning skin. "Do it again." He begs as his eyes latch themselves to the spot between my collarbones.

So I do. I swallow the lump in my throat. The man is pleased with the movement, the feeling of me beneath his palm. Then, his thin lips curl into a devious grin. His eyes are no longer on me. He finds what he is looking for somewhere behind me. "I told you I would be back." I can't tell who he speaks to.

The hand around my throat tightens before he retreats. He stands, placing his hands in his pockets and leaning back as if to get a better look at me. His piercing blue irises seem to glow as he stands against the black.

Blond hair and blue eyes—the same man as before. He really meant it when he said he would be back for me. We stay like that, staring at each other for a few uncomfortable seconds before I look down, and the man disappears behind me. I let out a heavy breath and brace myself for what comes next.

Just like that—*bought*.

Is this what Jez felt like when she was chosen to be taken to Jericho? Did she lie about knowing B before she left? If it was a situation like this, it would have been the first time they ever met. He paid Corey for her and took her to Jericho, just like what is about to happen to me. How many times did she lie to make it easier on me? How many times did she lie to make it easier on *herself*?

No more men stop at my spot. They don't even look at me. There might as well be big red letters on my forehead—*Sold*. Chairs shuffle and scrape against the floor around me. I stand to leave with the others. I try not to look around too much even though I so badly want to find the man who has laid his claim on me. We return to the dressing room, where shouting comes from Corey's office. "It's been years!" Cherry screams. I can't see the tears, but I know they are there. "What's so fucking special about *her*." She puts a wicked twist on the word *her*. Me, she means me. Corey says something I can't make sense of, followed by "You goddamned liar!" *Smack*. The sound of flesh on flesh. I cringe. Then, silence.

We all knew Corey had a special interest in Cherry. We just didn't know he was denying every offer *because* of his obsession. The office is quiet for what feels like a long time. Then, the handle clicks, and a red-faced, make-up-smeared Cherry comes out. As usual, she adjusts her dress and holds her nose in the air. Then, she walks right past me like nothing happened. I do feel bad for her, but there is nothing more important than getting to Jez.

I linger outside Corey's office for a moment, but I know I can't avoid him forever. After giving Corey enough time to reign in his anger so it does not attach itself to me, I hear the click of a lighter and smell the weed. That's when I head in and sit in the chair. The one closest to the door in case I need to leave quickly. Corey huffs a laugh when he sees me cross my legs. A trail of smoke follows from the brown rolled paper between his fingers as he moves behind the desk like I'm not even here. "I bet you're happy." He moves papers around, looking for something. "I hope you find what you are looking for in Jericho." It's not quite sarcastic, but he might as well have spit in my face.

He opens a drawer and pulls out familiar paperwork. The same ones I signed when I started working here. A deal with the devil. When you work for the club, they provide their services to you, but it also means you are their property. You belong to the club, you can be bought and sold as they please.

Corey slides it over and leans back in his chair. I sign the spot beneath my other signature, dotting the I in Knight with an X. Slowly, I slide it back to him and stand, prepared to make my exit. Corey stands as well. I freeze. Of course, he will not make it easy. He makes his way to the door, a cloud of smoke in his wake. He brushes me with his shoulder as he passes. Just as I thought he would, he stands between me and the door to block me from leaving.

*Déjà vu.* He digs his hands into his front pocket and pulls out cash from the leather. He counts slowly, antagonizing me. Then, Corey catches my eyes before dropping the wad of hundreds on the floor. "Pick it up." He says too calmly.

He won't get the reaction he wants from me. I roll my eyes before raising my leg to step over the discarded cash. I am not going to need his money where I am going. Corey takes a step to the side, stopping me dead in my tracks. My head nearly hits his shoulder. "I said, pick. It. Up." He now looks down past his pushed-out chest at me. No matter how many inches in height I gained this year, I am still shorter than Corey Bronze, but now I feel insignificant. His hand comes to his mouth as he takes another uncaring drag of the blunt between his fingers.

I stare at the spot between his brows, not letting him see how scared I am. When he does not so much as blink, "You are exactly who I thought you were," I spit at him. His movements are quick. Before I know it, his fingers are wrapped around my hair at the base of my skull.

He pulls me in so close I can taste the cologne he sprays on his neck. "And you're just like the rest of those whores." He breathes as evil flashes behind his eyes. With the leverage of his hands in my hair, he pushes me down. Forcing me to the ground to pick up the bills from the floor. I obey, gathering them into fists. When I am done, he drags me back up and holds me close again.

Just when I think it's over, he pulls me into him. He takes no precaution, crashing down on me like a tidal wave. He parts me with his tongue as he forces a kiss. He holds me so tightly it hurts. My head stings with pain as some of my hair is ripped from my skull. I try to deny him, holding my mouth closed as best as I can. He doesn't care. In fact, he smiles against my mouth, pleased with the amount of fight I put up. His other hand comes up from beside him. The one that once had a blunt in it now holds a knife.

The cold blade pushes against the side of my face in a threat. He continues his assault, shoving his tongue inside of my mouth. He tastes like smoke and gasoline. *I hate him. I hate him.* I have no choice but to give in, letting him take what he wants. Once he is satisfied, he pulls back but keeps me in place, moving the blade from my cheek down to my throat. "It gets worse." He warns. Then he pushes the blade into my flesh. Ignoring the pain, I force our eyes to meet, making sure he can see every bit of his reflection in my eyes like I can see my own in his.

Warmth drips down between my breasts. "I wonder if I will have the same fate as my father." he queries as he follows a drop of blood down with his eyes. I don't try to make sense of his drunken ramblings. Especially when he drops the knife back to his side, he releases me and steps to the side, giving me room to leave. I hurry for the exit, only letting myself fall apart when I am on the other side of the club's back door, and the low hum of pink neon is in my ear.

# CHAPTER 9

There is little time to sleep, but when I do, I dream of brown eyes in the corner of my room, disappointment on his face. The gun stays tucked beneath my pillow and the mattress. Since Riley left, it has gone with me everywhere. I've gotten very good at having it on my body where no one can see it. The silver is cold against my flesh as I strap it to my thigh.

The rest of the night is spent packing. Most of our things will stay here. I can't very well take my favorite mug or the old radio along with me to Jericho. I take one more long look at the kitchen with all its memories. Jez's dance lessons and Riley's annoyance at our loud music.

"You're going to be late." I whip around to find Corey standing in my door frame. A woman stands behind him, peeking around his large shoulders into the apartment that is now hers. She looks all too eager, not to mention her not-so-subtle once-over as Corey leans against the wall.

I try my best not to reach for my gun even though I want nothing more than to put a bullet through Corey for what he did to me. What he probably does to Cherry every single day. "Why are you here?" I ask instead.

He sighs and takes a few steps forward that almost have me retreating before he grabs the bag out of my hand. "You're still mine until midnight." He tilts his head slightly at me.

Right, we take the midnight train to an inner city, Warshaw. Then, a plane into Jericho. I have never taken the train further than the next town over to shop with Jez. Certainly not the Inner Ring. Of course, I also haven't been on a plane. I feel my nerves getting the best of me.

Corey stands over me with that look he gets when he wants something. "I was never yours." I remind him. It is my last day, what's the worst thing that could happen? He already made the deal. I already signed the papers. He can't do anything to me unless he wants to owe the man who bought me. And it's more than even Corey can afford.

His confident mask slips, and his nostrils flare, letting me know I have said something to upset him. God, men are so easy to read. Then he places that mask right back on, unaware I even saw it move. "All set?" He asks as he looks around at the empty apartment. Then, before I can answer, "Jez never let me in here." He takes in the curtains made of patches of clothing. Internally, I laugh. *Yeah, no shit, she never let you in here,* I want to say but don't. "It's... homey." Corey decides on the word at the last minute.

*It was.* I correct him in my head. It hasn't truly been a home since Jez left. When there was music for dancing and not drowning out unwanted thoughts. When there was coffee in the morning while Jez sang in the bathroom, and not the coffee I use to keep me awake until sunrise. It *was* a home, but it's not anymore. It hasn't been for a long time.

Corey takes my bags down the five flights of stairs without a sweat. I guess all that time at the gym really paid off. No amount of attractiveness could make up for his personality, though. I suppose I should get used to men like him. Maybe I should thank him for training me in how to deal with assholes.

The men shake hands as we arrive at the station. My buyer, Ben, seems to have had a long night. He reeks of booze and sex. About three different shades of lipstick color his face and the collar of his shirt.

Ben leans over into my ear. I can hardly hear him as our train approaches. It squeals against the rails before coming to a stop. "Ravishing, Blue." he hiccups. He straightens his shoulders but still keeps his eyes trained on me. I'm surprised he can even stand with how much alcohol comes off his breath. It's almost enough to make *me* drunk. "Ravishing." He says again with a shake of his head like he can't believe it. Then he turns his attention away from me again.

I'm used to compliments. It's what happens before men ask for what they really want.

I turn to see Corey watching us like a hawk. My face feels warm with embarrassment even though nothing has happened. But I have seen that look before. It's the type of pinched features and heaving shoulders that come before the rage. Before he throws hands or holds you at knifepoint while he shoves his tongue down your throat. It's the same expression Riley gets. I usually run from it. Today, I have nowhere to go, nowhere that will get me closer to Jez anyway.

A high-pitched woman's voice comes over the intercom. You can't understand what she says. It is of no importance because there is only one train that runs from Harmony to the Inner Ring, and it's this one. Ben takes my bag from Corey's hand. I stiffen, waiting for a fight to break out between them.

Nothing happens, but still, I'm frozen, waiting. Until Ben grabs my hand and leads me towards the open train doors.

One more look at Corey, but it's not him I seek. I stare right at his bushy brows and honey eyes, and imagine Riley standing there. *Bastard.* That is for both of them.

I'm careful over the gap between the train and the broken cement of the station for fear my shoe will fall in. Ben places the bags overhead clumsily while muttering something to himself. When he sits he immediately checks the time on his watch before he crosses his arms and closes his eyes. The other men also take their seats, watching Ben the whole way. They even lean over to each other and whisper something at his expense. Ben is oblivious.

I hesitate to take a seat but am forced to when an attendant comes in and points next to Ben. "No standing on take-off." She sounds like she has said the phrase a million times. If she has to repeat it, who knows the kind of wrath we will endure. So, I sit.

Ben sinks down into the chair, leans his head against the back, and falls right to sleep. I wish I could do that. More quiet words are exchanged between the two across from us.

The train makes a noise like it's exhausted from shuttling people around all the time. With a few shakes and rattles, it hums with whatever energy runs this old thing. Then, we are off. I try to ignore the thumping of my heart.

It's finally happening. I am going to Jericho.

I shift under the gaze of the men, who roll their eyes and continue their secrets. I wonder if it's about me or the man beside me they speak of. It's not the first time I have endured such things, and it looks like it's not the first time for Ben, either.

The best way to deal with it is to avoid it altogether. I make sure to look down at my hands, twiddling my thumbs and braiding a few strands of hair to pass the time, all while Ben sleeps. His way of ignoring the not-so-subtle glances and fingers in our direction, if I had to guess.

This isn't exactly how I thought this part would go. My brain just skipped over the boring travel and went straight to Jericho, where I will find Jez.

There is a loose string on the hem of my skirt I pull at until a booming laugh fills my ears as one of the men runs past us to the back of the train and through a door labeled *lavatory,* a much nicer name than the one Jez and I gave our own bathroom. He throws his hands over his mouth as he goes. When he reaches the room, he has no time to shut the door before he bends over, hugs the toilet, and empties his stomach. I glance between the lavatory door and the two men in time to see them exchange money. They snicker to themselves. A bet has been won.

The commotion was enough to rouse Ben from his not-so-peaceful slumber. He was twitching and sighing every few seconds. "What's so funny?" he asks as he straightens his jacket and sits up.

A smile I hadn't realized I was wearing fades away. Ben looks at me expectantly, his face falls into its natural flatness, unamused. "Someone lost a bet," I say quietly as the man walks back slowly to his seat, holding onto every rail and rope he possibly can to keep from falling over.

Ben trails him with his blue-flame stare. "Nothing better to do with their money." He mutters in their direction. An observation he has clearly made before.

One snaps their head in our direction. "Got something you want to tell me, Ben?" This man's face looks as if it's made of plastic, all sharp features and clear skin. It's strange, they all look like that. It's as if someone has pinched their faces in all the right places and pinned the skin to the back of their heads. It's unnatural. These things do not extend to Ben, whose features are soft in most places but sharp in others, the way it's supposed to be.

I put my head down to avoid their heated conversation. Especially when I see the two of them stand. They walk past their friend, who is nearly passed out now. I watch only their feet as they near us, perfectly polished brown shoes with an emblem on the sides, some fancy company. "Come on now, I'm listening." One says to Ben.

Ben says nothing. "Maybe *she* will tell me what you said." I know he is talking about me, but I can't bring myself to look at him.

"*She* won't say anything to you," Ben replies for me, bored. "You know the rules." He reminds the man.

I can hear the man's smile as he talks. "Who would believe *you*?" he huffs.

Ben wipes his hands on his jaw, leans back onto the headrest once more, and sighs. "I'm too hungover for this," he says as if he is done with the conversation.

The man on the left isn't done, though. He reaches out and touches my chin, lifting it until I meet his eyes. "Dance for us, girl." The other man agrees with a slight nod of his head. "No rules against that, eh Ben?"

I try to turn my head to Ben, but the man I now see has brown greased-up hair and green eyes that lock onto me and don't let go, keeps my head in place. "No, no rules about that," Ben repeats lazily. I don't want to know what rules they speak of. With a deep breath, I agree with a nod. Assuming I cannot disobey, or at the very least, I *should* not, not if I want to get to Jez.

The black night sky and bright white train lights make me feel exposed. We can't see out, but anyone could see in. Just like when the lights were on the chairs at the club. We were in a cage made of it. Our predators could see their prey, but we could not see them. Just the way they want it.

*For Jez,* I remind myself as I stand in front of the men. I do not plead for them to change their minds. No, I know how much worse it can get if I do not do as they say. Many lessons from Jez on how to give, and how to take when the time is right.

I begin the same, memorized routine I have done every night for the last five years. Although not with a gun strapped to my thigh. I think of my next steps carefully. Greasy is first.

My first and most important rule: They do not touch without guidance. I choose the spot, the timing, the pressure. The same was true at the club. I brace my hands on Greasy's chest, gently pushing him to the seat across from us. "Sit and watch until it's your turn," I give a low command to the other man from over my shoulder, taking note of the hickeys on his neck as he watches with desire in his eyes. He obeys with a smirk, he likes that—being told what to do, they all do.

Ben sits up straighter and crosses his arms before him. They both wait to see what will happen next. I ignore them and turn all my attention to my John. It doesn't matter his name.

I make sure to look past those green eyes as I lift my leg to straddle him, searching for his soul. I think Jez was wrong because every man I have ever danced for has no such thing. No matter how hard I look, I can't seem to find *anything* behind their eyes, certainly not a soul.

Each move has been practiced over and over, making them come out perfectly timed. First, I grab his wrists and guide them to my hips, holding them there so they do not slip to my thigh. As I grind up against his middle, he looks down at my exposed skin and licks his lips.

I'm not dressed in the attire I would usually wear at the club. My loose skirt hides the gun well, but it's long and in the way of my dance.

Luckily, I have other assets I can use to my advantage. My cropped top fits nicely to my figure, giving the men across from me something to look at.

I slowly move up and down, rocking my hips, even letting him get a small taste of flesh when I push my breast up against his face.

Just as I timed it, one of his hands runs up the length of my stomach to the middle of my breast and back down again. He is satisfied, obvious by the tent in his pants that presses up against my ass. It's all so simple. They all want it the same way.

Next, I spin around so I am facing the two men across from me as I press into the man below me. Hickey is practically touching himself. Some men like to watch more than they like to play.

Ben keeps his face neutral as he takes it all in. He seems unphased by the whole act. Doesn't even look at the goods I have set out before him.

I take my Johns hands and wrap them around me so he palms my breast. I lean forward slightly so they are pushed up and nearly spilling out of my shirt. All while keeping a steady circle around the cock beneath me with my hips.

My hands go into my hair. I pull at the ends, creating a mess of brown strands. I had almost forgotten I dyed it until it falls into my face. Hickey smiles, all his too-white teeth showing, clearly enjoying himself. I'm not even surprised when he snakes a hand down his pants. I make sure to keep his attention, letting him in on the dance without actually touching him.

A small moan of pleasure escapes me. It's not even fake. You would be surprised how easily you forget the men and focus on your own pleasure. Which I have found adds to theirs. It took a while for me to come to terms with the fact I might just be fucked up enough to enjoy it. I thought it rather strange when I first started dancing and I would end the night with soaked panties. Then I started to like working at the club, the taboo of it all, the way the men were so malleable. I could use them in any way I wanted.

When I find release, I close my eyes, imagining another face. The man beneath me also grunts his pleasure. Across from me, Hickey is finishing himself off. The only person who does not move is Ben.

He has no reaction at all. He just sits there with his arms still crossed. I catch my breath, keeping my attention anywhere but on him. It's impossible when he begins to clap. Slow and pointed at the three of us for our performance. My cheeks heat as I scramble off of the lap of the man beneath me. I pull at my shirt that has ridden up and fix my skirt that miraculously didn't give away the weapon strapped to my thigh.

Ben continues his sarcastic clap. He ignores the men as they smile at each other. Then Hickey hands my John, Greasy, some cash. He takes one of the hundreds from the pile and holds it out to me. I was one of their bets, I realize.

My breathing becomes even as I look between Ben and the hundred-dollar bill in the man's hand. Finally, after what feels like forever under the stare of Ben, I take it.

A moment passes after I sit down. A very long, sit with yourself and who you are, *what* you are kind of moment. Ben leans his head over to the side lazily. "Truly disgusting." He tells me what I already know. My body is on fire with anger and embarrassment. I don't regret it. Who knows what would have happened if I hadn't? I ignore him, turning my head to the other window, where I catch a glimpse of myself.

If who I have to be to get to Jericho is *her*, then so be it.

It's not long before Ben is back to his twitchy sleeping. I force myself to stay awake. It's not hard. All those nights at the club have me on a nocturnal schedule. Soon, the other men are all asleep as well, which puts me at ease. Not for long, though.

The sun rises slowly, bleeding into the night sky with its red and orange. Finally, I can see out the windows, only for a second, because soon we pass through a long tunnel. The sound the train makes echoing off the sides of the stone walls makes my heart race.

We come out on the other side to skyscrapers in the distance and beautiful brick houses on one side of us. They all have the same green lawns and various flowers in neat rows, bushes shaped into perfect squares. Each little box is exactly the same as the last. It reminds me of a song about houses made of ticky tacky—one of the many songs on the radio rotation in Harmony.

We are not in Harmony anymore.

Past Ben, through the window he leans on while he snores, what I see is nothing short of amazing. Rolling fields of wheat. Golden light reflects off the grass as it sways back and forth in waves. It's like what I imagine heaven to be like. On the other side of the field is another city. Identical to the one we drive through currently. The towers in the distance match the ones we near now.

The only difference between this city and its twin is a giant cloud of smoke that leaks from one of the buildings in the distance. It gets worse and worse the longer I stare at it, rising into the air and billowing out at the top where the wind catches it. It doesn't take long to realize the black smoke does not belong. Leaning closer, I rub my eyes to make sure what I see is real. It is. So real that I almost yell when the same building crumples to the ground, sending plumes of debris into the air. A whole skyscraper, gone in the blink of an eye.

We pass through another tunnel. The burning city disappears. My heart races with anticipation, and I can't help but press my hands against the glass as if I could capture the image in my hands. Gone, replaced by the dark stone of the tunnel. That loud noise that rumbles the train car fills my ears again.

We emerge on the other side to the same houses, *oblivious* houses, ones that could not have seen their twin city fall. These houses are adorned with willow trees in every yard, a small difference from the previous neighborhood.

"Not in the mood for one of your dances, Blue," Ben says as he rouses from sleep, probably due to the hand I have on his knee to balance myself. I'm still leaning over him to look out the window, still trying to convince myself I saw the building fall.

With a look of disgust from Ben, I retreat, hitting the back of the chair with a thud. "I—I was" I snap my mouth shut. "I'm sorry," Is all I say because *that* is what he wants to hear, not excuses.

Ben looks out at the houses and finally back to me. "Almost there."

# CHAPTER 10

*Warshaw,* the sign reads in fancy script. A huge bomber plane mounted on steel beams is set above the words. Warshaw is the oldest city in Palen. I remember a lecture in history about its birth. The construction of the first wall was made to guard a sacred treasure. A golden box said to hold divine energy. No such treasure was ever found, yet the city still put up its walls and built its army. Thousands of years have gone by since then, but there are still conspiracies about what Warshaw was really built for.

Riley once said not to believe any of the history books. That they just don't want you to know what's really going on. That the real secrets of Warshaw and Jericho are hidden beneath layers of propaganda. His paranoia never rubbed off on me. I mostly just liked to hear him talk.

Long past the plane, past the houses, and into the city, the station is filled with nicely dressed people with somewhere to go. They filled the empty train seats before we were even out the door. These streets are intact, unlike the ones of Harmony. There is no trash littering the ground or men gawking as women pass by. The air doesn't reek of smoke or piss. There are patches of dirt with grass and flowers growing out of them. For the life of me, I cannot remember a single time I saw a flower in Harmony that wasn't made of plastic or paper.

I so badly want to walk over and pluck one from the ground, but Ben is already staring, probably wondering why I am standing still on the busy sidewalk. I ignore the huffs of frustration as I cut across a group of people to catch up to him. Ben's eyes narrow in frustration. "I've got a few things to take care of." He pulls out his wallet and hands me a clear plastic card with lines of copper running through it. I'm hesitant, but take it, even though I have no idea what it is. "The guys will take you to get some proper clothes." Hickey and Greasy nod their heads in what can only be described as excitement. They have other plans, it seems.

I peek over my shoulder at the two men who are all but touching their dicks. My head snaps back to Ben. "I'd rather go with you," I tell him, and it's true. I even grab onto his arm to emphasize how little I want to be alone with those men, not that Ben is much better.

Ben's eyes trace down my arm slowly before returning to my face, his expression barely masking his disgust. He pulls from my grip as if my touch has left a lingering, unwanted mark. "Oh, but I know how much fun you three have together," he remarks with a glance at the men behind me. Ben turns without another look in my direction.

Greasy and Hickey exchange words at my failed attempt to get Ben to take me with him. Suddenly, I can only think of Riley. All the subtle things I missed. Was he disgusted by me the same as Ben? You do not have to like someone to fuck them.

The men know exactly where they are going. I follow closely behind. Women hold their breath when we pass and peek over their shoulders to steal a second glance at the men. At first, with heat in their eyes. Then jealousy when they get to me. I guess the men from Jericho are well-known in the Inner Ring as well. It's not hard to pick them out of a pile. They all look eerily plastic. Different from one another in the slightest but well-manicured enough, well-dressed enough you know they do not belong.

The further we walk, the more the air fills with unease, my own, but also those around me. I am missing something. I just don't know what it is. All I know is something is unsettling about this place, even with all the beautiful windows with intricate displays in them. Gowns and jewelry, odds and ends I can't imagine wearing or keeping in my home. Everywhere we turn, there is something new to look at. Distractions.

We reach what can only be the heart of the city. The buildings turn old, from black and white to color. No more matching brick and perfectly paved roads. These buildings were here first. Oh, how they have stood the test of time. Unlike the old buildings of Harmony, no these were taken care of. No squatters or teenagers in search of a place to party. No smell of decaying flesh. Not a single used needle littering the ground.

The prices on the sleeves of mannequins in the window become increasingly expensive the further we go. I hear the two men ahead of me making bets on the amount of money they think Ben has. They seem to be taking us to the place where it will cost Ben the most.

The card he gave me must link to a bank. We only used checks or cash in Harmony, and most of the checks bounced, so we all dealt in the thin paper bills. If you didn't pull it from your account, then you didn't really have it to begin with.

Hickey thinks the card will be declined. Greasy takes the bet. He always does, I realize. I put that piece of information about him to the back of my unorganized head for later.

It's always important to know what the men like and dislike, their addictions, or lack thereof, and what is important to them. Jez told me to make what is important to them important to you as well. She had all kinds of tricks that made men topple over themselves to get to her.

They walk into a store, not a glance in my direction to check if I follow. *Confident bastards.*

Beautiful, tall women emerge from seemingly nowhere, all dressed the same. Black shirts tucked into a tight black skirt and silver dainty jewelry. Aside from the one on their left ring finger, that piece of jewelry has a giant diamond in the center, surrounded by smaller ones on the left and right of the big one. Ugly things, but pretty is not what they strive for.

A brunette walks up to Hickey and kisses him on the cheek. "O." she coos. *What kind of a name is O?* Then on to the next man at my side. "Samson." She provides the same kiss for Greasy, before turning to me. She gives my clothes a once over, noting all the imperfections, I'm sure. Then she looks back at O and Samson, who give her a simultaneous shrug. "Go on in," she instructs them. "We have some work to do," she says. Again, combing over me until her eyes land on an imperfection at my middle. I don't bother finding what she looks at.

She then holds her hand out to me, palm up, waiting. I'm not sure what for. Finally, after a few beats of silence, Samson takes pity on me. "The card." He points to the hand that holds the plastic.

As soon as I plop the plastic in her greedy palm, the woman drags me to the other side of the room, crowded with clothes made of silk and soft cotton. "No touching, please." She reminds me like I should already know. Wouldn't want my grimy Outer Ring fingers on their fine clothing. I roll my eyes at her backside before I turn to see Samson and O have disappeared.

We return to the front with bags of clothes I didn't try on *or* choose. All beige or white. Black is more my color.

Samson and O stand there in new suits. Samson wears dark green to compliment his eyes. While O is in black trousers and a white shirt with the first couple of buttons undone, he slings his suit jacket over his shoulder, showing off the muscles in his bicep.

Samson is no longer Greasy. The purple bruises around O's neck are completely gone. Which no longer makes him Hickey. These men are dangerous, I see it now—why women swoon, and men get a pinched look of frustration around them.

The card Ben gave me gets put through a machine. When she hands it back, Samson places cash in O's palm. O wears a proud smile as we walk out the door and across the street. There is no point to it all, I realize. They have more money than I will ever see in my life, and yet they pass back and forth what could only be considered change. Is life in Jericho that... boring?

We enter the side door of a salon with even more beautiful women. *Do they only hire leggy blondes and sassy brunettes in this city?* They all take notice of the two handsome men before me. O leans into one's ear, whispering something sweet because her eyes roll to the back of her head. Then, O's eyes shift to mine as he continues his secret with the woman. He moves his hands in a circular motion that has me confused. Her cheeks turn red before she nods her head in understanding.

Women pull me into a room with a chair and a mirror. There is a door to the left that looks like a bathroom.

Again, the men have disappeared. *Why do they keep doing that?* It's almost insulting how trusting they are. They know I won't run. No one ever has because they do not know what I know. There is something *else* going on in Jericho. Something they hide from the rest of Palen. I will not run either, but not for the promise of paradise. *For Jez.*

The air fills with the scent of roses before the water turns on. Not a word is spoken, just the poking and prodding of perfectly manicured fingers until I go in the direction they desire. They leave the room with one more look to tell me how disgusting I am. It's a common theme today.

My palms sweat as I carefully unstrap the gun from my thigh and hide it under my clothes. I hadn't thought this far ahead. Riley told me to take it everywhere with me, just in case, and so that is what I have done. Now, it might be the reason for my demise. *Stupid, Emerson.* I scold myself.

Steam comes from the water. There was no hot water in our apartment building or in all of Harmony. So, when I run my hand under the warmth, I can't help but get excited. It feels so good to just stand under the heat, but I remember I should not be enjoying my time. I should hurry and find Ben so he can take me to Jericho. To Jez.

My eyes go wide when I step from the shower. I throw myself at the space where my clothes used to be as if I had just misplaced them. They are gone. My heart jumps into my throat, and panic threatens to take over. But the gun remains. Right where I left it. Taking a deep breath, wrap a towel around myself, and open the door a crack. "She won't last a day." One of them laughs to the other. "And that shirt?" She scoffs. The shirt Jez made for me from one of her old dresses. My favorite shirt, in fact, is now gone.

The other woman nods her head in agreement. "Cheap clothes for a cheap whore." She snorts back. *Whore,* a word used to describe me since before I even knew what it meant.

I clear my throat. The women turn slowly, annoyed by my presence and not at all ashamed of themselves. "O said to wear this." One tosses a cream-colored dress that was picked for me. She sets a pair of heels on the ground in the same shade. "The rest of your things will be in Jericho when you arrive." She turns back around to continue her earlier conversation about me.

Holding my tongue for the sake of keeping my plan on track, I shut the door and dress. This tight fabric leaves little room for my weapon, but I manage. Not that it matters at this point because they clearly left it for me to keep.

What kind of game are they playing? Whatever it is, I will gladly play it if that is what it takes to get to her.

The fake blonde drags me to a chair in front of a mirror. She begins to run a brush through my damp hair. When I meet my own eyes in the mirror, I hardly recognize myself. Not only my features surrounded by brown hair but the clothes, the jewelry. It's all so *not* me.

They make no mention of my dye job. Not even when they brush through it with a fine-tooth comb, searching for lice. They are almost surprised when they dont find any. Then, they use hot air out of a machine to dry it until it's barely curled at the ends but straight near the top, just like theirs.

Finally, we are done, and I feel like a doll—not in a good way, either. I've been used and abused. Everything about me now screams Jericho. I stand uncomfortably in my heels as we wait for O and Samson, who appear from a side door labeled *Massage.*

O slaps one of the blondes on the ass as they leave. She turns a shade of red before he drops a wad of cash in her hand. Then he looks at Samson who is also holding out his hand, waiting for his payment for an unspoken bet between the two. *What a strange pair.*

Samson sucks in a breath at my appearance. "I think another dance is in order," he says as he swipes at his jaw.

O watches the interaction with that stupid smirk on his face. "Let's get out of here." He says with one more glance at my exposed thigh. His features darken like he is having some kind of internal debate before he strolls out the door.

I take one more look around, reminding myself of how Jez was mesmerized by Warshaw. How she was on this very ground where I stand before she was flown to Jericho, where she has been trying to reach me. I push back the sting of tears.

*Guilt is not beautiful*; I remind myself of Jez's words.

# CHAPTER 11

Smoke, I smell it before I see it. Thick and black as coal as it rises to the left of us. Men and women scramble.

Everything happens so fast. We are suddenly caught up in chaos as stores lower bars over their windows and lock their doors.

A low vibration emanates from the ground. It sounds like something is snaking its way around down there, through the sewage.

The smoke lays over the city like a blanket, filling my lungs and causing me to choke. I do not move, I can't. My mind screams to run, but my legs don't obey.

Samson grabs my arm and pulls me in the opposite direction in which we came. He tugs at his jacket, covering his face with the fabric. My head whips back and forth as I take in the sight of men and women racing to get away, pushing others out of their way in the process.

Then, *boom—an* explosion in the distance—so loud it keeps a low ringing in my ears as we go.

My heart races. Men appear from the direction of the explosion. They look like they belong to the Palen Army, not like the residents of War-shaw at all. Most of them split into different directions, disappearing down side streets or alleyways. Three men make their way towards us before deliberately turning down a street.

They walk with ease, black masks over half their faces, leaving only their eyes. Guns are slung across their bodies casually. They wear black uniforms with a vest over the top that seems to hold all sorts of weapons. I was wrong. These men are not part of the Palen Army. No names on their sleeves or golden angels pinned to their chests. It's not Navar or Canaan either.

The three men walk like they know exactly where to go. They make another right turn, heading straight for a café. A left would have taken them right to us. They stop and look around in search of something. I swear their eyes pass right over us. Thankfully, the debris and smoke must cover us well enough, but I see *them*. In fact, I can't take my eyes off them. Not even with Samson's death grip on my wrist as he pulls us between two buildings with a warning on his face that I am to remain hidden.

Still, I watch as the three men stand over a family that has taken shelter under a table. The same table where they were enjoying lunch, not but five minutes ago. One of them, the tallest of the three, pulls a large older man up aggressively by his arm. The leader exchanges words with the others I cannot hear. A command, because the other two usher away a screaming girl, leaving the old man alone with the tall one. The man's wife, a woman with equally grey hair as the man, goes much more willingly with the others. It's almost as if she knew this day would come.

The old man lets out a cry as he shakes his head profusely. I can't hear what they say, but I can see the pleading on his face. The kind you do only if you are about to die. The leader leans in close, telling him of what I already know. He is a dead man. You quickly memorize the actions that come before death when you live in the Outer Ring. I would usually look away at this point, but I can't bring myself to.

Another plea comes from the old man, but the leader doesn't care. He brings the gun from his side and pushes it against the man's head. More pleading and begging, but it does not matter. Nothing the old man says will save him now.

Time seems to slow down after the loud firing of his pistol. Blood sprays from the side of the man's head, and his body falls limply to the ground.

There is no time to register what I have just seen because another explosion has my attention wavering. The ground vibrates the same as before. I know what happens next. I've seen it. Across the field on the way here. My prediction is correct.

Beyond the men in black, the tallest tower in the heart of Warshaw begins to crumble and sway. I don't take my eyes off of it. Objects, *people,* fall from the windows in an attempt to save themselves. A series of loud noises echo off the brick. "It's going to fall," I say, but it comes out strained and too quiet for anyone else to hear.

O pulls a device from his pocket and presses the screen. He holds it up to his ear, and soon, another voice fills the space, mumbled and electronic sounding. "He's here," O says to the person on the other end. More words I can't quite understand are exchanged. O nods once, then pushes the device back into his pocket in frustration.

Samson gives O a nod of understanding. I don't try to make sense of any of it because, past them, the tower sways. It's *going to fall*. It's the only cohesive thought in my head. "Fuck." Samson checks the time on his watch before turning to me.

"It's going to fall." I try again, but either Samson and O are not listening or they do not care. More explosions. More smoke. I stand, prepared to run *anywhere* but towards the giant skyscraper threatening to kill me.

Samson's brows scrunch together in confusion as I step away from them. "Sit the fuck down," he demands, but I do not listen. "Did you hear me, bitch?" He tries again from behind me because, without realizing it, I have put distance between us. My body knows something my mind does not.

My eyes go from the tower to where the men in black once stood. Where did they go?

Red pools beneath the tables and coats the ground. The man's lifeless, *headless* body leans against a chair. Behind that, the same swaying of the tower with a logo on it I have never seen before. Back and forth.

Someone speaks behind me, Samson, I think. I don't listen. *It's going to fall.*

Before Greasy and Hickey can stop me, I make a run for it. *Away. Get away from here,* I repeat in my head. I hear the men cursing and stumbling to catch up. One of the storefronts blows up right in front of me. My arms go in front of my face but I keep moving. I can't hear, I can't think, I just run. The useless heels I was given are long forgotten. Glass slices the inside of my feet, but I don't stop.

A series of explosions come from behind me. Then, the sound of what can only be described as the screaming of metal against metal in a high-pitched whine cuts through the ringing in my ears. When I finally look behind me, Samson and O are nowhere to be found. Only the settling of dirt, remnants of what used to be buildings and stores, and...people. Or at least pieces of them.

*Smack.* Something stops me dead in my tracks, *someone.* Ben towers over me, his hands wrap around my waist. My arms flail in an attempt to get out of his grip. He looks over my head for a split second at the destruction behind me. *It's about to get so much worse.* I can't say my thoughts out loud. I scramble, trying to go around him but he holds firm.

*No, it's going to fall.* Ben pulls me towards a door. Still, I struggle, trying to fight against him, but he wins when he lifts me over his shoulder with ease, my arms dangling behind him. Something doesn't feel right.

"It's going to fall." Was that my voice? It sounds so distant.

He carries me over the debris of what used to be a store before he stops and throws me on the ground while he fidgets with a rug. Ben lifts it to reveal a hatch door built into the wood. "Get in," he tells me. A siren wails from somewhere far off. My head snaps to the noise and then back to Ben. "Get in, Blue." He pleads with his eyes, but his words have a bitter twist to them. There is blood on his shoulder and down his chest. Not his own.

Go with Ben or wait for the whole city to fall? I am out of options. I choose the one where I live, where I get to Jez.

I peer down at the narrow stairs, wondering where they lead. I take each step carefully. The adrenaline is starting to wear off. My feet are on fire, and my dress is damp with blood, but I can't seem to figure out where the wound is because everything hurts. Small sounds of pain escape me with every movement.

Ben's breathing is steady, his hand is on my lower back as we make our way further down. There isn't much space above us or around us.

I reach out for another stair with my good foot, but there isn't one there. The harsh step causes pain to shoot up to my hip. When I find my balance again, my eyes immediately catch on a distant flickering light. The tunnel widens.

The sounds from the city above, the sirens, everything is muffled. Ben whispers something under his breath before scooping me into his arms. Much more gently this time.

He carries me further down a hallway, towards the light, around a corner to a grey metal door. He reaches one hand out and knocks a sequence. The door unlocks from the inside. Three distinct clicks before it screeches open.

My body feels heavy, like right before you fall asleep. That sounds nice right now—sleep. I let my eyes close at the idea.

Warm air hits my face. A man I can't see mumbles something before ushering us through the door. It's difficult to keep my eyes open long enough to see books piled high on both sides of a couch and coffee mugs set atop each of the piles being used as side tables. We make our way through a maze of magazines and trinkets. Some of the piles come up to Ben's hips where he has to lift me up and over the collection of...things.

We make our way to a colorful room with packed bookshelves that reach the ceiling. Nothing has ever felt more painful than when Ben lays me down on a bed. My back stings with a sharp pain, which quickly has me writhing. Suddenly, I feel much too warm. I can feel the sweat drip down my face and stick to my hair. My words become incoherent even to me, so I say the only thing I can. "It's going to fall," I tell Ben as he stands over me. It's the only sentence I can get out. His brows pinched together in either confusion or frustration.

Another man, the same one who opened the door, walks slowly to the other side of the bed. His back is arched slightly. His face seems crooked, like half his jaw is gone from beneath the flesh. My mind is playing tricks. *This* is what the world looks like before you die—distorted.

My vision blurs. That crooked face comes in and out of focus as he retrieves something from a drawer. I look back over to Ben, ignoring the dizziness that comes with movement.

Ben holds a knife in his hand. *No.* I think I say out loud, but my voice seems too loud to be anywhere but inside my head. I try to move, to stop him from doing whatever he is about to do. My movements are too slow, too weak.

Death fills the room. I felt it once before. In the back of the pawnshop after the death of a Bronze. It was lingering there for weeks. What would Riley think of me now? He would kill me for my lack of thought before throwing myself into this life. A failure, that's what he would think of me.

It's true, I *failed*. I curse at myself for it. I hate myself for not knowing. I couldn't feel it. Shouldn't you be able to feel when a part of you is broken? Jez is the voice inside my head, the eyes that stare back at me in the mirror. I should have known.

*Jez, I'm sorry.* I don't think the words make it past my tongue.

Ben's mouth moves, but I don't hear any words. He looks at the man across from him. I follow his eyes. Only to be met with the terrifying sight of a needle in my arm. When did he do that? Then, the pain starts to disappear. I look down at my toes. The dress is no longer the ugly cream color that it once was. It's dark red, almost black. My legs are covered in the same red substance that can only be blood.

*"You don't see it do you?"* Riley's voice is in my head as I replay our last night together.

I reach out for life, but I do not find it. And that's okay because I'm not scared anymore, not with Riley's voice in my head. *"You don't scare me, Riley Bronze,"* I think I say out loud. *Death* does not scare me.

# CHAPTER 12

Riley

By the time I make my way to the pawnshop, I've already made up my mind. I pass the dark window, catching my reflection in the glass. Beyond my determined gaze, beyond the reflection of a child who knows exactly what he needs to do, is the light from Father's office.

He's gone too far this time.

Father has always had his grimy fingers in every pie here in Harmony. I had my suspicions, but now I have proof.

Nothing ever comes into Harmony without Father's knowledge. He never misses a beat, always one step ahead. Not this time. This time, *I* am the one thinking ahead.

I push the back door of the pawnshop open. It's not quiet. I *want* him to know I'm coming. "Ri." Father doesn't even turn his head as he sits at the desk. How he always knows it's me, I will never know.

The room smells of whiskey. He's been drinking since morning, as he always does. His book is open, filled with fake numbers that all add up to one thing: *trafficking*. I spent countless hours, while Em sat oblivious beside me, reading and rereading those numbers until I understood what they meant.

There are piles of cash on the desk he counts greedily every night. Father grips a pen in his meaty fingers, swollen from drink. He shakes his head when I don't say anything. Instead, I pull the pistol from my waistband. He laughs. Father just added fuel to the fire. He doesn't get to laugh. He doesn't get to do anything at all. Not anymore.

"What's so funny?" I ask him, mostly to see if he'll answer truthfully. He won't. He never does.

I hear the click of a pen, but I am focused on the back of his head as I stare down the barrel of my gun. The chair squeals under his weight as he turns to face me. Father ignores my question, *and* the gun pointed between his brows. "Back out of the deal." I give him a choice. The choice between life and death.

He shakes his head before reaching for the glass that sits within arm's distance, always. It's filled with brown whiskey, accompanied by the open bottle nearby that never lasts the day. My arms are steady, held out in front of me, ready. He's far too calm as he drinks, tipping his head back, then against the cold metal of my gun once again.

"What deal would that be, Son?" He asks, pretending to be ignorant.

Father knows as well as I do what deal he plans to make. He can't talk his way out of this one. It's a nice try, though.

"How much?" I want to know the price he's put on her head. How much is a fifteen-year-old girl with white hair and icy blue eyes worth? To me, more than anyone could ever pay in cash.

"Riley—" Father begins.

"How. Much?" I shout when he tries to explain away the unexplainable.

Father stands, and my body moves accordingly. I brace myself for an attack. It never comes. Instead, Father grabs the other glass from the desk. He fills it with the same pungent, cheap whiskey.

He holds it out, offering it to me. "It's about time you knew how the world works. How business works," he tells me. I do not take his offer.

I clench my jaw. "I know how it works. I know everything." I say.

Father smirks, setting the glass on the edge of the desk. He leans back in his chair, the smugness radiating from him as he crosses his arms over his chest. "Do you, now?" He says, his voice dripping with condescension.

I tighten my grip on the pistol, my finger over the trigger. "I do," I reply, my voice steady. "I know what you've been doing. I know about the girls. I know about *her.*"

For a moment, Father's expression falters. A flicker of something—fear, or anger maybe—passes through his eyes. But it's gone as quickly as it came. "And what do you plan to do about it, Son? Shoot me? You think that will solve anything?" He narrows his eyes.

I take a step closer, placing the gun back where it belongs. "It'll stop you," I say, my voice low and menacing. "And that's enough for me."

Father sighs as if he is tired, and not just from lack of sleep. "You're just like your mother," he says, shaking his head. "Always thinking you can change the world with a single act of defiance."

"Don't talk about her," I snap, my anger flaring. "*You* don't get to talk about her," I say more calmly.

He chuckles, a dark, humorless sound. "Look where it got her."

The words hit me like a punch to the gut, but I don't let it show. I can't afford to show weakness now. "Back out of the deal," I repeat, my voice like steel. "Or I swear to God, I will pull this trigger."

Father's eyes narrow, and for a moment, it seems like he might comply. But then he shakes his head again in disbelief. "You don't have it in you, Son," he says, his tone almost pitiful. "You're not a killer." He tries.

My heart pounds in my chest, the gun suddenly feels very heavy in my hand. I know he's trying to break me, to make me doubt myself. But I can't afford to hesitate. Not now, not if I want to save her.

With a deep breath, I steady my aim and tighten my grip. "Maybe not," I say, my voice barely more than a whisper. "But I'm willing to learn," I promise.

I squeeze my finger until I feel the shift of metal. The sound echoes through the room, a deafening crack that seems to hang in the air.

Harmony won't be the same after this.

I can't say I believe in a God, but I pray *this* single act of defiance *will* somehow change the world.

If it doesn't. I will.

# CHAPTER 13

A sweet melody plays to my left. It's quiet, beautiful, and calm. An arrangement of violin and piano—a song I have never heard before. *Heaven*, I think to myself as I watch the lights dance behind my eyelids.

Then a door shuts, and the whirling of a fan covers the sound of the lullaby.

I feel heavy. You don't feel heavy in heaven, do you? I always imagined it differently—lighter.

This is not heaven, not when blinding light seeps into my vision. Not when footsteps approach in a slow crawl, one foot dragging on the wooden floor. Especially not when I open my eyes to my gun lying nicely next to a stack of books. *Shit.* I sit up. It's so fast I nearly double over to puke.

"Lie back down," a man says. "Worked hard on yer' stitches." His voice is gentle but coarse. It makes you want to listen to what he says. When I make no such effort to lay back down, he stumbles towards me. There is a limp in his step. That same dragging of his left foot I heard earlier. His arm is also in an odd way. It bends in places it's not supposed to. All to match the side of his face with no structure to it.

He smells like earth and coffee. When he bends down, all I can do is stare. The man takes the blanket off my legs and inspects them. White bandages cover my body from the waist down. My back no longer burns with pain, only a slight pinch to match my heartbeat. My dress is gone, along with the homemade sheath that held the pistol close to my thigh.

My head pounds. My memory is spotty when I try to remember where I am and why I have all these bandages. "Where am I?" I decide to ask the man.

He continues to peel away the many layers of white fabric surrounding my leg, dabbing it with a towel and rubbing a salve onto the wounds. He isn't like the men who touch for their own pleasure. He has the hands of a healer.

Small indents fill my skin where open wounds used to be. There are wild and random marks all the way up to my thighs, some with stitches, and some melded together with a type of glue. From glass, I realize. I remember running through shards of it down the sidewalk. It felt like a dream until I ran into—"Ben." I say aloud.

"You're in Warshaw, in my bunker," The man finally replies, annoyed. "Ben is talkin' to the Mrs." He laughs then. "Good boy, he is." I almost laugh, too. *Good* is not the word I would use to describe Ben. I think better of my decision when my breath catches in my throat due to the pain in my lower back. I wince, cursing as I shift into a more comfortable position.

The man finishes his job, rewrapping my wounds and checking my temperature before covering me again with a blanket. "Felix." He holds his good hand out. I take it in my own.

It takes all of my strength to grip his hand with a shake. I can't help but think it's some sort of test as he inspects my fingernails with a twist of my hand. "Emerson," I reply.

The door opens, and Ben walks through it with a mug in his hand. He takes a drink casually as he watches Felix wipe his hands on a white towel. The room grows unbearably quiet as the two men exchange a glance.

Felix nods before he heads for the door, shutting it gently behind him. His gravelly voice trails off as he speaks to someone on the other side, The Mrs. I assume.

Ben walks to my side and sets the cup beside the gun. Suddenly, the memory of Riley setting his coffee near that exact weapon as he slipped into my bed comes to mind. Why does he keep popping up? I shake my head to rid myself of that stupid memory. My head is all kinds of messed up from whatever I was given.

Ben pushes his hands into his pockets. His blonde hair is perfectly placed atop his head. He smells the same as when I first met him. Floral and spice. The scent fills the room. I suddenly feel warm again as I wait in awkward silence for him to speak. Whatever they gave me before must be wearing off.

"We are headed to Jericho first thing in the morning," he says simply. The city was hit hard, but there is still a flight going to Jericho," he tells me.

The city, the tower that was swaying in the distance. "What was that?" I ask before I can stop myself. I wish my head would clear.

His lips form a thin line. "Nothing you have to worry about. They can't get into Jericho." He dismisses me, but he didn't see what I did. He didn't see the men in uniforms that did not belong to the Palen Army. They were something else entirely. They killed someone right in front of us.

*Us.* "What happened to Samson and O?"

Ben sighs. He pulls his hands from his pockets and reaches down towards the gun. I flinch, which hurts. He grabs the cup instead. *Of course, Emerson. If he wanted you dead, you wouldn't be here.* His lip twitches upward at my discomfort. *Asshole.* "You outran them." He answers my question vaguely. I know what he is saying. They are dead, caught in the explosions that also took the city.

"The tower." I feel my brows push together as I put the pieces back together.

Ben clicks his tongue. "You were right. It fell." He takes a swig of whatever is in his cup. "Along with about four others throughout the Inner Ring. All government buildings. Sending a message." It sounds more like a question at the end than a statement. Because Ben doesn't know for sure, but he looks determined to find out.

I don't mention what we saw before the tower fell, mostly because I do not wish to think of it all over again. Blood, so much of it. Also, because if anyone knows what is going on, it's Ben. The men from Jericho always have information. Corey and his father paid thousands to learn what they know.

Besides, I can't risk planting the seed of doubt in Ben's head. That will not get me any closer to Jez. It does not matter who those men are or what they are doing. Nothing will get in my way. If anything, I need to expedite the process.

Ben looks down at me, his eyes snaking from brow to covered feet. He doesn't give much away, a hard read. When I can usually guess what men will say before they speak. "What's with the gun, Blue?"

That was *not* going to be my guess. "A gift," I blink up at him with fake confidence, but he does not care or even look at me.

He huffs a laugh, his gaze still steady near the end of the bed. "A contraband weapon as a gift." He says more to himself than anything before shaking his head in disbelief or amusement, I can't tell. He lets out another breathy laugh before walking towards the door, the mug still in his hand.

The gun remains. Just like it did before. We are still playing this strange game.

Ben has a grip on the glass knob before he decides to turn his head over his shoulder like he had a last-minute thought. "Don't go getting any ideas, Blue." He glances at the gun one more time. A devious grin takes over his features because what he really means is *I dare you.*

Before I can answer, he is out the door. I hear the rustling of papers before his footsteps are far enough away I can no longer hear them.

Felix comes to check on me throughout the day. He instructs me on how to change my bandages. Tells me the wounds will heal in no time, but even he doesn't seem to believe it. There was a shard of glass that somehow punctured through the flesh on my lower stomach and came out the other side, just below my ribs. That must have been where all the blood came from. I have to fight the urge to wince every time I breathe in too much air.

This will be my greatest performance of all time. No amount of pain will stop me.

Felix gives me clothes that look like they belong to a woman, his wife, I assume. They are not in the fashion of today's clothes. The grey shirt has words on the front in a font that makes it impossible to read. The pants are black, loose around the legs, with multiple pockets on the side. The boots they give me have some caked-on mud around the soles, but they fit. It's still painful to walk, but I make sure not to let that show as I walk out of the room. I won't give Ben a reason to leave me behind.

I'm unsure why Palen is being attacked, but I know I need to get to Jez before they do. Ben assures me it's not a problem. That one does not simply *get* into Jericho— *a fortress*, he called it. I have never believed the words of any man, and I won't start now—not until I see it for myself.

My heart pounds as I leave the room. Out the same door I saw Ben open and close after his warning. It's disorienting and dark, aside from a light around the corner of a hallway. I go around piles of newspapers and step over the top of discarded boxes with odds and ends in them.

The light glows over the top of a woman the same age as Felix. She sits with a book open on her lap. Her silver clouded eyes almost look like they pop out of her head due to the thick glasses that lay on her nose.

You can tell she was once a beauty. Her long, greying hair still has long strands of black. It's all piled on top of her head in a perfectly round bun. Every square inch around the woman is covered in posters or picture frames. A large map is between two comfortable-looking chairs, one for her and one for Felix.

The map shows the rings of Palen, the walls, the railway that connects the two Outer Rings, and finally, the mountain. At the very top, nestled safely between two peaks, is Jericho. No wonder you need a plane to get there. It's much farther up the mountain than I thought. Maybe it *is* an impenetrable fortress, as Ben said.

I hadn't realized I had gotten closer to the woman as I poke at the word Palen at the top of the map in fancy script, until she peeks over her glasses at me. Her eyes do not seem to latch onto anything. She is blind or at least nearing it. She lowers her head again to resume her reading.

My eyes slide down the map in search of Harmony. When I find it, I place a gentle finger over the city I called home. A red X marks the letters. Does that mean what I think it does? There are others with the same mark over the top, including a brighter, fresher red over the city we are in right now. *Warshaw.*

I swallow the knot in my throat. Palen is being targeted, but by who? The woman turns the page of her book. Her movement has my hand retreating back to my side.

Somewhere behind a door to the left, I smell coffee and hear Felix and Ben exchanging words. Every now and then, they laugh—a low rumble for Ben and a large booming howl for Felix.

*Smack.* The woman closes her book abruptly, making me nearly jump out of my skin. I suck in a harsh breath to keep myself from letting out a cry of pain from the quick movement. She turns her attention to me. "What do you need, dear?" She asks. At first, her harsh words make me think I have done something wrong. But when I look at her, I see she wears a genuine expression.

"Oh, I don't need anything." I look around and make a gesture with my hands. "I was just looking at all your... things." I feel embarrassment warm my face as the last word escapes me. "I mean, you have so much," I say quickly. I want to hit myself. "It's nice." I try to amend.

She shakes her head as she stands. The chair groans beneath her weight or lack thereof. "Lots of things to keep us busy down here." She tells me as she places the book on top of all the others piled at her side. She stands beside me, also facing the large map of Palen. She places her hands on her hips before declaring. "A shit world we live in these days."

Surprised at her colorful words, I let a smile creep to my face. I stare at the map again with her, although I don't think she can see it. There is a small, dotted line that passes through Warshaw, through the gates, and continues up to Jericho. It looks long with all its turns and curves, even on the map. "What's that?" I question, tracing my finger from Warshaw to Jericho.

"Used to be the road to Jericho." She points a crooked finger at the map as if she has memorized the spot. I follow her finger to the small mark. There is a drawing of a house. Beyond the inner wall, between here and Jericho. "That used to be the old safe house. Before they closed off the road. Felix was in charge of blowing the damn thing up."

I hardly pay attention to that end part. "There is another way into Jericho?" I ask in awe.

"You'll never make it to Jericho going that way, dear." She takes a step closer, squints, then slides a finger between the inner wall and finally to the circle that represents Jericho. "That's approximately fifty miles of pure snow and ice. No one makes it through on foot. Not anymore." She nearly spits before she makes a clicking noise with her tongue and turns to face me.

She sets her clouded eyes upon mine, all the way to my center, to my soul. So that's how you do it. How can she see so little and so much at the same time?

"Doesn't stop people from trying." She shrugs. "Don't know why you all are so keen on the place anyway." She waits for an answer, but I do not have one. Not one I am willing to share anyway.

Thankfully, we are interrupted as Felix basically slams the door open with a laugh. He has two plates of food in his hands. "Eat up." He pushes one of the plates into my hand forcefully before wobbling away to his chair. Ben saunters in behind him, his hands in his pockets, his face still holding the remnants of a smile from their conversation.

I find a seat on one of the few chairs without something set on top of it. Then I begin to eat the mush that is supposed to be food. It tastes good but feels like a slug crawling down my throat. Still, I force myself through the whole thing before watching Ben clear off a seat beside me. He watches as I scrape at the remnants on the sides of the plate. "We have a very limited amount of time to get to the plane. My guy will be waiting there for us. Do you think you can walk? It's not close." he says honestly.

Nothing will stop me from getting to Jez. "Yes," I tell him while nodding my head for emphasis.

"Good." He looks down at his watch, a vintage Rolex with gold detail. I almost can't stop myself from rolling my eyes. Thousands upon thousands of dollars. More than I will see in my entire lifetime, wrapped around his wrist like it's nothing. Ben follows my eyes to the watch before placing his hand down at his side. "Sleep well tonight. We leave in 7 hours." He clears his throat.

Ben stands before he reaches a hand down quickly, causing me to flinch. I relax slightly when I see he is only reaching for the empty plate in my hand. Ben then leans down slowly. Ben's anger is easily felt but not seen. He whispers into my ear so only I can hear. "They think you are my wife, Blue. Act like it," he says harshly. All with a fake smile on his face so Felix and The Mrs. are none the wiser. He takes the plate from my grip before standing as if nothing happened. I do what I do best, I pretend. I smile like what he just whispered to me was honey and I am a fly, desperate for more.

Ben disappears behind the door that leads to the kitchen, leaving me with the couple. "He's a good man." Felix slaps his knee. The Mrs. peers at me over the top of her glasses before nodding in agreement. My forced smile feels like needles. If only they knew.

# CHAPTER 14

With the covers pulled over my face, I let Ben think I am sleeping. Which is impossible because my stitches pull with every breath, and my bandages are rubbing up against my skin uncomfortably.

When he lays beside me in the bed, I make sure to take even breaths, ignoring the pain. To my surprise, Ben settles into the bed after turning off the lamp and falls right to sleep. He reeks of alcohol, which must aid in his deep slumber.

Before I decided to hide away in the bedroom, I saw Felix excitedly reach into a cabinet and pull out two dusty glasses along with a bottle of whiskey. The two men sat down at a very small, very cluttered table and began to drink. It lasted well into the night, and I am grateful for that.

Night turns into day quickly. It feels like my eyes hardly have time to close before Ben pulls at my covers to wake me. "You're bleeding," he tells me. *Did I hear that correctly?* I rub the sleep from my eyes to look up at him. Ben clocks the confusion on my face. Then, he runs a finger down the T-shirt Felix gave me. Ben's finger comes away red. "You're bleeding." He repeats.

He's right. The shirt is soaked, blood has leaked right through the bandages and onto the bed. Ben balls his hands into fists. He is upset. "It—it's okay. I must have just moved wrong in my sleep." *Please do not leave me here. Please do not get on the plane without me.* I plead in my head.

I watch as Ben's blue eyes shift from me to the door. Felix enters and sets a mug on the stack of books near the door, nodding to Ben before he leaves.

Ben places that mask back on. The one where he pretends to be kind because his anger turns to worry as he begins to lift the blood-soaked shirt up in an attempt to help me. When I push his hand away, telling him I will take care of it, he doesn't argue.

Ben's hands shake as he buttons his shirt. He gives up halfway, leaving the top two buttons undone. A small tuft of blonde peaks out from his chest. He is acting strange, more than usual.

I carefully wrap bandages around my waist, making sure to angle my body so he can't see the damage. It's worse than I thought. The bandages are completely soaked, and my side seems to have its own heartbeat. Felix's white sheets are stained red. I throw the blankets over the mess before Ben can see.

He is too busy muttering under his breath to pay any notice to me anyway. He doesn't even grab the mug Felix left for him as he leaves the room.

Am I missing something? He is not his usual self. Before whatever has got him in a twist, he reminded me of Jez in a way. Always there with the right words and the fake smiles that make people believe what isn't true.

Today, he is missing a few of those practiced steps, as Jez would call them. The ones that make it look like the confidence is natural. Like the smile is always there. Like nothing could knock you over or change your stride. I only practiced those steps in my dances. They don't transfer well outside the club.

Ben fidgets and paces the room twice before Felix hands him a plate with the same slop that was given to us last night. Ben scarfs it down within seconds. Then he is up and pacing around the room again. Felix quirks a crooked brow at him, then me.

*They think you are my wife*, Ben's words ring through my head. So, I am the perfect picture of a wife in front of Felix and the Mrs. I stand and make my way to Ben. Mostly to see if he has changed his mind. But also to stop him from wearing a hole in the carpet. "Let's go." he practically runs into me as he says it. "We should go." his voice a bit lower this time. When his eyes meet mine, I can't tell if it's nerves, fear, or something else. He holds me with his gaze for a few seconds as if he is searching for something, *someone.*

I hold his arm at the elbow, "Yes, let's go." I agree with him in a soothing voice. His jaw clenches, and he runs a hand over the blonde stubble on his chin.

Felix opens the locks on the inside of the door. The same three clicks I heard on the other side as Ben held me in his arms while life slowly leaked from my body. Only now I can see it in action. The door must be at least a foot wide. So nothing can get in.

I turn to see Felix one more time, memorizing the strange curve of his face before I look at his wife, who smiles softly in my general direction. How long before her eyes fail her completely? I smile back, even if she cannot see it.

The trip is shorter on our way up than it was down. Maybe because I am not walking with glass in my feet or a gaping hole in my side. Soon, we are back in the shop, or what used to be a shop anyway. Some walls are missing, and piles of debris seem to have flooded in from the street. It is eerily quiet, aside from the slight crunch of our footsteps on the ground.

I look down at the door that now lies beneath my feet. Where Felix and The Mrs. will spend the rest of their days.

It's still so early the sun has not risen all the way, casting a grey hue over the entirety of the city. Which I am thankful for because if I had to see the carnage again, I don't think I would be able to get the images out of my head. I already see the man's head when I close my eyes, red spraying to the ground as a black figure towers over the body with his arm stretched out, a pistol in his grip.

Ben seems to know exactly where to go. He crosses streets and goes through alleyways, all without a word. The whole place smells like burnt asphalt and plastic. There are no more beautiful women occupying the windows of stores. In fact, there is no one in sight at all. It seems as if people have long since ransacked the stores and their belongings. I didn't think those kinds of things happened in the inner city. Harmony was full of thieves, beggars, and all sorts of unsavory characters. Here, everything seemed so clean until now. Tragedy brings out the worst in people.

The buildings become sparse and the ground turns from concrete to manicured lawns, the same as we saw on the train. Up close you can see the fake green when the season would usually turn the grass brown. If you look close enough, everything and everyone is imperfect in some way or another.

Ben's head is on a swivel. We turn down a series of long pathways, nearing a large building that looks run-down. Its red brick is crumbling, and all the widows are broken. Lifeless vines grow up the sides; they look like they have been growing for many years to be able to reach the top and cascade off the other side. I guess not all of Warshaw is as pristine as they would like people to think.

By the time we round the corner, I can barely stay on my feet. Every step sends a jolt of pain through my legs, and an unsettling warmth radiates from my core, threatening to bring me to my knees. Even if my legs give out, I will drag myself to her, inch by determined inch. I close my eyes and picture her face. My favorite image of her, with rags in her hair and coffee in her hands.

Then, I see it—an airplane. It's smaller than I thought it would be, and it looks nothing like the bomber plane that holds the spot above the sign at the entrance of Warshaw. It's white with red lines on the wings and nose. There is what looks like a fan on the front and a tail that goes up into the air on the back.

A man stands near the door, checking his watch impatiently next to a short stack of stairs leading into the cabin. He looks to be in his late thirties, reduced with the help of whatever the people in the Inner Ring do with their faces to keep their skin from falling or wrinkles building around their features. He nods to Ben, who keeps his eyes but leans down to my ear. I quickly fix my uneven breathing so he doesn't hear. "No dancing on this one, Blue. He doesn't play fair." Ben pauses, thinks for a moment, then lets out a small laugh. " Actually, he's not even in the game." Ben warns. I hardly hear him when I nod because there is a pounding in my ears now that we have stopped.

We approach the man who ushers us onto the plane with a motion of his hand. "Ben," the pilot greets him from under a baseball cap with a nod of his head. The air around this one is dark, more so than Ben, Samson, and O combined. A chill runs down my spine, followed by a bead of sweat.

His black hair flips at the ends, sticking out the back of the navy-blue cap with an old baseball team logo on it—of course, that team has ceased to exist in more than a hundred years.

The man with black hair watches Ben take the steps with ease. Ben turns and gives him a light pat on the shoulder. "Debts repaid, Adam." He tells him before disappearing with a sidestep into the cabin.

Adam spies at me from beneath the hat as I take the stairs, much less gracefully than Ben due to my injuries. Adam watches, amused. His gaze drops to my middle, where the soaked bandages lay beneath a black shirt. He licks his pink lips, a scar on the top left, before he slips in behind me. Then he shuts the pressurized door, releasing a whoosh of air. *Did it just get smaller in here?* I wipe the sweat that has accumulated on my brow.

Suddenly, I am terrified—not only of the men. Ben is already in a seat, with a fake mask of confidence on his face and in his posture. Without realizing it, I now face the exit, only to be met by Adam's dark features. Trapped.

Adam towers over me, blocking the door I wouldn't know how to open even if I tried. He watches me like a hawk, with a pointed nose and narrow brown eyes. He looks hungry, searching for his next meal as if it will suddenly appear on the spot between my eyes. "Women are bad luck," he mutters. I swallow away the knot in my throat as he pushes past me. "Especially liars," Adam hisses down at me. I try not to let my face show what Adam already knows.

*Liar.* I am that. I would lie, steal, *kill* to get to her. But right now, what I have to do, is live.

I turn swiftly away from him. My feet thank me when I take the seat next to Ben, between him and the window. Ben studies the Rolex on his wrist too intensely, as if he has gotten lost while trying to read the time. I take a deep breath, not caring about Ben's strange behavior, to look past my reflection in the window. To Palen. What will it look like from up there? I search the sky.

No matter how many times I unclench my hands from the seat or swallow the lump in my throat, nothing could hide my nerves. I have never flown. Never even saw a plane until I got here aside from a dot in the sky with a white streak behind it as they flew over Harmony once or twice. Jez would make wishes on them, like a shooting star. *Those* were impossible to see from beneath the pollution of Palen's Outer Ring.

Adam watches me squirm with a satisfied look before he sits at the front, flipping switches and checking gages. Then, another flip of a switch and the pull of a lever makes the engine roar with life. The whole plane vibrates before lurching forward, towards a long stretch of asphalt. Weeds grow through the cracks of the road. I watch as we pass reflector lights on poles. They pass slowly at first, then faster and faster.

Ben lays a hand on my thigh. His touch stops it's absentminded up and down. At first, I want to rip his hand away, but when I peel my eyes from earth to look at his face, I realize he is not comforting me. His chest heaves in tortured in and outs, and his mouth is set in a line as his jaw muscles flex over and over again.

The plane speeds up faster than any train or car I have ever been in.

I close my eyes, clawing at Ben's hand like it will tether me to Palen. The speed puts strange pressure on my body that is uncomfortably heavy. I hear the engine and the wind as it slides over the wings. My stomach lurches. It seems to go on forever. I think I'm going to be sick.

Then, weightlessness.

My eyes slowly open to reveal a sea of clouds below, rolling like a picture of the ocean a woman once brought into the pawnshop. I loved that painting. I looked at it every day, pretending I was at that beach in the sun. Riley didn't much care for it.

I search this side, then the other. The scent of floral spices and whiskey fills my senses. My fingers are still wrapped tightly around Bens, my nails nearly embedded into the skin on the top of his hand. He doesn't even notice. His eyes are squeezed shut, just like mine were just a moment ago. "You can open your eyes now," I tell him, releasing him and leaning back in my seat with a wince. Only to be met with brown piercing eyes in a large mirror Adam peers out of.

"A storm and a woman on my plane." He huffs with a shake of his head. Ben opens one eye, then the other.

He makes a noticeable effort to keep his attention away from the window. "You could ask for forgiveness another way." Ben grins at Adam's reflection, quickly switching from scared to confident.

Adam angrily clenches his mouth closed but doesn't let go of Ben's eyes in the mirror. Ben stands his ground, never wavering, not even a blink. Slowly but surely, Adam's eyes go from Ben to the open air before him. *Forgiveness, for what, I wonder?*

My body becomes accustomed to the new height the longer we are in the air. The adrenaline has worn off, replaced with a wet heat radiating from my side. I knew my stitches were torn when I left the bunker. I hope Felix forgives me for staining his nice sheets I left covered in blood. I wrapped the wound tightly, but I knew it was only a matter of time before I bled through.

I have been careful not to place my hands near my stomach, turning away when a breath is too deep so no one can see the pain on my face. So far, Ben has either been too nervous or too distracted watching Adams' every move to notice the sweat dripping from my brow. My whole body is on fire, but we are so close. Soon, I will be in Jericho. I can manage until then.

Adam also looks back to make sure his passengers are behaving. He has this look on his face that makes me think he wants me dead. He clearly hates women. He has only mentioned it about a dozen times. He keeps mumbling under his breath. *Bad luck. Devil woman. All the same.* I ignore him.

None of it matters because I am on my way.

Finally, things are going to plan.

I will save her.

# CHAPTER 15

Turbulence.

That's what Adam calls it. Every now and then, the plane shakes. At first, I braced myself against the seat, closed my eyes, and waited for the inevitable fall, explosion, or whatever causes planes to crash, but it never came.

Ben has moved from beside me to the front with Adam. Now, both of their faces are in the mirror, giving me nowhere to hide.

The plane shifts, forcing me to lean to the side against the window. Luckily, my sharp breath could be mistaken for awe when my eyes latch on to a patch of black that offsets the white sky.

Sticking above the clouds in the distance is a towering mountain, jagged and unmoving, despite the optical illusion that happens as we approach it, making it seem as if it were coming right for us. We continue to circle around it, revealing what is hidden on the other side. Another nearly identical jagged peak to the one beside it. The clouds seem to turn liquid as the white descends off its ridges like a waterfall, pooling into the lower clouds.

Adam presses more buttons. Then, lifts us further into the sky with a pull of the control wheel. He whispers a string of curses as he watches the screen set on the dash between the two men. A green square with a digital hand circles round and round. Sometimes, dots appear on the screen to signal nearby objects. The mountain must be the dots near the edge. Occasionally, a bird or two will appear, and the green dots will come and go as quickly as the birds.

While Adam continues to wrap around the mountain Ben begins to take notice of the screens as well, but you can tell he cannot make sense of it.

Ben does, however, have a better view out the front window. We make another obtuse left turn. My weight shifts again, and there is that sting of pain. Ben finally speaks up, "You're going in circles, Adam." He says through gritted teeth. Adam looks over at him, annoyance on his face. Then Adam returns to the task at hand with a roll of his eyes. Ben turns to Adam with death in his eyes, "What the hell is happening?" Ben asks. Adam continues his constant left turn. You can't see much behind the wall of white clouds.

It's not until some time passes before I see the same jagged spot of the mountain I saw before. Ben is right. We are going in circles. "Adam," Ben says in a warning growl.

"Give me a damn minute." Adam nearly shouts as he fidgets with what looks like a radio. Ben snatches it out of his hand before he can use it. "What the hell?" Adam throws his free hand into the air.

"They might be listening," Ben informs Adam. Who is *they*? I catch my mind often drifting from one thing to the other easily when I should be paying attention to what is happening in front of me.

Adam peeks at me through the mirror, his eyes darken. When the plane begins to shake again, I can't help but bite my lip to keep curses from coming out. *Turbulence*, I tell myself. Adam's lip twitches upwards when he spots my arms wrapped absentmindedly around my waist. I have given myself away, or maybe he already knew. "You have no idea what you have done, Ben." He still curves the plane to the left, around and around we go.

Ben's mouth falls open slightly at his words. "I know *exactly* what I am doing." He snarls, his voice loud. You have to shout to be heard over the engine's rumbling.

Adam's lips curl into a cat-like grin. "Really?" I think he looks at me again, but my vision is starting to blur. *I do not feel so good.* "Girl!" Adam shouts back at me. I forgot he doesn't know my name. I await his next words, straightening my shoulders so he does not see my weakness. "Do you know what awaits you in Jericho?" He asks, that same shit-eating grin on his face.

The pain coming from my side is so bad I can't get words to form, so I nod carefully. But when my vision clears, Adam's attention is not on me. He looks at Ben. The question was not for me. It's all to get under Ben's skin, and it's working.

Ben shakes his head in warning of what he is about to say next. "You are no longer part of the society, Adam. You have been absent, *awol*. You. Don't. Exist." His words radiate anger. "Thanks to me," he adds as a reminder to Adam.

Adam still takes that same wide, sickening left turn. "Thanks to you." He agrees with a nod. "Thanks to you, *I* know what you have brought with you. Do you?" Adam asks. Again, his gaze meets mine. Dangerous.

Ben's features pinch together in confusion before he moves so quickly towards me I nearly jump out of my skin. I let out a strangled groan of pain as my body relaxes, but not before I feel the cool touch of Ben's hands on my calf. He lifts up the fabric of my pants. I wish I could stop him, but I think if I tried, I would pass out. When he grabs the gun from my boot, I am helpless.

Adam curses when he hears the click of the hammer. "You'll kill us all, Ben." Adam almost sings. Ben braces his hands on the gun as if he has done this a million times before. Riley's hands come to mind, wrapped around the same gun, his arms outstretched as he warned me of second chances. The image is gone just as soon as it comes.

Something is definitely not right. I feel like when the radio antenna gets knocked to the side, static starts to play instead of music.

"Take us into Jericho. Now." Ben pushes a bit further, pressing the gun into Adam's temple. "Lo will be expecting you, and you will never come." He spits. "That would be a shame," Ben says.

Adam's nostrils flare, his jaw clenches, and his hands tighten on the control wheel. His eyes narrow in on mine in the mirror. "*She* will die before then," he says quietly. I could only understand because I was watching his mouth move in the reflection.

Ben cocks his head in confusion before looking over his shoulder at me. Noting all the things that are wrong.

I see it, too, in the mirror, right next to Adam. My skin has paled, my eyes feel heavy. There is a throbbing in my head that doesn't go away, forcing me into a permanent scowl. No matter how many breaths I take, I never seem to have enough air.

Ben purses his lips together before turning back to Adam. "Take us into Jericho." His blue daggers pin Adam. "Now."

"I can't," Adam replies as if it is final.

"You will." Ben returns.

The plane shakes again. I close my eyes. Somewhere near Adam, an incessant high-pitched beeping begins. Soon, it becomes a more urgent, longer version of the sound.

"Fuck." I hear Adam say.

"What was-" Ben starts. Then my stomach is in my chest.

We are falling. I can't make myself look.

There is a terrible scraping of metal on metal coming from somewhere to my left.

"Sit down." Adam half shouts. Followed by the clicking of a seatbelt.

I squeeze my eyelids as tight as they will go. *No, no, no. This can't be happening.*

We must have stopped falling because the feeling in my stomach disappears, but the sound is still there. The plane is still shaking in a different way than before.

I grip the seat in a failed attempt to steady myself. When I open my eyes, I see nothing but white on the other side of the window. We are inside the clouds instead of atop them like we were before. I look to Adam, who is lost in concentration. Ben still grips the gun with one hand, pointed at Adam. "Land the fucking plane. We will walk." Ben spits.

Adam huffs. "She will never make it to Jericho." Then, "Hold on." He tells us as the plane forces its way through a much darker part of the sky.

We violently make our way through the clouds. The green dots on the bottom of the screen start small and grow as we continue. At this moment, I am thankful for the pain because I have no time to think about anything else.

When we emerge on the other side, below the white, we are met with a whole other problem. We are too close to the mountain. The snow is falling at the same rate as we are, making it look suspended in the air around us.

Everything happens in slow motion. The ground comes up to meet us. My head lulls back and forth. Someone yells my name. I can't tell who. I'm frozen, unblinking, waiting for the impact as I stare at those green fucking dots.

The wings scrape against the tops of trees, knocking the snow from the pine. There is that voice again. My name, my real name. Emerson. Not Babe, or Blue, or bitch. Then, we continue our assault through the trees. They snap and break, slowing us down with jolts of pain.

When we finally hit the ground, the plane crumples with the impact, and the windows shatter into tiny pieces all around. Something flies past my face, brushing against my hair before landing with a thud on the seat behind me. The cool air rushes in all at once.

Ben's body sits limply in the chair, his shoulders slumped, his head to one side.

Adam is moaning and groaning as he looks back and forth, disoriented. He inspects his hands and then places them on top of his head. You can see the breaths he takes from the cold that surrounds us. Long in and outs before he finally looks behind him, to me. Those same puffs of air do not come in such large quantities from Ben. Instead, they are short and labored.

My body shakes with fear and the cold. Slowly, I unbuckle the belt, falling out of my seat and grabbing at my middle when I reach my feet. When I lift my hands from the damp shirt, they come away red. I make my way to Ben, who has a gash on his forehead that leaks down his face, staining his pale skin.

I push my hand to his face, his eyes barely open enough to see me. "Jezebel." He whispers. My head spins, and my eyes feel like they might pop right out of their sockets.

I must have hit my head. "What did you just call me?" I desperately ask, shaking his head in my hands when his eyes close again. "Ben!" I shout. A hand wraps around my wrist but I am too weak to pull away from it. "Ben," I try again. Adam pulls at me until I am nearly in his lap.

I scramble away from his touch, but it's too late. "You are coming with me." He stands, knocking against me with his body.

"No." I cry.

Another violent pull has my insides curdling. "Yes." He takes a bag out of an overhead compartment and wraps a coat around my shoulders. Long, grey, and painful against my side. He shrugs on his own coat before gathering supplies from under a seat. The wind howls, flowing through the aircraft along with bits of white caught in the draft.

I don't take my eyes off Ben. His head falls to the side, but he picks it back up. I try to go to him, but Adam won't have it. He is already pulling me towards the back of the plane, where there is a hole big enough to get out of.

*Ben knows Jez.* I can hardly think of anything other than that vital piece of information. I know I heard him correctly. He called me Jezebel. I fight against Adam, but he is stronger, uninjured.

"Let me go." I plead, but it's no use. Adam ignores me, walking us farther back.

The plane lets out a strange squeal from beneath us. The sound disappears before echoing back at us again when it hits the mountain. Adam flinches but keeps going, pulling me from the seat I have a white-knuckle grip on. The same noise rings in my ears before the back half of the plane shifts. It begins to move, taking the whole thing with it, until finally, we are at an incline.

Adam slams against the back wall hard but is up and moving again in an instant, climbing the side of the plane.

I hold on tight to the seat, using the backrest to lift myself up until my feet are on it. Adam climbs up the side, using whatever he can get his hands on to lift himself up to me. We move again, sliding along the ground. You can hear the knocking of rocks and the screeching of trees up against the bottom and sides of the metal aircraft.

I suck in a breath, preparing myself for what comes next. We circle around as we go, drifting over the snow until we hit something solid again. I cry out in pain as my body slams against the seat. Light hits my eye, a reflection from something on the ground near my feet. The gun. My gun. Riley's gun.

Adam is holding his arm. There is a gash on it from the fall, but it doesn't stop him. He reaches for me again. I ignore the pain and bend down to grab the silver pistol. Holding it the way Riley taught me, outstretched in front of me, steadied by my other hand, ready to shoot. The hammer is already back. All I have to do is pull the trigger.

So I do.

# CHAPTER 16

*Click.* The hammer falls. Nothing happens. I pull it back again. *Click.*

Adam laughs. So does Ben, who now stands behind me.

I'm not sure how he got there. Things are still fuzzy. How I, myself, am standing, I'm also not sure. Ben looks to be finding his balance, and his wound is still leaking a deep red, but his confusion is long gone. "Put the gun down, Blue." He tells me—*Blue*, not Jezebel.

I lower the weapon and watch as Adam licks his lips. I let the gun fall to my side in defeat. "Do you know what you are doing, Ben?" He asks through heavy breaths.

"You should know better than anyone. I *always* have a plan." Ben's reply comes out strained, and I notice he favors his right side.

Adam crosses his arms and shakes his head. "You're in too deep this time," Adam explains. I look to Ben to see his reaction. I have no idea what any of this means. Ben pushes his lips together as if he is thinking carefully about what to say next. He comes up with... *nothing*, apparent by his quick glance in my direction. He doesn't say anything at all. A few uncomfortable seconds pass with no further information. "You don't know," Adam says in awe, finally breaking the silence.

Adam also looks at me, the same as Ben did just a moment ago. As if I have the information he seeks. "Don't know what?" I ask quickly. If this is about Jez, I need to know what's happening. Adam doesn't care. He keeps his attention on Ben. I also take the time to find the answers on Ben's face. "Tell me what's going on," I demand of Ben. "Where is Jez?" I basically cry. "I need to know. I need to get to her." God, I sound like a broken record.

Ben doesn't even flinch, doesn't move a muscle until Adam speaks again. The men only keep their eyes on the other, daggers slicing through flesh. Unease fills the cabin. "They will come for you," Adam says to Ben as if it's common knowledge. *Who?* "If you do somehow make it to Jericho. If you exchange her, you won't live long enough to be happy with your girl. You will be tortured, killed." *Exchange? Me?* I want to scream. I want to tear into Ben's mind and pull out the information he refuses to share with me.

"I have to try," Ben says before he grabs the gun from my hand and holds it out. Adam moves so quickly I barely have time to dodge his assault. The men fall to the ground in a mess of limbs. Adam climbs on top of Ben, punching his head into the hard surface beneath. Ben's arms are pinned beneath the weight of Adam.

Soon, Ben goes still, but Adam continues pulling his arms back even through the exhaustion that has taken over his body. He slowly brings them back down again to collide with Ben's face. Wet smacks of bloodied flesh on flesh fill my ears. Ben's face swells and bruises. "Stop," I scream. It's so loud in this small space.

I need Ben alive. He knows so much.

My head feels light, and I know I don't have much time before Adam kills Ben. I say a prayer and grab the gun from Ben's loose grip. Adam doesn't even realize what's going on. He is lost in his own rage. My shaky arms lift the weight of the weapon until I am aiming the barrel at Adam's head.

I pull the trigger.

A shockwave starts in my hands and travels to my shoulders before pushing my whole body back slightly. My ears ring from the sound of the blast. Adam's body falls sideways to the ground, dead.

I suck in a breath. Then another, and another, but it's not enough air. I *killed* him. With a gun that only had one fucking bullet in it. Ben *knew*. He must have taken the rest of them out. *Stupid fucking games.* My mind catches up slowly. Finally, I see the spray of blood, the smell of it, all around me, on me—my own and Adam's.

My head feels light. Loss of blood, maybe, shock, the realization I am a murderer, it doesn't matter which you choose.

The gun slips from my fingers and drops to the ground beside Ben. He coughs up more red to match his face. Blood. The whole cabin is painted in it now. It's a red nightmare. And when I close my eyes, red, red, red.

I fall to my knees beside Ben, pushing back the urge to expel my guts. Ben groans, his fingers twitch. He swallows over and over again due to the liquid that pools and spills from his mouth. His blue eyes hardly open wide enough to peer up at me, or past me, I can't tell.

Frantically, I search for life, for the soul Jez promised me would be there. "Tell me about Jez." My voice cracks.

Ben's brows push together, "I would have loved you too." He says through shallow breaths.

That's not good enough. "How can I get to her?"

"You can't." He tries and fails to shake his head. I wait. He has more to give, I can tell. *They all talk if you wait long enough.* "You were never go-

ing to see your sister again. You were meant to *be* her, her replacement."
He chokes out before his eyes slowly close before opening weakly again.

*Replacement?* There is so much I do not know. I will not get the
answers here. I have to make it to Jericho.

Ben clocks the determination on my face and smiles, perfectly white
teeth, blue eyes the same as mine. The same face Jez knew once, maybe
even loved.

"There she is," Ben whispers. Then, his lids flutter before closing all
the way.

There is nothing quite like the silence that happens right after death.

The plane's cabin has supplies, enough for one person. The person
whose face is etched behind my eyelids as I pulled the trigger that ended
his life. Only replaced when I think of the map that hangs on the bunker
wall above a woman who will read, drink coffee, and laugh with her
husband until the world ends. Which feels imminent at the moment.

The plane slid and stopped at a row of trees before a ravine. You can
see the marks on the otherwise white forest floor. The air is so cold as I
step onto what is now half a wing. The other half is nowhere in sight.
The grey coat falls just above my knees keeping my center warm, but my
toes quickly become numb from the snow beneath my feet.

My head pounds, and my vision blurs when I move too fast or breathe
too deeply.

*Just keep walking.* Jez's voice fills my head.

That's what I do, I keep going. Stopping only to throw up or rewrap
the scraps of shirt I have tied around my waist. The bleeding has slowed,
but not enough. The world goes grey when the sun begins to hide behind
the clouds. Even more so as it falls behind the mountain. I feel like I am

on the dark side of the moon. I curse at myself for letting another day pass. Another day Jez has to endure in Jericho.

Riley's voice fills my thoughts like it often does at times like this. Times that feel like death. *"Don't cry."* Riley's words come as a tear falls to my hand.

If my mind isn't playing tricks on me. If I am not just making things up in my head as I did Riley's voice. Then *that* is a split in the trees that could only have been man-made.

The mountain range is to my left, two peaks mocking me, watching me fail. The road has to be to my right, which means the safe house is along it to the west. Time is running out. I can feel it. If my memory fails me now, I will not make it to the safe house. I will not make it at all. The Mrs. was right. So was Adam.

I slide on my bottom down to the open area, where trees do not grow in the same rows as the others, cursing to myself when pain shoots up my spine. The ground is uneven, but I am sure this is the same long and winding road I saw on the map.

Behind me is a trail of my own blood, staining the perfect white that falls from the sky. I imagine Felix traveling the same road, to the safe house and beyond to Jericho, with a mission to destroy the one remaining path. You can tell where the road cuts out and begins again, like what is underneath the snow has been removed by force because it has.

The road narrows ahead, swallowed by the evergreens at its sides. Just beyond that, a dark building with chipping red paint that once made it stand out among the snow-covered evergreens. I don't let myself rejoice just yet as I take my final steps towards the cabin.

The wind howls, stinging my ears, freezing the liquid that has built up around my eyes and nose. The path to the door has drifted over, making it hard to get to. I trudge through the snow that now comes up to my knees in some places. It looks like this place hasn't been used for years.

Riley's voice is nowhere to be heard. Maybe death will wait? I hold tight to my stomach, telling myself once I am inside, I will be fine. I will live. *So close.*

With my arms wrapped around my middle, I push through the snow slowly, dragging my feet because it hurts to lift them. I reach for the handle on the old wooden door. "Who the fuck are you?" That is not Riley at all. Whose voice would be in my head now? Not one I can remember. Hypothermia, lack of blood, a hard hit to the head. Take your pick. I'm dying. *Hallucinating.*

*So close.* I reach for the door again, shaking my head to get rid of the voice. "Stop." The voice demands. If I stop, I will die. I need in this door. I need to live. I shake my head again. "You won't have a hand if you reach for that again." He warns.

I shake my head. "You're not real," I say to the voice inside my head. The sound of wood being dropped to the ground makes me second-guess myself. But before I can turn my head over my shoulder to see if my mind is truly playing tricks on me, my hand is being ripped away from the handle.

The wind catches in my hood. It falls so I am revealed.

My brows come together. "Real," I say to myself. Then I blink, making sure if I close my eyes and open them, he will still be there.

The man moves a string from the side of the door frame. An invisible line. He lifts his head and points above the door, where a snow-covered slab of metal blends into the side of the cabin. He unwraps the string from the handle as he huffs his annoyance at my actions. The metal falls at our feet.

I watch all of it while trying to maintain my balance. It doesn't help when the man lifts my hand into the air, holding it in front of my face for me to see. "Gone." He scolds with a shake of my wrist in his grip. I stare at my hand like it's the first time I am seeing it. My head falls to the side, it takes all my strength to keep it in focus. My fingers are purple and lifeless. How long have they been that way?

Then, past my hand to the man's face, which is mostly covered. I can spot the anger in the space between his green eyes, a wrinkle just above his nose. "You're hurt." I can't quite tell if it's a question at first. He waits for a response. I nod my head because talking feels like too much work.

He twists the knob and opens the door. I was expecting it to be warm. It's not. The sun has almost disappeared, making the one-room cabin very dark. I can hardly make out a couple of bunks, a fireplace with nothing in it, and shelves with what looks like old board games and books with broken spines.

The possibility of someone being here was never zero. It's a public safe house for those who try to make the journey, or at least it used to be. The Mrs. said those who try, fail. Yet here he is.

He brings in the wood that had spilled due to my almost lost hand. Now I am no longer moving, my limbs almost sting as they regain warmth slowly, too slowly.

I am so cold that when I fall onto the bed, my body shivers violently. My eyes close for much longer this time. I can't seem to talk myself into opening them again. I try to grip at the blankets but fail. My fingers don't curl around the fabric the way I want them to.

Nothing is working the way it should.

These are not the usual shivers I would get from a cool day in Harmony. No, it's unending chills that make their way into your bones, making you think you will never get warm again.

I almost forgot someone else was here until, "Take your clothes off." The man says. I squint at him from the comfort of the bed. Enough to see him as he peels away his own layers. Starting with the gloves and the scarf that was covering his face. *No.* I want to say, but nothing comes out. My jaw is making an incessant clicking noise as my teeth hit against each other.

He nears me. Again, my body does not respond to my demands when I try to move. The man lays his coat over a chair and pulls up his long sleeves, revealing forearms filled with intricate tattoos. He reaches a tattooed hand out in my direction. I try to pull away, but only a whimper escapes. After he lays it on my head, he turns away quickly, mumbling something under his breath.

Soon, there is warmth and light at my side. A fire has been started in the hearth. Then he is back. Peeling away my coat, then my boots. I can't move. Can't fight. My blood-soaked shirt is being ripped away from my skin. This is really happening. Did I choose this life? The one that ends with a man using my body in any way he sees fit. What Jez had warned me of without outright telling me of what is to be my fate?

I will never make it to Jericho.

# CHAPTER 17

This time, I do not have the luxury of whatever liquid Felix squeezed into my arm. The man pours a liquid over my stomach and onto his hands. It stings in a pain I have never felt before. I suck in a breath that hurts even more. "Put this in your mouth." The demand comes with no inflection, a practiced phrase even. Then, a piece of fabric is being shoved between my teeth.

For a moment, nothing happens. He leaves for what feels like a long time. I am exposed, both warm and cold. I am sweating, but goosebumps appear on my skin, and I still shake from the hike to the cabin.

I am dying, I decide. Where is it? His voice? If I am going to die I at least want to hear it one more time.

My chest heaves in ragged in and outs as panic sets in. I try to sit up but something holds my shoulders to the bed. Brown hair falls into my vision before disappearing again. I would know that hair anywhere, it's long now, not the short hair he had when he left me—Riley. I try to reach for him, but he's no longer there. A soothing voice floats through the room. "Brace yourself, sweetheart." It seems to come from nowhere. Not the man or Riley.

Then, an object is lifted above my body, barely within sight. It glows orange. The image blurs. When it falls, my jaw tightens around the fabric in my mouth, but the scream is hardly muffled from behind it. My back arches, and my hands ball into fists at my sides.

Pain. What I felt before is nothing compared to this. Then darkness. Only for what feels like a few seconds before I am rolling over on my side to throw up whatever is left in my stomach, which is nothing—just yellow bile.

My mind is foggy. Everything begins to bleed into each other while the room spins. I have to close my eyes to keep from heaving again.

Only the crackling of the fire remains.

Time passes, I am uncertain of how much. I begin to think I may have imagined the whole thing. But when I reach my hand down to my side, I feel fresh bandages.

The door opens, I don't try to look, but a rush of wind fills the cabin before the door closes with a slam. Then, the sound of trickling water before a wet cloth is placed across my forehead.

"Who are you?" I say maybe to no one because there isn't an answer.

Then, a chair scrapes across the floor from one spot to another.

More silence. "Who are *you*?" If I could see his face, I know I'd see a smile. While I feel like I'm dying, he is smiling, which enrages me, but I play along because I have no other choice. I need to do what I do with all men, pretend. *Pretend that their words are honey, that their touch is wanted, and that their lies are truth.* Jez's words fill my head.

I grit my teeth, "Babe," I tell him my name. The name Corey gave me, not my own.

He huffs a laugh. "Hello, Babe." He drawls. "Why are you here?" There it is again, the smirk that bleeds into his words. I gather all my strength to look over at him. Lazily my head falls in the direction of his voice. My eyes open slowly, I let them adjust to the light before I hook onto him. Mostly for something to stop the spinning, but I hope he sees it differently.

He is, in fact, smiling, like he can't help himself. "Jericho." That is the only answer I can give to his question. He wears a white T-shirt that reveals the same tattoos as before. From this distance, the darkest pieces of the art make it look like his arm is concave in those spaces, offset by the white that wraps around roses and over the wings of birds. He searches the table next to him before picking up a pack of cigarettes, pulling one out, and holding it between his lips, unlit.

He then pushes his boots up onto the table and leans back in the chair as he looks down his nose at me. The chair balances on its two back legs. Again, there is silence as I stare at him, waiting for a response. "I gave you my name. Now give me yours." I barely get it out without coughing. My throat is dry and scratched from heaving. My head pounds and my eyes start to become heavy again. My body is trying to heal itself with rest. I force myself not to move my attention from him, not to show weakness.

He grabs a book of matches from the pocket of his shirt. When he lights the match, his face illuminates in yellow for only a few seconds as he holds it to the end of the cigarette. His green eyes concentrate on the task at hand, only straying when he notices me watching.

My brain betrays me because, for a moment, I am lost in the image of him. Not caring of his name, or why he is here, or why he saved my life. Every man I have ever seen now seems mundane, plain, compared to the one who reclines by the fire, a living work of art that renders all others ordinary. His branded fingers curl around the cigarette, removing it from his lips. Smoke spills into the air. Seconds later, the smell drifts into my senses. How I love the smell of burning tobacco.

"Bash." He says as he inhales more sweet smoke. This time, Bash leans his head onto the back of the chair and closes his eyes, leaving the lit cigarette to balance over his bottom lip.

His arms cross, and I am left staring at Bash like there will be more, but there isn't more. He doesn't say a word. His brows crush together at the center as if he is deep in thought.

I nearly shake my head at the absurdity of it all but think better of it when my head pounds again, reminding me I am incapable of doing *anything* right now, which puts me at the mercy of Bash.

Bash, whose dark hair falls in perfect waves over his bushy brows. Bash, whose teeth are exceptionally white for being a smoker. Bash, who saved my life. "Bash?" I decide to ask, noticing my eyes are becoming increasingly heavy by the second. "Why are *you* here?" I ask him with a slight yawn, using the same tone he used when he asked me my name. This time, I give in and let my lids close while I wait for his answer.

"Jericho," he says simply. The same answer I gave.

I inhale as deeply as I can through my nose. That smell reminds me of home. "What's in Jericho?" I ask next. He shifts, which I can hear but not see.

Just when I think I will not get an answer, just when the only sound is the falling of a burning log, just when I am about to drift into sleep. "A girl," Bash tells me. His voice soft. A melody.

"It's always a girl." Is my last thought before I am pulled into nightmares.

# Chapter 18

"You have some explaining to do."

My mind reaches for consciousness, but I come up short. This has to be a dream. I shake my head and bury myself back into the pillow. Any minute now, Jez will come and wake me up for school. I will be late, as usual.

"I know you're awake."

No, this can't be happening. The blankets are pulled from my body. I lift myself onto my elbows, groaning on the way because I had forgotten about my injuries. *Fuck that hurts*, but I keep going until I am painfully leaning onto my hands behind my back.

Bash holds onto the wood of the top bunk, his arms straining against his shirt. We stare at each other while I try to remember what he just said. His smile from our previous conversation is nowhere to be found. There is a rage behind his eyes that is poorly hidden.

In the daylight, those eyes look like emeralds against the white light that spills in from a small window behind me. Even brighter in contrast to his black brows, which push together angrily. "Why are you looking at me like that?" I finally ask, noticing how much effort I have to put into every word.

Bash all but rolls his eyes. "Like what?" he says through clenched teeth. Almost like he is ashamed I could see right through him.

I have practice in finding out the true thoughts of men from their facial expressions alone. "Like you're going to kill me," I answer him.

Bash crosses his arms over his chest and leans back just as he did the last time we spoke. "Maybe I am. Depends on your answers." he shrugs.

Now it's my turn to roll my eyes, or at least I try. "I'll answer any question you have." I peel my right arm up from the bed and cross my heart. Even though I don't remember the last time I answered anything truthfully.

Bash follows my finger as it lays over my left breast. Over the white shirt, I now notice belongs to Bash. His eyes linger for only a second before he is back to scowling at me. "Let's start with the two corpses in the plane." His left eyebrow rises involuntarily.

I don't let myself be surprised. "What about them?" I ask almost daringly. Challenging him to ask what he *really* wants to.

His face goes as still as stone. He is unamused by my challenge. "One beaten to death. One shot." He states the facts. Then he reaches into his pocket and pulls out a card. The same kind of card that was used to buy clothing in Warshaw before the city was attacked. Not the same kind, *the* card. He holds it up, then he slides another one from behind it, holding the two out where I can see them. Ben's face in a black and white photo. His ID card.

I hope Bash doesn't notice my shutter when I remember his words. *You were meant to be her. Replace her.*

"You really were headed to Jericho. Huh?" His lips flatten into a line. "Bought," he adds with a nod of his head. He doesn't need an answer to know it's true.

I nod anyway before looking down at the blankets to avoid eyes that seem to see everything. Jez had the same talent. "You're lucky." Bash states.

My head snaps back up, sending a twinge of pain down my spine. I ignore it. "Lucky?" I ask, dumbfounded. I have to reign in my anger. He has no idea just how *unlucky* I really am.

Bash looks down at me in confusion. "Yes." He moves his eyes between mine, searching. Then he thinks about what to say next. You can see the careful planning on his face. "It's not what you think it is," he states.

Yes, Jericho is not what it seems. That's what Jez was trying to tell me in her letters. I should have known when I received them and they were censored. I should have known a lot of things, but I figured it out too late.

"What is it then?" I ask the question that has been on my mind since the beginning. I need to know *exactly* how my stupidity has affected my sister.

"Answer my question first." He places the cards back in his pocket for safekeeping.

I close my eyes, and there it is. Adam's lifeless body. The life I took. And for what? Ben died, my way to Jericho, my only connection to Jez—gone. I swallow hard, and when I open my eyes again, I think I see a flash of pain cross the face of the man before me. As if he knows the weight of someone's life and what it feels like to take it. "I had no choice." Those are not the words I had expected to come out. Yet there they are.

Bash just nods his head, satisfied with my answer. I look away, fearing he might see more than I am willing to give. "Jericho is filled with filthy motherfuckers who trade women and children like candy." He says nonchalantly as he walks towards the fire. He grabs something from the table.

His smokes. I hear him slam the box against his palm multiple times. I look over at him, confused, forgetting the question I previously asked.

He lights the cigarette, taking a long drag before "You asked." He reminds me, shrugging his shoulders slightly.

I force myself to sit upright with my legs dangling off the bed. "Is that why you are going? To save your girl?" I ask next.

Then he lets out a low laugh that has my stomach in knots, maybe from lack of food. "Oh, she isn't mine." He says, like he can't believe I would even ask. He takes his usual seat next to the fire. *Not his.* I repeat in my head, tucking away the information for later.

I lean over onto the post that holds the top bed onto the lower one, using it to steady myself as I twist my broken body toward Bash. "Whose is she then?" I ask.

Bash leans his head to the side. He looks over at me as well. His eyes roam from my unruly, *unnatural* brown hair down to my stomach, where his handy work has undoubtedly saved my life. Then, as if he regrets his decision to look at me he drops his eyes. *Strange.* "She belongs to someone that you don't want to know. Someone who has killed for her before and would again."

"Why doesn't *he* go to Jericho then?" The words come without thought.

He sighs and lifts the handle next to him, placing a black pot over the flames. "Let's just say I owe him a favor," Bash says before he goes deep into thought. Smoke billows around him as he sucks in tobacco. I do not push further. Besides, I feel I have already gotten all the information about the subject he will give.

Soon, the room erupts with the savory scent of whatever Bash has put in the pot. My stomach growls. Finally, I am feeling well enough to get out of this bed. My body is sore in places I didn't even know it could be—whiplash, along with the addition of my previous injuries. The plane went down so quickly and with such force, but I was losing blood long before that.

I keep a blanket around my shoulders, even though I know Bash has already seen what I now hide. I sit in the chair across from him, tucking my legs into my body tightly. It's more comfortable this way. He waits for me to settle into the seat before passing me an empty mug. "Still want to go?" His abrupt question surprises me.

My eyes go wide. I don't even have to think about my answer. "Yes. I have someone who needs saving as well." I tell him. He nods his head, dips a metal ladle into the pot, and fills my mug with some type of stew. There must not have been any bowls.

I hastily drink the brown liquid. It burns as it goes down, but I don't care. It warms me from the inside out. I barely notice Bash staring at me. "Who?" He asks.

I smile into my mug. "A girl," I say mockingly, to which he flashes his white teeth—the kind of smile that pulls at his eyes. I wonder when *I* last smiled like that.

The man across from me shakes his head. "We can't go anywhere right now." He says. His smile disappears just as quickly as it came. He speaks in a strange way. The kind of way men visiting the club from the army base closest to the wall would speak to each other. Always in short, to the point sentences. All with an air of mystery behind them.

Bash nods towards the window. "Benjamin A. Mor," he says slowly. Ben, his full name. My heart drops into my stomach. The food there sits uneasy. I wait for Bash to say more. "He will be expected in Jericho," he says more to himself than me. I see the gears turning behind his eyes. I'm almost amused until my palms begin to sweat, and there it is again—Adam's death, Ben's last breath.

When he turns all his attention back to me, half white light, half orange from the fire, I hold my breath. "This could work." He says assuredly.

I have either hidden the panic that threatens to take hold well, or Bash does not care. "What could?" The words come out separately and strained.

"They only let you in with a member's name." He checks to make sure I am following. "Ben is the answer. If they don't look too closely to the picture." There's that smirk again as he shrugs his shoulders. "You'll need a change of clothes." Bash and I both look down at my bare skin. My legs now rest on the floor, my thighs peeking out from beneath the blanket.

In this very moment, I feel... ugly. My legs are scarred to high heavens from glass and shrapnel. There is still sweat, blood, dirt, and God knows what caked to my flesh. Not to mention the stretch marks and cellulite most men, men who pay for their women, never minded. If it moves and talks, has tits and a place to stick it, they don't care.

But in front of Bash, someone who seems to have no intention of harming me or selling me or using me, I have this need to cover myself. This is new. The club has all but stripped me of being embarrassed by my body. Now, it's all I can feel.

Jez was always the beautiful one. Perfect in every way but one.

Bash reaches out almost as if on instinct, tugging the blanket until it's past my knees, covering the entirety of my legs. His calloused thumb scrapes against my skin, causing a shiver to run up my spine.

When he retreats, he immediately finds something in the distance to latch onto so he doesn't have to look at me. All my thoughts come crashing to the surface.

*Clarity,* he sees what I see, a mess of a woman that has no value outside of the club. *Bought,* he said it himself. Bash clears his throat. "There are some clothes in the pack." He waves his hand lazily.

I stand so fast part of my vision clouds in black. When I catch my bearings, I notice Bash busies himself with the fire, poking at its embers with a metal rod. I huff as I turn, now angry he is making such an effort to avoid me. He doesn't have to make it so obvious he can't stand to look at me.

I dress quickly, noting all of the clothes in this particular pack are women's garments, none of Bash's things are in here. They must be for the girl Bash is retrieving from Jericho. They fit a little small, but they are better than the blood-soaked hand-me-downs that came from Felix.

The white long-sleeved shirt provides the warmth I was missing. It lays right above my hips, meant for someone much shorter, I assume. The jeans are comfortable, made from a material that stretches around my thighs, which I am grateful for. I made sure to choose from the more casual outfits. The other option was a black silk skirt that obviously goes with the blouse made from hell, with lace and a corset of the same dark color.

Bash is now mumbling something to himself. His shoulders are tense, the muscles in his back are basically tearing out the back of his shirt. I am not blind, his looks have not passed over my head. It is not the kind of attractive Corey or Riley possess. Bash isn't just muscle and man. Bash has much more delicate features. Ones that are offset by his bright green eyes that almost look like they do not belong to his face. Of course, someone who looks like Bash would not be interested in me.

Those outside the club often have that mentality. They think us to be dirty, *used*. I will not try to change his mind. It won't work anyhow. I decide not to let it get to me. The view from down here, beneath the nose of yet another man, is all too familiar.

I interrupt Bash's thoughts when I push the chair out and take a seat in front of the fire next to him. He only lifts his head slightly, showing his displeasure. When I reach back to the table to grab his cigarettes, he watches from the corner of his eyes but does not stop me. I slowly pull one from the pack, using my pointer and middle finger to bring it to my lips. Bash gets this strained, almost worried look on his face. "Will slow the healing process." He sounds like he has recited it a million times before.

I just place my hand before him, palm up. To which he lets out a huff I think is supposed to be laughter before he places the matchbook into my hand. "'Tis a different kind of healing I need," I say through my teeth while I keep the cigarette balanced between my lips. It moves up and down as I speak.

Bash nods his head once before leaning back in his chair. He watches me strike the match before I hold it up to my face. I breathe in once, deep, to get the thing burning. Then, I use a trick I picked up from Corey and pass it to Bash. On Corey, the gesture seemed fake, although I hardly turned down his offer. Wouldn't want him to think I was onto him.

When Bash takes it, I am pleasantly surprised. He, too, takes a deep breath, holding it, savoring it, before releasing it into the air. "Want to play a game?" He asks, seemingly out of nowhere. I keep my eyes on the fire, but I feel his emeralds burning a hole into the side of my face. He only looks if he thinks I am not.

"What kind of game?" I ask, letting the corner of my mouth rise. If we are truly trapped in here until the storm passes, then we will need to do something to fill the time. Besides, I've never let a man beat me at a game. Ever.

"A drinking game." I see the end of the cigarette glow orange in my peripheral.

"You're on."

# CHAPTER 19

Bash sidesteps me and heads for the kitchen—if it can even be called that. The sink doesn't work, the stove and oven that once ran on gas are out of order, and the counters are piled high with empty bottles and cans from I don't want to know when.

He pulls open the cabinet beneath the sink. Revealing rusty plumbing and more trash. Bash sticks his hand to the side, and sure enough, when it reappears, there is a large jar with clear liquid sloshing back and forth. Moonshine.

Jez would sometimes show up with a jar that looks all too similar to the one in Bash's hand. We would take it to the roof along with all the blankets in the apartment. Then we would just lay there, staring up at the clouds and listening to the sounds of Harmony. Making plans for when we get to Jericho.

I shake my head, clearing out the memory and pulling myself back to the present. Bash grabs two clean mugs—there seems to be a never-ending supply around here. He fills his own, then mine, and slides one in front of me. The smell is putrid, similar to gasoline—not quite the quality Jez would get from our neighbors in Harmony.

"What game are we playing?" I ask, grabbing the cup with two hands, cradling it close to my body like I would a hot cup of coffee.

Bash flashes those pearly whites. "It called who can get drunk the quickest." He takes a swig and lets out a slow, satisfied breath.

His attention goes to the fire, they always do, the only thing in the room that isn't me. "Oh, come on." I roll my eyes. I need more information about Jericho and what is going on there. Not to mention, if his friend is as important as he made it seem, then perhaps getting to know Bash isn't such a bad idea. Any information could aid in rescuing my sister. "Let's play never have I ever." It's more of a demand than anything else.

He makes a low growling noise before he holds out his cup, using it to point at me. "I always lose that game." he shakes his head. Even though he faces me, I notice he still does not meet my eyes.

I cross my legs and lean back in the chair, matching his cool demeanor. I curl my fingers around the mug's handle. "Then you will win your game *and* mine." His game where he gets drunk the quickest.

Bash doesn't say no. He doesn't exactly agree either. Still, I start the game, whether he is playing or not. "Never have I ever seen the Eastern lights." First, I will find out where he might be from. He looks like a middle-ringer. Handsome as they come. Maybe the most attractive man I have set my eyes upon since Riley left. Yet, he doesn't seem to have the edge most do in the Outer Ring. The world is harsh to those who come from poverty. They stick us all out there together like dogs. Like our lives are worth less than theirs.

When he doesn't drink, I nod, making sure to hide my frustration. That is most of Palen. The Outer Ring can't see the lights at all due to the pollution, and the Inner Ring can only see them from its easternmost border. Of course, Jericho is right in the center. From what I have heard, they can see them from almost everywhere if it's the season. It's a part of its magic, its allure.

There is the second option, the one where Bash is not participating in my game. He doesn't say anything for a long while. I don't either. This is one game I am very good at winning, the quiet game. Then, he crosses his arms, cup in hand. Finally, he looks up at me. *Finally* meets my eyes with a cocky smirk. "Never have I ever used a fake name." My heart races. It's not like it was hard to figure out *Babe* isn't my God-given name. I just didn't think he would call me out on it. Bash holds the space between my brows, waiting patiently for what he knows comes next.

I take a drink, a big one, because I think I'm going to need it. That was a mistake. It burns all the way down, causing me to cough in a fit that lasts too long. When it ends, Bash is laughing. He does that a lot. Sometimes, they even feel genuine, like right now.

I grin back at him, laughing at myself as well. "That one was easy to guess." My face feels warm from just one drink. Pain meds be damned. Next time I get a piece of glass through my abdomen, I'm asking for this.

Bash nods his head in agreement and takes a swig as well, telling me he has also used a fake name before. I don't ask him if the name he gave *me* was fake because 1. I like it, it suits him well. And 2. If I ask for his real name, he will ask for mine.

So, instead, I play on. My next question will have me drinking another sip of Deaths Moonshine, as I have decided to call it, but I feel like it's worth knowing the information. "Never have I ever killed someone," I ask quickly before I lose my confidence.

Bash looks almost proud. He silently takes a drink before watching to make sure I do as well. That puts me no further ahead, but I had to make sure I really saw what I thought I did after he asked about the plane crash.

He saw right through me when he asked about the corpses—the corpses that belong to Ben and Adam. One's death by my hand. Riley had his reasons, ones he never shared with me. Maybe Bash had his reasons as well.

Bash pours himself another glass. While mine looks like I haven't made a dent, I learned my lesson after the first drink. Too much of this stuff, and I will be on my ass.

When Bash leans forward onto the table, I slide back. On instinct, of course, although I am stopped by the chair. He tightens his jaw. It seems like he has to work very hard to keep his eyes on mine. I am not used to men being so... disgusted by me. I will not let him win this game, either. I also find the table with my elbows, leaning close to Bash, waiting. He looks down into his drink to help him find whatever it is he is about to say next. "Never have I ever." A pause. "Broken a promise." He seems to decide last second.

He doesn't drink, though, doesn't move. I do, though. Because I have broken many promises. Starting with my promise to keep away from the club. Ending with the promise I made to my sister to make it to Jericho, to be with her. Instead, I let her suffer alone because I was too dull to put two and two together. So, when the mug comes away from my lips, I stare at Bash who doesn't look at all surprised. His brows raise, they do that, I have noticed, against his will, it's his only tell. I laugh "I'm not a saint." I try to lighten the mood, but it doesn't work.

Bash scoffs. "What are you, then?" He asks as darkness surrounds him. It's not visible to the naked eye, but it's in the air, his aura.

When I don't answer, Bash takes the opportunity to finish his cup, lifting it into the air and downing its contents. Clearly, he has had more practice in the art of drinking than I.

"What kind of question is that?" I ask, a slight jest to my voice even though Bash is completely serious, still as a statue, and definitely not in a joking mood.

I place the fake smile gently on my face, the practiced one that keeps men from doing what Bash is about to do.

"Never have I ever." Bash slurs his words, I guess Deaths Moonshine is getting to him, too. "Slept with someone for money." He reaches for a cigarette clumsily, patting his chest to make sure the book of matches is still there.

My mouth falls open before I quickly snap it shut. *How dare he.* My face warms with anger, I try to reign it in, but the alcohol mixed with the audacity of the man before me, makes it impossible. I stare at his right eye, then the left. "There it is." I nod to him.

Then, I sit back and wait for him to say what he *really* wants to say. *Stay quiet long enough, and they talk,* I remind myself. It comes to my mind in Jez's voice. Bash finally finds his mouth with the cigarette and lights it up. Then, when he looks up at me, my stomach turns in on itself. Because what I see behind those eyes is the opposite of a soul. "Aren't you going to drink?" He says with a hint of arrogance.

I swallow. The air is so dense it could be cut with a knife. My features contort to show my anger. I shake my head. "I have done a lot of things for money, but that's not one of them." The words come out in a half-whisper. "Sorry to disappoint you," I add a little more confidently. I don't know why I feel the need to explain myself. Bash might not even remember this in the morning.

When my anger gets the best of me, I push the chair back. For no reason, I realize, because there is nowhere to go. "Maybe *now* you can look me in the eye," I say as I stand. The lack of food and the absurd amount of alcohol has my head spinning until I find the table before me with my hands. Which, unfortunately, has me leaning closer to Bash. Who just watches me through his long black lashes before he raises his head.

I probably look crazy as I search his face, forcing him to see me. I don't find what I am looking for, but I find something else. Something I only see in the mirror. Shame.

At first, I am confused. Then, Bash raises the jar, which is almost empty, and drinks from it. He drinks.

He drinks.

When realization dawns on me, it's too late. "Fuck." The word leaves my mouth without thought. I push my fingers through my hair "Fuck." *Really, again Emerson?* "I'm sorry, I just assumed-"

"That you would somehow be below me if you had to use your body to survive. Just like I am below you for using mine." he finished my sentence, but that is not at all what I was going to say.

I'm quick to defend myself. "What? No-"

He cuts me off again, "Then what did you *assume*?" he puts emphasis on the last word.

I'm a mix of anger and guilt as I try to put my thoughts into words. Was this all some test? "You couldn't even look at me earlier." I decide to say, but it's so... unhelpful. Bash also looks confused. I try again. "I just *assumed* you thought I was a useless whore. The same as everyone else." I have to turn my head to get away from what I might see on his face. He doesn't say a word. "I don't want to play this game anymore, Bash," I say to the fire.

A few seconds of unbearable silence. "Me either." Bash takes another drink he definitely does not need. I stand as straight as my broken body will let me. I have never had a problem with what people do to survive, my sister, Riley. Shit, even Corey was just trying to live in this fucked up world. The only life he knew how to live.

I don't know what game Bash was playing, but it certainly wasn't the same one as me. Whatever it was, I have clearly lost.

Bash's words cut through my thoughts. "Never have I ever made an assumption about someone without really knowing them first." I nearly roll my eyes but think better of it. Nothing could change the words that were already said by me, by him. Bash takes a timid drink first. Then I follow. Actually, I down the whole thing. Then I slam the mug back onto the table. I don't look at Bash before storming off to the farthest bunk.

# CHAPTER 20

When I wake up, I rub the sleep from my face and let my eyes adjust to the bright light that spills in through the window. My retinas may never recover. I didn't take into account the bunk I chose to be as far away from Bash, being this close to the window last night.

My head pounds with a hangover, but I am thankful for one thing that happened last night. Moonshine. I slept without nightmare for the first time in a long time. My breath puffs into a cloud above me. Cold.

I take a look around the room from under the warmth of the blanket. When I realize Bash is nowhere to be found, I sit up in a panic. A mistake for many reasons. The main one is a sharp pain in my side that was once dulled by liquor.

Bash's pack is gone. Was *that* the game? To get me drunk so he would have time to get his things and leave? He left me and is probably well on his way to Jericho. Without realizing it, I had given him everything he needs to get in.

Quickly, I pull the coat that belonged to Adam over myself and slip into my boots, which were discarded by the door. *Bastard.* I need to get to Jez. If my memory serves me right, Jericho is not far from here. A few miles at most. I can do it. I can make it. *Bastard.*

When I pull the door open, my lungs fill with cool air, making my nose run, and my ears burn. This is going to suck. *Bastard.* Still, I have to try. So, I gather all my strength and head for what I think is the road. Adam knew what kind of storm this would be. It's dangerous.

As I trudge through snow, I curse the name of every man who has wronged me. Starting with Riley and ending with Bash, with many in between.

I only make it a few steps before something eerie happens. The mountain goes quiet. Noises that usually fade into the background, ones you only notice when they *aren't* there—gone. Even the wind seems to stop its incessant howling. The only sound left is the crunching of snow beneath my feet. So, I stop too, waiting the same as everything else.

It starts small, a high-pitched whining sound in the distance. It's like nothing I have ever heard before. Slowly, it gets louder and louder until it vibrates the ground beneath me. The trees begin to shake, clearing their branches of white. Then, the earth begins to shift. The tightly packed snow begins to slide from beneath my feet.

"Move!" a voice shouts. From where? I can't tell. "Run!" Bash says again. I turn to see him barreling towards me, a dark figure in a sea of bright white. The sound from above becomes so loud it drowns everything else out. Including whatever Bash is currently shouting as I stand there, frozen.

We collide, his hand wraps around my arm, and I am being pulled away from what I now see as an avalanche, right where I stood, swept away down the mountain.

My ears ring as Bash pulls me to the ground with him until I am on a knee. He holds my shoulders tightly as if he is checking to make sure I am truly in front of him and not at the bottom of the mountain under a pile of snow. His eyes quickly move from my face to the sky as the sound becomes unbearable, drawing nearer. I cover my ears, but it's of no use.

One, two, three, jets streak the sky above us. We watch as they are there one second and gone the next.

Behind us, a part of the mountain explodes, followed by another and another down the path that leads to the safe house. Another explosion, and it's gone. Nothing left but scattered brick and pieces of wood—just like that.

I'm stuck, staring at the remnants like an idiot, waiting for the other foot to fall. Nothing happens. Still, I stare, mouth agape. Then my body is shaking. It takes a moment to realize it is Bash, *he's* shaking me. He turns me to face him. His mouth is moving, but there are no words coming out. His eyebrows pinch together unwillingly.

Wet, hot tears fall from my chin. Bash's voice goes from distant mumbles to a loud, painful barrage of sound before I finally put the noise and the movement of his mouth together. "Let's go." he breathes. "We need to leave." He is trying his best to convince me as he pulls the pack onto his shoulder.

The tears keep coming. They fall and fall, tasting of salt, reminding me I am angry. "You left me," I say to Bash, who makes the biggest mistake of his life. He smiles. A small, almost nonexistent smile, but I fucking saw it. My arms act on their own, pushing Bash as hard as they can. "You left me!" I shout. God, is that my voice? It sounds so...broken.

Bash shakes his head, lifting us both up. My legs feel like they might collapse on themselves. "I came back." He tries. "We really need to leave, Babe." That stupid name. I hate it. I don't know why I chose to give Bash that name.

I shake my head. "Why?" I ask a little quieter, letting my voice readjust now that the ringing is gone.

"Why do we need to leave?" he asks as he wipes away the snow from his knees.

"Why did you come back?" I clarify. He straightens back out, meeting my eyes. Which seems to be an accident because he immediately busies himself with whatever is in his pack.

Bash pulls out a knit hat in the ugliest green and places it on my head, tugging it over my ears. "You won't like the answer." His hand lingers for just a second, brushing away a strand of hair caught on my lashes.

I back away from him only a few inches, enough to really look at him. "Tell me anyway." I demand.

He sighs. "I realized you were a key part of the plan."

"What plan?" I ask.

He sighs again, this time to give himself more time before he answers. "It will be easier to get into Jericho." As he speaks, he drops to one knee before me. "After last night-" he begins but changes his mind mid-sentence. "I thought I could do it myself. I was wrong." He takes the bottom of my coat and pulls the zipper up to my chest. I had not realized it had come undone. "You see, they don't care about Ben. They only care about his buy. *You*." Bash runs his hands down my legs, clearing the cold snow from my jeans. His warmth is there for only a second before it's replaced with bitter cold.

When he stands, I swear I see regret in his expression. "You are using me." I half-whisper.

Bash's eyes close for a bit longer this time, but I am ready when they open. Hoping to see that soul Jez always promised would be there. "Yes." He looks to the empty, much too quiet forest to his left before I can finish my search. His jaw clenches, and his breath hitches. "I didn't want to." He admits. "I wanted to do it alone so you never had to-" he stops himself. His face goes from soft to harsh, like he had to stop it before it took over. "Whoever you have on the other side is in danger. It was selfish of me. You have someone you love in Jericho." His words are kind, but his voice is not.

I nod my head in understanding. "Come on." I pull the hood of the coat over my hat for extra warmth. Bash leads the way. I step only where he has stepped, in the holes he has made in the snow with his boots. My body is tired, but I am eager to get going. To Jericho. To Jez.

He stops every few seconds to make sure I am still behind him. The further away from the safe house we get, the worse I feel. "Why did they destroy the safehouse?" I ask to distract myself.

Bash peeks over his shoulder at me. "Someone is cutting off the entrances to Jericho," Bash tells me, sure of himself. *Someone.* Something tells me Bash knows more about who than he lets on.

"Maybe they are cutting off the exits," I say absentmindedly. Jez is trapped there. She would have left long ago if she were not. They not only want people to stay out of Jericho, but they also want to keep them in. My head runs into one of Bash's shoulders. "Why did you stop?" I ask.

Bash peers down his nose at me. "Why were you on that plane, Babe?" His mouth makes a line. There is that name again. Before I can tell him how much I hate it, he speaks again. "It wasn't one of Jericho's." He informs me.

He said it himself, but I will remind him. "I was bought," I say.

"Right. Convenient." He all but rolls his eyes.

I push his shoulder with my own, turning slightly to face him. "I would get on *any* plane, *anywhere*, *anytime*, to save the people I love." That is the truth. I have done much worse for much less.

Bash eyes me suspiciously. I guess he also thinks I know more than I am letting on. I don't.

I knew only that Adam owed Ben a favor. I know Ben told me Adam didn't follow the rules. The rules I know nothing about and don't care to memorize. And last, I know Jez doesn't do anything she doesn't want to. She's stronger, smarter, and more calculated than anyone I have ever met.

The image of my sister floats to the surface. "Anything to get to Jericho." His sarcasm is palpable. I laugh. I *actually* laugh at him. I don't need him to believe me. The how's the whys, it doesn't matter as long as I get to Jericho.

But since I am under fire, I will make sure Bash gets burnt as well. "You don't hear me questioning *your* motives." I match his sarcastic demeanor. Bash's shoulders straighten. I take it as a challenge. "Should I?" I ask but give no time for him to answer. Besides, he has the start of that smirk on the left side of his mouth he can't quite seem to get rid of, and it pisses me off more than I'd like to admit. "You just so happened to be at the safe house? Just so happened to know how to cauterize and care for a wound?" I shove my finger in his face. "Your friend must be pretty important to have the disposal of the Palen Army at his fingertips. Isn't that right, *Medic*?" I basically spit the last word. I've thought about it before. I could be wrong, but I doubt it. I saw men just like him come into the club. Pawn their things at the shop. One even patched Corey up in his office once.

They talk the same. They act the same. They. Are. The. Same.

I know my answer when Bash meets my eyes for a split second. Still, he tries to deny it. "You have no idea what you're talking about." He says under his breath, casting clouds of vapor into the cool air. What a terrible liar he is. "You should be careful what you say about him." Oh, now he is going to try and scare me, predictable. "He has made less important people disappear." He says right on queue.

"I'm quaking," I say flatly, unafraid, before I take a step, letting him know I am done with the conversation. But his arm is out in an instant, stopping me.

"If you know *anything*, you should tell me. It would be a shame if you ended up on the wrong side of this thing." He says like he almost cares.

This *thing*, whatever, is burning cities and destroying government buildings. Killing people and sending trained soldiers to extract people from Jericho, the center of it all. The place that is supposedly impenetrable?

What's worse than knowing nothing is having other people *think* you know nothing. They can use your incompetence against you. So, I just nod my head. Hopefully, giving nothing away while still giving him what he wants. Bash seems satisfied because he continues on. I follow.

# Chapter 21

It's both exactly how I thought it would be and completely different. Where the mountain was once cold, it became tolerable. The snow melts the further we get. The ground becomes soft, and mud sticks to the bottom of my boots.

Bash has removed his layers. He's down to a white T-shirt tucked into his navy jeans. He places a hat over his head, which fails to cover his black hair as it curls out the bottom. I also strip off my jacket, thankful for the heat in any amount. When my body was shivering, there was a constant pulling in my middle. In the place where I will forever bear a scar in the shape of Bash's knife.

The land is now dry, the trees have become sparse, and before I know it, we are overlooking a lush valley. Jericho is hidden somewhere behind the green. Jez was right. It's paradise. Or at least it seems like it from the outside.

Bash catches me gaping, "Keep moving." He says like a soldier.

After a downward struggle, we reach a clearing. The walls are made of simple stone, with places for guards to watch. Not quite the elaborate kingdom I had thought it to be in my head.

Men in uniform hold large guns in their hands, which, upon closer inspection, are pointed right at us. A reflection from the scope on the left as proof. They watch as we walk to an opening, understandably wary. Somehow, aside from the stubble that has grown down his neck, Bash looks like he hasn't been hiking up and down the mountain all day. I would hate to see what I look like. With my hair in a loose braid and sweat leaking from every crevice. Admittedly gross, but true.

Bash is deathly quiet as we approach a large gate that looks like it belongs in a castle. The structure doesn't quite fit the technology hanging on the hips of the guards and at the entrance. A small metal box with knobs on it. And they each have the same cord hanging from their ear, which disappears down their shirts somewhere.

I try to remember to breathe, but it's getting more difficult when I see how serious it is. "You better have a good excuse for showing up here." The fat one says. His navy suit, along with the others stationed along the wall, is unlike the rest of the Palen army's tan and green I have seen in Harmony.

Bash leans down into my ear. "Don't say a word," he says through his teeth. "Follow my lead," he adds before straightening his shoulders as he continues his confident steps in the guard's direction. "Our plane crashed on the south side of the pass." Bash doesn't hesitate for even a second as he calls out to them.

Tanner, his last name, is strapped across his left shoulder. He steps forward and passes me like I'm not even there, holding out what looks like a scanner. Tanner waits impatiently. "I.D.," he demands. Bash reaches into his front pocket and pulls out Ben's I.D. I hold my breath. After what feels like an eternity, the screen on the device flashes green. Tanner clears his throat. "And do you have anything to declare?" He turns his head and runs his eyes over my body.

"Outer Ring. Almost wasn't worth the fucking work." Bash spits.

Tanner, along with the men that now surround us on the wall and past the gate smile at his little joke. I watch them each carefully.

"Well, you know the rules." Tanner looks down at the screen again. "Mr. Mor." His brows scrunch together, and I can't help but think we have been caught. But then he looks back up at Bash, who is cool as ever. "Your *own* purchase. Not for Edwards?" Tanner asks amused but does not let Bash answer. "Hell of a first, son." he tells Bash who agrees.

I remember O and Samson treating Ben the same way. Making bets about his money, like they didn't think he had his own.

Ben had bought from the club before, when I sat for Corey the first time. *Edwards*, I make sure to memorize the name. Did he buy Jez for this Edwards person as well?

My mind races with thoughts of what this could mean until I am interrupted, "We need to do a search, blood test, and questioning. You know how it goes. We will take her separately. You can wait out here." Tanner is back to ignoring me and only speaks to Bash. Then, he turns to leave.

I do not look at Bash because I know what role I am to play, and it's not the one where you question your owner. "No," Bash says too quickly. Tanner's head snaps back to Bash. My eyes go wide. "I will go with her. She's a rule breaker." He amends.

Tanner looks like this information pleases him. "The best ones are." He tells Bash. *Disgusting pig.* I think to myself. Bash makes a face at me that has me readjusting my features from disgust to neutral.

Bash then puts on his best smile. It doesn't quite reach his eyes, not like the toothy grins I have witnessed before. "You're telling me." He agrees with Tanner.

Then we are being ushered into a small building with white tile floors that quickly dirty from our boots. We are shoved into a room with a medical bed and a mirror.

Bash's pack is emptied and inspected carefully. It contains a few articles of clothing, rope, and a pair of gloves, followed by gauze and bandages—the things you would see in a medic's bag. A picture falls to the ground, face down. Almost the same white as the tile. Riley used to have a camera that would push out those same square photos. No one seems to notice it, not even Bash. I quickly look away from the photo and back to Tanner, who licks his lips as his eyes roam.

Then Bash is frisked. They lift his shirt, revealing lines and shaded designs I can't make sense of without seeing the entirety of his tattoos.

Next, they pat around his hips and then down to his ankles. I don't miss the death stare he gives the man who takes his time around his middle, checking the inside of his waistband. Then, before I can blink, it's gone. He is back to being unphased, pretending like this is all normal, a part of his fake life in Jericho as Ben.

My heart hurts for that person behind the mask of Ben. The one that doesn't want to be touched like that ever again. I know the feeling well. "Strip." I flinch when the soldier near Tanner approaches me. I do not see the badge with his name printed on it. My eyes go wide as he waits. *Strip,* it's a word that was said to me often at the club. I would oblige, taking off my dress, walking around in my lace and nothing else. It's not the same, not in here, in this confined room with strangers. If Bash still counts as a stranger after our confessions at the safe house. It feels... wrong.

Bash clocks my discomfort, his face softens. I made it here, I'm so close to Jez I can feel it. I just have to get through the gates. I close my eyes, and when I do, I see her. Hair in rags, dancing in the kitchen. When I open them I am met with emerald green. Bash has knelt before me. "One last time." He whispers.

"We don't have all day." A voice from behind him says. Tanner.

Bash's face flashes annoyance, but not at me. "Told you she wasn't one for the rules, boys." Bash's anger does not match his face. His eyes plead with me. My breath catches, and my hands shake uncontrollably. I know tears come next. I do everything I can to stop that from happening. More words are exchanged between the two men behind Bash. I don't hear what they are. I only watch as Bash's hands reach under my arms, lifting the white shirt from my body. It's for show, of course. Men in Jericho do not coddle their women. No, they take, and they do not ask permission.

I meet Bash's eyes with understanding. "I can do it." I spit. It comes out harsher than I thought, but it helps the act.

Bash backs up with his hands in the air. "I have shit to do, you've already cost me too much time."

I can't help but shiver as I finish pulling the shirt over my head. My boots and jeans slip off easily, revealing the black panties and matching bra that were in the pack Bash gave me paired with the bandage that feels like it's the only thing holding me together.

My face heats when I look up to see the faces before me. They spy at every ounce of bare skin, stopping at my breast, not even trying to hide their hideous smiles as they pat Bash on the shoulder. "Good buy," one of them says. I don't know which, because my eyes are stuck on Bash's black boots, black laces, and black socks.

"Do the blood test," Bash says impatiently.

A strand of brown falls into my face as I keep my head down. "Doc will treat her right." The door opens, and I watch as the feet before me shuffle out into the hallway. Black boots, Bash hesitates at the door before he, too, is gone without another word.

Here I am, practically naked in a room, alone. A tear falls onto my bare thigh. At least Bash isn't here to see it. When the door opens again, a tall man in a white lab coat enters. He has a medical mask over his face and a blue hat to match. His freckles along his nose are sparse but apparent against his pale skin. He slides latex gloves onto his hands in a hurry.

He doesn't look at me the same as they did. He looks at me like a chore, and he treats me as such. "Lay down, hold your arm out." He instructs. I slide up onto the bed until my back hits the uncomfortable pillow. My whole body has goosebumps, both from the cold room and the fear that is building in my chest.

The doctor turns around, opening a drawer next to the door. When he faces me again, I see a needle, like the one Felix used in the bunker. When he shoved it through my skin until I couldn't think, couldn't move.

My mind races. I move on instinct.

They just need a little blood. They *always* just need a little blood, but they take and take until it's all gone. Panic consumes me. Before I know it, I'm off the bed and headed for the door.

*Smack.* I hardly have time to register the hit to the side of my face. Then the doctor is in front of me, anger reflecting in his eyes, and I am on the ground, flailing. I hold the side of my face like it will stop it from hurting. "No." I cry. It's no use.

The doctor wraps his cold hand around my arm and pulls. I let my body weight do the work, not letting him win. "We can do it the hard way." If I could see the lower half of his face, I think I would see a smile there. He *wants* to do it the hard way. I hear the shuffling of feet outside. Then, silence for a moment before it stops. Two guards I haven't seen yet come barreling in the door. "Hold her down." He says to them while still looking down at me, like dirt on his shoe. They lift me onto the bed once more. My feet kick in protest, but I am easily subdued.

*Where is Bash?* "Please," I beg as one pulls my arm straight while the doctor ties an elastic band around the top. "Don't."

I thrash, failing at pulling my arm from his grip. "Hold her still, you morons." He yells to the men.

"Fuck you." I spit.

The one to my right climbs onto the bed, placing a knee at my middle. A gut-wrenching half scream half cry rips from my throat. Hot tears fall down my face. I can't fight these men any longer. I don't really know why I tried in the first place. I was never going to win.

There's a painful pinch in the crook of my elbow. When the men finally untangle themselves from me, I watch as deep red fluid fills the small tube. Bile rises into my throat, I have to lean over the side of the bed to heave. Emptying the contents of my stomach.

"Dramatic little thing. Aren't you?" The Doc says holding up the vial to inspect. "Won't last a week." He laughs to himself. Then he moves closer to me. I wipe the saliva from my mouth and stare him down. If I can't kill him, I can at least wish him dead.

He takes his free hand and gently places a finger just below my belly button. He runs it down to the edge of my panties and tucks it into the band. I look at his companions, who are ready to hold me down again if I fight. "You surprised me." The doctor practically sings. "Must be worth it," he says to my center. I want to bite his finger off, but I can hardly breathe, let alone do anything to stop him.

There is a commotion outside, followed by a few loud bangs. Bash's voice fills my ears. "Are you fucking kidding me?" The sound of metal hitting the metal as instruments hit the floor. Other men join in, asking him to keep his voice down.

Then, the guttural sound someone makes when they have been punched in the stomach. Unfortunately, I have heard it many times before. "You're next if you don't move."

The two guards step towards the door in anticipation after hearing the threat. The doctor takes a step back as well, but his eyes do not leave my body. I can't see his face, but his eyes are scrunched from a smile hidden beneath the mask. "Let him in," he says loud enough for them to hear from the other side.

Bash crashes in, sending the door into the wall behind it. He immediately goes for the person closest to me, which is now the shorter of the two guards, the one that climbed on top of me. Bash pins him up against the wall, his forearm on his neck. "She's mine." He tells the room before he lands on me. As much as I want his anger to be for me, I know it's not. It's for the inconvenience, he has a job to do, and I am screwing with his plans. We need this to work, and I almost ruined everything. "You don't touch what isn't yours. Understand?" He reiterates. "I don't share." And with that, he is releasing the man.

Bash's eyes catch on my cheek, where there is sure to be a swollen bruise later if it's not already there. Bash bends down and picks up my clothes, throwing them in my direction.

"She's all yours." The doctor says, bored. The vial that was once the deepest red is now a pale-yellow color. They must have mixed my blood with a solution to test it. "Newbie." He huffs in Bash's direction. "You will get used to sharing soon enough." Everyone follows the doctor out who narrows his eyes at me before he is on to the next one. His job here is done.

Bash waits until the door clicks closed before he moves in front of me. I somehow managed to make it to the edge of the bed, my legs dangling off the side. He lifts my chin and pushes it to the side to inspect my cheek. He raises his thumb to stroke the spot beneath my eye, wiping away a tear. "Afraid of needles?" He asks. A smirk appears on his face, but I don't feel like joking. His smile fades, but we remain like that. My head tilts up to him as I slow my breathing, and my heart rate returns to normal. I am thankful for his acting skills. And whatever *this* is. Maybe a mutual understanding, his past and my present, the same. *Used.*

He seems to have just realized I am still down to my underwear because he takes a large step back and adverts his eyes, as usual.

I can hardly stand, let alone dress, but Bash doesn't dare help. He waits patiently as I struggle to lift my legs and tie my laces. I am grateful for that simple gesture. I needed to do it on my own, to prove I am still capable, strong enough to make it to Jez.

As we leave the room I bend down and pocket the photo that had fallen out of Bash's pack.

# CHAPTER 22

On the other side of the white room with its white tiles is a long corridor. The same windowless doors line the walls. A camera moves with our steps, following us to the exit. Bash doesnt even seem to care. In fact, I swear I see him tip his hat in the direction of the lense with a knowing grin, like he can't help himself.

The men glare at him. One of them has a blackened bruise on their cheek, the same as mine. Bash really did a number on these guys. I wish I was as confident as him, walking past them like he owns the place.

Instead, I hesitantly walk behind him, not letting him get too far ahead of me. The doors open, and I hear birds chirping and smell the sweet scent of fresh flowers from the other side.

It's finally happening, I made it. *We* made it. Bash is out the door with his arm around my wrist as if I won't come with him if he doesn't drag me.

Each house is more elaborate than the last. Vegetation falls from the roofs, coating the sides of the buildings in beautiful greens and yellows and reds. The trees are filled with fruits I have never seen before. I want to reach up and grab one from the branch, but Bash keeps going. "Forbidden fruit." He mumbles. Whatever that means. My stomach growls.

Every painting that has ever come into the shop is pale compared to the colors around me. Paradise. That part Jez was right about.

Cars pull into gated homes. Not at all like the abandoned vehicles of Harmony that were often used as makeshift homes or a safe place for druggies to shoot up. It's not like the car Corey drives, either. These have none of the rust spots or broken mirrors. There is no dust to dull the color or dents in the doors.

Soon, we are at a split in the road, one way with what looks to be a village up the hill, with perfectly placed evergreens on each side. The other way, the way Bash takes, leads to luxury condos and high-rise buildings. The windows reflect perfect images of what is across from them. It's quiet, even as men and women walk by. The men on the right, the women on the left. That's how Bash has positioned us as well.

One man tips his hat to Bash, the woman doesn't look up, or break her stride. The man on the other hand runs his eyes up and down my body, he even licks his lips. It's all very strange. I remind myself *this* is what will get me to her. So, I act accordingly.

I quickly realize Bash knows exactly where he is going. He is walking the streets like he has done it a million times before. Taking the perfect turns until we end up in front of a grey building with tinted windows and marble statues to match.

Bash clocks the look on my face. "Ben's apartment." He whispers to me as he scans the card on a panel to the left. I wasn't questioning where he was taking me, though. I was questioning *him*. His unwavering steps and knowledge of the city. Suddenly, I am very suspicious of the man before me. Bash, the medic. Bash with a mission to get into Jericho. Bash told me what they do here is nothing short of disgusting, and yet it's as if he is a part of it in some way.

The large door clicks, signaling that it's unlocked. Bash holds it open for me. Where else do I have to go? So I take a step into a hallway with gold detail and dreary paintings along the walls. At the end, there is an elevator. Cameras are all around us. I wonder who sits on the other side of the lens. Another reason to be wary of Bash. It was easy to get past security and into the city. Too easy.

Won't they know he does not belong? That his black hair, green eyes, and broad shoulders do not belong to Ben? "Just keep moving, we belong here. It's *my* place." I can't see his face, but I can tell he is wearing that signature grin.

I push forward, the walls seem to close in as we near the elevator where Bash reaches over my shoulder and pushes a button. Thirteen. Then, my stomach flips in on itself as we are lifted into the air. My chest heaves with ragged in and outs. The space is much too small.

Then the metal box shakes, and the light at the top illuminates behind ornate number as we pass each floor.

When the feeling in my stomach goes away and we stop moving, the world that shrank around me is now back to its original size. My mind was playing a cruel trick. It had happened once before when Riley locked me in the closet in the back room of the pawnshop. His father's voice was muffled as I pushed my palms against my ears. When he finally opened the door, I had already believed myself to be dead.

Bash clears his throat. "Babe," he pulls me from the memory. "What is it?" He asks. His head slightly to the side in concern.

I shake my head. This isn't one of those times when I will let the world crush me. *This* is the day I made it to Jericho. One day closer to Jez. "I finally made it." I didn't mean to say it out loud. It almost sounds like I am trying to convince myself. Like if I pinch myself too hard, I will wake up in front of our tiny window covered in homemade curtains that don't match.

Bash looks like he wants to say something, but the doors have split open to reveal an immaculate apartment that once belonged to Ben. It's the opposite of what Jez and I called home for all those years in Harmony. It's pristine, someone must have spent hours cleaning every inch. The floors shine in large tiles of black and white, and all the accents are deep red or marble. The whole city is visible from beyond the window a couch faces. The couch looks like a cloud, fluffy and white. I can imagine Ben there, sunken into the cushions with a glass of whiskey in his hand.

Bash takes a few steps to the edge of the window, looking down. He hates it, and you can tell. "Fucker." He says to himself. It is quite absurd, the amount of useless objects and unnecessary pieces of art that probably cost Ben a fortune.

I laugh from behind my hand. Bash's head snaps up from the city below at the sound. A smile threatens to take over his face before he looks away quickly.

I turn swiftly on my feet, ignoring the warmth that rises to my face. Then, I walk down a perfectly lit hallway in search of a bathroom. When I pass a room to my left, curiosity gets the best of me. Ben's room.

Forgetting the shower, I desperately need, I walk into the charcoal room. Red sheets are on the bed, and red curtains hang from the window. A marble-top desk and a bookshelf lay against the wall opposite the bed. Each of Ben's things are lined up perfectly atop it. It doesn't even look like he lives here. The only thing out of place is a pen that seems to have been thrown down after scribbling on the pad next to it.

Ben knew Jez. She might have even been here in this apartment. Something feels right when I pull the string attached to a lamp on the corner of the desk. I lift the notepad to the light.

There etched into the paper: *Will be back before Sunday. -B*

B, as in Ben.

B, as in the man who bought Jez.

How many days past Sunday has it been? Either way, Ben never returned. I know in my heart this note was meant for Jez. From her lover, who was willing to trade me for her. She couldn't have known his plan involved me as her replacement. She would never do that to me, would she? As if I could see more into the lives of Ben and what feels like the stranger who used to be my sister, I study the blank white pad for a moment longer.

Bash clears his throat, which has me jumping out of my skin. He leans against the doorframe, crossing his arms as he watches me intently. He studies me in the same way I was studying Ben's rushed note. Like there is more under the surface, his brows are set along with his jaw. "Shower. Your bandages need changed. They are on the counter. If you need help, let me know." He says, showing his military side once more. Demands, short and to the point. I have no strength to argue. Besides, he is right. I saw the same sight as Bash did in the exam room after my blood was drawn. My fight accomplished nothing aside from harming the wound Bash worked so hard to mend.

I take one more look around the room, hoping to see any sign of Jez. *Nothing.*

So, I nod my head. Walking past Bash down the hallway once more. A thought dawns on me when I am finally behind the bathroom door. One that would ruin everything.

Bash could leave me again.

This has me pulling the door back open and peering out, fearing I will not find him on the other side. But there he is, with his hands on his head and his hat on the ground like he was mid-struggle, the kind you have with the thoughts in your head.

He swings his whole body in my direction, and for the first time, I see he is not confident, cool, or collected. "Is everything okay?" He asks when I don't say anything.

"Uh, yeah. I just-" I stumble over my words. "I wanted to make sure you were going to stick around, that you weren't going to—" My eyes finds the direction of the large window with a view of Jericho. Even though I cannot see it behind the walls of Ben's apartment.

Bash shoves his hands into his pockets. "I'm not going anywhere, Babe." He assures me. I cringe at the name. This has his left eyebrow up in the air. Babe does not seem to fit who I am anymore, but it's the name I gave him. It's the name I have answered to for years.

As I stare at Bash to make sure his words are true, I can't help but wonder what Emerson would sound like from those lips.

Instead, I slowly close the door, turning for what looks like a bath fit for a king, with large shower heads on each side and intricate designs covering the entirety of the room from floor to ceiling. My heart feels heavy at the thought of those in Jericho living like *this* while the Outer Ring is suffering, starving, *dying*.

I undress and unwrap my bandages. I get caught by the reflection in the mirror of a girl who looks nothing like me. Messy, now unbraided brown hair. Bruises line my arms, face, and side, along with a crimson scar the size of Bash's knife. It hasn't had time to properly heal, especially not under the weight of that guard's knee.

Blood, dirt, and God knows what else seep into the drain at my feet as water falls over my skin. This shower reminds me of the one in Warshaw, but this time, I take my time, washing everything away and letting the water run down my back even when I am clean.

The water never runs cold. So, I stay. For so long, by the time I get out, my fingers are shriveled, and I have washed away the sins of everyone but myself.

This time, I face away from the mirror as I wrap the clean bandages around my abdomen the same way Bash did, wincing when they tighten around the middle as I bend to grab my jeans. I wish I didn't have to put these back on. They are uncomfortable, not to mention dirty. I don't like the idea of putting Ben's clothing on, so I slide them over my legs anyway.

As I pull them over my hips, I run my hands over the back pockets. The photo I had picked up is still there. The one that fell from Bash's pack.

I don't know why I didn't give it back to him or why I took it in the first place. Maybe I didn't want that man having anything of his, anything he could take from someone like he takes blood.

I pull the square out, curious about what I will see. Maybe Bash's lover, which has my chest tightening for reasons I cannot explain. Or maybe it's his family. Many soldiers keep pictures of their loved ones to remember them. Few get to see their mothers or fathers, brothers and sisters, ever again. This also has my body doing unwanted things as I think of the last time I saw Riley and how I will never see him again.

That is until I turn the image over. There on the other side is a beaming fourteen-year-old Riley, next to... *me*. A round-faced twelve-year-old that didn't quite fit right in her clothes. I am staring up at Riley with a stupid love-stuck grin on my face. My hair is pulled back in a perfect Jez braid. I can't believe what I am looking at.

Bash has a picture of *me*.

# CHAPTER 23

In an unorganized mess, Bash has piles of papers on the coffee table and spread along the cushions of the couch. He doesn't hear me enter the room as he reads through what looks like a ledger with lots of numbers that would mean nothing to me. Riley's father had one on the desk in the back room. It means something to Bash because his attention does not waver. He leans back onto the couch that swallows him up and marks the page with a pen. Whatever he sees on the page upsets him because when he is done, he throws it down, creating a large thud on the table before him.

I watch him carefully. A picture of *me*. He had a picture he was keeping in his pack. I can't give anything away. He clearly has no idea who I truly am or we would not be here.

I already hid the photo of Riley and me in the back of the toilet for safekeeping, a place where no one would think to look. Now I only need to know one thing—why?

Before I can say anything at all, my stomach growls. Bash turns to me, the anger is still on his face, but it slowly softens as he takes note of my wet hair. "I found an address. Ben's employer—Edwards." He says as he hops over the couch to get to the kitchen. I follow timidly.

Bash begins pulling a bowl from one of the cupboards. He reaches past me, grazing my side to get to a drawer where he takes out a spoon. How does he know where everything is? I guess it is getting pretty dark outside. I must have been in the shower longer than I thought. And by the looks of it, he has done his digging.

He continues speaking as he moves again. "We will start there. To find your girl." He winks before he turns to open a door and comes back out with a box.

"You are going to help me?" I ask, surprised. Bash pours the contents of the box out into the bowl. Little, round, brown dots I have never seen before. Is he going to eat that? It looks putrid.

Bash stops with his hand on the refrigerator. "I will help *you* if you help *me*." He opens it, his top half disappearing for a moment. He pours milk into the bowl, places the spoon in it, and slides it over to me.

I eye the bowl suspiciously. This gets me a crooked smile from Bash. "How could *I* possibly help *you*?" I speak with the same emphasis on the words he used as I stir the mysterious food.

"Eat." Bash does not answer my question, not right away anyway. I pull the sloppy food to my lips. It's sweet, delicious. I practically shove the next bite into my mouth. Bash is satisfied with my reaction. Is this what they eat in Jericho? Nothing but sweet bits of milk and sugar?

He takes a seat on the stool across from me and folds his hands, leaning on his elbows in my direction. "There are rules here. You will have to stay with me. You will have to blend in. Got it?" He asks. Blend in like those women that were walking. With their heads down and their mouths shut.

I nod my head in agreement. Whatever it takes.

"The women usually keep track of who has come and gone." He thinks about it for a second before deciding on different words. "Who has been bought and who has been sold." He cringes visibly, a small amount of emotion I haven't seen from Bash. Aside from his act to get those men away from me and his occasional fake smile, "Maybe your sister has some intel." He says nonchalantly.

I stop the spoonful of food before it can reach my mouth. *He knows.* I think about it over and over again. Not a single word has been shared where I have revealed the girl I am after is—"My *sister*," I say out loud, confused. My mind races. I have indeed made a huge mistake in coming here with Bash. A picture of me. *He knows.* I swallow the lump in my throat. This is bad. This is so *very* bad.

Bash smirks when he sees me squirm. Finally, he takes mercy on me. "You talk in your sleep." That is all he says before continuing. "If we can find her, she might be able to point me in the right direction," Bash says to his hands. I let out a relieved breath. Thankfully, he does not see because he is back to being his usual self, looking anywhere but at me.

Finding Jez is top priority, but now my mind is occupied with what I might have said to Bash unknowingly. My cheeks heat, and the hunger that was once in my belly is gone. I push the bowl out of reach. Bash notes my discomfort as he peers up at me through his lashes. Then he pushes the chair back and stands. "Don't worry, the rest is safe with me." He jokes as he nears me. I look up at him in horror to see his devious smile. Oh, God, just kill me now. Bash grabs the bowl and places it in the sink. I make a mental note to sleep as far away from Bash as humanly possible tonight.

Bash braces himself on the counter, giving me a good look at the tattoos that run down his forearms. I drop my eyes in an instant before he can catch me. "You need to be prepared." He says, all serious again. How does he do that? "She might not be the same as you once knew her. Jericho changes people." He tells me. Does he know from experience?

If I let myself think about it too long, guilt will take over. One thing at a time. I don't want to know what Jez has suffered in the last few years. I just need to get to her, and if she chooses to tell me what has been going on here, I will listen.

I change the subject. "What about the girl you are after? Why is it so important to get her out?" I ask. Time to get answers for myself.

"I think you know," Bash says softly.

My heart speeds up again. I can't help but think I am in way over my head. Pretending I have no idea what he is talking about, I tilt my head as if I am confused. "Your scars, the plane." Bash looks at me like I know what he is about to say. I don't. "I know Warshaw was attacked. I know you had to have been there. Seen the damage. Suffered in it." He glances down towards my middle, which is hidden behind the table.

I understand now. "They are after Jericho next," I say as Bash nods his head once. "How long do we have until the city falls?"

"Not long. It's going to be big. They are doing the world a favor, trust me." *Trust* him. Trust Bash. Do I?

"*They*, as in your friend?" I ask carefully. Bash nods his head for a second time in confirmation. "Tell me about him." I am relieved when the words come out so casually.

"The only thing you need to know about him is that he doesn't do anything halfway." Bash seems proud.

He keeps his head down to avoid me, but I see him go somewhere else. The place people often go as they think of a memory. "He is lucky to have you," I say, and I truly mean it.

Bash goes quiet. He doesn't say a word as he pushes the chair back into the table before he heads for the couch. He begins to shuffle through the papers rather aimlessly. Maybe to stop me from prying, or maybe he didn't want to admit his worth.

Most of the men at the club would beam when given a compliment, lie or not. Not Bash. No, he isn't the type.

He is clearly done with me, so I head back to the now-destroyed bedroom. All the books are off the shelves. The bed, the dresser, and a few of the smaller statues have been moved. Bash really tore the place apart. As if I could find something Bash missed, I walk around the room, sifting through Ben's things a second time.

There is a suitcase on the bed that looks like the others, but this one was left out for me. When I open it, there are women's clothes. Ben must have packed this bag for Jez. *Her* clothes, *her* toothbrush, *her* comb. I hold one of the shirts up to my chest. It does nothing. It has no life to it. I thought I would be able to feel her here like I felt her in Harmony after she left. When I was alone with all the things that were hers.

I slip on the shirt along with a pair of shorts I found at the bottom. By the time I build up enough courage to go back into the living room where I know Bash is, it's late. I couldn't bring myself to sleep in the bed that belonged to Ben. Actually, I don't think I could sleep at all, not knowing how close I am to her.

Thankfully, Bash is asleep on the couch, still in the same clothes from our journey. He is still surrounded by all of Ben's paperwork. He has a death grip on the paper in his hand and a pinched look on his face. He must not have gotten the information he needed. A glass of what looks like whiskey is within arm's distance.

I find the most luxuriously soft blanket that hangs over the arm of the cloud couch and lay it over Bash. Who grumbles and readjusts in his sleep. I down the rest of his whiskey before I attempt to pull the papers from his grip. It's impossible. Even in his sleep, he is trained to keep his wits about him.

I give it one last try, but as I am pulling the papers, Bash is pulling in the opposite direction. Before I can let go, my feet are being swept out from beneath me. Bash is mumbling something under his breath, a string of curses followed by a name, a woman's name. Something that starts with an A, Amber, I think.

With all my strength, I push off of him at his shoulders. He has my wrists in his grip in an instant, trained to do so. Soon, I am being flipped to the side as one of Bash's giant arms wraps around my throat. He pushes the back of my head against his arm, sending me further into his choke hold. I claw at his forearm, but it's of no use.

"Bash." I hardly get out. "Bash, stop, you're hurting me." but he doesn't let up. My vision darkens, and all I can think to do is pull at his hair and kick with my feet in hopes something will wake him.

A small scream escapes as he releases the slightest of pressure. I scramble away from him onto the floor, knocking things over as I go. The empty glass shatters to the ground. "Fuck." He growls. You can see the sleep leave his body as he sits up. He moves quickly. A tattooed hand reaches out for me. Reflexively, I move away from the hand that just tried to kill me. Tears from the struggle fall to my knees I have tucked into myself. "No," Bash says with regret and another emotion I can't make sense of right now, but it has his features contorting in pain.

My hands go up to my neck. I try to speak, but it hurts so much that the words get caught in my throat. "No, no, no." he shakes his head as he slides off the couch towards me. It takes my mind some time to catch up. *You're not in danger.* I repeat in my head.

Bash runs a timid hand through his hair as if he doesn't know what else to do. Then he looks around at the mess, at the glass. "Can I touch you?" He whispers. All I can do is nod my head. Soon, I am being swept into Bash's arms. I've never gotten close enough to smell him. Now, with my head in the crook of his neck, I smell sweet tobacco from his cigarettes and sweat from his shirt.

When he places me down, we are on the same cold slab of marble we were sitting at earlier. He pulls out one of the stools and gently positions my legs one by one until my feet are flat on the seat. "You have to know how sorry I am, Babe." He tries. There it is again. That stupid name.

"Don't call me that." The words come out in a pained whisper and without thought, surprising me.

Bash also looks surprised. He searches my eyes but comes up short. Then, "What would you like me to call you?" He asks gently.

"I haven't decided yet. Just not that." I say. Then, I lean back on my hands to relieve some of the pain from my middle.

Bash looks like he wants to help in some way, his hands twitch like he should be using them to mend me, but he doesn't move. "I understand." Bash looks down at his feet, then back up at me. "I'm not going to ask if you are okay because I know you are not. Today, you have experienced so much-" he pauses, balling his hands into a frustrated fist. "Shit. From me, mostly. I-"

"You don't have to apologize for doing what you need to do to survive." I cut him off. I wanted to tell him before, during our game of never have I ever. I wanted to tell him that I wasn't one to judge and I would never shame someone for things out of their control. Still, even now, I keep those last thoughts to myself.

Bash just nods his head. I can see he is slowly accessing me. The way medics do to their patients I suppose. "I'm fine." I try, but he doesn't seem convinced. "Just scared me, is all." I try again.

What I think is a laugh escapes him. "*Scared* you?" Now I see the smile creeping to his lips, the way it always does. I am starting to think it's his way of keeping out the bad. "I almost *killed* you. Twice," he says incredulously.

Once when he left me for dead on the mountain, again when he had his arm around my neck like a vice. I can't help but laugh, either. I *really* laugh, a sound I have not heard in a long time. It hurts me to do so, but I can't help myself.

Bash is staring at me like I am crazy. He crosses his arms and leans up against the counter at my side. I could move my leg a centimeter and hit him. My brain is permanently wired to notice just how close I am to men at all times. Where to touch them and how. He looks over his shoulder at me. "You think it's funny?" He asks with his eyebrows raised.

I shrug my shoulders at him, which has him placing a hand on his chest as if to calm it. "Who almost dies twice in one day?" I breathe as my smile softens.

Bash shakes his head in disbelief. "People who hang out with me." He keeps his eyes on mine, and his smile fades as well. As if he catches himself doing something he shouldn't, he looks away.

I clear my throat, pretending like it doesn't hurt when he does that. "Technically, you saved my life before you tried to take it, so we are even," I say. When Bash opens his mouth to argue, I don't let him. "Thank you.

For what you did at the wall. It was a good act." This has his head turning again. If only I could figure out how to keep it there.

"What act?" Bash says sarcastically.

"Oh, please." I push him with my knee as I roll my eyes.

We stay like that for a moment before Bash holds out his hand. "Your sister is lucky to have you." He tells me the same words I used earlier. I'm starting to think the man he works for is more like a brother. The same as Jez is to me, my other half.

I take his hand as he helps me off the counter. "Oh, so *you* can compliment me, but *I* can't compliment you?" I ask seriously once I am steady on my feet.

Bash looks down at me with those stunning emeralds that catch in the light behind me. "What other nice things do you have to say about me?" He bats his eyelashes. I take another step in his direction. We are so close now I have to lift my chin to see his face. He is looking at me, *really* looking at me, and not trying to find another object to latch onto like he did before. Good.

My hand betrays me, reaching up to poke at the start of a tattoo peeking out from the collar of his loose shirt. How badly I want to see what intricate design decorates his chest.

I hadn't realized we had not spoken in a long time until Bash lets out a breath that moves the ends of my hair. Quickly, I snatch away my hand, embarrassed. I force my eyes from his chest to his face. His features are deathly serious, jaw set, waiting.

My brows involuntarily push together as I find something I was not even searching for.

There it is. Behind his eyes. A soul.

# Chapter 24

*Knock, knock, knock.*

I could sleep here forever.

*Knock, knock, knock.*

When I realize what is going on and where I am, I sit up in a sweat. Bash had switched places with me last night when I couldn't bring myself to sleep on the same mattress, in the same sheets as Ben.

The knocking has stopped, but feet shadow the other side of the doors. They move back and forth, pacing the length of the elevator. I keep expecting the doors to open, but they do not.

Ben's ID card, the one Bash used to get into the building, must have a code that only lets those with it into the apartments.

I go silent so as not to reveal myself to whoever is on the other side. If Bash and I are caught, they wouldn't wait for an answer, right? They would simply destroy the doors to get to us, the way they often did in Harmony when the police were after someone.

Movement from the hallway catches my attention. Bash takes careful steps in my direction with what looks like a bat in his hands. Upon closer inspection, it is just a piece of wood that seems to have come from the desk chair.

I stare at him, my eyes wide in terror as he approaches. He places a finger to his mouth in a silent demand to remain quiet. My arms cross over my middle as I watch the door, waiting.

A booming voice comes from beyond the metal doors. "I know you are in there, Ben." The man must place his hand against the metal wall of the elevator because there is a large thud. Then he sighs loudly. "The guards told me you arrived yesterday, you little shit." He says impatiently.

I look to Bash, who seems to be deep in thought. He twirls the object in his hand, waiting.

"Fine. The shipment will *still* be delivered. Whether you are there or not." He waits again as if we will change our minds and let him into the apartment. "I'm done, Ben. I held up my end of the bargain. You said it yourself, I'm free." His voice breaks. A pleading with Ben, whom he does not know is no longer with us.

It seems Ben had a lot of people who owed him favors. He told Adam he always had a plan. I wonder what plan he had for Jez and how it's all connected. I was obviously a part of it. How many people would he hurt? How many bridges would he have burnt to get what he wanted—if he were still alive that is. I can't help but think his death has placed Bash and me directly in the fire Ben started.

Bash and I stand there, staring at each other. Bash looks like he wants to kill someone. The same look he gave me when we first met after he found the bodies in the plane. There is silence from the man on the other side of the doors. Then, the whirling of the elevator as it descends. Silence.

It's a few seconds before either of us move. Bash goes first. The wooden leg falls from his hands as he heads for the couch, where I remain frozen, staring at the elevator doors. My legs are shaking. When did I become so weak?

When Bash places a finger on my chin I instantly relax, letting myself breathe fully again. My relief only lasts a few seconds. "I have to leave," he whispers, still not risking being heard even though no one is there.

I look up at him, confused. "To where?" I ask. What could possibly be more important than finding Jez?

As if Bash sees the thoughts as they pass behind my eyes. "We can still find your sister." He assures me. "But if they are delivering what I think they are, I need to leave now."

I take a step back, away from his touch. My heart sinks. I can't tell him. I can't tell him what I now know for certain.

That this delivery will not help him find what he is looking for.

That who he seeks is standing right in front of him.

Stuck. That's what I am, between doing whatever it takes to get to Jez and telling Bash who I really am. I can't risk it. I can't let him take me out of Jericho before I find her.

So, I will let him go.

Bash's features contort into something similar to pain as I nod my head. "I will be back," he says, turning back into the medic, the soldier. "Do not leave. Do not let anyone in." he gives his demands.

"What happens if you don't come back?" I ask without thinking, without knowing why I care.

Bash places that falsely confident smile on his face, which I see through immediately. "I always come back." He says. I can't help but think there is double meaning to his words.

I want to grab his hand, to stop him. *Do not risk it, Emerson.* He will be back after he has failed at getting closer to the impossible—*finding me.* He will come back, and we will find Jez. I will tell him, just not now.

After Bash leaves, I use the first few hours to put the bedroom back together. The blankets and a pillow are on the floor. Maybe Bash also didn't want to sleep in the same bed as Ben.

Next, I rummage through the kitchen until I find what I am looking for. Coffee, my connection to Jez.

There is nothing left to do but wait. I sit on the couch facing Jericho, watching the small people walk through the streets of paradise—or what looks like paradise on the outside. I now know none of that is true.

I think of Jez and her letters about Jericho. Especially when it rains. The sky is clear one second and grey the next. She mentioned fresh water falls every day here. She could be looking out her window right now, seeing the same predictable rainfall. Perhaps even with a cup of coffee in her hand, the same as me.

Day turns into night.

I begin to worry if all of this was for nothing. The city will fall, and I will be dead along with it. Maybe I am a part of Jericho in some small way. Part of the problem that whoever Bash works for is trying to fix. Playing my part, just as Corey said.

The night goes on and on. My coffee soon turns into whiskey. Glass after glass until the bottle is nearing the end of its life. My thoughts become dull, which is what I was hoping for. My eyelids become heavy, but when I give in and close them, the room begins to spin. So, I keep myself awake. First, I count the black tiles, then the white ones.

It's well past midnight now, all the lights have shut off replaced with a glow from the city lights.

I have given up, accepted my fate—the one where I am trapped in a city that is soon to be destroyed. So close to Jez, yet unable to reach her. Hopefully, my death will be quick. Maybe the city will fall in one fell swoop, taking Jez, Bash, and I with it.

Was it worth it? Yes, I think it was. Jez and I made a deal once that we would make it to Jericho. *No matter what,* we would tell each other. "We made it." I hold my now empty glass in the air. "Cheers, Jez," I say to the world below.

Now that my head is nice and quiet and my face is sufficiently numb from alcohol, I hardly even flinch when the doors slide open and a familiar voice fills my ears. A voice I would have liked to hear had it not been for the labored breathing followed by "Help." Bash hardly gets out.

# CHAPTER 25

I push away the fog of alcohol long enough to stand. It's clumsy, sending yet another glass to the ground.

Bash holds his shoulder with his hand, pressing into a wound that the black fabric of his shirt would otherwise hide. His face contorts as he stares at me. Then he falls to his knees.

How I got over to him so fast is a mystery. God, I am so stupid. I shouldn't have drank so much. No, I shouldn't have let him go in the first place.

He points to the kitchen with a shaky finger. Yes, I remember seeing a first aid kit under the sink. I run to it. My legs do not move as fast as my mind would like them to. Causing me to stumble as I go.

My mind sobers when I return to Bash, especially when he rips the black fabric off of his body. A bullet wound. One side a small round hole, the other a bloody mess of torn flesh. "It went straight through." He says calmer than I would ever be in his situation.

I basically tear open the kit and watch as Bash finds a clear liquid and hands it to me. "Since you seem to have had the rest of the alcohol." He says through gritted teeth.

I ignore him. "What do I do?" To my surprise, the words come out clean and not slurred at all.

"Go get some water." As soon as he says it I am on my feet. I grab a bowl and fill it to the brim, spilling it on the way back to Bash.

As I kneel down, I see he has set a few things out, including a sewing needle and thread for stitching. Something I am familiar with as I would mend Riley's wounds often, but none as bad as this. Gauze and medical tape lay to the side.

He takes a cloth and dips it into the water, using it to clean the front of his shoulder. Then he hands it to me. "Take a few breaths. You're shaking." When I look down at my hands, he is right.

I take a few even breaths before beginning to clean where Bash could not reach. He winces in pain with every stroke. "Anymore whiskey left?" He asks me. I go to the cabinet and bring the near-empty bottle back to him. He drinks it down like it's water.

Bash instructs me on how to sterilize the needle. Poor Riley never got the same courtesy aside from holding it over a flame. Then I pour the clear liquid over his wounds before I move behind him to start the stitches on his back. "You have lost a lot of blood," I note the puddle that pools at our knees as I reposition. It soaks into Bash's jeans and coats my bare legs. Bash doesn't answer. He grinds his teeth so hard I can hear the bones crushing together.

I push the skin together with the first stitch. Bash lets out a low growl. I try to take his mind off of the pain as I go, this part I am quite good at. "Did you find what you were looking for?" I ask carefully, already knowing the answer.

He shakes his head. Beneath the blood, a tattoo takes up the entirety of Bash's back. Something drunken me did not notice at first.

Men with wings and creatures with eyes made of purest black. A man being caught by demons, dragged into the fiery pits of hell. The depiction of someone falling from grace, I decide. "It's beautiful," I tell him as I continue the task at hand.

"Hurt a hell of a lot less than this." He spits but he doesn't seem to mind talking, I take that as a good sign.

"Almost done." I lie. I used to do the same to Riley so he would stop asking. It's almost on instinct.

Bash huffs a laugh, even through the pain, at me. "I have given more stitches in my life than you could ever dream of, Sweetheart. You're nowhere close to being done." He tells me. My face heats at the new name he has chosen to call me. Thankfully, I am behind him, so he cannot see.

I change the subject back to the tattoo. "What does it mean?" I ask.

He thinks for a moment, or maybe he just needs more time to speak as I take another bit of skin and run the needle through it. "The Last Judgment." He tells me as if I will know what it means. When I do not reply, he sighs. "It's a reminder of sorts. The painting was hung above the hearth of my mother's home." He says it like he did not belong to the same house as his mother. "It burned, along with the rest of them." He says with another groan, and this time, I really am almost done with the stitches, the ones on his back anyway.

Maybe it's the liquid courage coursing through my veins, but as I finish the last stitch, I take a look at the now complete masterpiece on Bash's back. Beneath the beauty and the ink. Raised scars. Something he has worked hard to cover. "You lived in Jericho, didn't you?" I say without thought.

I had noticed how he seemed to know exactly where he was going. He also left for a place where he knew deliveries had to have come into Jericho. Not to mention the art on his body, obviously depicting pieces that would not be hanging on the walls of homes in the Outer Ring. *I always come back,* he told me before he left.

The only question I used to guess where he came from was the Eastern lights. I should not have assumed everyone in Jericho had the fortune of seeing them. I get my answer when Bash tenses. I pull the knot tight. Moving with the needle in my hand until I am in front of him.

The smile that hides his pain is nowhere in sight as he locks eyes with me. He might have read my mind, or maybe I spoke my thoughts out loud because of the alcohol. Because he says, "Never got to see them. The lights." His brows scrunch together.

I smile at him. "You always come back," I repeat his own words to him. He just nods his head. I now know a little about the man across from me. The reasons he had to do what he needed to—to survive. Broken but alive. Like me.

These things are not easy to talk about, so I don't.

Bash basically burns a hole into the side of my head with his intense stare as I reach for the smaller wound on his chest. This one does not take long to mend, which I am thankful for because I don't think I can ignore his gaze any longer. This is the longest he has ever looked at me, and I can't look back.

Finally, I take my attention away from the blood, running my fingers down his chest in the same fashion as I did the night before. When I so desperately wanted to see what is now right in front of me. "What is this one?" I ask about the scene on his chest and stomach. Another distraction for him.

This one of a bleeding heart. Knives through its center. The hilt is the piece that travels up the center of his neck. It bleeds into something else I cannot quite see as his torn shirt still hangs loosely on his body around his center. The design goes onto his shoulders, where it turns to the roses and birds around his arms—the ones that I have already memorized from our walk here and our time at the safe house that no longer exists.

I was so busy tracing the lines of one of the swords I did not realize how much time had passed in silence. He has not answered my question, but it does not matter because I already gave my own meaning to this particular piece of art.

I pull my hand back to myself, where it belongs. Before I can finish my retreat, Bash grabs my hand and pulls it to his face. My fingers gently touch his jaw, they are coated in his blood, but I do not say anything as he pushes my palm into the side of his face.

My body warms from the touch. Everything is on fire, and it feels so good until I remember the amount of blood beneath us and the alcohol we have both consumed. Bash doesn't need this, not after what I have done to him. This wound is *my* fault. "You need rest," I whisper.

"I don't need anything but this," he tells me as he grabs the same hand and uses it to pull me into him. He winces when my body hits his, but he doesn't stop as his other hand comes crashing down on the back of my neck. He holds me in place, my mouth so close to his that I can feel each word. "I have had enough of looking at you and doing nothing." Bash finds my eyes as he speaks.

I swallow the knot in my throat. "You do not look. Every time. You look away." My words come out desperate and choppy.

Bash has that same pained look on his face he gave me before he left. "Only to stop myself from doing this." his hand balls into a fist, holding my hair as he pulls me into him. His lips are soft, salty from the struggle of getting back. Back to *me*. Sweet with the taste of expensive whiskey.

Somehow, my knees end up on each side of him as I fall into the kiss. I wrap my arms around his neck, careful of his new injury. My fingers go through his hair. The hair that feels just as I thought it would.

My lip's part, letting him further into me with methodical twists of his tongue. It's everything I thought it would be and more. It's gentle but unending and passionate. I know it cannot go further than this. Not with both of our injuries. Not without making sure we complete our missions.

Not without the truth.

Not without my name on his lips. My *real* name.

Bash doesn't put up a fight when I gently push our bodies apart. His hand rests gently on the back of my head. "As soon as we get out of this damned place," he falls forward until his forehead is against my own. "You are mine." He finishes, and my heartstrings pull until I think they will snap. I have made a colossal mistake, lied my way too close to the sun and now I will burn for it.

*If you will still want me.* I think to myself.

*You got shot because of me,* I want to scream. *You wouldn't have had to come back to Jericho, where you so obviously suffered if it weren't for me!*

Bash won't want anything to do with me once he finds out *I* am the girl in the photo with blonde hair and blue eyes.

# Chapter 26

Bash

Seventeen. Finally, I received my shipment date. Mother has no idea what I have done. It's too late. My request to get to the outer wall has been accepted.

I am free. Of Jericho and Mother.

I will serve my years rebuilding the walls of the Outer Ring, the lowest of the low. But at least I am not seen, no one pays attention to the builders. It's easy, the way life should be. I don't worry about when my next meal will come or whose bed I am to sleep in.

Every day, I do the same thing, and every night, I sleep in the same cot with the same men who occupy our tent. They treat me as an equal. They do not look down on me.

It's hot, sweat drips down my back as I do my daily quota of miles. A group of sergeants walks past my unit with their chests pushed out. They have been gathering men for what they are calling a trial run of new automatic weaponry. The chosen soldiers never come back, so I make myself scarce.

Wrong place, wrong time.

The wall crumbles, and bricks fall. It happens all the time. The damage is usually minimal. This time, it isn't. Part of the falling wall hits a bomber car that explodes on impact, causing half a mile or more to fall. We all scramble, but it's not fast enough. Certainly not for the sergeants who are now under a pile of rubble.

I prefer to stay where I am. Not seen or heard.

My mind is changed when I hear the screams. The same as the ones from Jericho where my brother and sisters would beg for help, and I could do nothing to stop their pain. It's not like I didn't try. The punishment for it was substantial. Worth it every time, but soon they caught on.

Mother knew I would not stop, that the lashing and beatings were doing nothing to keep me from them. When I was taken out of the house, *sold*, it was the last time I got to see my siblings. Mother would visit often. For no other reason then to tell me of my failures. The biggest one being that I would never make it out of Jericho.

That's where she was wrong, but at what cost? I had left my siblings at Mother's unmerciful hands.

That day the screams from beneath the rubble became my brothers. It's like I couldn't stop myself from going to him.

*Bronze*, the name tag on his left shoulder read. His head was bleeding, and his arm was bent in an odd way. His hand was limp at his side. I was used to blood and broken bones. Mending them all with a smile on my face in front of my brother and sisters. If I was smiling, then they were too.

Bronze didn't care that he was broken as he plunged himself back into the mess, dragging me with him. Pulling body after body out as I did all I could to mend them. Many died but if it weren't for Bronze, they *all* would have.

After a few hours the medics got there, took over. They had to be convinced by Bronze to do so. The Palen Army doesn't care about those stationed in the outer walls or its citizens, but *he* does.

Riley Bronze is working his way up the ranks and fast. Whatever needs to be done, he is your guy. No matter how dangerous or dirty the job. The Palen Army isn't known for its fairness. They are known for breaking men and turning them into weapons. It's almost as corrupt as Jericho. And Bronze knows that.

That's why he keeps me by his side, even still, as captain of the Medic unit in the Palen Army.

I know now what I did was wrong, that I should not have left Jericho. That I should have fought. Bronze left, too, for a different reason, of course. He left so he could start something bigger than all of this.

Riley has big ideas, bigger than anything I ever dreamed of. He tells me of all the ways in which we could change the world. That there is something bigger out there we just don't know about yet, far beyond the shitty walls of Palen.

It started out small, just the two of us. Then it grew when soldiers caught wind of our plan.

First, I went back for my sisters. They are so little. They wouldn't have lasted long in that place. My brother on the other hand can handle himself. Or so he says.

It took almost four years, but I had them back. With me at the base outside the wall. Safe. Bronze brought back every person that was dear to me and more. That's why I owe him my life.

We were pushing our limits, but it was almost time. Time for us to destroy the world that has taken so much from each and every one of us. We were met with success around every corner and things were going exactly to plan.

Until *her.*

The girl Bronze never shut up about. Emerson.

She was the reason Bronze wanted to save the whole damn world. Must be a hell of a woman. I could never imagine being so bent up for someone. I have no lack of women throwing themselves at me. Not a single one of them has ever made me feel quite like that. Never will.

Not the way Bronze described it, anyway. "Kill for her, live for her." He had said to me that day.

We were so close. He was going to save her along with everyone else. It was supposed to go smoothly. The way we planned it so carefully, but she ruined everything. Because when we got to the Outer Ring, a drug-infested shithole called Harmony, she wasn't there.

I've never seen Bronze like that. It was like his life had just ended right before me. She wasn't in Harmony. She wasn't on the list of women headed to Jericho either. Someone had either erased her, or she was dead.

Bronze went the dead route, blowing up every city he could get to with the limited amount of ammunition we had gathered from The Rebellion. There would be more of course, but we would use that on Jericho, take it out in one fell swoop. No survivors.

Bronze had given me everything. I couldn't let him think she was dead. Not without getting into Jericho one more time, to make sure. I had my suspicions long ago that the people of Jericho were trading women under the radar. It was a way to get what you want without paying your dues. How even the most despicable humans can steep lower than low, I will never know. If there is one thing those bastards do well, it's break the rules. Trafficking wasn't even close to the top of the list when it came to the atrocities the citizens of Jericho had committed.

I asked for a week, just one, because that's all it would take, and he agreed. I just wanted to give him what he had given me. I had nothing to go on but a feeling—maybe some faded memories of my mother talking with her husband about a vague delivery of unmarked women. I couldn't be sure. I just knew I had to try.

Blonde hair, blue eyes. A useless picture of a little girl looking up at a young Riley Bronze.

# CHAPTER 27

After a quick breakfast, or at least what I made a quick breakfast when I shoved the food into my mouth so fast I almost choked, Bash pulls out a set of keys. I look at him, confused. That smirk starts at the corner of his mouth before it consumes his entire face. "Ben-" he begins but clears his throat. "I mean, *I* have a car." He winks.

My mouth falls open slightly. We are so close. Sometimes, I forget the world as I know it is about to end. That Jericho and the whole of Palen are on a time limit. Especially when Bash is good at making things seem bright. Like our lives are not on the line. He seems to have lots of practice in the art of pretending.

It's not hard for Bash to find the house of Ben's employer. We roll down a side street with many houses behind gates. Ben's car must get us through what Bash is sure to be the house Jez is at because the metal gates open right up. The lawn is lush and manicured. Birds sing, and butterflies float nearby.

Soon, past the greenery is a large tan house. It's more like a castle, actually. It even has a rounded turret that shoots up into the sky. A huge balcony overlooks the drive. I have to crank my neck just to see the point at the top that has a strange symbol on it. The same twisted foreign letters that were on the building in Warshaw, I realize. The one that fell.

It has everything Jez ever dreamed of. A garden, lots of shade. Water falls from a fountain nearby. All of it is a beautiful façade. My stomach suddenly feels queasy. I knew Jericho was not what it seemed long ago. This place, this house, it feels as if there is something sinister hidden behind the lush green.

Bash signals for me to walk by his side. "Eyes forward, straighten your shoulders." He reminds me. The part I play is exhausting, which has me thinking of how Bash must have felt for his entire life. How Jez has probably felt for so long. Guilt threatens to eat me up from the inside out.

It's silent.

Even as we near the door, there is no chatter from the inside of the house, no music or footsteps. Nothing. Bash takes a step in front of me and rings the doorbell. His shoulders straighten even though I know it hurts him to do so.

He wears a suit jacket and matching trousers, the same fashion as the men we passed on our way here. The deepest shade of black he could find in Ben's closet. I wear the spare clothes from the bag I am certain belongs to Jez. They are as uncomfortable as they look, with an itchy white collared shirt and matching linen pants.

It's too quiet, the kind of silence that comes from emptiness. My suspicions are correct when no one answers. He pushes the button a second time to no avail. My chest tightens. "No, no," I whisper to myself.

She has to be here. *She was supposed to be here.*

Bash peeks into the intricately designed window next to the door. "Let's go," he says, turning on his heels. His good shoulder hits mine when I do not move. Even he is upset. I can see behind those silent eyes, but he still does not budge.

"I'm not leaving," I tell him, my attention still on the knob, as if it will twist open and my sister will be on the other side.

Bash's voice is low. "You are." He gives his demand through clenched teeth.

I shake my head in disbelief. When I try to pass him to get to her, he pushes his hand out, catching me at my middle. I wince. I look up at Bash to show him my anger, but he doesn't care. "Don't make a scene, Sweetheart. They are watching."

My shoulders fall in defeat as I look up at the door frame, where I spot a camera. It seems to dial in on my face. It takes everything in me not to stare it down, letting the person on the other end know exactly what I feel.

Then I turn. Not even a shard of glass through my stomach or the glowing heat of Bash's knife pressing down on my skin feels as painful as this. The further we get from the door, the more I feel it. My heart pounds into my ears, my chest tightens. This is a feeling I have never felt so deeply before. Failure.

I failed Jez, Riley... Bash. The man who stands before me, watching me fall apart. He can see it all. I do not hide it well. "I'm sorry." I think I hear him whisper, but my mind is elsewhere. To a memory of Jez, one where she would fall apart just like I feel as though I might. With her shoulders shaking and her eyes swollen from tears. She had not seen me walk up to the bathroom door while she stood in front of the mirror. It was like a switch flipped, and she was back to being my big sister when she noticed me watching. The one that never wavered, never second-guessed herself. How much did I miss? Was I so naive? Those letters were not the first time I had ignored her pleas for help, were they?

Bash stops dead in his tracks, pulling me from thought. I look up to see his black brows pushed together as I knew they would be. Then his eyes go from anger to something else I do not recognize. His hands go from his sides to my shoulders in an instant. The touch brings every emotion to the surface, and suddenly, I want to scream, fight, do anything besides give up.

I begin, but my words are cut off. "You shouldn't be here." I hear a voice so ingrained into my memory I can't believe I didn't get to hear it for seven years. My legs buckle as the anger spills from my body, replaced with something else. Bash is there, holding me together.

When my body finally catches up to my brain, I turn.

There she is. Jez, but not my Jez. She looks... different.

I'm making a list of all things that are so so wrong with her, but Bash's body is in front of me in a second. He pushes me to the side so hard I nearly trip over myself. He walks straight to her and doesn't stop until he has Jez pushed up against a wall with vines on its side by the door. "Stop," I say, but he doesn't listen. "Stop." I cry, forgetting about being the perfect submissive woman.

Bash grabs her by the chin, inspecting her. First, he pushes her head to the left, then the right. She looks scared, but she doesn't say anything. Which is so *unlike* the Jez I know. My feet move on instinct. I rip his hand away from hers, but he still has this look of determination on his face. "What are you doing?" I ask through my teeth, enraged. "Don't touch her!" I spit at him before wiping the anger off my face to turn to my sister.

My sister who just stares and stares at me. A strange, wild look takes over her face as she looks at my hair. "It's really you." She finally whispers. "You look so grown up." She says, and it sounds a bit sad. Even though she is the one who predicted my late growth spurt, Jez told me I would grow into my curves, and I did.

I take her all in now. Hallowed eyes and small frame. She was always petite, but this is past what is considered normal. It's unnatural. When my eyes fall past her protruding collarbones and down to her middle, there is a small bump she cradles with one hand. Pregnant.

Quickly, I catch her eyes again. So sad. I realize that's just how she looks now. Jez attempts a smile, but I do not reciprocate. When I do not say anything at all, she speaks up again. "You shouldn't be here, Emerson." Worry contorts her features, and she begins to shake her head almost violently.

I had almost forgotten Bash was standing behind me until his voice fills my ears. "Emerson." He repeats my name. It sounds so good for all of two seconds until I remember what comes next.

I brace myself for what is about to happen. The anger, the betrayal I will see on his face if I turn around. So, I don't. I ignore Bash, who makes a noise I think is supposed to be a laugh. "We need to leave," I tell my sister.

Bash's footsteps sound behind me, to the left and then to the right, as he paces back and forth.

Jez continues shaking her head. My brows furl in frustration and confusion. Tears well up in her eyes, threatening to fall any minute if she gives them a chance. "I can't go," she tells me.

"You *can*, Jez. Let's go." I grab for her hand, but she snatches it up to her chest.

Then she looks around. "Where is Ben?"

I try not to close my eyes, or his face will pop up behind my lids. Dying in my arms.

I'm somewhere between screaming and crying. She should not care where Ben is. Not when her sister is standing right in front of her. The sister Ben planned to trade for her freedom, if you can call it that.

"Jez." Her name comes out harsher than I thought. The tears she was holding so patiently fall down her cheeks and onto the ugly grey dress that hangs off her bony shoulder.

Then she seems to retreat, stepping back into the house as if to get away from me. "You have no idea what you have done." She tells both of us. "You should leave before he gets back." I can't believe what I am hearing. Who is this person, and what has she done with my sister?

"If you don't come with us now, you won't have another chance," Bash says harshly. Finally, I look at him. Yeah, there it is, just as I thought it would be, pain, hurt. He keeps my eyes, searching. I look away first to my sister. My *broken* sister.

It's supposed to be the other way around. She was perfect, always. Now she is just...here. A shell. Her lack of effort pisses me off. The Jez I knew would never do this. She would fight, she would *live*.

If she won't do it on her own I will make her. "Ben was going to trade *me* for you." I spit at her in hopes it snaps her out of whatever trance these people have placed over her.

Jez's eyes go wide like she can't believe it, *won't*. "No, he wouldn't have done that. You don't know him like I do. He loves me." She says and truly believes it.

My face falls flat. "Loved." I correct her, my anger getting the best of me. Anger at her, at Riley, at the fucking world. We were supposed to be together. I was not supposed to be left behind or forgotten.

She shakes her head, not believing a word I say. So, I continue, driving home my point. "It's true." I take a step in her direction. Removing the distance she put between us. "He was going to take you away. Then I would become *this.*" I push my hands out, pointing down her body. "Your husband's personal whore. Someone to pump out more children so he can sell them. Someone who he can beat and rape, just like he does to you. You want that for me, Jez? You want me to become *you?* Become whatever *this* is?" I make sure to emphasize the disgust in my voice.

And it works because it's all over her face. The same face that stares back at me in the mirror every day. Guilt.

Bash's hand is on my shoulder, but I don't stop. "It's time to leave. It's time to go *home.*" I plead, reaching for the locked door.

"This *is* my home, Em," Jez says, but it's not as believable as she wants it to be.

I shake my head at her. Then I pull my arm from Bash's grip. He does not try to stop me. "It's not, and you know it," I scream.

Then she steps back, tears falling, her body so frail it seems as if she might shatter into a million pieces right before me.

She grabs the door behind her, the one that would force me to be walls away from her again, maybe forever this time. Before she closes it, she stares me down. As if the old Jez is there, fighting to get out. "Let me save you." Her eyes close for a moment too long, and when they open, my heart breaks. "Let it be the last thing I do." She smiles weakly.

Before I can ask her what that means she looks past me, to Bash. "Take her to him." She tells him.

My brows come together in confusion. "To who?" I barely get out before Bash pulls me back towards the car. *No.* "Wait, I'm not done! She can't stay here!" I shout to the door that is now shut. Each word hurts more than the last.

"She made her choice. It was a good one." Bash says through his teeth as he shoves me forward.

"No, no, no," I say all the way to the car. Now, my own face is soaked in tears as we drive the opposite way.

Bash drives silently. I do not dare look at him. I wouldn't be able to do it all over again, have someone look at me the way Jez did. "Why?" I ask. "Why didn't she come?" I'm nearly doubled over in what I think is pain or sadness.

Bash punches the steering wheel as he looks in the rear-view mirror. I twist my head to see what he sees. Black smoke. I know what happens next. "She's an informant. She just saved our lives." He tells me. I suck in a breath, one I very much needed.

"Informant for what?" I look at a blurred version of Bash.

"The Rebellion." Bash says.

# CHAPTER 28

I have no time to ask Bash for an explanation before an explosion sounds behind us. So loud it hurts my ears and has the car shaking. I look behind me to see the neighborhood up in flames.

Jez, up in flames.

That's when everything turns off. The tears stop falling. My chest no longer hurts. It's all so numb. All of this, for nothing at all.

I could not save her.

Another explosion in the distance, as if the first one triggered something. The same song and dance as before. Jericho will fall.

Bash mumbles something under his breath as he takes a sharp turn. We are headed to the wall. He strategically takes side streets and back roads, swerving around cars and pushing his way forward.

The world seems to slow as planes fly above, dropping things as they pass. They fall slowly to the earth before detonating on top of buildings. Taking out huge portions of the city. I watch it all like a movie. With all the loud noises and excitement. All while I sit, helpless.

A helicopter flies to the left, Bash notices it too, he drives in its direction. A part of the road collapses in front of us. We are going too fast. Bash does all he can to stop but we are running out of places to go as cars pile up and pavement falls into the earth. The car makes a terrible squealing noise before we hit a tree on the side of the road.

My head hits the dash. I ignore the dull pain that emanates from my head as Bash grabs my arm, pulling me so I face him. He inspects my eyes carefully with a finger in front of him that I follow as he checks for a concussion. He grabs my chin like he has done before to be sure I am without injury. A feeling that would usually send butterflies to my stomach. Before I hurt him.

I swallow away the guilt. His brows push together as he runs a thumb over my lower lip. For a split second, he drops his guard, and there it is again. A soul I do not deserve. "I'm sorry," I say so quietly I do not think he hears me with all the noise around us—the *carnage.*

Bash turns from me to open his door. When he gets to mine and offers a hand, I do not take it. His kindness, all wasted on me. "Can you walk?" He points beyond the wall. I nod my head in answer. He takes a step in that direction.

I look back. At the broken city, the fallen city. I take a few seconds to say goodbye to my sister's grave.

Bash grabs my hand when I do not move. I want to hold onto it forever, but he releases mine immediately.

We walk for a long time in silence. All there is to hear is the slight ringing in my ear and the remnants of Jericho's bones shattering. They did not leave a single brick stacked on another. As soon as we are over the wall, another explosion, larger than the rest, takes out what was left.

Bash stops in a clearing, leans against a tree on the edge , and wipes the sweat from his brow. His jaw clenches as he stares at me with that same pained look in his eye. His mouth opens, then closes again.

The silence finally gets the best of me. I do not listen to the voice inside my head that usually tells me to wait it out. *They all talk*. Jez, *her* voice and *her* lessons. I force myself to meet Bash's eyes, ready to break the rules and ask for his forgiveness, beg for it.

Before any words can get past my lips, "I know why you did it." Bash reads me like a book.

My eyes widen, which hurts because my head feels like it might fall off my shoulders. He lets the corner of his mouth rise when I hold my head between my palms. "I would have done anything to save my siblings." He huffs a laugh. "I *did*. I got them back. I had to lie and cheat and kill to get them." He sighs as he remembers it. "I would have helped you either way." He shakes his head at me in disappointment. Hurt more by my lack of trust in him than my lies.

I take a step in his direction as I nod. "I found the photo," I admit to him. I'm kicking myself for hiding it. The only copy in existence is gone, under a pile of rubble that used to be Jericho.

Bash studies me for a second. His emeralds fall from my hair to my toes. "I can't believe it's you." he pauses. Bash must think of Riley next because he shakes his head, "He is not going to be happy." He runs his hands through his black hair. "Fuck, he is going to be more than unhappy."

"Riley?" I ask but do not wait for an answer because I already know. "How is he?" I can't help but ask.

Bash lets that grin devour his face. "Miserable," Bash says without thought. I laugh. Glad for the distraction from my sisters death as I think about Riley.

I can see it now—A brooding Riley that joined The Rebellion. "Of course he did." I accidentally say out loud. Bash gives me a strange look

217

to which I give him an explanation. "When we were little, he had all these ideas. He always wanted to change the world. Change his fate." I smile at the memory. "Of *course*, he joined The Rebellion. To do just that." I tell him.

Bash lets out a laugh I don't think I have heard from him before. "Join? No, no." Bash looks at me again as if to make sure I am serious. "He runs the damned thing."

"Riley? *My* Riley?" I ask in awe as I try to wrap my head around it.

Bash nods his head but his smile fades as he looks somewhere else. Just as he did before, making sure he looks at anything but me. "Your Riley." he seems to say to himself.

The hurt on his face confuses me for a moment. "Look at me." I basically plead. He does. He looks at me with every emotion that I don't quite know what to do with. I can't decide if it's hate or something else entirely.

He keeps me pinned beneath his gaze before he steps forward and braces my neck with his hand. He pulls me so close I can feel his breath as he speaks. "He is going to kill me." He says so seriously it hurts. I close my eyes, wishing for a different world where I meet Bash under different circumstances. One where I tell him my real name. Where I show my real self, not this jaded, selfish version of me.

"I won't let him." I open my eyes and try to hide the hurt with a smile. A smile that gets eaten by Bash's lips as he crushes himself into me.

"You have no idea what you have done." Bash whispers into my mouth when he finally pulls away after what feels like forever and yet not long enough.

"Tell me." I plead.

Bash thinks about it for a moment. "Bronze has spent his entire life waiting for you," Bash explains. Bronze. Riley's last name. A name Bash must call him often because it falls from his mouth with ease. The name Riley wore on his shoulder in uniform, I'm sure. I think about all the times I convinced myself I hated him—Riley Bronze. The man who left me. I let that hate to the surface, *I* was the one who waited, not him.

When I look at Bash, it's hard to think of Riley at all. It's easier to think of what's happening right now, in this moment. Bash's body pressed against mine. His arms around me. It feels safe. Not the way I felt with Riley. Where at any moment, he could change into this dark entity with a matching aura.

"Is Bash your real name?" I ask, curiosity getting the best of me.

Bash nods his head with a smile. "Sebastian Stone. But just call me Bash." he drawls.

"So you gave me your real name." I manage a smile. A smile that feels wrong under the circumstances and is gone as soon as it comes.

Bash nods as he sees the expression on my face. Then, as he always does, he attempts to lighten the mood. "I thought you were going to die," he winks.

Then the wind picks up, swirling my hair all around. Bash pushes it from my face as he holds me in place. He holds it so tightly I can't help but think it's for the last time—like he is trying to see me, hold me before he no longer can. When he releases me, my heart breaks all over again.

I watch as a black helicopter appears from behind the trees. That's where the wind was coming from, it's so strong that it bends the branches of trees before it comes down slowly over the top of us.

The chopping noise fills my ears painfully. When the ladder falls, and the door opens. Those same figures of men in black who were in

Warshaw spill out. Maybe not the same ones that killed the man at the café, but they are dressed in the same black, the same weapons fall over their shoulders. A black mask over the lower half of their faces. Bash grabs my hand and pulls me to them.

One of the three with the same green eyes and bushy brows embraces Bash. They look too similar to be anything but brothers. I look to the other two, who watch me like I am a snake, like I could strike at any second. They are protective of their own.

I study each of their faces but none of them are him. I become increasingly aware that if I get onto this helicopter, I will be taken to Riley. That is something I am extremely unprepared for. To look into the same eyes I see all the time when I close mine. What will they see?

I take each step carefully. Wary of another flying object that could hurdle towards earth as it did before. Bash places a helmet onto my head, gently pulling the latch at the bottom to tighten it. He guides me to a seat where I am stuck facing two of the three men who have a strange way about them, stare at me. They look as if they have seen a ghost.

When I close my eyes to avoid their curious stares, suddenly, Bash's voice is in my head—in my helmet, actually. "Breathe, Emerson." I turn my head to him to see the smile I knew would be there.

Then, another voice fills my ears. "*The* Emerson." The man laughs.

I struggle to find the match to the voice until Bash kicks his brother. "Leave her alone, Daniel." He says, but it doesn't come out as seriously as he would have liked it. He looks so happy to be around these men. His brothers. Blood or otherwise.

We shift on the ground as we ready for takeoff. The taller one is in the pilot seat, with blonde hair that peeks out from beneath his helmet. Then I begin to panic. Thinking of the last pilot that sat before me.

Adam, the man who has one of Riley's bullets in his skull as he rots on the mountain. I squeeze my fists into balls.

*Breathe, Emerson,* I repeat in my head over and over. I close my eyes and begin to pray for my life. "So, we shouldn't tell her that we know how she lost her shoes at the park when she was ten? Just up and forgot where she put them." When I open my eyes, I see the man next to Daniel, deep blues, pinning me to the wall behind me. His words confuse me at first, but these men know things about me, and I know why. Riley never could shut his mouth.

The helicopter moves, I grab at the seat in fear. Not again. Flying is not for me. It's decided. If I never do it again, it will be too soon. My breaths come out so loud and fast I know the others can hear it.

I swallow my heart, which has somehow made its way up to my throat. *Breathe.* "Or the time she swallowed her last baby tooth with a bite of bread." I don't know who says the words. For a moment, I am caught in the memory. Jez's worry and Riley's laugh as I cried over a plate of food. Riley told me it would be inside of me forever which sent me further into tears.

Bash places a steady hand on my thigh. This pulls me from the memory. When I look out the window, we are far above the trees. The man in the pilot seat peaks at the men behind him and nods his head.

They were distracting me.

I grab Bash's hand tightly in my own. The two men across from me stare like I have gone mad. Like Bash has, as well. Even the man in the front takes a second glance at the mirror to watch the two of us. One of them clears their throat, the one with piercing blue eyes. Then, they all find something else to look at.

The *only* thing to look at—a smoking Jericho disappearing into the distance. There is a look of relief on all the men around me the further away we get. We pass the walls that seemed huge and unmoving from down there. Now, they are jagged and barely visible. The further we go, the more destruction we see.

Until finally, it's all behind us. Palen, in its entirety, stands no more.

"What now?" I ask the collective. All but Bash look at me. I try not to think much about what that means.

"Now we take you to Bronze. He will decide what to do after that." Daniel says before looking from me to his brother.

# CHAPTER 29

Riley

Corey is sitting back in his chair, not a care in the world, like he always does. In his office where he pretends to be Father. Where he drinks and smokes and fucks. It's like seeing Father all over again. The same road with all its twists and turns.

The club is empty. It smells just the same as it did all those years ago.

The last time I stepped foot in here was when I came to pick up Emerson. Corey had one of his goons stop by to tell me she was here. She was going to sit in for the Jericho boys. The one night of the year where she should be the furthest from here as possible.

It was too late. By the time I showed up, she was already being poked and prodded by one of the men. I wanted to cut each and every finger off one by one. Whichever parts of him touched her would be gone. Whatever words he spoke to her would never be spoken again because his tongue would be on the floor at my feet.

I almost did it, too. Walked right onto that stage to tear him to ribbons in front of everyone. What a beautiful spectacle it would have been. But that's exactly what he wanted, and I don't like giving Corey the satisfaction.

We made a promise after that. After I stupidly left Emerson without an explanation. One where he gets what he wants, and I get what I want. *Her.*

Now I am here to collect.

Corey doesn't see me, or he doesn't pay any attention. He never does. I fold my arms as I lean on the door frame. His eyes flutter up in annoyance before he realizes who stands before him. Someone he never thought he would see again. Oh, how wrong he was. "Ri." Corey fakes a smile at me. I narrow my eyes at him. I hate that name, and he knows it.

When I step into the room without a word, Corey stands. I return his smile with one of my own, but mine is genuine. I am having a hell of a time watching Big Bad Corey slowly lose his cool. *Afraid,* that's what he is, as he should be.

Now, I know Corey is a coward at his core. He never stood up to Father. He did as he was told out of fear of punishment. I've just never seen it on the surface, right there on his face. "What are you doing here?" He asks, quickly pulling on a more confident mask.

"You and I have a deal, do we not?" I cock my head at him. Oh yes, this is interesting. Corey is shaking in his boots. For good reason, he is staring at a dead man. Or at least who he thought was dead. I can see him trying to make sense of it.

"No: Nice to see you? How have you been?" He attempts a joke.

I watch him study me for a second too long. He might be drunk or high or both. Probably checking to see if I am real or not. That shit he has been on for years rots your brain away, makes you see things that aren't really there. "It's *not* nice to see you, Corey." I sigh, bored. "I also know how you have been. The same as you have been for our entire lives." I tell him. He doesn't respond.

Instead, he pulls a flask from the drawer, takes a healthy swig, and holds it out to me. The way I knew he would. I ignore it. "Is it nice to see *me*?" I ask with a devious grin as I see my words work their way under his skin.

Again, no answer. I click my tongue three times. "Clumsy. That's the word I would use to describe the men you sent to kill me. Couldn't do it yourself?" I don't need an answer. I didn't expect to get one from coming here. I watch as his eyes dart back and forth between me and the door. He swallows audibly. It's fun to watch him squirm, but I am here for a different reason. "So. Where is she?" I ask.

Corey runs a hand through his hair. Then he closes his eyes, and when he opens them, he is shaking his head and staring at me like he wants to kill me. "You can't have her." He then informs me with a smug, satisfied look in his eyes. To which I laugh.

"Funny. Where is she?" I ask again. This time, I raise my voice slightly to get the point across.

When I lean forward onto the desk, Corey leans in the opposite direction. He crosses his arms defensively. "She's not here." Corey responds vaguely. I slam my hands on the desk, sending things flying. "What the hell does that mean, Corey?" I ask impatiently.

I should kill him right now, but I will wait until he gives me what I am after. "It *means* she's gone." Corey breaths out slowly. "Sold to one of the Jericho boys. I couldn't pass it up. He paid double." He shrugs like it's all just business. *She* is not business.

My mind races but I do not waver, do not let him know how it affects me. "You've made a huge mistake," I warn him.

Corey takes another drink. He doesn't stop this time. He knows his fate. Drunk until the very end. Just like Father.

"Just like Father." He repeats my thoughts out loud. I raise my brows in surprise.

"Tell me everything you know, and I will make it quick," I promise.

# CHAPTER 30

It's dark when we descend into a field of lights. The Rebellion's camp. It's larger than I thought it would be. Riley has been very busy. He has always been like that, driven.

Bash is particularly quiet. He lets his brother, Daniel, take the lead as we walk through the camp from the field where we landed. There are children running back and forth through string lights attached to each tent. Women watch them play. They look happy. An expression I haven't seen on someone in a long time. The look of freedom, I decide.

Jez could have become one of those happy women. She should be here. The guilt turns my stomach in on itself.

Daniel pulls the gun from his back, and the others do the same. Finally, their masks come off, and I can see all their faces clearly. Hardened features from years in the service paired with muscular arms and lean bodies. "Liam." The pilot holds out his hand to me. His blonde hair is tucked behind his ears, and it flips out at the ends. His hand is rough and stained with black as if he has been working on something mechanical. His eyes are light brown, kind.

"There wasn't much time for introductions. Michael." Says the man with eyes that are an almost impossible shade of blue. Jez would have fawned over him. Michael holds his hand out, and when I step closer to take it in my own, I take note of a single tear-shaped tattoo over his left cheek. His greying dark brown hair is shaved, much like Daniels, and placed perfectly even though it was under a helmet. He has perfect white teeth and a stare that keeps you in place. He knows it, too, because he has me frozen with a look that tells me he planned it that way. "It's nice to finally meet you, Emerson." His words come out like honey. The same calming voice I heard in my helmet on the helicopter. His words were a good distraction.

Bash and his brother are nearly identical. Daniel's hair is cut short, while Bash's falls over his ears in waves. The biggest difference is when Daniel takes his jacket off, there are no tattoos on his arms. Bash doesn't have an ounce of flesh, aside from his face, that isn't decorated with beautiful designs. I catch myself wondering what other permanent works of art might be hidden beneath his clothing.

My face warms as I realize I have been basically undressing Bash from across the space. I'm tired, and all my thoughts are scrambled. It's like I can't help but dissociate from what I have seen today, even though I know I shouldn't. Bash's eyes are on me as well, his brows pushed together in concern.

Daniel watches us intently. His head snaps back and forth between the two of us. Then Daniel's face gets swallowed up by the same smile I often see on his brother's. "Let's go." Daniel waves to us to follow him. Then he looks at Liam and Michael, who also wear a strange look on each of their faces. "Go get him. We will be in South Camp." They nod their heads and continue shedding their gear before they leave.

I follow Bash and Daniel through the rows of tents until Daniel stops us outside one. Shortly after we enter, a woman brings in a bucket of water with steam coming off of it. Bash quietly thanks her. Then he shoves his hands in his pockets. He is acting so strangely. "Clean up a bit. Bronze—I mean Riley will be here soon." Bash orders before he turns to leave with his brother. I grab his arm almost on instinct. Bash goes rigid, which has me releasing him immediately. I clasp my hands tightly together in front of me. I don't trust myself not to touch him again if I don't.

Daniel clears his throat. "I'll be outside." He raises his brows as he turns.

Bash stares at the water in the bucket until it stills. The space becomes dense with tension. My eyes never leave his brows, which crush together the same as before. If he keeps them like that for too long, they might get stuck.

Finally, he speaks. "I'm sorry." He whispers. "About your sister."

I shake my head, not prepared to speak of her so soon. "You said she saved lives." I still look at him, but he does not look back.

When he finally peels his eyes from the water, it's to look towards the rest of the camp. "She saved everyone here. You should be proud."

I nod my head, which he does not see. "I am," I say as I step in his direction. He takes a step back. My shoulders drop, and my heart falls into my stomach. Bash finally meets my eyes. I let him see the hurt there. To which he just shakes his head like it will explain anything. "You didn't have this problem with Babe." I laugh, but it's only to cover the pain.

"We can't do this right now." He continues with his head shaking. "He—I can't do this to him." Bash hardly gets the words out. I take another step. He doesn't move this time, so I take another and another. Until we are so close I can see the outline of a matchbook in his pocket.

His jaw tightens as I touch it, placing my hand flat over his heart. It's so quiet I can hear his breathing. It's comfortable. I know he feels it, too, because his features soften, and he leans into the touch. But quickly, the softness twists into regret, followed by anger. He stutters a breath and grabs at my wrist, using his grip to distance us. Bash stares down at me, which has me taking my hand back. "Coward," I hiss at him.

His chest moves in heavy ups and downs. His nostrils flare before he grabs my shoulders. Bash's fingers dig into my skin. I don't think he realizes his own strength. I don't react. I don't let him know he hurts me. Bash pulls me close to him, his breath on my face. "I owe him my life. Don't you get it?" His voice is low and dangerous.

"I get it. I have *always* gotten it." I spit, letting anger take over. "I have never had a day where I was not reminded of it." Bash's eyes shift from one of my eyes to the other as I speak. "Never had a man look at me without seeing *Riley* first." I breath. "Like you are looking at me *right now.*" I look into his eyes deeper, until I find it.

Bash searches my face, then releases me and takes a step back. "Talk to him. Spend time with him." He pushes his hands through his hair. It looks like every word is painful as he speaks. "If you still feel-" Bash turns around and mumbles a curse under his breath. "If you still feel this way, then come find me." He says to the fabric that surrounds us.

Someone enters behind me, but I can't seem to take my attention away from the back of Bash's head as I try to will him to turn around. He doesn't. "Am I interrupting something?" That particular voice tears my eyes from Bash.

Gravity, the way it's always been, I find myself nearing Riley without even realizing it. I turn quickly and suck in a breath when I see him. He looks the same and yet so different at the same time. His hair is buzzed on the sides and pushed back on top with gel. The lines around his eyes are more prominent, and he has the start of a beard around his jaw.

Now, I can feel Bash burning a hole into the side of my head. "No, I was just leaving," Bash tells Riley. I squeeze my eyes shut to avoid both of them. Maybe *I* am the coward.

Bash's heavy steps fade as he leaves the tent.

Now it's just me and Riley. When I open my eyes, I simultaneously want to hug and hit him. I love and hate him. He left me. He used me. Tears sting at my eyes. "You are elusive, Em." Riley takes two tentative steps in my direction.

When he nears me, I can smell him, and I hate it. I remember this smell. Being sucked into my lungs in sensual in and outs as we spent what I didn't know at the time was our last night together before he left to join the Palen Army.

He lets out a low hum as he moves a strand of hair from my face, tucking it behind my ear. It's familiar—soft, the way he always was with me and no one else. "Your hair," he remarks. I shiver beneath his touch. Suddenly, I can't think of anything else *besides* that touch.

My mind slowly catches up as I understand what he just said. I had almost gotten used to seeing my reflection as a brunette.

Blonde is the old me, the girl in the photo Bash carried to Jericho with him. It would be all too easy to slip back into my old self. Attached to Riley like bees on honey. He feels it, too. Evident when I finally look up at him, Riley places a finger over my bottom lip. He pulls down slowly. "Don't." I stop him by pulling back just enough to be out of his reach. "You don't get to do that." I wipe away a tear that has escaped down my chin. "You don't get to pretend everything is back to normal." Every word gets louder as I go. "You left me!" I scream at him.

Riley looks down at my feet, then slowly back up to my face. He crosses his arms, waiting. I am not done yet. He doesn't get to be the old

Riley while I have lost so much. Done so much only to be rewarded with so little. "Everyone left me, Riley." I feel as though I might collapse in on myself. "My mother, Jez, you." *And now Bash*, I do not say out loud.

"I couldn't say goodbye," Riley admits. "I know I shouldn't have done it that way." He sighs. "Look around you, Emerson. It's all for you." He says proudly. His arms outstretched to show me.

"You don't get to ruin my life, then build me a new one." Now, I am talking so quietly as every emotion eats away at me.

Riley holds a hand out towards me, but I push it away. Then I look into those eyes that I wished would look back at me for so many years. I search, and I search. He seems to be looking for something as well. We do not speak or move. Hate, that's what I want to feel, but instead, my heart swells, and that makes me even more upset.

When I find what I am looking for, I push past him.

Daniel still stands outside the tent entrance, like the perfect guard dog. He watches my every step carefully. I have a feeling if I walk, he will follow, but I do it anyway. Whatever gets me far away from Riley. I need space. Air that won't suffocate me.

It's quiet now, so late now people have retired to their tents, fast asleep. My footsteps are echoed by the sound of Daniels behind me. Every step I take he takes as well. I walk and walk until the ground becomes soft, and I am stopped at a lake. After a moment, there is only the chirping of crickets and the song of frogs. Something I have never seen or heard before.

This is all so overwhelming, but *this* I could get used to. If there wasn't a stalker on my heels. "Are you all like that?" I ask over my shoulder at him. His white shirt lets me know where he is in the dark as it reflects the moon.

He laughs. "Like what?"

"Loyal," I say, hoping he understands what I mean.

Daniel doesn't say anything. Maybe he is deep in thought. Maybe he was instructed not to talk to me about such things. Riley has always dictated what information I was allowed to hear or rather *not* hear.

He will be sitting there in silence for a long time, I decide. I plop down on the cool ground. Listening to all the new noises. It has been so long since I have had to do this, and I am not sure if I still know the words, but I look up at a clouded, dark sky to say a prayer for my sister. One she taught me when I was small: "Raise her rank amongst those who are guided. Take care of those who she has left behind." I put the words into the world with intent, just as she told me to.

Daniel sits down at my side. I ignore him. Jez's smiling face appears in my mind. The words are right there, the ending of the prayer, but I cannot seem to remember it. I search my memory again but come up short. This pisses me off. I can't even do *one* thing right. I drop my hands in frustration. "Forgive her and us, oh lord of the worlds. Expand her grave and illuminate it for her." Daniel finished the part of the prayer I had forgotten.

My attention falls from the sky to him, but his head is up. His arms dangling over his knees as he pushes the prayer into the world.

My shoulders sag as my body relaxes. Every emotion seems to rise and fall. When I become angry or sad, there is nothing I can do to stop it from taking me over entirely. Greif, it does that to people.

Daniel doesn't move, so neither do I. We stay like that for a long time. With our knees on the ground and our hands open to the sky.

So long my eyes close and my dreams are filled with Jez.

# CHAPTER 31

When I wake up, I am staring at the green fabric of one of the tents. It's hot, so hot my clothes are now damp with sweat. I sit up so fast my head goes light. Right, I haven't eaten in almost two days. Weird, I didn't even feel hungry yesterday. There was so much going on.

My vision clears as I sit up. There on the chair is a sleeping Liam. Slumped in a foldable chair as he snores. A piece of his blonde hair that has fallen in his face moves back and forth with each breath.

My feet are moving before my head can catch up. I don't try to find the boots that have been removed for me as I quietly slip out of the tent, only to be blinded by the glaring sun. I move my hand up, providing shade. When I can see again I am met with a towering Riley. Not as towering as two years ago, I notice. "Going somewhere?" He asks. I try my best not to roll my eyes.

Then he holds a canteen up to me. Water sloshes around inside. My mouth waters, but I don't want to take anything from Riley. I begin to pull my hair into a braid as I walk past him. Of course, he catches up to me with a few strides. We walk for a minute in glorious silence. Then, "You reek." He tells me. To which I side-eye him as I make my way... somewhere. I don't know where anything is.

Riley places his arm around my shoulder and guides me to what I think is a bathhouse. A compilation of tents with steam coming out of the tops. He gets the attention of an older woman who grabs a towel and hands it to him. Everyone stares at us as we walk. This is nothing new for me. You are never truly alone in the streets of Harmony. There are always eyes on you.

Riley opens one of the larger tents and prompts me to enter. When I do, he shoves the towel into my hand and winks as the flap shuts. Now I am alone in darkness. At first, I am confused and moving for the exit until a woman opens an inner part of the tent. She guides me wordlessly into a steam-filled opening.

There has to be some type of spring beneath us. A sulfur smell emits from the hole in the ground where women gather warm water before they retreat into a back room. The woman hands me a bucket the same as the others. I follow their lead, filling it before entering the back where I wash the grime from my body. Riley was right, I reek. Not only that, but my middle aches from yesterday's activities. There are new bruises and scrapes around the wound. This damn thing will never heal if I keep getting into situations like that.

When I am done, the woman and I walk back to the exit together. "Thank you," I tell her. She nods her head. Then she pulls the grey hair from her face, revealing smooth skin where her ears would normally be. She turns her head left, then right to show me she cannot hear.

Before I can do anything else, she grabs my hand and holds it flat. I nearly pull it away before I understand her intentions. She bends my elbow, forcing my hand to my chin before she pulls on it lightly. Thank you, she mouths. I understand now. I make the motion again, my hand falling away from my chin flat. "Thank you," I say again with the gesture.

A small smile crosses her wrinkled face.

I knew what was waiting on the other side of the tent before I even reached the door, another guard dog. Sure enough, there he is. Far enough away to make his presence known. So I don't run, but close enough if I *do* run, he can catch me. I roll my eyes but see no use in doing anything but approach Riley.

The sun will dry my damp hair in no time. I push it so it lies in the middle of my back as I walk. All eyes are on me—I noticed it before. It's so obvious and annoying. I stare down a man to my left, making him regret that decision. He averts his eyes quickly.

Riley isn't as easily deterred. In fact, he is quite amused by my antics. He watches my every step as if he is trying to memorize my walk. As I get to him, he makes a strange noise that comes from somewhere deep in his chest. I don't give him the satisfaction of asking him what is wrong.

Besides, I don't need to because Bash walks towards us in his usual confident stride. The same military-issued black pants. He doesn't wear his with the matching jacket as Riley does, though. He wears a white T-shirt with a pocket over his heart, a matchbook inside, as usual.

Bash walks past women who nearly break their necks as he passes. He is clean-shaven, and his black hair is pushed out of his face. A pack is slung across his muscular shoulder. Not the shoulder that had a bullet through it less than two days ago.

When Riley strategically moves in front of Bash I glare up at him. "Jealous isn't your color, Riley." I spit Jez's words out at him. She would often tell me that about Riley. Women would constantly throw themselves at him. Right in front of me, like I wasn't even there. Now it's his turn to feel what I felt all those years—alone.

Riley crosses his arms at my words but says nothing about it. Instead, "Bash told me you were severely injured." His eyes narrowed in on me. "Any reason you neglected to tell me that?" I give him the same look he is giving me. Was he always like this? Controlling?

I look up to Bash instead. Doing my best to ignore Riley's tightening jaw. "I just knew someone else would tell you." I practically sing. Ignoring the glare Riley gives.

"It was important information, Emerson." Bash replies. My name off his tongue sends butterflies to my stomach.

I stare up at those glistening emeralds in the sun for only a moment longer before Riley interrupts with a hand on Bash's good shoulder. Gentle. "Bash here is the best medic in the camp." Is that pride I hear in Riley's words?

Bash returns his friendliness with a joke. "Camp? Try again, Bronze. Remember, you'd be dead if it weren't for me." Bash smiles wide before adding. "Twice." He winks down at me.

I look between the two, and I can't believe I actually have a smile on my face. Riley notices it, too. He is happy. It makes my heart hurt for him. I don't think he has ever smiled like that before. Not in front of me, anyway. Bash makes people do that—smile.

"He will check your wounds every morning until you are completely healed, understood?" He asks but I know I do not have a choice.

Then, he is back to brooding. *No, no, no.* I want *that* Riley back, he was here only seconds ago. I just nod my head in agreement. It's not like I can tell him any of that.

Riley escorts us back to the tent, *my* tent. There is a change of clothes on the bed, folded nicely. An awkward silence falls upon the three of us as we stand there. Bash sets out his things, a much nicer set of medical supplies than what was in Ben's apartment. Riley folds his arms near the exit. "Do you want me to stay, Em?" He asks timidly.

I shake my head at him. He nods in understanding before turning his attention on Bash. "Bring her to The Kitchen when you are done." He orders.

"Yeah," Bash says, looking down at the bandages in his hands. Riley hesitates before he steps through the exit with a shake of his head. His heavy steps fade from us. I get a glimpse of another person on the other side of the tent as the flap closes. Riley doesn't think Bash and I should be alone. I roll my eyes in disbelief.

Bash peeks up at me and crosses his arms. He takes in a breath like he wants to say something but changes his mind. "What?" I let curiosity get the best of me.

His brows rise slightly, but he lets no indication of what he is thinking cross his face. Instead, he gets right into it. Serious as a heart attack. "Take it off." He points to my shirt.

This just will not do. Serious Bash is no fun. "You first." I tease. He doesn't move, not even a blink. "Fine," I say, pulling the shirt off my body, leaving me in only a black lace bra. I throw the shirt to the ground. If I never see that stained white shirt again, it will be too soon. It's just another reminder of my failure.

I hadn't noticed I was staring at said shirt on the ground for far too long until Bash's soothing voice fills my ears. "Good, now turn around." He instructs.

My heart skips a beat at the words, distracting me from the memory of Jez. I do as I am told. Mostly so I do not have to face him as warmth rises to my face.

He runs a hand down my back, inspecting the wound. Goosebumps fill my skin at the touch. "You are lucky it's not infected." Bash whispers. His breath smells of sweet tobacco.

"*Lucky,*" I repeat the word with a huffed laugh. "I hate that word." I have decided. Bash remains silent as he dabs at a tender spot with some type of liquid on a gauze pad.

When things go quiet for far too long my mind goes back to Jez. "Do you think I could have done more?" I ask him. He was there. He saw her leave. Dragged me away. Then, the world blew up right before my eyes.

I almost think he isn't going to reply, but his hands stop for just a moment before he answers. "You did more than I ever would have." He breathes again, sending his intoxicating scent into my nose once again. My brows come together in confusion that Bash must be able to sense because he clarifies. "I never would have gone back on my own. Bronze was the one that made me realize I couldn't leave them there." He tells me, his voice low.

Bash grabs clean bandages. His large hands push my arms into the air gently. I lift them above my head as he begins to wrap my middle. "I was stationed south, rebuilding the outer wall for years before Bronze came along." His thumbs scrape up against the skin on my stomach, which has me sucking in a breath. Still, he continues. "I don't think I ever would have done it on my own." Each word sounds like it hurts him. "Gone back to Jericho."

I know what he is doing. He wants me to get to know Riley again, to see the good so I can see past the bad, as I have always done.

Bash needs to know he is good as well. That what he did was nothing short of heroic. "You would have," I tell him. Bash finishes the last wrap, securing the fabric tightly at my side. I turn around to face him. Ready for the pain I knew would be there. A pain he and I share. Guilt. "The Bash I know would never leave someone behind. Not even a girl he barely knew. A girl who forced her way into the safehouse with you and gave you a fake name."

"Would have saved me a lot of trouble if I had." There is that half smile. Meant only for situations like this. For when he doesn't want to show his true emotions.

"I'm sorry," I say, holding his eyes. He doesn't have to give me emotions or words. I just need him to know how truly sorry I am. "I'm sorry I didn't tell you. I'm sorry you got shot. I'm sorry I was a coward." I get them all out at the same time.

"Don't do that." Bash places a hand in the crook of my neck.

I lean into it and close my eyes. "Don't do what?" I ask.

"Apologize for doing what you had to do." He tells me. There is that warmth, the kind that starts wherever Bash is touching me and spreads all over. I open my eyes, met with unwavering emeralds. Finally, he is looking at me. "We don't say sorry for that shit." Bash continues. "Michael, Liam, even Daniel. We all follow Bronze because he makes sure we will never have to be sorry for it again."

My eyes widen as I recognize something in Bash. The same thing I saw in Riley earlier. "You love him," I say without thought.

Bash clears his throat. The left side of his mouth curls up as he looks at me. "You do, too." He says plainly. "You just won't admit it." Bash's fingers twitch in my peripheral, the way they did at Ben's apartment when he didn't know what to do with them.

"I will admit it." I look down and smile at the lack of space between us. "I've loved him for my entire life." It feels strange to tell Bash, of all people, the information I've always kept to myself. Jez knew. I didn't have to tell her. She just knew, Jez was just like that. Riley was not as perceptive. Not until I was being looked at by others. Not until he thought he would lose me. That's not what love is, is it?

"I can see you questioning it. Him." Bash leans his forehead against my own. Finally, the touch I have been craving from him. "Don't. He loves you. We all do. In our own way." I make space between us to look up at him in surprise at those last words.

He searches my eyes. Back and forth as if it will make me understand. "What does that mean?" I shake my head. All? As in Bash and his brother. As in Michael and Liam? As in Riley?

Bash clears his throat. "I can't speak for everyone." He straightens his shoulders, wincing slightly at the movement. Then his brows come together like they always do. He seems to prepare himself for what he is about to say next, "I think I loved you before I even met you." He finally admits.

I search those emeralds for truth. "How could that be?" I ask, almost terrified of the answer.

Bash pushes his hands through his hair. Putting distance between us. "Br—Riley." he corrects himself. "He told us everything about you. It's what got us through."

"Through what?" I ask, my voice shaking.

Bash's mouth sets in a perfect line before, "Something terrible." That's all he *will* say about it. I can tell. I nod, letting him know he does not need to go into detail.

Suddenly, I am very hot. I need to leave. Space. I need space. I take a step back. From there, I get a better look at Bash. He is sitting there with regret written all over his face. This was not the reaction he was expecting. *Love?* I repeat in my head.

I can't help it. I turn away from him. Then, I pull on the new shirt, a black tank top to combat the heat. It's still paired with these fucking linen pants I despise, but it's better than standing in front of Bash, exposed.

"Michael." I hear Bash call out. My back is still turned. "Take Emerson to The Kitchen." Then I hear the sound of his bag shutting before a few beats of silence. I swear I can feel his eyes on the back of my head. Then, he is gone.

# CHAPTER 32

Bash

"Bronze," I call out to the dark. There is no answer.

It was his turn to take the punishment for stealing. But he has been gone for far too long. I swear I heard the door close. The turn of a lock. The click of a key into metal chains. The same chains hang from my own hands and feet.

Liam cries from beside me, a nightmare that often has him flailing, fighting. We all live the same nightmare. Every day. Liam lives it through the night as well, in his dreams.

My throat burns with each word, my mouth long since dried of its saliva. "Bronze. Answer me." I try again.

It takes what feels like hours, but finally, metal scrapes on concrete. It echoes off the walls. "I'm here."

We are finally free, but not out of danger. Our sister camp has been overrun with refugees. They are running out of resources. Even if we leave now, we won't be able to reach them in time to be of any help. On top of that, those who didn't join our efforts are now causing problems, trying to find their place in a world where Palen stands no more.

I know what we have to do now. We have to reach out to Navar. Technically, they are our ally. Navar helped us in the past, but it came at a price—a price we have yet to pay fully. Bronze might have started The Rebellion, but Navar's technology finished it. Without them, we wouldn't have been able to take Jericho down. Our agreement was simple: they assist us in toppling Jericho, and in return, we find them something they have been after for hundreds of years. The Ark of The Covenant.

It was supposedly hidden in the walls of Jericho. However, we haven't found it yet, which places us directly under Navar's thumb.

Bronze has a lead. He suspects someone in Jericho knew we were coming. If we don't find the Ark soon, Navar's patience will run out, and all of this will have been for nothing.

Michael clears his throat, knocking me from my thoughts. "You are thinking loudly again," he says from his post. I'm supposed to be taking Michael's shift on our western border, where I can look into the darkness and think clearly without her soft voice in my ear—the voice that makes me want to kiss her whenever she speaks. Here, I can only think of one thing: on the other side of that darkness are our people, helpless and afraid.

Nothing I come up with helps. "A message is on its way to Navar," I tell Michael.

Michael clocks the look on my face before turning his head. "It won't help, will it?" He says into the void.

I take a deep breath, feeling the weight of our situation pressing down on me. "We have to give them a reason to help us," I reply. "We have to find the Ark."

Michael scoffs. He has never outright told us about his experience with The Ark, but it doesn't take a genius to know his disagreement at every turn is to keep himself distanced from it. He was imprisoned after an attack on his troops in the Canaan Army. They had it in their possession. Apparently, they weren't the only ones after it.

"The bloody Ark of the Covenant," he mutters, shaking his head.

# CHAPTER 33

Bash disappeared last night, and I haven't seen him since. So much for Riley's instructions for Bash to change my bandages every morning. Not that I needed it anyway, the wraps are still dry and clean. Besides, it's not my body that needs the healing as much as my mind.

Things haven't been the same in my head since Jez's death. Things aren't as clear. People aren't as easy to read. Especially Riley. I used to know what he was going to say before he even got a word out. He has always been secretive, and I knew why. The club was keeping him that way, his father, Corey.

Now, there should be no reason for Riley to keep secrets, but it seems as if there is something much bigger going on—something I *should* know about but don't.

After Bash disappeared last night and Michael took me to The Kitchen to meet with Riley, everything seemed normal. But then Riley stationed a woman outside my tent instead of one of the guys. When Riley returned, he seemed off.

He had this look on his face like he was at war with himself. When I asked about it, Riley brushed me off as if nothing was wrong. I couldn't tell if I was missing something then, but I sure as hell knew when he didn't speak the rest of the night.

If I am being honest, it was a nice break from the nonstop questions about my life. Trying to make up for what he missed, I guess. Sometimes, it makes me think he might *actually* be sorry. I spent so much time convincing myself he *wasn't* sorry. That I hated him. It's going to take a while to feel anything but hate.

I've been in the darkness Riley strategically placed me in for too long, and it's time for answers. They can't avoid me forever. If Riley doesn't want to talk and Bash is making himself scarce, I will find someone who *will* tell me what is going on.

In the short time I have been here, I noticed Liam spending most of his time in the field where we landed the helicopter. He only makes his way back to camp to switch places with Michael at my tent. Where Michael goes after that, I haven't figured out.

With Michael hot on my heels, I make my way towards the field. Where I knew he would be, Liam has his head inside an open compartment on the outside of the helicopter.

His white shirt is stained with black. You can see each and every drag of his fingers across the fabric. His long blonde hair is under a cap pulled on backward to stay out of his way.

Michael eyes me suspiciously as I walk through the open field to where Liam works. Just the way I planned it. The three of us, here, without the attention of Riley or Bash.

Liam pays no attention to us as we near him. In fact, he is completely oblivious to our presence. I would love to sit here and watch Liam work. He knows exactly what to do with each moving piece of machinery. His back muscles tighten with every turn of a wrench. Liam is someone who is good at their craft. That alone is attractive in a person. My craft is dancing. I don't think it is of much help out here, though.

Michael doesn't let us go unnoticed for long because he clears his throat, which has Liam's shoulders straightening. Liam grumbles something to himself before: "I told you I need to concentrate on this if we—" Liam stops when he turns and sees who is accompanying his friend.

I latch my hands behind my back because I don't trust myself not to touch as I peek around Liam's shoulder to see what he is working on. I can't make heads or tails of it, but it's fascinating all the same.

"If we what?" I ask Liam as I peer up at him from his shoulder. He smells like whatever black liquid coats his hands and shirt—oil.

Liam peers down at me and narrows his eyes suspiciously before twisting his head to Michael for answers. I also look over, only to see Michael with his usual piercing stare and his arms crossed over his chest. Those are not normal blue eyes—not like mine or Jez's. No, they are deadly, predator eyes, watching our every move. "What is she doing here?" Liam asks Michael.

Michael shrugs. "Beats me." he dismisses the question. Michael looks past us to the open, empty field, pretending he isn't paying attention anymore.

Liam wipes his hands on a red rag slung over his shoulder before giving his full attention to me. Brown, knowing eyes. "Ask what you want to ask," he says impatiently, his face serious.

My brows shoot up before I can stop them. "Can't I just see what my favorite pilot is up to?" I blink up at him, trying to get the line of his lips to curve. It doesn't.

"No," Liam says flatly, uninterested. Michael huffs a laugh at our interaction. "Now, what do you want?" He pauses and looks back at the helicopter. "I need to get back to work."

I crossed my arms in defeat. Liam didn't even budge. I see. Once he has his mind set on something, that's the way it is. "One of you is going to tell me what that meeting was about," I looked between the two men. Michael wears a curious half-grin. I have a sneaking suspicion he knows all too well what I am up to.

Of course, I am unsure if they had a secret meeting, but I get my answer when Liam makes eye contact with Michael. So it's true. "Come on," I say seriously. "Something is going on you aren't telling me about."

Liam makes sure not to give anything away while I search those kind eyes. "There is always something going on you don't know about, Emerson." Michael cuts in. "Now, let's go before Bronze takes apart the whole camp looking for you."

Liam grabs a wrench and tries to get back to work. I shake my head at them. It's time to switch my tactic. "Bash told me you all know everything about me," I tell them, making my voice soft, just like I used to do at the club for private dances. It makes them feel more inclined to give me what I want. Then, it was money. Now, it's information.

Michael looks like he already knows, probably because he was listening outside the tent when Bash told me he loved me. My face flushes as I remember his words. *We all do, in our own way.* "Don't I get to know anything about you two?" I ask.

"Jesus, just tell her, Liam." Michael spits.

Liam laughs. A dimple appears on his cheek. I smile up at him for a moment, pleased *someone* got him to break.

Then, he turns to me again with a straight face like that smile never happened. "I'm not telling her shit." he looks at me but talks to Michael. As he stares me down, a smug look takes over his face. It tells me I lost, my plan failed. That is not true, though. I got information, just not all of it.

I roll my eyes in frustration. My feet are moving before I can think. I see Michael give Liam one more pleading look. Michael might be on my side on this one. Even if he is, these men mean more to him than I ever will. That is plain to see. His loyalty trumps my peskiness.

I do get one thing from Michael before I enter my tent again in a huff, and he takes his spot outside. "Bronze will tell you, Emerson. Once we figure out all the details, he will tell you. I will make him," he promises. I touch Michael's arm and nod my head in a silent thank you.

*Good dog,* I think to myself.

# CHAPTER 34

Riley

"Tell me something good," I ask Bash. I let him in on our game, mine and Emerson D. Knight's. Her name appears behind my eyelids when I close them. Bash has never met Emerson, but he knows her well. One day, they will meet. When we get out of here. When we save her.

Regret eats me alive. It's all I think about down here. I should have figured out a way to get to her. I should have taken her out of there when I had the chance.

Not just her, Liam, Bash. They are only here because of me, because of Corey. Thankfully, Michael and Daniel weren't with us on this mission. How Corey figured out where we would be is beyond me. Father always knew things he shouldn't, as well.

Bash's movement echoes off the walls of his cell. They keep me separated from Liam and Bash. I thought those men were going to kill me. Corey must have given them different instructions. He never seemed the torture type. I guess I was wrong. Whatever, it just gives me one more reason to kill him.

Bash's answer comes moments later. "I found it." he rasps.

We have been taking turns getting punished for stealing. It's just a distraction, though. Shove whatever is near you in your pocket for them to find so it doesn't look suspicious when we find what we are *really* after.

"That *is* something good," I reply.

"I can't believe it." Em huffs. Michael knew what we all did. And he is right, as he often is.

I need to do it right this time. Tell her goodbye.

Her brown hair still catches me off guard. With white growing out of her head the way it should be. Em crosses her arms before she turns to the lake. Daniel told me she would be here. That she has been here every night since they brought her to me.

Praying—for Jez, for me. For Bash. I push down jealousy. I left her. I do not get the right to be jealous. I knew when I left that the possibility of her finding someone else was high. Little did I know it was going to be *him*. Stone, Bash, my brother. More of a brother than Corey ever was to me.

When I don't answer, she throws her hands into her hair. She does that when she is angry. "You are leaving me," she pauses, but I know there is more. "Again," this time, her voice trails off. This isn't just anger. This is much more than that.

"This isn't the same as last time." I watch as she rolls those big blue eyes. I love when she does that. It's part of the reason I tease her. So I can see *that*. Emerson clocks the half-grin I accidentally let onto my face. I continue, "Our people. They will not survive without the help of Navar." I explain to her. It's about time I did it, too, because she deserves to know. She deserves the world. I could give it to her if she would let me.

"What do you have to do?" She practically begs. I know I wasn't always so willing to tell her what was really going on in the past. So when she asks me something like she just did, with broken promises in her voice, my stomach twists with regret. I should never have done that to her.

I step towards her. To my surprise, she doesn't try to get away from me in the same way she has these last few days. "They hired us to find something in exchange for the weapons that helped us take out Palen," I tell her. I watch her nod her head up and down. She bites her bottom lip to stop herself from speaking. She wants me to tell her more. So I do. "They originally thought it was in Jericho. We searched everywhere." I sigh because what I am going to tell her next is going to break her heart.

She waits patiently. "One of my informants told me there was a man there who knew where it was." Her eyes go wide, the way I knew they would. "Liam sabotaged the plane to get to him," I admit.

"Ben." She breaks her silence. I nod my head. Bash told me about the men in the plane. About how one of them had their head blown off with a .38 special. My revolver. The one I gave Emerson for her sixteenth birthday. The man was Adam. A rogue that we would often pay for intel. He knew all, saw all. Like a hawk. Em's voice dissolves the image of Adam from my head. "Jez was an informant as well." It's not a question because she already knows. Still, I nod my head.

Then, she must be deep in thought because she doesn't speak for a long time. I don't say anything either as I let her process. "But the safe house got blown up," she tells me. I nod again. "That was you?" She asks, another question she already knows the answer to.

I am quick to defend myself. However, nothing I can say could ever make up for what I did. "I didn't know. Bash was supposed to be in Jericho, I thought I was helping him. Getting rid of the exits so no one could escape with what he was after." I shake my head at the thought that someone might use Emerson to get to me. "Our men had been removed from the wall. Replaced with guards in the Palen Army. So he had to circle back. He knew the deal. He had a week. He knew on the third day it would be destroyed." I tell her. Em's cheeks turn a bright red. Something happened at the wall, with Bash. I just can't figure out what. Bash didn't say anything, and I can't ask Em. Whatever it was, it was enough to have her in a panic right in front of me. Fuck, I messed up so bad.

"I thought for sure that Corey-" I stop myself from continuing. It won't do her any good now to know what Corey had in store for her if she doesn't already. "I went to him, and he told me you had been sold. I already thought you to be dead. When Corey told me you had gotten on a plane using a fake name, I knew what I had done. So I started with Harmony, and the rest followed." I didnt just think her to be dead, I thought *I* had been the one to kill her.

I watch her reaction—or lack thereof. "It wasn't until Jez sent up that signal that I realized what a huge mistake I had made. Realized you were alive. That Bash had succeeded."

Em places her hands on her hips. "When do you leave?" She asks. She has no other questions? That's it?

Em is not the same girl I knew in Harmony. She knows what she wants and how to get it, too. "As soon as Liam says we are in the clear. He used words I didn't even know existed. Something about air tracking." I tell her.

"We?" She then asks.

I force myself not to react. What Em means to ask is if Bash is going. "Bash is my best medic. I need him with us. Liam pilots the helicopter. Michael won't stay here even if I ask him to, not again. And I—" I run my hands through my hair. "I got them into this mess. I have to get them out."

Em pushes her bottom lip out in that pout I hate. The one I get rid of every chance I get. My finger twitches as I do everything possible to stop myself from doing just that. She looks up, and I so badly want to grab onto her and never let go—the way I did before I ruined everything. "Tell me something good," Em says. My relief is immediate. I hadn't realized my brows were pushed together until they unfurl. Or that my hands are in fists until I release them.

This time, I can't help myself. I close the distance between us with one more step. I pause, waiting for her to move, to do anything. She does nothing as I wrap my hand around the back of her neck and pull her into me. "You, it's always you," I whisper into her mouth.

# CHAPTER 35

Six. We all sit around a table in one of the larger tents—the same tent they used to have these meetings without me only days ago. This time, that isn't the case. Riley promised to include me in all further decisions. There were no complaints from the guys. Michael even patted me on the shoulder on the way in. His way of welcoming me. I have a feeling it was his idea.

While everyone seems to be in agreement about my presence, there is someone in this room with anger pouring out of every crevice. Daniel and I will stay here while they go on their mission, but he isn't happy about it. Apparent by his dagger-like stare across the way at his brother, then to Riley.

Bash avoids all of us as best as he can. His face is straight, his shoulders back as he leans into the chair beneath him.

I try not to watch Riley as he speaks. If I look at him for too long, my mind will go back to this morning when he found me at the lake to tell me they were leaving. Even now, my face warms.

Only for a second before I catch Bash peeking at me from the corner of his eyes, and guilt takes over. I swiftly avert my eyes, focusing on a knot in the wooden table.

"Emerson will be in charge of whoever comes from the west camp. Give them jobs. Navar has promised more supplies, but only for a limited time." My head remains down as I peer at Riley from beneath my lashes. His face says everything I need to know. Navar has only promised us resources until he presents them with the Ark of the Covenant.

If they fail, we have nothing. We will die out here.

I can see the severity of his decisions and how hard they are for him to make. But he is a leader, always has been. When it comes to making hard decisions, he will always do it because if he does not, then who will? Who will care? Palen certainly did not care, not for its people.

Riley continues when I nod my head in agreement. "Daniel knows the ins and outs of the camp. He is also our sole connection to Navar, as he is the only one who speaks their language. They will give him information and supplies. They trust him." Riley looks to Daniel for the same assurance that I gave him. Daniel sighs as he crosses his arms. He is not happy about any of this.

Finally, after a long silence, Michael is the one to speak up. "Someone has to stay here, Daniel. You know that."

Daniel side-eyes Michael but immediately returns his attention to Riley. "You can't be serious. After what happened last time? What if this time it's worse? What if I can't get to you this time, huh? What then?" Daniel finally lets his anger get the best of him. "How many times, Riley? How many times are you going to risk the life of my brother?" Daniel dares a brief glance at Bash. Bash's jaw is set, but he is unbothered. He doesn't say a word.

Bash mentioned something terrible had happened. I haven't asked what. I'm not sure I would get any answers even if I did. It's none of my business anyway. Whatever it was has made Bash loyal to Riley in a way I cannot explain. Liam and Michael are the same way.

Guilt takes over Riley's features. I have seen it there before many times, but it's gone in less than a second, replaced with practiced poise. "What would you rather have us do?" Riley replies calmly. I was wrong about him before. He *has* changed. This isn't the same Riley.

Daniel shakes his head. "We should reach out to other nations. Even if Navar helps us, they are fighting a losing battle. You can't put us in the middle of that. We could lose everything." Daniel's voice breaks at the end. My heart hurts for him.

"Losing or not, it's the right side." Michael cuts in. Everyone's attention goes to him. Bash pushes back in the chair until it balances on its back legs. He is sitting right beside Michael, making it hard not to look at him. Michael takes a moment to gather his words. "They might be blinded by The Ark, but they are only after it so it doesn't fall into the wrong hands," Michael tells us. He is as serious as a heart attack. He knows something I do not. The tattoo on his cheek might have something to do with it. A branding, from where I do not know.

Actually, everyone seems to know exactly how he would have such information besides me.

Michael's blue eyes shift to mine. I must have let the curiosity show on my face because he gives me a look that tells me he will tell me about it later. For now, he continues. "If there is even a small chance we can find it, we should. Not just for our people. For the world." Riley nods his head and scans the rest of us to make sure we are in agreeance, even me.

No one speaks for what feels like a long time. "Liam, we leave at your command." Riley ends the meeting.

Bash is quick to leave. He doesn't even glance behind him as he goes. Daniel tries to get Riley's attention. There is still that air of anger around him. I get it. They are leaving us. It's not the first time for Daniel, either. Riley's eyes are on mine instantly. Without thought, I look at the empty space where Bash had been just seconds before.

I'm suddenly torn between chasing after Bash, who strangely had nothing to say before disappearing as quickly as possible and staying with Riley to find out more about my part in it all. When Riley sees the indecision on my face, he turns away from Daniel. His shoulders fall in disappointment, but an understanding falls between us. Then, he gives me a nod—one that tells me to go after Bash. So I do.

When we entered the tent, the sun was falling. Now, it's completely dark outside. The only light is from small solar-powered string lights that make the camp look like twinkling stars resting just above us. That doesn't mean they light up the entire space. This makes it hard to find where Bash could have gone.

I check the now empty Kitchen and The Bathhouse. I made sure when I arrived, I knew which tent was his. That was empty as well. How could someone possibly just disappear? Unless they do not want to be found.

So much time has passed. There is no doubt in my mind, I am being avoided. I give up. I would not want to be around someone who ran after what was probably a difficult admission. I wasn't ready, I still am not. If I open myself to the possibility of loving someone, I will end up hurt when they leave, just as I was when Riley left.

The only person who I have no doubts I loved wholeheartedly is my sister, Jez, and her absence has my heart in pieces. I can't let history repeat itself, or I might not be able to put my heart back together again.

Riley must have told the guys not to trail me because, by the time I make it back to the row where I can see my tent at the end, there isn't a soul stationed outside my door.

The camp has gone quiet. The lights have even started to dim as they run out of their battery charged by the sun.

Bash wins. He did not want to be found.

I near my tent, exhausted and disappointed. With each step closer, I think of how little time I have with Bash and Riley. I could lose the last two people who mean anything to me in one fell swoop. The start of tears stings at my eyes. All day, I kept it in. I didn't let anyone see my fear or anger or heartache. I have lost so much already, and now I have to be prepared to lose it *all*.

My head spins. Between what Riley and I shared this morning and their plan to leave, which has my heart in knots about Bash, I just don't know what to think or feel. How could my entire being possibly be split perfectly in two? *Sleep on it.* Jez would tell me. By morning, everything will be clear.

That is what I planned to do until a figure came out of the darkness.

A hand grips tightly at my wrist as it pulls me away from the safety of the camp's light. At first, I fight it, pulling away and grasping at the hand that holds me. I nearly scream, a hand falls over my mouth, making it impossible.

Sweet tobacco fills my senses. Bash's words are low and in my ear in an instant. "Come on, Sweetheart, I'm not going to hurt you," he tells me. My heart settles as I turn to him. A wicked smile takes over his face as he looks down at me. My eyelids flutter as I focus on his face, at his green eyes barely visible in the dark.

It's so easy to get lost in those eyes, and I do. I forget the world for just a moment—the impending doom, all of it—the cloud that hangs over us like a storm about to drop hail and tornadoes. For just a second, it's just Bash and me. His brows push together, and worry replaces his smile. My head falls forward until I am resting on his chest. I breathe him in and listen to the steady beat of his heart.

Calm, something I only feel around Bash.

# CHAPTER 36

"Let's go." Bash lifts my head with a finger on my chin. This time, it's not to check for injury. He doesn't search my eyes for anything other than *me*.

He pulls me up the hill behind my tent. My favorite view of the lake is right here, where the moon is cast in a perfect reflection on the water. There isn't much moon to see tonight, but it's still beautiful.

Bash doesn't stop, though. The further we get from camp, the darker it gets. He continues around the left side of the lake. There is a sandy shore over there. I know because I have spent many nights walking around the water, mostly with Daniel trailing behind me, sometimes Michael.

Daniel doesn't let me out of his sight when it's his turn to play guard dog. That's probably why Riley has given the task to him more often than not. Riley was always good at finding other's strengths. Daniel's is that he doesn't let others suffer alone. I found out when he prayed for Jez with me that night, right across the bank from where we stand. That is why it is so hard for him to let go. To let his brother leave without knowing what awaits him, without being there.

Bash's footsteps slow. I peer over my shoulder to see how far we have come. Farther than I have ever gone. "Don't you think we are getting too far from camp?" I say to Bash without looking at him.

He chuckles, hardly loud enough for me to hear. "No," he replies matter-of-factly. I know the feeling well. Not wanting to be near the people who will suffer if you do not play your part perfectly. It's too much weight. Out here is where I feel light.

Finally, we stop. There is an unfamiliar sound of wood knocking on wood. It's hard to see in the dark where it comes from. Bash knows precisely where he is going. Like he has practiced the steps many times before.

Bash stops, he pulls his boots and socks off before rolling up his trousers. "What are you doing?" I ask. He does not reply. My eyes adjust enough to see him move for the water. He pulls at a rope attached to a small wooden boat that he pushes until it is right at my feet. That's where the noise was coming from.

My face contorts into a real smile. Bash's white teeth reflect what little light there is. I step into the boat carefully, feeling the back and forth of the water beneath it. "Where are we going?" I ask.

Bash pushes the boat out into the water further before he jumps in as well. I laugh nervously as it rocks back and forth wildly. I grip onto the edges as I sit on a ledge that goes from one end to the other. Bash sits on the opposite side, our knees knock together. I am grateful for the lack of room in this small boat. After so much time spent with Bash before we got here, it has been strange to have him so far away. Even when we are in the same room, it feels like we are miles apart. Sometimes I catch his eyes, but they aren't the same eyes that look at me right now. "You will see," he says mysteriously.

Bash reaches into his front pocket, grabs a cigarette, and holds it between his teeth as he lights it. Then he paddles us further into the center of the lake. I laugh at him as I watch him blow smoke into the air above us.

Above us. My mouth falls open slightly.

Bash's grin tells me the answer of why we are here. "The lights," I say to the sky, a smile takes over my face entirely.

Bash stops his paddling. The world goes silent for a long time as we watch the purple turn to green and then back again. It's magical. It doesn't belong in the same world as Jericho, as the war. Its beauty is too pure.

By the time my eyes fall back to Bash, I realize he hasn't been watching the lights at all. His face is illuminated by the orange glow of a cigarette, his eyes set on me. I laugh again. I can't stop myself. "I could listen to that forever," he tells me. Then he clears his throat as if he misspoke before taking another drag and forcing his eyes to the sky.

I lean forward. It's my time to stare. There is so much to see as he leans back onto his elbows. The roses that wrap around his arms—the goosebumps that have accumulated there, even though it's not cold.

Every move is deliberate and practiced. I saw it before in Jericho. How he walked and postured himself. It's the same as I did at the club. It's a defense mechanism—something learned from mistakes. If I strayed from the exactness of my plan, then things would go wrong.

Each step of my dance was perfectly tuned to who was in front of me. I had it down to a science. Every drink, every fake smile, and bat of my lashes. Every hand that touched me was placed right where I wanted it. It was necessary but draining. Each man took a piece of me. I suddenly became desensitized to it all—so much so I had forgotten what it felt like to be wanted for more than what was on the outside.

"You are supposed to be watching the lights." Bash's words knock me from thought.

"I prefer this view," I say as I grab the dwindling cigarette from between his fingers, ignoring the butterflies as my hand skims his. "I'll have to memorize it," I tell him, pointing to my temple.

"Then I should get a good look as well." Bash goes still, all but his emerald irises that start at my brows and slowly, too slowly go down my body. He stops at my middle for a second too long before moving on. My breath hitches as his features go from light to dark. His jaw tightens, then his fingers curl in on themselves as he makes his way back up to my face. A sound so raw leaves his body, the hair on the back of my neck stands on end.

I would give anything to know what he is thinking right now, what has him in such a state. "You know so much about me." I finally take a full breath. "When do I get to know about you?"

Bash flashes those emeralds at me, and he lets out a breath as well, one I hadn't realized he was holding. "You know more about me than most." He shrugs.

I shake my head. " It's hardly fair," I half-whisper. "I bet you know my favorite color, and I don't even know your middle name." I look up at the sky again, catching it change colors again.

"Blue," he says smugly. My favorite color. Then he pauses as he leans forward. So close I could reach out and touch his face. "And I don't have one." He gives me an answer to a question I didn't even mean to ask.

My head falls to the side, "You don't have a middle name?" I ask.

Bash places his elbows on his knees. That darkness that took over him just moments ago, the kind that has me warm under his gaze, is back. "Mother never gave me one. Daniel, either." He leans onto a fist. So close.

Too close. I watch him carefully, and he watches me right back. His shirt pocket falls open with the weight of the pack of cigarettes. The one in my hand is getting near its end so I discard it before grabbing the pack. Any reason to touch Bash again, if I am being honest with myself. I reach in again for the matches.

Bash keeps me under his gaze the entire time. He blinks slowly as I illuminate the space between us with a strike of the match. Our eyes meet. When Bash licks his lips, a fire starts in my chest and travels down to my center.

I try to think of *anything* else. When I come up short, Bash offers me more. "Ada and Esther came up with their own." He lets the corner of his mouth curl.

Riley had pointed out two young black-haired girls who often looked like they were getting into trouble. Before he even told me they were Bash's sisters, I could tell, especially from the way they hang all over Daniel. They all have the same eyes. "Your sisters," I said, mostly because I don't have any other words.

Bash nods his head. "Don't ask me what those names are. Daniel would know." His face falls. I don't like that face—the one I saw at the safe house, the one I saw when we arrived—defeat.

Now I am putting the pieces together. "They are who you went back for," I say out loud.

Bash closes his eyes for a second too long. "The first time," he nods only once. "Then for Daniel." His brows push together. "The third time-" He pauses as if to gather strength for his next words. "I went for me. To take back what was stolen from me. From all of us." I can tell Bash is forcing his eyes to keep mine, but they don't latch onto anything. It's as if he is looking past me. I don't say a word. "I burnt it all to the ground.

My sisters loved the paintings, so I kept those—in a way." He finally lets his head hang. He looks down at my boots. His shoulders relax.

I give him all I have for his sorrows, which is the cigarette that burns in my hand. He peers up at me through his eyelashes and huffs a laugh. Then he takes it between his pointer and thumb and inhales its contents.

I offer him a smile next, the same as he often did for me when I needed it most.

He does not return the gesture.

Suddenly, the orange glow of his cigarette, the last remaining light between us, falls into the water. I follow it down, surprised by the act. When my attention returns to Bash, I can't help but tilt my head, wondering why he would do such a thing.

I get my answer when his hands are on my thighs, gripping at the material. "It is a different kind of healing I need," His voice is low and dangerous.

Then, the weight of him rocks the boat so much I think we might spill over as he falls to his knees. Bash settles between my legs, and his middle presses up against the inside of my thighs. I slide forward so that as much of him can touch as much of me as possible. "Let me have you." He lays a gentle kiss along my collarbone. "To see if it cures me." He whispers into my neck.

I need more of him, as much of him as I can get before I have nothing at all. He needs it too, I know it, I can feel it. Bash catches my chin with his finger as he searches for an answer. I don't give one, but he sees it on my face, in my fingers that now glide along the bottom of his jaw. He hears it in the moans that escaped when his flesh met mine.

Bash applies pressure to the bottom of my chin until I am no longer looking at him. Instead, I am looking at a dark sea in the sky. Threads of pink and violet and green dance above us. "Beautiful in every color," Bash pushes my hair so it falls to the middle of my back. I feel every movement as his fingers trace the curve of my waist, over my hips, the length of my thighs. Every caress is a promise for more. I suck in a breath as he finds my center.

Then, the touch is gone.

There is that wooden scrape against wood again, and when my head falls, we are at a dock. It must be on the other side of the lake because I have never seen this landscape before.

Bash carefully steps out of the boat and onto the dock before offering me his hand. Which I gladly take. My eyes do not adjust quickly to the dark as I try to find his face, his eyes. When I find them, I begin my search, to see if what I saw before still remains. My heart hammers against its cage, which Bash can most likely feel now that our bodies are pressed against each other. "Have you found what you are looking for?" Bash asks.

I blink up at him in surprise. "Yes," is all I say before Bash lifts me effortlessly, carrying me to the edge of the dock where the grass meets wood. He lays me down gently. The cool ground is welcoming—a nice contrast to the fire that has spread to the entirety of my body. Bash hovers over me. Is this the picture he has promised to memorize?

When he finally moves, his hands work quickly. He strips away the barriers between us, until there is nothing left but skin against skin, heart against heart.

I arch into him reflexively, like I can't help myself because I cannot. "Bash," it comes in a plea. He responds with a knowing growl. It feels like we have waited far too long for this.

The world narrows to this moment, this connection, the rhythm of our bodies moving as one. Bash's mouth moves along my jaw softly. He whispers something I can not hear because of a pounding in my ears. Then he fills me completely in one hard thrust of his hips. My lips part, and my back arches further. *More,* is all I can think. I hadn't realized what was missing until this moment.

We become lost in each other. This is the image of Bash that I will keep. The one of him bare yet completely covered in black ink. He looks like a mosaic, with all the colors behind him. Perfection.

Bash's pace quickens, his control slipping as he nears the edge. I cling to him, my nails digging into his back, my own release building like a storm. When it comes, it's unending, like a damn breaking. Flooding its surroundings.

When we collapse together, our bodies entwined, the world slowly comes back into focus. The lights still dance above us. Bash holds me close, his breath evening out, his heart still racing against mine.

I run a finger down his chest, over the heart of ink. Four swords, I count. Then I lay my head upon it. "Have I cured you, Sebastian?" I ask Bash, his heart beating loudly in my ear.

His chest rises and falls. "If you have, every man in all of Middle World will want the antidote." Bash's fingers tangle with my hair. His other hand pushes my chin up until I am looking at him. What I see when our eyes meet is nothing but need, desire. The same that I feel. I straddle his body, pushing my hair to my back. His hands instinctively grasp my hips.

It is my turn to find a cure in Sebastian Stone.

# CHAPTER 37

Michael

I don't speak the language. I don't know what they say before they spit between the bars of my cell. Prisoners of War. Our country does not care how many are tortured or kept. They want one thing and one thing only—the Ark of the Covenant.

It started as a rumor, what it held, how much it was worth. All of it was wrong. It held no treasure.

Which somehow made it more valuable to Canaan, my birthplace. Where my mother raised my brothers and I. Where I saw my father turn into the same dark entity as his father and his father before him.

When word quickly spread that The Ark brought darkness and plague wherever it was kept, they sent their most expendable soldiers after it. Death followed us wherever we went. If it wasn't just leprosy or plague, it was a different kind of illness it brought. The kind that turns men into monsters.

It holds pure evil. Canaan knew. Jericho knew.

I want nothing to do with it ever again.

I had heard about prisoners being bought. Whether it be labor or something else they buy us for. So, when a man who went by Bronze had an interest in me, I made it clear I would not be a good purchase. I started fights, got myself a reputation for being insubordinate, did anything to make me unwanted.

Still, he showed up every third Saturday to visit. He spoke of a new way of living, of a new life that I could help him build. I wouldn't hear it.

There is no life outside of this, not one I want to live anyway. There can't be, not for me. I won't be another slave. Not to my family, not to the Army. Now I am in prison, and I know which one is worse, which one I deserve.

Soon, I realized our meetings were a nice break from the monotony of prison life. A room with just Bronze and me, where I didn't have to look over my shoulder every second. He spoke in my language. I didn't speak back.

Persistent. That's what Riley Bronze is.

He told me stories, ones that made life more tolerable. They were often about a girl. I didn't know her name. Bronze wouldn't tell me. He described her, though. She had long blonde hair, often in a perfect braid. Her blue eyes were much lighter than mine, so much so that he often referred to them as ice.

After months of our visits and of his stories, I would see her in my dreams. Standing over my child body with tears in her eyes. Or smiling through the bars of my cell.

I found myself looking forward to his visits. To hear more about her. Whatever stops the nightmares, I told myself.

Finally, when he asked me if I would assist him in his plan, I agreed.

The guards wake us at dawn with a clanging bell. The harsh sound leaves our ears ringing as it bounces off the cold stone walls.

We are herded like cattle to a cramped courtyard for breakfast —a watery substance that barely sustains us. I eat in silence, surrounded by other silenced men. Whether it be their tongues were cut out, or they have nothing to say.

Work follows breakfast. We are assigned various tasks, from breaking rocks to digging ditches, laboring under the eyes of the guards who seemed to get off on our misery. I don't mind this part. My concentration on the task makes those pesky thoughts go away.

I knew my target. Who I was supposed to get close to for Bronze.

Berkley, the man who knows a way into Jericho.

So I followed him every waking hour, noting his every move. He walked differently than the others, with more confidence, like he owned the place, because he does. Every guard is wrapped around his finger, and every person in his block gives him extra food for his fat belly.

Canaan had tried for years to get into Jericho and failed. This man just walked in? If Bronze is right, then he knows more than just prisoners and guards.

When getting close to him became more difficult than I thought. When men would meet me in my cell and beat the shit out of me. When my meals went missing for a week, I met with Bronze with the intention of telling him I was out. "Why me?" I asked Bronze. "Why not just pretend you want to buy him instead, not me?"

Bronze's expression is unreadable. "Because Berkley is smart. He knows the game, knows how to manipulate people. If I approached him directly, he'd see right through it. But you, you're different. You've been here, you've suffered. He won't suspect you. Earn his trust. Find out who his contact is and how they get into Jericho. We need that information, Michael. Without it, we're stuck."

"Who is we?" I ask.

Bronze leans forward onto his elbows. He does that sometimes when what he is about to say next is no joking matter. "I have someone who is in desperate need of redemption."

I shake my head at him. "When do you get *your* redemption?" I remember every word out of his mouth about her. Bronze told me his girl would never forgive him for what he did to her, that he would save her, that *all* of it was for her. Will it all be worth it in the end if she still hates him?

Riley visibly considers this. "It just so happens getting into Jericho has multiple benefits. Because after he does what he needs to do, after he gets his people out. We are taking down the entire city."

The city that holds The Ark. Using it to do unspeakable things to people. "I want in," I say without thought. It's decided. Because of her, because of Bronze. I don't want to live this life anymore.

Riley grins, "You're already in, Michael." Bronze sets his brown eyes on mine. "There is just one more thing."

I keep his attention, my shoulders fall. I know what he is about to say. "There is nothing you could ask of me that I have not already done," I admit. I am ready to do what it takes. I have hope now.

"Good, because this can't be traced back to us." I knew what it meant. I was going to get the information and *kill* Berkley.

There will be consequences. No one kills in this prison and gets away with it. The guards do nothing, but the inmates have taken to branding those who have wronged one of their own, but this task ends with more than just a tattoo on my cheek.

273

I learned her name, Emerson Knight. I couldn't get it out of my head. Then, I saw her. It took too long. Longer than I wanted it to. Emerson, *the* Emerson was right in front of me. I looked at Bash, only to see something there that we all felt but were too smart to admit. Love.

# CHAPTER 38

It's happening all over again. I am being left behind.

Liam has given them the okay, and soon, all four of them will be on their way to Canaan—Michael's birthplace. The only place Michael thinks would house The Ark of the Covenant. They had tried it once before.

Michael 's unit in the Canaan Army was attacked. There were many people after The Ark during it's short time away from Jericho. He just happened to be in the midst of it, wrong place, wrong time. All nations collided at once. Jericho got back what they were missing.

Canaan is full of barbarians and savages that live as if morals do not exist, a life I am glad Michael is out of.

He told me all of it, how Riley bought him from the prison. How he saw The Ark and how it affected people. I saw the fear on his face and the tremble in his words when he was trying not to remember the terrible things he saw.

No secrets. That's what Michael said. He doesn't want me thinking their mission will be easy because in truth, it will not be. There is a war going on, a fight for power. It seems as if The Ark plays a role in who wins.

There is nothing I want to do more than to hold on to them, force them to stay. I cannot. If what Michael says is true, they need to go.

Not only will our people die without the help of Navar, but worse things could happen—plague and death.

Navar's tactics might be aggressive, but they are a holy city—one that knows more than they are letting on. They claim to have divine power. A connection to a place beyond this world. "Secrets that go so deep into history they won't see the light of day for another thousand years," Riley tells me as he shuffles playing cards in his hands.

This time, I listen. This time, I won't let Riley's words go in one ear and out the other. Not like when we were young, and his words seemed like the ramblings of a madman.

Liam and Riley sit at the table with cards in front of them as we spend our last few hours together. I lost almost immediately at a game they call Hold 'em. I lean back on the cot in the corner as I think of all those days in the pawnshop with Riley, playing cards. He let me win each and every game. He never would admit to it, but I know it's true now that the blanket of childhood has been lifted.

The last few nights have been nearly sleepless for one reason or another. A mixture of guilt and racing thoughts about what to do about Bash and I fills my head. "Place your bets," Riley says past me to Bash and Michael, who entered the tent quietly. I had been so deep into thought I hadn't noticed. It startles me when Bash breezes past. Sweet tobacco fills my senses. I keep my eyes forward on the cards being flipped down the middle of the table by Liam. Bash has been standoffish the last few days since *that* night.

Bash has made it clear. Riley deserves the truth, but it has to come from me, not him. I haven't found the right moment to tell him, especially with their departure hanging over our heads. Tensions are already high, and I am not going to drop this on an already stressed Riley.

The other side of Riley's anger is something else entirely. I have seen it one too many times. That's not what they need right now.

Again, I am startled when Michael's words force me out of my head. "Liam hasn't lost a game since I have known him," he says, placing his bet.

They all look to Bash, awaiting his bet. "I don't make bets." Bash shrugs. I have to force my eyes forward again, or I will get stuck on those roses that peek out beneath his white shirt around his biceps.

Riley stares Liam down, trying to read his mind as if the cards will show up in those honey eyes. Liam laughs. My mouth falls open slightly. Maybe the first person to stare death in the face and *laugh*. I'm not sure if anything gets under Liam's skin, but so far, it doesn't seem like it. Liam clicks his tongue and shakes his head. "Bronze, all muscles, no brains." He flips his cards face up. This time, I laugh. Loud and out of my control. Then, I watch all four sets of eyes land on mine.

It's easy to feel small with all these men around, but I've been surrounded by men my whole life—the kind that will force you into a box, make you fit into their distorted version of perfection. It's how they see all women. These men are not the same. No, they all have a grin on their faces as they turn back and wait for Riley to flip his cards—cards I know are a losing hand.

The slight widening of his eyes, the clenching of his jaw. I just know. I know *him*. I know his tell. He might be able to hide it well when the stakes are low, but sometimes he slips.

Everyone watches, all but one person. Bash does not care about the game. His emeralds glint as he leans to the side. A sliver of light runs down one side of his face from an opening in the tent. He crosses his arms, and his eyes narrow at the spot between my eyes. Bash has a way of making it seem like it's just the two of us. My whole body warms.

After what feels like a long time under Bash's stare, "Next time, Bronze." Michael slaps Riley on the shoulder—a losing hand, just as I thought. I blink away the feeling of Bash's eyes, returning my attention to the game.

Later, as everyone goes to bed, I walk around the camp. I often do, ending my nights at the lake or on the hill. Jez might not be here, but she walks beside me. There is a part of her that is still around. I feel it in the silence of the night or in the prayers Daniel teaches me.

Daniel has found me many times wherever I end up. In Jericho, Bash and his siblings were forced to learn the sacred prayers. Daniel often describes this as a comfort for him and a punishment for Bash, whatever that means.

Daniel is more intelligent than most. His interest is in languages. From other countries, along with signing with his hands, which I have been learning slowly. His tent, which he shares with his sisters, is filled with books he often lends me to pass the time.

He wanted nothing to do with our last meeting. His mind is set on finding a different way. I watch him now, reading to his sisters, as he does every night. The twins are wild, running around without a care in the world, the way Riley and Bash worked so hard for them to be able to do.

They look so calm when lying there without mischief taking up space on their small faces.

Past that, to my favorite place in the camp, The Bathhouse. To the woman who has no name. It was never given to her because of her disability. I guess they did not deem her worthy. She is more than worthy, more than kind.

The children call her Grams, so the camp has followed. I sign that to her as she sees me. "Grandma, hello." Her wrinkled cheeks lift into a soft smile as she waves back.

Our conversations often last long into the night. Pen and paper for most of them while I learn her language.

We sit with coffee in our hands, Grams reminds me of Jez in more ways than one. She is blunt, she sees all, knows things before you have even said a word. These same qualities in Jez that I took for granted. In fact, they would lead to fights between my sister and me. It took me too long to realize how valuable those moments were.

Grams and I talk about her life and mine, about our shared difficulties in the Outer Ring. Her home was on the other side, a city called Serenity. We both laugh at the names Palen decided to give their cities. She cannot hear it, so she does not know her laugh is long and low—it's the best sound in the world.

Tonight, our talk is brief because something else catches my attention. A hunched over Riley with a needle and thread in his hand. He mends what looks like a stuffed teddy. A child cries from nearby, followed by the soothing words of a mother.

I walk slowly up to him, inspecting his work. It reminds me of when he would be tinkering on a watch or fixing a broken TV at the pawnshop.

"Em," he grunts as he shoves the needle through the torn arm. How he knows it's me behind him is beyond me.

I lean over his shoulder further. "What are we working on tonight?" I ask him just as I would at the pawnshop.

Riley doesn't look up from the task. "There are important things to do before we leave." He says seriously. Riley takes everything seriously. Even something as *unserious* as fixing a teddy. When his large fingers fail him, and the needle falls to the ground, I sink down onto the grass with him and hold out my hand, palm up.

Riley takes the defeat and places the toy in my hand. He finds the needle and hands it over as well before settling beside me. We sit like that in silence as I work.

We have company. The child keeps poking his head out of the tent to see our work. When I am done, the boy with tears down his face takes the completed work from me and wipes his face with the head of the bear. Rather disgusting if you ask me, but Riley has this look on his face. Something I have never seen before. A mix of love and fear. He smiles before patting the boy on his head. The child's mother gathers him and takes him into the tent.

When it goes silent, "What other important things should we do?" I whisper to Riley.

Riley lets his head hang, and his arms rest on his knees lazily. It's finally showing. The toll all of this has taken on him. He looks... tired. I rest my head on his shoulder, feeling him relax beneath me.

"I don't know," Riley murmurs finally. "I feel like I've done all I can. What about you?"

I don't answer right away. The weight of what I have shared with Bash presses down on me. "Riley," I begin, my voice barely a whisper. "There's something I need to tell you."

He shifts slightly, I take my head from his shoulder and turn to look at him. That gold fleck I used to try to find is now staring me in the face. His features soften. Acceptance. He sighs, *he knows*. He has to know. Just as I knew he held a losing hand, he sees the truth on my face.

When he notices what I have discovered, he begins to nod his head. "I...I shouldn't feel this way," my voice trembles. Those are not the words that should have come out.

I want to say more, but my throat is on fire as I hold back tears. "Don't tell me, I couldn't take it." Riley puts his hands through his hair. *Speak.* I shout inside my head. *Just say anything, anything at all.*

Riley speaks instead, "I have loved you since you walked into the pawnshop, hiding behind Jez." He presses his hands together in front of him. *Love,* a word I have only heard within this camp, and not until my arrival here. Not even Jez and I spoke the words outright.

Finally, words spill from somewhere deep inside, "I didn't know." I say, because it's true. *I* loved Riley. Everyone knew. For so long, but that's the way it was, *one-sided.*

"Well, now you do. What will you do with it?" Riley looks over his shoulder at me. He glances from my mouth to my eyes over and over again. My bottom lip juts out, out of my control. Riley's thumb meets my mouth before I can stop him. It lingers there as I think of an answer to his question. I come up with...nothing. Actually, my mind is blank. How could I possibly think about anything else with his hand on me, the way I always wanted him to be—*near.*

I close my eyes, hoping it will clear my mind. It does not work. "Love me, Emerson." Riley pleads. My heartbeat jumps into my throat. It's so loud in my ears. I squeeze my eyes tighter still. There is nothing I can say to convince myself that what I am feeling is not there. The facts. It's what I feel for him, what I feel for Bash. I open my eyes at the realization, only to be met with those all-knowing eyes. A tear falls onto the hand that remains against my cheek. "You can't." Riley shakes his head. "You can't have us both." Riley's voice is low. We are so close his breath pushes a strand of hair from my face.

I want both. I want the calm that comes from Bash and the confidence that Riley gives me.

"Come with me." Riley lifts us both up. I don't fight it. I go with him. It's better than sitting here without any words, not ones that would help anyway.

We make our down a row of tents. Until we end up right outside of Riley's. I stop.

"Come on, Em. I won't bite." He holds the tent open for me to enter. When I don't move, he tries again. "I have a gift for you. I was going to give it to you tomorrow, but I think now is the right time. Since I am trying to convince you I am in love with you and all." His jaw clenches. I cock my head at him. He sighs. "I just want you to have all the facts before you choose." Riley concedes.

This time, I am teasing him when I don't move my feet, just to see what he will say if I remain. His arm is still outstretched as he holds the fabric in his hand so tightly his knuckles turn white. "Goddamit, Emerson, you're embarrassing me," he says through his teeth. I smile wide before ducking under his arm.

I have made it a point never to enter Riley's tent. I knew if I smelled the scent often left on my sheets in Harmony, I would forgive him for everything. Just to lay down and be surrounded by him.

Thankfully, I have already forgiven him. It started after I found the photo Bash had dropped. He said he would find me in Jericho, and he did. Now, everything I tried so hard to keep buried under a layer of ice, is melting away.

The turn of an old wooden knob, the static before music plays. My mouth falls open slightly. *My* radio. He saved it from Harmony. Where I was supposed to be. I snap my mouth shut. Fuck, I messed up so colossally. He came back for me, and I was *gone*.

Memories of Jez and I dancing in the kitchen flash behind my eyes as I listen to the song on the radio. Riley staring at us from the broken couch with this stupid grin on his face. *Love.*

I am, was, forever will be in love with Riley Bronze.

# Chapter 39

Riley's voice is low, as is the song, so we don't wake his neighbors. "I had Liam fix it for you," he shrugs. This is a side of Riley I have only seen once before, after his father's death. Vulnerability.

He is always so good at keeping a dangerous aura, the one he needs to be a leader, to have people follow him, listen to him. They know as well as I do what makes him great is that he shows no fear.

I stare and stare at the radio. I know it's mine, but it looks completely different. It's perfectly polished. There is new brass around the speakers, and the hand on the front moves when Riley spins the knob. Liam must have spent hours on it. It looks brand new, as new as a hundred-year-old radio can get.

I think Riley is talking, but I am busy thinking about all the times I missed it. Riley's love. Every wish since I met him, every birthday candle, every star, was for this.

So why does it feel... wrong? To have what I have always wanted? The answer is so simple, yet complicated in every way.

The song switches, just as I knew it would. We are picking up the only station left in Middle World. The same predictable loop I listened to over and over again. It's slow, Wine and Dandelions. At least that's what I call this one. Riley turns it up just enough for the two of us.

He steps forward, I step back with the slight shake of my head. If he gets too close I will never let him leave. Not tonight, not ever.

He takes another step.

This time, I have nowhere to go. Riley has a smug, satisfied look on his face. I can't help but feel as though I have fallen right into his trap. "Come on, I learned just for you." He stares down at me as his right-hand goes to my waist, a feeling that has my heart thumping.

"You did?" I look up at him finally, and all my fears are gone. The what-ifs vanish. Riley grabs my other hand and holds it inside his own at our side. Jez taught me the steps. Of course, it was just us, no male counterparts to lead. We took turns, learning both sides. One of my favorite memories of her.

Riley takes a step back. I take a step forward in the space he made. "All those trips to Jericho, did you get to talk to her?" I ask, and for some reason, my chest feels tight, like talking about her will make her death all too real. It's not like talking to Daniel about the prayers for her afterlife. This is her *being*, the person who still exists inside my head. Not dead at all, not to me.

We take another timed step, "Yes. Many times." He sighs.

My eyes start to well with tears. They have been uncontrollable lately whenever I think of her. Riley peers down his nose at me. He is deadly serious, the way he always is. "She wrote you every day." He tells me.

"I know. I got the letters." My brows push together. "All at once, actually. It's strange." I say as I think of Jez's perfect script, her name with a heart to dot the *I* in Knight.

Riley nods his head. There is something else there on his face, more to the story I have not been told. "What is it?" I ask, but as the words come out, I understand. "It was you, wasn't it? *You* sent me her letters." It's not a question.

Riley searches my eyes as he finds the right words. "I just wanted you to know she was there, that she was alive, that she cared. That—" he pauses. "She didn't abandon you." Riley shakes his head. *Abandon,* that's what *he* thinks he did. "I didn't think you were going to—" he clears his throat. Regret floods his features.

We stop just long enough for me to catch that golden fleck in the small amount of light in the tent. "Thank you," I tell him as a tear falls to my shirt. Just as he has done a million times before, he dries my tears with the back of his hand. I get lost in the touch as I stare into those familiar eyes.

The corners of Riley's mouth curl into a small smile. "I see it," he whispers. I lean my head back to peer up at him. I hadn't noticed how close our bodies are now and how slow our dance has become. "See what?" I ask, confused.

"Your soul." His words come out softly, and his brows push together as if he is surprised I would not know. Another tear falls, but a smile takes over my face. He really did speak to Jez and learn her tricks. Now, we have stopped our dance altogether.

Is *Riley* my last remaining connection to my sister?

My body acts on its own. I lean up until our faces are nearly touching. I close my eyes tightly. "Love me, Riley." I plead with him the way he did to me.

His breath catches. "Easy," he tells me. It's as simple as that for Riley. For a moment, there is only the sound of our breathing. Then his lips brush mine, feather-light, testing, tasting. I respond instinctively, my hands sliding up his chest to clasp behind his neck, drawing him closer.

A noise, deep and masculine, leaves Riley's body before he drops to his knees in front of me, his eyes never leaving mine. His hands travel down my sides, fingers tracing the curves. I can feel the heat of his breath against my skin as he presses a kiss to my stomach, then another lower. His hands fall to the drawstring of my pants. He pulls each one slowly. "I dreamt of you," each word sends heat to my middle. "That night, I climbed through your window," he kisses me again, getting closer and closer to the wet heat he has created so easily with the lay of his hands and the tickle of his breath.

I bend towards him. *Touch me more. Love me more.* I want to say. It's killing me. "It wasn't the first time," he admits, but I'm so lost in his touch it hardly registers.

He speaks again, but it's covered by whatever noise leaves my body when his fingers grip the flesh around my sides. He pulls me to him. I fall, my legs spread so he rests firmly beneath me. Wait, what did he say? "Not the first time," I repeat the last thing I remember. "What?" I breathe, I can't think, I can't do *anything* but push myself desperately further into him.

He kisses my neck, and soon his words are in my ear. "I watched you." his breath catches as his hand snakes down the front of my panties. Riley parts me with a single finger, then two. "Did you see *my* face, feel *my* fingers inside of you when you would touch yourself?" On his last word, he enters me. His large fingers fill me completely.

My eyes roll to the back of my head at the feeling. "Yes," I swallow after my confession. It's true. I saw only him, called his name, wished for it to be him, and now it is.

"Say it again." Riley moves inside of me again, sending waves of pleasure through my body.

"Yes," I say more clearly, understanding his need for consent. I laugh to myself. *Consent,* that's funny, for someone who watched me touch myself through my window. It doesn't bother me at all. I would gladly let him watch again.

My word sparks something inside him because he removes his hand and lifts us onto the bed. There is something urgent about our movement.

Our last night together, *again.* Just as it was before, but now I know. I know he is leaving, and I can give him all of me before he does. Just like this, with our skin pressed up against each other. It could be all we have. If what Michael says is true, this mission could claim their lives. My head spins. Bash, Riley, along with Jez, dead. Do the people I love always have to die? "Don't," Riley pulls my lip into his mouth for a moment before releasing me and pulling away so I can see the seriousness on his face. "We will find our way back to you. How could we ever not."

# Chapter 40

Riley's arm finally releases me as he sleeps. His chest moves in rhythmic ins and outs. After what was the perfect night, the night I dreamt of for years. Finally, the face I would pretend was on every man I ever danced for is lying right beside me.

But that feeling is back, the inevitable weight of the decision I *have* to make but is *impossible* to. My heart aches for more reasons than one. Guilt is swallowing me whole. I could not save Jez, and now I will be losing the people I love most. Not to mention the strings of emotions I am pulling on.

My breathing speeds up, along with my heart rate. It's like I'm underwater—pressure where it's not supposed to be. I quickly throw the covers off of myself to alleviate some of the panic. It doesn't work. I search the ground and find Riley's black long sleeve, which I tore off of him last night as the music was playing, and my mind was nowhere but with him.

I need to leave. I need to get the hell out of this tent now that the walls are closing in. Taking one more look back at Riley, I whisper my apology. He won't be happy when he wakes up, and I am not here.

It's still dark, but an orange glow tells me the sun is coming up in the distance. I follow its light. My legs wobble beneath me, but I know I have to keep moving. To get rid of this feeling.

I walk until I reach the lake. There is no one to disappoint here, no one who looks at me with love I can't give back fully because my entire being is split in two.

The world blurs as I go. Somehow, I find myself right at the edge of the lake, my knees in the cool water, mud covering my bare legs. I pull some of its contents to my face, forcing the heat out of my blood.

Much bigger things are happening, a war, The Ark. All much more important than *this*.

Crickets sound in the distance now I have settled. I open my palms with the intention to pray but what could I ask for? God does not grant such petty wishes.

So, I give up.

I pull my knees to my chest as I watch the rising sun. Footsteps approach from behind me. "I don't need prayers today, Daniel," I tell him without removing my eyes from the blinding sun.

He doesn't move, but I have no energy to fight. "What do you need, then?" My head falls into my hands when I recognize the voice—not Daniel at all, but his brother, Bash.

I breathe out slowly. "Time," I answer so quietly Bash does not hear.

Bash's black boots are beside me in an instant, half submerged in the water. "Play a game with me," he says. I don't dare look up at him. I huff a laugh at his words. I am not in the mood for a game.

He remains. "Never have I ever loved two people at the same time." He starts the game. Then a flash of silver falls beside my face. A flask. I take it, tipping it into the air as whiskey burns my throat. Still, I don't think I can look at Bash after last night, so I hand it back with my eyes forward.

When he takes a drink as well, curiosity gets the best of me, and I tilt my head up until I can see his face. Bash smiles wide. He knew exactly what he was doing, that his confession would pique my interest. *Asshole.*

Then, Bash clumsily falls to the ground beside me. *Drunk,* that's what he is. I laugh. "Never have I ever still been drunk at sunrise." I say. Bash laughs too, but not just any laugh, a sad, fake one. He drinks, telling me what I already know.

Then, he sinks to the ground and lays back with a thud. When I look over my shoulder at him, he has his hands behind his head as he looks up at the sky from his back. The flask rests on his chest. His emeralds flash to mine, I turn my head back to the sun. I don't deserve to look. To see what I already know is there.

"I told Michael and Liam to meet me here in five minutes, so I don't accidentally profess my love to you again." His words hang in the air, a blend of jest and sincerity. My heart skips a beat. I curse under my breath. That is not the reaction I should have.

I look down at Riley's shirt—a clear sign I shared a bed with him last night. "You couldn't possibly," I say in disbelief.

Rushing footsteps come hurtling towards us. Michael and Liam run into the water, splashing it over Bash and me. "Come on, Emerson. Water is fine." Michael's octave is even lower in the morning, especially with the help of liquor.

Daniel walks up behind us slowly. Bash tenses at the sight of him. "This water is supposed to have healing properties," Daniel tells us. It's his way of letting Bash know he is calling a truce. That he won't say anything, won't try to fight anymore. Today, they leave, and there is nothing we can do about it.

The sun is up, and the world warms. I kind of liked the cold. I'd rather feel anything other than what I am currently. Michael and Liam whisper something to each other before they head for shore. "No, no, no," I tell them when they approach me. "I'm not even dressed." Liam licks his lips at my words, and his eyes travel down to my legs. "You're drunk, all of you," I scream as I am being lifted into the air.

Liam is on my right, Michael is on my left. "You can't fly a helicopter drunk," Liam says with a look that tells me I should know better. I turn to Bash to see if he will save me, but he has a devious half-smile on his face that tells me he will not be doing any such thing. Bash's eyes run down the length of my body, Riley's shirt parting precariously down the middle, only my panties underneath, before I am tossed into the water. Thankfully, I can stand in the shallow water because I do not know how to swim. Not a lot of pools or fresh water in Harmony.

The cool water is just what I needed. When I reach the surface, Liam is waiting for me, a grin on his face, a dimple on his left cheek.

Now, even Bash has joined in. His shirt is off to reveal those tattoos, the one on his back still covered by a bandage from where he was shot. Bash and Michael might be trying to kill each other. One's head goes under the water, then the other. Daniel watches from the shore, shaking his head.

Liam pushes his blonde hair to the back of his head with both hands. "Do you feel healed?" He asks me. He must have heard Daniel's fact.

His eyes are sad, just as Bash's laugh. "Do *you*?" I answer with a question.

Both of our eyes go to Michael and Bash, who still play their game, if you can call it that. "Sometimes," Liam admits. "When it's like this. When out there doesn't exist." He looks into the distance, then to me. "You know they don't care, right?" Liam says plainly.

My brows come together, confused. "About what?" I lift my head up to look at him, ignoring the blinding sun.

Liam leans toward me so Bash and Michael cannot hear what he is about to say. "Who you choose." He crosses his arms over his bare chest. "Hell, choose me, Emerson." He pleads jokingly, but his *'I don't care'* mask slips for just a moment. "As long as you stay with us," he says seriously.

Liam looks away from me again. I can tell he is dreading this day as much as I am. I lean my head against his shoulder. I'm not sure if he needs the comfort, but I sure do. "I'm not going anywhere," I promise.

# PART 3

---

SELFLESS

# CHAPTER 41

Michael

Canaan is just as I remembered it. Cold, dark. This is a place where nightmares are born. Where men pump their wives full offspring every year to build their army. Children begin training at the age of ten. The way my brothers and I did. We learned to sneak, lie, cheat, kill. There were no rules. There still aren't.

My name comes with honor. Michael is the family name. My father and his father are all named after the archangel. An angel who was said to lead armies in the battle against evil. To lead his people into heaven. There is no doubt we helped place many souls in heaven, but it was without wings. Instead, it was with daggers, swords, and poison. Or, when all else failed, our fists.

"Santo Michael," the man at the gate says to me. His face is pale, and his hands tremble. I thought I would never come back here. To them, I am a ghost. Someone who should not exist. The rumors of my death spread quickly, the way I knew it would. No one gets thrown into Philistine prison and makes it out alive.

Riley mumbles something under his breath as we pass through the gates. "What's that smell?" Liam steps beside me. I see him place his shirt over his nose from my peripheral.

"Home," I say as I continue walking. That is a lie. It's not home. Home is where Bash and Liam spar until one of them bleeds. Home is Daniel's annoying habit of knowing literally everything. Home is where Bronze gets to take the weight of the world off his shoulders. Home is where Emerson is.

I push those pesky thoughts to the back of my head. My chest feels tight here. Every sound has my head on a swivel. Every time someone's footsteps close in behind me, I have to fight the urge to get into an attack position the way I always had to when I was young.

As we continue walking, I can feel the guys getting more and more curious. It's not something I broadcast to the world—that my father is the Duke of Canaan. It's not like it matters anyway. It didn't save my brothers and me from the war. It didn't place us above the rest. Soldiers, that's what we were, and that's what we will always be in the eyes of Canaan. Expendable.

There are consequences to my coming here. As the oldest and last surviving son of Michael Brigadier, I was supposed to take the family title. I never wanted it. It was better to let them think me dead. That's why I never returned, why I devoted my life to Riley's cause, doing as much good as I could to offset the bad that is Canaan.

For the world, for Riley, and for the many people we have worked so hard to save. I will make my presence known. I will take the title when my father dies.

Everything is going exactly to plan. In no time, we will have The Ark. We will bring it to Navar, and the world will be slightly less evil. If becoming Duke is what I have to do in return, so be it.

It was all so easy. Or so I thought.

# Chapter 42

Days, weeks, months. No one came. There was no word from any-one—not Riley, not Bash. The camp on the west side of what used to be Palen, the one that Riley assured me would join us, never showed. Daniel sent messengers to Navar, but they never returned. We have run out of options. Our people are running out of supplies, and there is nowhere for us to go.

I push the small wooden boat into the middle of the water. It's usually where I do my best thinking, but today, when I look up at the sky, all I see is Bash—the usual image of lights dancing behind him—the way I promised to memorize him. He seems to occupy my dreams as well, always with the demons from his tattoo peeling off of his skin and standing over him. They try to grab him, take him. I do all I can in my dream, but I am always too far away. The closer I get, the further the distance between us.

Daniel has it in his head to leave in search of Bash. Something isn't right, I can feel it in my bones, but going after them won't help anything. Leaving our people will do more harm than good. They have grown to look at Daniel as their leader. Rightfully so, he has kept us afloat in the times where it felt like we would drown.

The boat knocks up against the side of a rock. The water has pushed me all the way back to shore. My thoughts were so occupied with all the things I *can't* do I hadn't even realized how long I spent staring up at the sky. I am no closer to an answer than I was before.

Just as I place a foot in the water and begin to pull the boat to shore, something strange happens. A familiar silence befalls me. The birds stop their song, and the frogs quiet like when you first disrupt their peace. My heart begins to race as I scan the surroundings, looking for any sign of what could be causing this unsettling calm. Unlike the time on the mountain, there is no obvious danger.

Before I know it, my feet are moving back to camp before my mind can catch up.

That's when it happens. A blood-curdling scream. My lungs burn as I sprint back to camp. Branches claw at my skin as I tear through the underbrush, my mind racing as wildly as my heart.

Another scream. I follow the noise until I reach the far end of the camp. Men and women scatter in all directions. Grams peeks out of a tent with a confused look on her face as she watches the chaos unfold before her. "Hide," I sign to her. Another head appears from behind her. Long black hair and green eyes, her hand around her sister's. Esther and Ada duck behind another tent, taking Grams with them.

My world spins as I see men in uniform holding Daniel at gunpoint. Blood runs down his face. His eyes lock onto mine instantly, a warning etched across his face. When I don't move, "Run!" He shouts, but I can't leave him. Riley and Bash would never forgive me. His words are followed by a nauseating guttural sound as one of the men kicks him in the stomach, sending him to his knees.

His eyes close for a second too long. When they open again, the man who kicked him follows his gaze to me. Daniel tries to say something, but his words dissolve into a pained grunt. His eyes roll back, and the gun that was aimed at his head now points to his motionless body.

One of the men approaches me. He spits something in my direction, but I don't understand. His tongue clicks in a foreign manner. Daniel is in and out of consciousness. They point to him as they shout what can only be demands at me.

"Don't," Daniel coughs.

I swallow away my fear as best as I can. "What do they want?" I ask Daniel.

"They want a reason for Riley and Bash to return The Ark." He looks at me expectantly.

*Me*, they want me.

The men start dragging Daniel towards the center of the camp, his limp body leaving a trail of blood. The sight of it ignites something in me, a desperate anger.

"Let him go!" I scream, but they do not understand. One of the men backhands me, sending me to the ground. Pain explodes in my cheek, but I force myself up, stumbling towards Daniel.

That's when I take a look around at the destruction. The camp is in ruins. Tents are torn apart, and supplies are scattered everywhere. Bodies lie motionless on the ground. *No, no, no.* The air is thick with the smell of blood and smoke.

"Stop!" I cry out again. Instead, one of them grabs me, pulling me roughly towards him by my shirt. He searches my face as if he is looking for something.

Daniel's eyes flutter open, filled with desperation. "Don't let them take you," he whispers, his voice barely audible. The man must think I can get Daniel to give them the information they are after because at his words he releases me. I go to Daniel, grabbing his swollen face. "There has to be a reason." Daniel pauses as he gathers his strength again. "There has to be a reason. They wouldn't keep it from Navar if they didn't think it should not be in their hands." He tells me.

When the man hears him speak of Navar, he spits onto Daniel's face. A string of foreign curse words leave the man's mouth.

From behind one of the tents, another guard pulls a woman by her hair. Her head bobs, and her grey hair falls in front of her face. Grams. She looks like she put up a fight, one that left the man holding her with scratches on his face and a torn collar. My pride only lasts seconds because the man holds out a bat to the side before it comes crashing down, hitting the back of Grams's knees. She falls to the ground with a thud. A sound leaves my body that I think I have been holding back for far too long.

No sign of Esther and Ada, that has to be good. Grams must have saved them.

Grams closes her eyes as a pistol is pushed up to her head. "Please," I beg them. The man looks at Daniel and repeats the same words I heard him say when I first arrived. A question Daniel refuses to answer. Daniel looks straight ahead, he does not speak. Does not move. All I can do is wait.

My eyes go back and forth between the man with the gun, his finger curls around the trigger, and Daniel who does *nothing*. "Do something. Do *anything*." I plead with Daniel but his mouth is set in a line.

My whole body collapses in on itself, or at least it feels like it as a shot goes off. I can't make myself look. My breath comes in rapid in and out. Fuck, this can't be happening. Grams' body hits the ground hard. Something deep inside me tells me I will never forget that sound.

I look at the men, their eyes cold and merciless. They want me as leverage, a bargaining chip to force Riley and Bash to return the Ark. So they will have me. I take one more look at Daniel, at the bodies and the destruction. All because I was nowhere to be found. It's my fault. Somehow, it always is.

"I will go with you." I make sure to look one of them in the eye. Begging him to understand me. Then back to Daniel. "Tell them I will go with them. Tell them who I am." My words come out broken. At first, I don't think Daniel will say anything at all. His face goes flat. "Bash would. He would not let you die. No more deaths, Daniel." It's a low blow, but it gets me what I want: a reaction. Daniel's eyes flick to mine with either anger or pain. I don't care which.

I tilt my head to the side. *Please, please.* I beg in my head. Then, a silent understanding passes between us. Daniel says a barrage of words that end with my name. He looks at me but he talks to the men.

They waste no time, tying my hands with a coarse rope. I do not fight as they lead Daniel and me far away from the camp. Past the hills on the west end of camp. The same place I stood every day in wait for our people who never came.

We are forced into a windowless armed car. The air inside the vehicle is stifling, filled with the scent of sweat and fear. Daniel's body slumps beside me, his breathing shallow and labored. I want to reach out to him to offer some comfort, but my hands are bound.

The men sit across from us. Smug satisfaction on their faces. One of them keeps his gaze fixed on me, his expression unreadable. I make my face as neutral as possible, not showing the fear they want me to feel. On the inside, I am trembling. How did it come to this?

Michael warned me of what this mission could mean. The lives of the people I love. It's better me than the rest of them. Who is left anyway. I make sure not to think of Grams or her lifeless body. If I had not agreed to go with them, I knew Daniel's fate would be the same. They are trying to send a message to the guys, wherever they are. Maybe Daniel is right. They wouldn't break their promise to Navar, to *me*, if they didn't have a good reason, but they will understand when they see what these people have done. I had no choice.

After what feels like hours, the vehicle comes to an abrupt halt. The men throw black fabric hoods over our faces before dragging us roughly from the car. Daniel whimpers. Thankfully, his body is pressed against mine, assurance he is still with me as we are led through the cool air outside. I hear the sound of a door squealing.

Then, stale, damp air fills my senses. Daniel falls onto me as another door closes behind us. He has lost too much blood. I try to keep him up as best as I can without the help of my hands, which are still behind my back.

More words are exchanged between the men around us. Someone places a hand on my shoulder and shoves me forward. We walk for a long time, through a series of turns, and up a set of winding stairs. Daniel's small groans of pain echo off the walls.

The sound of our footsteps change, making me think we have reached a larger room. I want to scream, but putting up a fight will only hurt us more. All I can do is stand in silence. There are other voices, small murmurs from a distance.

The cloth is ripped from my head. Light surrounds me, bright and blinding. When my eyes adjust, I am face to face with a man in a white robe. A tall hat of the same color, with intricate red designs, sits on his head.

Left of me is Daniel, whose head bobs as he comes in and out of consciousness. The guards hold him up by his arms. His eyes are swollen shut now, and blood pours from his wounds. I didn't have time to assess the damage before. It's much worse than I thought. Now, there is no doubt in my mind, they were going to kill him if I had not stepped in. The man in white says something to Daniel, but he cannot answer due to his injuries. When that fails, the man looks to me. I stare straight into his black eyes with as much strength as I have left.

He takes his eyes from mine first, a small victory. I watch him carefully, not taking my attention from him all while I keep a look of hate on my face. He is the leader, has to be, The one that sent these men to kill our people.

With a wave of his hands, people come rushing from behind us. This finally tears my eyes away from the man. They take Daniel away, his legs dangling from beneath him. I can see the fight in his eyes but it's gone just as soon as it comes. "Where are you taking him?" I ask anyone who will listen. The crowd behind me gasps at my words. They either do not understand, or they ignore me. When I move towards Daniel, the men at my sides take hold of each arm. "Don't touch me." I spit at them. "Don't fucking touch me!" I fight against their grip, but it's of no use.

I can't let them take him. Bash would never admit it, but losing Daniel would break him. Riley would never forgive himself for separating the two again. I know he would blame himself. I can't lose Daniel either, he is family, the same as Grams, Michael, and Liam. I have lost too many people. I won't let them take one more. Not this time.

The robed man holds up his hands. The guards retreat, but the door has already been closed. When I turn to the noise, I am ready to curse, scream, and fight until I get him back. I break away from the guards. They do nothing to stop me this time. But I only make it a few steps before I stop dead in my tracks, met with blue eyes—ice blue. My knees hit the floor.

Jez.

# CHAPTER 43

Bash

My dreams bleed into reality. The only time I can distinguish between the two is when I see her. Emerson. That image of her across the lake, her face cast in purple, orange, and green, haunts me. Her presence is the only anchor in my shifting world, but I stay away because the darkness that surrounds me mutes those colors. It takes over everything until there is nothing at all, leaving only shadows and voids.

This time, there is no lake. No Emerson. I wander through a forest, the trees towering above, their branches reaching like skeletal fingers. The air is thick with mist, the silence only broken by the occasional rustle of what follows me. An animal or man. I do not turn around to see. I have learned not to. The Ark uses your fears against you. It makes you see things that aren't really there. All your bad thoughts come to the surface and stay there.

The forest seems to stretch infinitely, the paths twisting and turning back on themselves, leading nowhere. The weight of the Ark's presence presses down on me, a constant reminder of the evil I carry. Its whispers grow louder, promising power and dominance, but I know better. I've seen what it does to those who give in. I have seen everything.

When I stood over the golden box, I felt a pull—a seductive lure of power. But as it opened, releasing a flood of darkness, I heard its whispers of promises I knew it could not keep. It's almost as if my body was working against my mind because I couldn't help it. I took a look inside. What I saw was evil—unadulterated evil. With it, who knows what Navar will do. I saw what it did to Jericho and the way the Duke of Canaan looked at it with lust in his eyes. Eyes that are no longer in his skull.

If I have it my way, it will never see the light of day again. The Ark of the Covenant, what it truly holds, will die with me.

Emerson

Her hair is in perfect curls down to her waist, and her face is full of color. Not at all the starved, *dying* woman I thought I was going to see behind my eyes forever. Tears stream down her face. A girl with white hair clings to her hip, another child is cradled in her arms. I shake my head. That's not possible. Jez is dead.

It took so long to convince myself. There were too many prayers said. Too many sleepless nights where I replayed our last conversation over and over. The way she looked at me, at Bash. Her skin and bones and the lack of light in her eyes. Followed by an explosion. So this, *this* cannot be real.

"Jez." I reach for her, but my hands are bound. I had forgotten where I was, what I was doing, *who* I was.

When I close my eyes, she is still at the other end of the room. When I open them, she is kneeling before me. My knees ache, and my stomach turns in on itself. "They will take care of him, don't worry," Jez tells me, her voice so soft and motherly I hardly register her words. All I can do is stare. The child in her arms lets out a soft coo, pulling me back to the present. It *is* real. All of it. Daniel's broken bones and swollen face, the blood, the bodies. Why we are here. It all comes rushing back.

My chest aches. I force myself to meet her eyes. "How?" I have so many other questions for her, but that seems to be the only thing that comes out.

Jez's brows come together. How did I forget how beautiful she is? How did I forget about that little line that makes its presence known when she is worried? "I will tell you all about it later. Right now, there are bigger problems. Riley has cut off all contact with Navar." She adjusts the child in her arms, his eyes open, and they are ice blue, just like hers, just like Ben's. "It's not how it was supposed to happen, but you are here. Help us." *Us.* That one word tells me all I need to know.

"After what they have done?" I shake my head at her. Then I look around the room, where the man in white waits. Everything is all gold and bright. Paintings line the walls until they collide at the top. Windows reach to the ceiling with colors and depictions of angels. A throne made of gold. It's all *so* much while we had *so* little. I raise my voice for whoever will listen, whoever will understand. "They are murderers!" I scream, my voice breaking from the force of my words. "All of you. You killed my people!" I turn my head back to Jez. "I will not help them." I spit.

Jez's eyes widen in shock but not at my outburst. She *really* didn't know about the attack. She was not a part of it. I can see the truth on her face, the genuine shock. The room falls silent, the echo of my scream hanging in the air. The man in white steps forward, his expression unreadable. "Take her away," he says to seemingly no one. So, he *can* speak my language. "Send for the healers." More people, where do they keep coming from? They gather around me, helping me to my feet. One pulls a knife from his side. I flinch, but the knife is lowered to my hands. I inspect the marks around my wrist after the rope is cut. Free, but not free enough.

Jez throws her arm around me, the child between us. "I have waited too long to hug my sister," she whispers into my hair. "Wait for more information before you react next time. Remember what I taught you." She releases me and holds my eyes for a moment. Her lessons are unending, even after so long apart.

The healers begin to move us to the same door Daniel must have disappeared behind. Before they can take me, I turn to my sister. "I'm sorry," I tell her—the words I should have said to her long ago. In Jericho, in Harmony.

"Never apologize for that again." Jez nods her head at me as the girl with white hair peeks out from behind her. A mother, Jez was always meant to be a mother.

Bash

The darkness within me grows, festers. My mind is a battlefield. Its whispers are insidious, promising power, control, everything I ever wanted. But it's all lies. I know that. Yet, resisting it feels like trying to hold back the ocean with a single hand.

"Bash." A voice calls from the distance. I make a turn, throwing them off my trail. There is no saving me this time, Riley Bronze. You will thank me later.

# CHAPTER 44

Riley

Bash's demons existed long before we came in contact with The Ark. They were always there, behind his eyes, along with his guilt, his shame.

Our first trip to Jericho, I saw those demons crawl out of his skin and into the room where his sisters lay bound and helpless. The darkness took over him, and there was no stopping it. Not that I wanted to. Those monsters got everything they deserved.

It had lasting effects. Esther and Ada saw that darkness and feared it. What I saw as strength, they saw as evil.

Em often told me I was good at finding each person's strength. What they are good at, what makes them who they are, at their core. Maybe I was wrong about this one. Maybe his rage, his darkness, is a weakness.

Emerson

I was expecting a prison cell, a place for us to rot while they hold us hostage. Instead, I was escorted into a room, small but comfortable. The walls are a soft cream color. A single high window lets in a sliver of sunlight. It cast a golden beam across the wooden floor. There is a small table beside the bed, holding a pitcher of water. There are even neatly folded clothes on the bed. I do not put them on. These things are not usually given to people who are being used as leverage, are they?

It all pisses me off, the fake hospitality, the calm after all the chaos I have witnessed. Now that it's quiet, my mind races with those thoughts. I hate it. So, I exit the small room in search of Daniel.

I'm not quite ready to see Jez again. She will give me her explanation, her side of things, and right now, all I want to do is hate. Hate them for what they did to Daniel. For what they did to Grams. Mothers, daughters, and sons were murdered in front of me. Everything I need to know about these people, this place, is that they will kill to get what they want.

The hallway is stuffy. I make my way back to the infirmary, where Daniel lies on a bed. They have a tube going into his arm, and his breathing is finally even. There is a chair in the corner that I pull to the side of his bed.

Gripping his hand in my own, I begin my prayer—the one Daniel taught me. The saint of healing, Raphael. "The medicine of God," I begin but pause. When I close my eyes, all I see is red. My prayers have never been answered before. Why would they be now? Still, Daniel's prayers were a comfort in my times of need. I should extend the same kindness. "Fuck," I shake my head, then start the prayer over again.

"There should be no cursing before prayers," a familiar voice says from behind me. My eyes widen. Liam.

He looks well. His hands have the usual dusting of black grease, but the rest of him is clean. It seems Navar has taken care of him as well. Along with Jez, and Daniel does seem to be getting the care he needs for his injuries. No amount of kindness they extend could make up for what they did.

"What are you doing here?" The chair squeals under my weight as I push it back. Tears threaten to spill as I rush toward him. His hands wrap around my neck, and he holds me in place as he inspects my face. It's almost as if he is having a hard time deciding if I am real or not. "What is it? What's wrong?" I ask.

"Nothing." He finally pulls me to his chest in an embrace. When I pull back, I look up to see a new scar on his neck, hidden by much longer blonde hair than he had when I last saw him. Instinctively, I look behind him for who usually follows. My heart sinks. No Bash or Michael or Riley. He is alone. When he clocks the look on my face, he tells me what I already know. "They are—" he stops and takes a breath. "I don't know where Riley or Bash have gone. Michael is—" There is pain in his voice. "Everything went to shit so fast, Emerson." Liam runs his hands through his hair. You can see the guilt rise to the surface. This is not the Liam that couldn't be bothered. This is a different Liam altogether, what happened during their time in Canaan? *One thing at a time,* I remind myself.

Sadness takes over his features as he looks at Daniel. "He put up a good fight," I tell Liam. "He thinks you guys had a good reason for not returning with The Ark. He was willing to give up his life." The words come out harsher than I intended, but I need answers. "So, is it true? Was not giving it to Navar worth *this*?" I push my hands out towards Daniel.

Liam's jaw tenses as he thinks of his next words carefully. I am growing impatient of not knowing. It's all I have ever been—in the dark. With Riley and now with so much time and distance between us, I couldn't possibly have known what was going on even if I wanted to.

Liam was wary of me at first, wouldn't tell me they were thinking of going after The Ark. Michael worked hard to convince all of them I was worth the truth, that they were going to leave the camp, risk their lives.

Liam seems to make up his mind, but before he speaks, he shuts the door. Interesting. He doesn't trust the people around us. That we can agree on. I'm not even sure if I can trust my own sister. Jez said I needed more information, and that is what I am trying to get.

For a long moment, the only sound is Daniel's breathing. Then, "Canaan had the Ark." Liam steps closer to me and lowers his voice. "Just as Michael suspected. We had a plan," he says, frustrated. "Michael warned us about what we might see, what we might feel. Bash—" Liam runs his hand through his hair again.

"He what?" I whisper impatiently.

"Bash saw what was in there and decided to take it. They tried to stop him. Before I knew it, half the estate was dead, a trail of bodies, starting with the Duke of Canaan, all the way up north into the forest. Then we lost him." Liam's voice shakes.

It all plays slowly in my head. "Bash took the Ark of the Covenant? Why would he do that?" I ask, but I know Liam does not know. No one does.

"When Riley finds him, we can ask," Liam says, plain and simple.

Riley

It took longer than we wanted it to, but all good plans do. We pledged our services to Canaan, hoping by the time we were called to duty, it would be Michael we served under and not his father.

Michael—damn him for keeping this from us. He didn't lie, but he sure as hell didn't tell the truth. When I decided to buy him from the Philistine prison, it wasn't because of his name or title. I didn't know any of that. It was because he was good at being invisible. He knew how to act, where to place himself on the food chain of prison life so he could live out his last days with no fuss.

It wasn't exactly random, but I sure did get lucky when I was invited to observe the prisoners with the facade that I was interested in purchasing one of them. Michael stuck out to me because he did not stick out at all. Not until he learned of my arrival did he start acting out, which only solidified my decision.

When I saw him place that crown on his head, with a whole room full of people, placing him directly in the spotlight, and saw the look on his face—that of a ruler, a leader, a role he never wanted but was forced to take—I knew in that moment how badly we had fucked up.

There were signs, but I chose to ignore them because we were so close. Bash was not on board, not after we saw it, what it held. It had a different reaction to him than it did to us.

It all happened so fast.

He had his own plans all along. Loyal Bash, my brother. He got close to Michael's father, the Duke of Canaan, Michael Brigadier—the same name he gave to his first born son.

An alarm sounded through the air of his estate early in the morning, before sunrise. It was the worst sound we could possibly hear. The night had been planned perfectly, down to the last detail. *This* was not part of the plan.

Liam and I searched everywhere for Bash, but he was nowhere to be found. My gut twisted in on itself like I could sense just how bad things were. I slipped right back into my role. Thanks to my time in the Palen Army, giving orders, assessing the situation, and how to best handle it, was easy.

I sent Liam to the west where Michael was already in position—the position I gave him for our departure with the Ark. Our escape.

I went to the throne room in search of Bash, who had been spending an unordinary amount of time there. When I got there, it was chaos. Bash had his knife to the neck of one of the guards as they tried to stop him from leaving. The Ark was nowhere to be found. The Duke of Canaan looked nearly unrecognizable had it not been for the bloodied crown next to his dismembered body.

Bash was right in front of me, but it wasn't him—it was the same darkness I saw in Jericho. Only now it was all around him. I put the pieces together quickly. Why he was so close to the Duke. Why he demanded to be the one to watch the Ark on the night we were supposed to take it and run. Everything we worked so hard for, gone. Along with Bash.

I put my arms up into the air as he slithered to the door. I couldn't do anything about it, not without killing him. That is something I cannot do, not to myself, but also not to Emerson.

Bash watched my every move like a snake about to strike—a killer. Before he left, he dropped the guard with a slit of his throat. All while keeping his eyes on me. That's when I saw it—Bash was still in there. Control—he had control. But for how long?

Then he said the words that will forever be etched into my mind: "If you love her, you won't try to find me." Bash told me.

Liam and I followed his tracks, his trail of bodies, the people who got in his way. Until the tracks crossed over a river where we lost him.

The rest of my time in Canaan was a blur of funerals, ceremonies, and damage control.

# CHAPTER 45

Riley

Michael sent Liam to Navar. We can't let this information get out.
Our mission has failed once again. The Ark of the Covenant isn't in
our possession, at least not the way it's supposed to be. We can only tell
Navar that Bash and I have gone rogue, cutting off our ties completely,
pretending we're keeping the Ark for ourselves. Liam knows the risks of
going to Navar. He made his choice.

When we finally received word back from Liam, everything was so
painfully wrong. Emerson and Daniel have been taken from the camp.
Our sister camp never reached Emerson. Those who weren't killed or
captured are now on the run. We can move them to Canaan with
Michael's permission, but what they've been through will cause tension.
There is already unrest due to Michael's new reign as Duke. The people
here are just as he described: wild, unlawful. They will not like the extra
company.

Threats. That's what Liam's letter contains. Navar will keep them
until we return the Ark. An eye for an eye. Emerson, Daniel, and Liam
won't survive unless I find Bash.

I follow every lead. Reports pile in when Michael gives out Bash's description with a hefty reward for any information on his whereabouts. It's all shit. They all lead me to the same place: nowhere.

Until one woman sends in a sketch with blood on it. Apparently, the man didn't like her capturing his likeness. There are witnesses. They describe him as a drunk, spending his nights at a bar in a town just outside of Canaan. The bastard always did drown his sorrows in alcohol.

This leads me here, outside a bar with no name, no windows, and abandoned cars littering the lot.

Every day, I wait for him. Each night ends the same. The bar closes, and the woman behind the counter tells me I have to leave.

Fucking pointless, that's what it is. I've followed a dead lead, just like the rest. There are probably hundreds of miserable men who drink themselves into oblivion in this God-forsaken town. In fact, I am one of them, sitting here with a fourth whiskey in my hand.

I tap my finger on the rim of my glass. Just like Father used to do. I curse him under my breath. It's time to break *that* habit. "One more," I tell the bartender. Her blonde hair falls into her face as pencil hits paper. She reminds me of Emerson. Another curse escapes my lips when I think of what she must be enduring in Navar.

The door slams behind me. I don't even bother to look anymore. It's never him. The woman peers up through her lashes as she pours me another drink. Her brows arch. She grabs another glass and fills it as well.

The stool beside me scrapes against the wooden floor before a very drunk, very angry Bash sits down. The blonde sets down our glasses before discreetly retreating. She is frightened for good reason.

Bash's tattooed hand grips the glass until his knuckles turn white. I huff a laugh. This infuriates him, exactly as I intend. "I told you to leave me alone." He spits.

I down the whiskey in my hand in one gulp. I have a feeling I'm going to need it.

"This isn't going to end well, Bash," I tell him.

Bash also downs his drink before reaching behind the bar and grabbing the nearest bottle. He refills my drink and his own. "Better I than her," Bash mutters. Then his head turns as if he sees something, but there's no one there. It's worse than I thought.

Finally, I search the mirror for his face, unprepared for what I might see. His eyes are almost hollow as he gazes down at the bottle in his hand. His black hair is unkempt, and his facial hair has grown long. Don't get me started on the stench of booze and blood emanating from him.

I've come here to tell him the facts, the truth, and that's what I intend to do. "Emerson—" I begin, but I'm cut off when the glass in his hand shatters under the force of his grip.

Bash's palm bleeds onto the wooden bar. "Don't you fucking dare. No lie of yours will make me turn it over. There are things you don't understand, Bronze."

That's quite enough. I turn towards him, but he turns away from me. I shake my head. "Return the Ark to Navar, or she will die. Her and Daniel. Liam. Ada and Esther. Dead. They've already raided the camps, *killed* our family, Bash. Do you want Emerson to meet the same fate?" I stand at my words. That's all I need to do. I saw him that day with the blood of Michael's father on his hands. He was there, fighting behind the darkness.

Before I turn for the door, I stare him down. His clothes don't fit properly, and his breathing is labored—all the signs of a broken man. Bash truly is willing to die with the whereabouts of the Ark.

The door opens, letting in the cool night breeze. Footsteps shuffle in, and before I know it, Bash is being placed in cuffs. He spins towards me. His eyes turn as black as night. I used to dismiss the stories of demons and devils, but now, I am staring directly at one. "What have you done?" Bash demands an answer.

"I am saving you from yourself, Bash." That's not all. I am saving everyone, Emerson included.

# CHAPTER 46

"Emerson," Jez's voice is soft as she cuts the brown from the ends of my hair. She had cut my hair many times before in Harmony when I was young. Then, she would gently pull it to the back of my head in a braid and tie it off with string or ribbon, depending on the occasion. Now, with the brown pieces cut off, there is not enough left to braid, so it lays messily on my shoulders. Jez speaks again, but I had been too caught up in memories to hear what she said. My mind drifts easily from one thing to another lately.

"Huh?" I stare at myself in the mirror before turning to my sister. Jez's eyes meet mine through the reflection, her expression soft and patient.

"The man you came with, it's not the same one I saw in Jericho." She places the scissors at her side, satisfied with her work. "He has the same eyes, a brother, maybe?" Jez makes a guess.

"Yes, Daniel is Bash's brother," I answer her question, trying to keep my voice steady even though Bash's name out of my mouth has my stomach in knots.

"Bash," she repeats his name slowly, thoughtfully. *Bash*. I can still feel his hand on my chin, see his emerald eyes watching me. There's something much worse than his betrayal—I can feel it.

I change the subject quickly, desperate to keep myself from thinking about it. About Bash and the dreams where I can't reach him. "Where are your children, Jez?" I decide to ask.

"Mm, Liam? I think his name is. He offered to watch them so we could speak." A smile plays on her lips. "He has kind eyes." Jez messes with a piece of her own hair as she looks into the mirror.

I'm glad she can't see me when I roll my eyes. "Wait until you meet Michael."

Jez spins to look at me, leaning against the vanity. "Ah, yes. Santo Michael."

Reaching into my memory at her words I pull out that name. Saint Michael, the archangel, Daniel had taught me his prayer for protection, but I do not know why she is calling him that. "You know him?" I ask. Come to think of it, Liam did mention something about Michael, but I brushed over it because I was too eager for information about someone else

"I do not. I only hear his name fluttering through the hallways. Women mostly." She pauses, searching my face. Jez is always doing that—a habit, I guess. "The same women who fled his father." My brows scrunch together in confusion, which Jez clocks immediately. "He didn't tell you?" She asks.

"Tell me what?" I shake my head lightly.

"Your friend Michael is the son of Duke Brigadier." Jez waits for a response, but I don't have one. These things mean nothing to me. I should have paid more attention in school. "Rumor has it, he has taken the place of his father with his return to Canaan."

"Michael is Duke of Canaan?" I ask her, even though I already know the answer.

Jez seems to go deep into thought. "You know Navar is not as bad as it seems." I laugh under my breath at her words. "Navar took them in when they had nowhere else to go," Jez speaks about the women as if they are her friends, her family. She waits for a moment before she speaks again. "You could stay too." My eyes widen at her words.

Stay here? With the people who killed Grams and tortured Daniel? "No." I spit as I run my hands through my hair, feeling the blunt ends catch on my fingers.

"Where will you go? Canaan?" Jez questions. "Where they use women as slaves to make more soldiers? I have seen the scars, the damage child after child causes." Her words are still in that quiet, motherly tone. It pisses me off. I just got her back, my sister, so I hold my tongue.

She doesn't know Michael. She doesn't know what he has been through and how thoroughly he hates Canaan. *I* didn't know. He was brave to go back. His willingness to put himself in a position where he would have to face his father again makes my heart ache for him. The Michael I know would never force women into bearing children. He couldn't possibly. Not after I saw the kindness, the love, the pain behind his eyes from his past. I *won't* believe it.

Jez's lips flatten into a line, as if she, too, is keeping her words from harming me. Her shoulders fall. This time, *she* changes the subject. "Philip needs feeding, I will go find Liam." She takes a step, ready to leave.

My heart skips a beat. "Philip?" I ask. I haven't heard that name in a very long time. "You named him after Dad?"

Jez nods her head in response. Her features soften. "You weren't old enough to remember, but he was kind. Who do you think taught me how to dance?" She winks at me. "And your niece would love to meet the woman she is named after." She looks towards the door.

"Emerson?" My own name leaving my mouth feels strange. Jez just nods her head.

Just then, a small but impatient knock hits the door. Liam enters the room with a child in his arms. He holds Philip like an explosive, far away from his body awkwardly. Liam looks between Jez and me before he clears his throat. Jez almost rolls her eyes as she gathers Philip into her arms and collects Emerson from the hallway where she hides.

"Thank you, Liam," she sings, ever the flirt. Jez looks back at me. "I will leave you two to talk." Another wink before the door closes behind her gently.

"What is it?" I ask, sensing the urgency in Liam's eyes.

"They found Bash."

*"They?"*

"Riley made a goddamn deal with Navar behind our backs. They are on their way now."

I had time, but nothing could have prepared me for this moment.

Riley walks in first, his demeanor calm yet determined, each step easy, or at least he is pretending it is. Riley has always been good at pretending. He looks straight ahead as guards escort him to the front of the room. His eyes are fixed and unwavering from the gold throne.

The High Priest, the man in white, waits for them to approach. Aaron of Word—that is what they call him. That is what Jez calls him. Supposedly, he is the link between earth and afterlife. Everything is coming together. Why they are desperate for possession of The Ark, why they believe others should not have it.

Whether I believe it or not is a different story. At this point, I do not care. Too many lives have been lost. Riley seems to have come to the same conclusion. The Ark of the Covenant should be returned to Navar for one reason and one reason only: to stop Navar from killing our people.

*Look at me,* I beg Riley in my mind. But he does not. There is that distant, unrecognizable look in his eye. Suddenly, I remember what Bash said to me outside the destroyed safe house on our way to Jericho: "*Someone who has killed for her before and would again.*" So, who is Riley going to kill this time?

A crowd of strangers lines the sides of the room. Their faces are a blur of curiosity as Riley stops before Aaron and bows his head. The men who surround Riley look familiar—maybe the same team that came to the camp and killed Grams right before my eyes. The memory sears through me, fueling my panic.

Riley reaches Aaron who still wears that flowing white robe. I am starting to hate the color white. Now I stare at Riley's back, my heart pounding in my chest as I wait. "A debt has been repaid," Aaron of Word announces, his voice cold and final.

Riley shakes his head in disagreement, his jaw tightening over and over. "We do not have it. We only have the man who took it." Bile rises to my throat. The man he speaks of is Bash.

Just as the thought crosses my mind, the doors open once more. Another set of guards waits on the other side. The crowd makes an unpleasant noise. I am pushed back behind broad shoulders and men in long black robes. I work my way past them, my breath coming in short, desperate gasps until I get to the front as the guards escort a man in black to Riley. A black hood covers his face, just like the one placed on mine and Daniel's head when we first arrived.

There is no mistaking who it is. Bash. When they stop, they tear the hood from his face. His eyes are sunken, haunted. Those nightmares that have kept me from sleep all those nights while they were away come to the front of my mind. It's the same man. The same darkness surrounds him as it did in my dreams. His shoulders are rolled forward in defeat, chains hang from his hands to his feet. He looks tired, broken, a ghost of the man he once was.

My knees feel like they might give out on me as I watch him. The room spins. Suddenly, Jez is at my side, holding me on my feet. Her firm grip is the only thing keeping me from collapsing.

Bash is forced to his knees. A pained sound leaves his body. He looks down at the ground with no life in his eyes, staring and staring until his head is lifted into the air by the hand of one of Aaron's men.

The room grows increasingly quiet until there is no sound at all. Riley stands beside Bash, as still as a statue, while Aaron seems to study Bash, his head cocked to the side.

Aaron takes his time, memorizing his subject down to the last detail. When he finally turns his head back to Riley, he smiles, a knowing catlike grin takes over his face. He is *happy?* Bash is literally dying in front of him, and he is *happy?* I want to claw out his eyes, make it so he can never smile again.

Riley takes in a breath and clenches his jaw in frustration. Something isn't right, Riley's deal has gone awry. Aaron lifts his hands into the air, the same way you would during prayer. "Take your friends, take your freedom, we have all we need." Aaron seems to dismiss Riley.

Bash's head falls again. *No, no, no.* My feet move on instinct, but Jez has a tight hand around my arm in an instant. She leans towards me, placing her mouth near my ear to whisper, "There is nothing you can do, Em. Riley made the deal. It's his cross to bear." I shake my head at her words.

Thankfully, Riley speaks, giving me hope he will not let this happen, that he will not let them keep Bash. But my heart sinks again when he doesn't even get a full word out before Aaron cuts him off. "You promised the Ark of the Covenant, and that is what you have brought us." His words are full of annoyance.

Then, Aaron sits on his throne and leans back like he is bored. "Your friend here was willing, ready to drink its contents and let it consume him. To let death take over his body until there was nothing left. Not he or The Ark, but *one.*" Aaron emphasizes the last word. His voice is soft, but it fills the room. What kind of riddle is that? What kind of *shit* is that?

"What does that mean?" Riley asks impatiently. The guards surrounding him have their fingers on the trigger of their guns. That darkness surrounds Riley, the kind I used to run from. The look of death takes over his features. Liam makes his way to the front to stand next to Riley to keep him from doing something he cannot undo.

"It means," Aaron begins, his voice dripping with cruelty, "That the Ark's power is not just in the physical object but in the willingness to surrender to its dark force. Your friend Sebastian was ready to make that sacrifice."

Aaron takes another long glance at Bash, who does nothing. This is not the Bash I know who would fight. "The Ark of the Covenant," he motions to Bash. Whispers spread around the room like fire. All of it untrue. Or at least I want it to be.

I fight against Jez's grip, making my way up the aisle until I am close enough to reach him. One of the men near Riley, with a gun in his hand, takes a stance as he holds the barrel to my face. I don't back down. I have to see for myself if what they claim is true.

Aaron clears his throat, and the man lowers the gun back to his side. I practically fall to reach Bash. I hold his face in my hands, forcing his eyes on mine. No words are spoken. It wouldn't matter anyway because who I look at is not Bash. Black eyes, and no soul.

# CHAPTER 47

After they drag Bash away, I force my eyes to meet Riley's. "What have you done?" I ask him. I can't help the anger that seeps into my words.

The throne room has emptied now. The only people left are Liam, Riley, Jez, and me. We have the night—that's it. We have been instructed to gather our things and leave by morning. Word has been sent to Michael, and we'll be on our way to Canaan.

Riley blinks before looking away, avoiding my gaze the same way he's done all my life. Fire burns in my chest.

I step toward Riley, but he shakes his head and takes a step back, turning his back on me. Liam reaches out, but I do not need comfort. I need answers. Jez's footsteps are light against the floor behind me.

Riley mumbles something under his breath I cannot hear. He runs his hands through his hair over and over again.

"Face me," I demand. "Look at me and tell me you didn't know what *this* was."

"You really think if I knew—" Riley shouts as he turns back toward me, his hands in the air. I do not move. This time, I will not hide from Riley's rage. It's all I have ever done. He lowers his voice as he nears me. Riley towers over me in silence for a moment before he grabs my shoulders and gives them a shake. "I thought I was saving him, not damning him." Riley's chest moves in and out heavily, and his grip tightens. His words are dripping in guilt.

Riley looks different. I haven't seen him in so long. His hair is long on the sides, and the beard on his jaw now grows down his neck, like he hasn't had time to take care of it amidst all the chaos. He is so close now I can see the speck in his right eye reflecting the golden light. Most notable is the look of defeat he wears. When I do not say anything, his head falls into his hands. Regret floods my senses.

When he looks up again, he takes his time, memorizing my features. "I can fix it," he tells me, but his words are broken. There is no fixing this, even he knows it.

Liam speaks from beside Riley. "Bash made his choice. We won't ever know why, but I trust his judgment. He clearly knows something we do not."

Riley's brows come together, and his hands ball into fists at his sides.

"We should go back to Canaan. We can make a plan from there. Michael's family might have information that can help," Liam says as Riley fumes beside him.

My mouth falls open slightly at his words. As true as they are, we can't do *nothing*. "We can't just leave him here," I say quietly, though I know we have no choice in the matter. Liam knows it, too. The only person who seems to think otherwise is Riley. I can see the gears turning as he tries to solve an impossible puzzle.

Before I can ask Riley what he's thinking, he storms off. Liam sighs and takes one more look at me before he follows Riley through the doors. I freeze, staring at the spot where I last saw Riley, knowing he won't be back. My heart breaks for him. There have been too many goodbyes.

My mind races, but I keep coming to the same conclusion over and over again. I turn to my sister. "Take me to him."

Jez's eyes widen at my words, and then she nods once. A silent understanding passes between the two of us. She knows, she always does. Before *I* do, usually. I think she knew in Jericho when I showed up to save someone who didn't want saving.

The guards stationed in front of Bash's cell move instantly when they see Jez. I want to ask her what she offered them, what she gave up to get us here, but the words die on my lips. There's no time for that now. I owe her. I always have, for everything.

The heavy door creaks open, and I step inside. The space is small, it's less of a cell and more of a room designed for someone in Bash's condition. There's nothing for him to get his hands on, nothing he could use to hurt himself or others. All the corners are rounded, and the hard objects are cushioned. Bash is slumped against the wall in the corner, his hands chained, his head hanging low. My breath catches in my throat as I take in the sight of him—so much pain and exhaustion etched into his features. Yet it's still Bash. Not the Bash I want, but he has to be there, *somewhere*. If *that* Bash can hear me, then that's all I need.

"Bash," I whisper. He doesn't move at first, doesn't acknowledge me. I take another step closer, until I am so close I could reach out and touch his hair that falls into his face. His head lifts slowly, and when his eyes meet mine, not emerald—but black. The same eyes I saw when I knelt in front of him in the throne room, in front of Aaron of Word, who told us exactly what Bash had done.

For a moment, confusion settles onto his face. He cocks his head to the side before it falls back down. He stares at the ground endlessly as he mumbles something under his breath. Then, he shakes his head as if what he's telling himself isn't true.

"Why did you do it?" The question tumbles out before I can stop it, my voice trembling.

He sighs. The sound is heavy. "It doesn't matter why," Bash spits at the ground.

My heart twists at his words, and I shake my head. Tears sting at my eyes. "No," I say firmly, stepping closer until I'm kneeling in front of him. "I won't accept that answer. You saw something the others didn't. What was it?" I sink down to the cold ground with him.

Bash opens and closes his eyes slowly. He stares at my hand that rests on my knee until finally, he reaches out. His fingers brush against mine. The touch sends a shiver through me. Then he looks up at me too quickly, surprised even. He didn't think I was real. Just how much torture is he enduring? How many demons are in his head?

He notices me staring. "You came here to say goodbye. Do it," he murmurs, his eyes searching mine. "Then," he takes a painful-looking breath, "I never want to see you again," he says with so much sincerity that it hurts. Bash pulls his hand away from mine and averts his eyes.

My face falls flat even though I don't believe he means what he says. "I didn't come here to say goodbye." I position myself in front of Bash, making it so he has to look me in the eye. Still, he does everything he can to avoid me. I am so tired of being ignored.

Bash lets out a low laugh that makes the hairs on the back of my neck stand on end. "Don't make this harder than it needs to be, Emerson."

"It's easy, actually. Not *hard* at all to love you," I tell him, and it's true. It's been easy since day one. Since he held a glowing knife above my body and marked me for life. It wasn't just a scar left by Sebastian Stone that day. It was something deeper than skin. It's all-consuming. Not in the way that The Ark has consumed Bash, but it has taken over my every thought, my dreams, the way I live.

Bash's head hits the wall beside him with a soft thud. I curl into him, placing my hand on his chest, over the tattooed heart that I know is there but cannot see. He doesn't move, telling me he has more control than I thought. I'll take whatever I can get. My head falls onto his shoulder.

"The future. That's what I saw," he admits. Inside the Ark of the Covenant—the thing Michael, Liam, and Riley must not have been able to see. Although, I know they saw something because Liam acted strange when I first saw him here in Navar. Like I was a ghost. Riley's reaction was almost the same. If I hadn't been so angry, I would have noticed how he retreated when I neared him. They have all been affected in some way.

"How do you know it's real?" I ask Bash.

"I don't," he answers plainly. "But if it is, I will do everything I can to make sure it never ends up that way."

I clear my throat. "What way?" I ask as I pull back to look at him.

"You don't want to know. I can keep it. It's not easy to control, but I can keep it away from you long enough. I can see a new future now. Through its eyes, I can see *you,* a happy life with your sister and Bronze by your side." Bash says, his words are void of emotion. He says it like it's fact. Plain and simple.

My breath catches as a tear falls down my cheek. "How could I possibly be happy if you are not there?" I ask him.

Bash peers down at me. We are so close I can feel his breath pushing the hair from my face. All I would have to do is tip my chin slightly, and our lips would meet. My heart speeds up at the thought.

Instead, he pushes himself away, forcing me away from him. The tears come freely now as anger takes over. I am mad at *myself*. For waiting so long. For not telling him how I felt. Out loud. When it was just Bash behind those eyes and not whatever occupies the space with him currently.

I stand, brushing off my knees. "You never want to see me again?" I ask, but I do not expect an answer or even give him a chance to. "I curse you." I spit at Bash. "I curse you to be haunted by my face. I curse you with the knowledge of my love for you. You will never find peace, Bash. Not in this life or the next." I take in a heavy breath for what I am going to say next. "The Ark might consume you, but I saw it first. *I* have laid claim on your soul."

# CHAPTER 48

There will be no sleep tonight. No dreams of Bash. Not when we are leaving tomorrow without him. As Jez guides me back to the room, up the countless stairs, I'm reminded of our apartment—the many steps it took to reach our door. It's the only thing that feels right in this moment. While everything else is falling apart, the piece of me that was missing is finally back together again. Now, I will have to deal with another missing piece in the shape of Bash.

Jez and my time apart feels like so long ago now, even though it's only been a few days since we have reunited. It's as if we could be separated by oceans, by entire worlds, and still somehow find our way back to each other. Perhaps the same can be said about Bash and me one day when we find a way to get him out of this.

"Jez?" I ask as we near my door, my voice trembling. Suddenly, I feel like a child again, retreating into that small, vulnerable part of me. But Jez's eyes meet mine with that familiar, understanding gaze, already knowing the words I haven't spoken yet.

"There are things you once knew nothing about," she says, her voice is soft. She gently tucks a loose blonde strand behind my ear. It stubbornly falls back into my face. "And there are things you still do not know," she continues, her voice barely above a whisper. "If there is a way out of this,

Riley will find it." She says it with such conviction I want to believe her. I truly do. But right now, everything feels so irreparably broken, like a teacup shattered into a million pieces—unfixable.

I hug my sister tighter than I ever have before. It's how I should have been embracing her all along. If I've learned anything, it's that love shouldn't be held back. You should give it freely, to those who matter most, before it's too late.

"Come with us to Canaan," I whisper, my voice pleading, my heart aching.

Her expression softens, like a mother's often does. "As if I would ever let you out of my sight again," she attempts to joke, but the smile doesn't quite reach her eyes. There's a sadness there. A feeling I am sure we will both carry for a long time.

When the door closes behind me, I smell him before I see him. How could I forget the smell I so often would find on my bed sheets? Riley is sprawled lazily on the bed, his eyes fixed on the ceiling, his thoughts clearly a thousand miles away. I take him in, his long hair and muscled shoulders, his large chest rising and falling. A sound I have found comfort in a thousand times before. "Emerson," he says to the air above him, using my full name—a sign this will be a serious conversation.

"Riley," I respond flatly so he does not hear the fear. He adjusts his hands under his head, and then, as if on cue, his gaze shifts to me. A cloud must pass in front of the moon, because the room darkens. I take a few steps to reach the lamp, pulling on its brass string. The bed creaks under

Riley's weight as he moves so suddenly I barely have time to react before his hand is around my wrist. "What if I told you I saw it too?" His voice is low, almost a whisper.

I pull my arm from his grip, a shiver runs down my spine. There's something strangely eerie about Riley, with the light casting shadows beneath his chin, giving him a menacing look. I always thought the Bronze boys were like angels—not the kind with white wings, but something divine all the same. Their hair too perfect, their faces too chiseled, too flawless to be of this world. "Saw what?" I ask, soothing my wrist with my other hand.

"The future," he replies, his words have a bitter twist to them. He spoke to Bash.

Whatever this is, it's more than just the pain we all feel for leaving Bash behind. It's deeper—jealousy, rage, and a type of understanding I'll never fully grasp because I don't know the true ways in which the Ark has scarred Riley.

I'm not in the mood for this. "And?" I prompt, knowing there's more. There's always more Riley never tells me.

"And I have played it over and over in my head. No matter what choice I make, it always ends the same," he tells me.

"I know," I say softly. "Bash told me." I tell him. Riley stares down at me. I can almost feel the sadness, anger, and guilt radiating off of him.

He's near a breaking point. The same air surrounds him as it did on the day Briggs came into the pawnshop and told me of my fate. The same air as the night he crawled into my bed with a faraway look on his face after the death of his father. The life *he* took.

"You love him," Riley says, his voice breaking. Bash once told me those same words about the man standing in front of me—Riley Curtis Bronze—the man I thought I would marry. Now...

Realization hits. Hard.

The truth crashes over me like a wave, pulling me under. I can see it in Riley's eyes—he knew before I did. He saw what I was too afraid to admit.

Bash. The man who had quietly, persistently become my everything.

Riley's words cut through my thoughts like a knife. "In my future, you look just like you do now. Scared."

I shake my head, struggling to find the right words. "I—I didn't mean to—"

Riley laughs, a genuine laugh that catches me off guard. I blink up at him once, twice. "You do, too," I say. Déjà vu. The same conversation, only with a different man.

Riley's smile fades, and he swallows hard. He only nods his head as if coming to terms with a reality neither of us wants to face.

Riley's family was nothing short of evil. He found his own family—in Bash, then in Liam and Michael. His brothers by choice. Riley gives everyone a choice. Just like he's doing right now for me. The way he has always done, but this choice feels heavier.

A tightness starts in my throat and ends in tears. Riley steps forward and pushes his forehead to mine while holding the sides of my face with his large hands. "Let me tell you something good, Emerson Knight." He begins. "There wasn't a day I did not love you. There wasn't a time I didn't close my eyes without seeing your face. I have loved you for a very long time." He breathes in. I close my eyes for what he is about to say next. "If the same is true for you. If Bash occupies the space behind your eyes, then *that* is good."

Daniel's chest rises and falls in slow even breaths. Finally, he is recovering, and he no longer has that pained look on his face as he sleeps. I gently take his hand, my fingers trembling as I begin the prayer I should have finished during my first visit. It's selfish because he is the one who is injured, but I am the one who needs comfort. Suddenly, his fingers curl tightly around mine. He's awake. My relief only lasts a few seconds before I remember the terrible news I have to deliver.

"Your hair," he murmurs, blinking up at me with a weak smile. Daniel wears a fake look of disgust.

Normally, I would have smiled at his attempt at humor—he rarely makes jokes—but it feels out of place now. My brows knit together in frustration. He notices, and his features turn into confusion. "What is it?" He asks, his voice broken. He inhales sharply, bracing himself, as if he already knows what's coming.

I force a gentle smile onto my face. "We leave for Canaan tomorrow," I tell him, deciding to start with the good news. "Michael—" I begin, but Daniel interrupts.

"Is the Duke of Canaan."

I stare at him, stunned. "How did you know?"

"I knew his father's name. I put two and two together a long time ago," he replies, his voice raspy and weak. Despite the dryness in his throat, he pushes through, his words slurring slightly. His face is still bruised, and there are stitches on his chin, but the swelling has reduced, and color has returned to his cheeks. "So Riley delivered the Ark?" He shakes his head, trying to make sense of it all. "I thought for sure they—" His voice trails off as he looks down at our clasped hands. I'm holding on so tightly that my nails have left tiny crescent marks on his skin.

"Tell me what happened," he urges softly. His patience is never-ending.

I close my eyes and press my lips together, trying to keep my composure. Tears sting at my eyes, but I know they won't fall. I'm too drained, too hollow to cry anymore.

So, I tell Daniel everything. Every detail, every horror, every heartbreak as I watch the understanding dawn in his eyes. The room feels smaller with every word. Daniel listens, his hand never letting go of mine.

# Chapter 49

The room is eerily silent, the kind of silence that feels alive. I can't see them, but I can feel them, crawling just beneath the surface, waiting for me to slip. My breath catches in my throat as I strain to hear their directions, but there is nothing—only the silence and the pounding of my heart.

I force myself further into the darkness. Every movement is a struggle against the invisible chains that hold me down. The air is thick, heavy with the stench of decay. I gag, the smell so overwhelming I can taste it, rancid and bitter. I know they're close. They always are. This time, I will not hide.

My eyes scan the room, searching for any sign of life. Shadows flicker in the corners, twisting and writhing like they have a life of their own. My pulse quickens as I realize they're watching me, waiting for the right moment to strike. Just as I want them to. I clench my fists, trying to steady my trembling hands. I know what I have to do next.

"Kill for her, live for her," I tell Bash as the guards carry him from the room.

# CHAPTER 50

Bash

Her eyes are bright and unblinking. Another dream. I hate this dream, the one she cursed me with. Her hair is chopped to her shoulders like it was that day. That's how I know it's not real. It's an exact replica of the last time I saw her. Emerson.

She tilts her head to the side, "What are you doing here?" She asks me. Her chest is moving up and down like she is having a hard time getting enough air. This is new. I have never been able to hear her voice. It's so clear and clean. Low and soft, the way it always is when she speaks. The words I often have a hard time letting her finish because I wish to take her mouth as my own. No words, only the deep moan she lets out when she has nowhere for words to go.

Emerson really *has* cursed me because no matter how many times I blink, no matter how many steps I take in her direction, she is still there. I hate that she is here. I hate her. Or at least that is what I have been trying to convince myself.

I look down at my hands, then past them to my chest, and finally to my feet. The weight of this dream is heavy—so heavy I collapse onto the ground, landing with a crack to my knees. Pain radiates up to my jaw, which clenches over and over again.

Then, Emerson is there.

I will take advantage of this dream. The one where I can feel her warmth, inhale her intoxicating scent. "I hate you." I tell her as I press my face into her neck, tasting her. How did I forget what she tasted like? It's like cream in your coffee, like honey in your milk.

My fingers trace the familiar line of her spine, and I can feel her shiver beneath my touch. Her breath catches as I wrap my hands around her back. Her nails press into my flesh everywhere she touches as if she's afraid I'll disappear if she doesn't hold on tight. I know the feeling well.

The warmth of her body seeps into mine, a sensation so real it almost hurts. My mouth trails up from her neck to the soft spot just beneath her ear, and I taste her again, a sweetness that makes my head spin.

"Hate me," she whispers, her voice trembling. Is she crying? Why would my mind present this Emerson to me? The Ark makes even the good dreams bad.

I don't answer. She wouldn't be able to hear me anyway. Not the *real* Emerson. The one I want to hear me.

Instead, I pull her closer until the space between us is gone. The way it should be, with the feel of her body against mine. I kiss her then so I never forget this taste again. Her lips are soft. There is that sound that starts in her chest and makes its way out slowly. That sound might echo in my head until the day I die. For a moment, I forget this is a dream. I forget none of this is real.

My heart hammers in my chest as her lips part beneath mine. Just the way I wanted them to.

Her eyes search mine the way they often do. Only this time, she finds what she is looking for. It took me too long to realize what she was doing all this time. When her blue eyes would pierce through the flesh and straight to the deepest part of me, this is what she meant when she spit her curse at me.

"Come back to me." She tells me. I realize I have not moved in a long time, my body had gone still at the discovery.

My hand moves to her cheek, and I brush my thumb across her skin. "I can't. When I open my eyes, you will not be here." It hurts me to say, even though I have said it to a million different Emersons in a million different ways in the same kind of dream. It must hurt her as well because she shakes her head in frustration.

"Don't I look real?" Emerson asks me with that fucking look on her face that gets me thinking about the first time I saw her. With snow falling around her, her lips were almost blue from the cold. I remember thinking I would drown in those eyes if I looked into them for too long.

My cock twitches at the memory. "Painfully real, Sweetheart." I push my hand into her white, short hair. I will miss the dark-haired beauty that appeared before me like a gift. A broken, *bleeding,* near-death gift.

Desperately, I lift her shirt over her head in search of the mark that will forever bind us together. Our bodies move together, igniting something deep within me, something I thought had died long ago. Then, I gently run a finger down that scar in the shape of my knife. Lower, and lower.

I force myself to stay. Sometimes, I wake up before I can get to the part where I am buried inside her. This time, I will not let that happen.

How she ended up beneath me is a mystery. Dreams are like that. They cut to the important parts. I pull her leg up with force, letting it rest in the crook of my elbow until her legs are sufficiently spread. Dream Emerson is much more malleable. I lick the spot between her breasts. The sound she makes is music to my ears.

Emerson's fingers travel from my hair to my middle and finally farther to undress me from the waist down. It's desperate. I almost laugh, who would want someone like me? Someone who is mostly darkness at this point. I have this strange feeling like this is the last time I will ever squeeze anything good from myself. It is a final goodbye to my life. The one I could have had with Emerson.

I pull her into me, lifting her hips up high. Her arms stretch over her head, giving me a full look at everything I have ever wanted to see. Her perfection. Only made more beautiful by the scar. My hands work on their own, touching all the pieces of her I will never be able to touch again. Starting with her breast before I plunge my fingers into her center.

When they come away wet, I stroke myself. It's everything I remember and more. I told her I would memorize her, little did I know my memory was so good.

With the grip I have around her waist, I pull her down onto my cock, it's easy, it's always been easy with Emerson. "Goodbye, Emerson," I tell her one last time because I can feel myself becoming dark again, becoming The Ark. It doesn't stop me from plunging into her over and over. I never let her look away or close her eyes. I hold her face in my hand, her cheeks pushed together from the pressure. "Say it." I urge her. "Say goodbye." I slam into her.

Her brows push together, and it's the most beautiful sight I have ever seen. She says nothing at all because her legs shake, and her breath quickens. There is a throbbing between my legs as she grips me tighter and tighter until a half-moan, half-cry leaves her body. My hand is around her neck. I push slightly upwards until her body is stretched as far as it can go. Bracing myself with the other hand, I lift away from her body so

I can see us. *Us.* The in and out, the puddle that leaks from Emerson as she comes again.

I take no precaution, releasing into her with harsh thrusts of my hips. Until finally, I collapse. Damn, this curse. It's too much. It's my entire soul, spilling into another person. How can that be? I thought I was lost. I thought I was too far gone.

Emerson watches as I fall beside her. My hand instinctively goes to her stomach. Her skin is as soft as silk. Her eyes latch onto mine. Then, as if something surprises her, her body jolts. Her lashes flutter as she blinks repeatedly. I am too tired to ask her what she sees. Maybe I don't want to hear the answer. It can only be the darkness that surrounds me that makes her eyes latch onto me, the demons that peel off my skin and into the space around me. I scare her. It's the only explanation.

My eyes close. As I start to drift, the dream begins to unravel, and I feel a familiar panic rising in my chest. I don't want to let her go—not again. My arms tighten around her, pulling her closer as if I can somehow keep her with me if I just hold on tight enough. That would not be fair. To keep her in this torment that is The Ark.

Emerson pulls back slightly, her hand coming up to cup my cheek. I force my eyes to remain open, no matter how heavy they feel. She smiles at me, a soft, bittersweet smile that makes my chest ache. "Wake up," she whispers.

"No," I say, my voice hoarse with emotion. "Not yet. Please, not yet."

More tears fall from her eyes. "I'll be here when you wake," she promises, her voice a soft murmur against my skin as she lays her head near me. *Liar,* I want to scream.

I want to believe her, I want to hold on to the hope that this time, when I wake, she won't be gone. But as the world around us begins to fade, as the dream slips away, I know the truth.

This was just a dream.

And when I wake, she won't be there.

# CHAPTER 51

"What are you doing here?" I ask. My head tilts to the side like a curious cat. I can't make it make sense. Bash is *here*. In the tiny room, leaving hardly any space between us. My heart thumps wildly. I try to steady it by taking in as much air as I can, but it doesn't help. This can't be real. I must be dreaming.

Bash takes a few clumsy steps in my direction, his feet dragging on the ground like the world is heavy upon his shoulders. There is a struggle in his mind. I can see it in the way his gaze flicks away from me, as if he's fighting the urge to run.

His response isn't in words, but in the way he drops his head, staring at the ground as if it holds the answers. Then, almost as if something snaps inside him, he sinks to his knees, his body folding in on itself. I can't tear my eyes away from the sight of him breaking in front of me. It's a raw, painful thing to witness.

I had almost convinced myself I truly *was* dreaming, but before Bash loses his balance completely, headed for the hard floor, I sink to the ground to hold him up, his weight on me completely.

He studies my face for far too long, trying to convince himself of something.

Before I can say anything, his hands reach out, pulling me into him with a force that almost knocks the breath from my lungs. His face buries in the crook of my neck, and I feel his lips against my skin. My eyes roll to the back of my head at the touch. "I hate you," he tells me with so much need in his voice that I know this has *nothing* to do with hate. Not at all. But if hate is what he needs to feel for me, I will allow it. I will let him hate me until the day he dies.

I don't flinch. Instead, I let my hands fall to his shoulders, gripping him just as tightly as he holds me. It doesn't matter what he says—his body betrays him. He presses closer. I can feel the warmth of him, the way his breath hitches as his lips move against my neck, tasting me like he's been starved for years.

He shifts, his fingers tracing down the line of my spine, and I can't stop the shiver that runs through me. It's like every nerve in my body is on high alert. His flesh scrapes up against mine as he licks my ear. "Hate me," I whisper. I say it with the same desperation.

I can't help the way my breath catches when his hands move lower, gripping my waist. For a moment, just like it happened before in the soft room with nothing to harm himself, I feel anger. Anger at myself because now I know for sure that my confession came too late. So late that he now is trying to convince himself he hates me. Hates himself.

But then he's kissing me, and all that anger melts away, replaced by something deeper, something more primal. It's not gentle, not the way it was at the lake. It's rough, hungry, as if he's trying to devour me, to make up for all the time we've lost. I don't resist. I can't. My body responds to him instinctively. I want to be closer, to feel him everywhere, to drown in this moment and forget everything else.

I can feel the desperation in his touch, the way he lifts me up before positioning me below him. His eyes are glazed over, eyes I can hardly see in the dark of the room. I only get glances at his body, the birds and roses that fill his arms as he moves in front of the sliver of light let in through the small window. I don't fight it, don't resist the pull of him.

His name slips from my lips, but it is muffled by his mouth, now on mine in a deep kiss.

When he pulls away, his eyes are caught in that white light from the moon that makes everything greyscale. It doesn't matter because the eyes that are there are just going to be that black color that makes Bash look like one of the demons portrayed on his back. Still, I do my search, looking past flesh and blood.

"Come back to me," I tell him when he doesn't move for too long.

He seems to think of what to say next as he brushes his thumb across my cheek. "I can't. When I open my eyes you will not be there," he says like the broken man he is.

This confuses me. I shake my head at him. I swallow the lump in my throat. "Don't I look real?" I ask with a cry. *Please, see me. I am real.*

He gets a frustrated look on his face as his jaw tightens. Then, "Painfully real, Sweetheart," he says, and I swear my heart stops at the name.

His hands move to the hem of my shirt. I don't stop him as he pulls it over my head. I know what he's looking for, and I see the flicker of recognition in his eyes when he finds it—the scar is a reminder of the past. The safe house. His mission to save a girl. He did save her, in a different way but saved all the same. His fingers trace it slowly. I stop trying to make sense of why he is here or how. All I know is I need him, need to feel him, to forget the world outside of this room.

I can feel his grip tightening on my waist, his fingers digging into my skin. I arch into him.

Bash pulls me down onto him, filling me perfectly. "Goodbye, Emerson," he says. I want to tell him this is not goodbye, but his hand moves to my face, gripping my cheeks, forcing me to look at him, to see him. "Say it," he growls, his voice rough, raw. "Say goodbye."

But I can't. I won't. My body trembles, and I can feel the tears welling up, but I refuse to let them fall. I won't give him the satisfaction. Instead, I close my eyes, letting the sensation of him filling me overwhelm everything else. It's too much, too intense, and I feel the pressure building, the tension coiling tighter and tighter until it snaps.

My body convulses around him, a moan slipping from my lips as I fall over the edge.

Then again as he dives deeper.

Until he finally releases inside me. Feeling his seed inside makes me convulse with pleasure.

Then, I watch as he collapses beside me. His hand instinctively finds its way to my stomach, resting there as if trying to hold on to this moment for just a little longer.

When I let my head fall to the side, we have made our way to the place where the light hits the wooden floor. Bash's face is illuminated completely.

There. It's Bash, the real Bash. Emerald-green eyes look back at me.

I blink to make sure I am really seeing it. His eyes close like a child who is trying his hardest to stay awake. But he is in his head, a dream. He needs to know the truth—that he is here, with me.

"Wake up," I whisper, the words escaping before I can stop them.

He shakes his head, his voice filled with an emotion I can't quite place. "No," he says, his grip tightening on my waist. "Not yet. Please, not yet."

The tears I've been holding back finally spill over, trailing down my cheeks as I look at him, really look at him. "I'll be here when you wake."

His eyes close all the way this time.

# EPILOGUE

Jez sits in the kitchen, a cup of coffee cradled in her hands, her legs crossed. Her hair is wrapped in the usual rags that create those effortless waves. She looks calm, but there is a heaviness in her eyes. We survived, but the cost had been high. Too high.

I close my eyes for a moment, and Riley's face comes to mind, as clear as if he were standing right in front of me. His deep brown eyes, with that distinctive fleck of gold in the right iris, a memory I can't seem to shake. His absence is an ache in my heart. Something I carry with me everywhere, in every breath.

Canaan has become home. It's where Michael leads. The title suits him well, though I know it's a responsibility he never asked for. He was born to lead, whether he wanted to or not.

It's where Liam gets to help rebuild, where he has his own space to work unless Emerson or Philip find him to ask endless questions.

It's where Jez is raising her children, who are effortlessly funny and too smart for their own good. Jez has found purpose in helping women who have been broken, the way she once was. She searches for them—women who need healing—and guides them back to a place where they can rebuild their lives. The women from Navar have returned to their families in Canaan.

Where Esther and Ada get into trouble.

It's where Bash and I find little moments to be truly happy, even after everything.

There is a bond between us all now. Loss and shared grief. We don't talk about it much, but it's there, a silent understanding that we've all been through something we'll never fully recover from.

We all know one thing for sure: Riley's name won't be forgotten. We won't let it be. He's part of this new world we're building, and his legacy will live on in everything we do.

Navar told us that Riley's body would remain intact, but his mind... his mind will slowly fade away. Just like Bash's was about to. Bash described it as standing on the edge of a cliff, looking down into an endless void. He knew that if he let himself fall, there would be no coming back. The thought of that still haunts me.

I take a sip of my coffee, trying to focus on the present. Before I know it, Bash is there, gently taking the cup from my hands. I hadn't even heard him come into the kitchen. I look up at him, then over at Jez.

The three of us. A soul seer, a soul seeker, and a soul for a soul.

# Acknowledgements

I am so glad you are *here*, at the end of my book. To anyone who has ever given me a positive word, a bit of encouragement, or even a smile along the way, you are all awesome.

A special thanks to my mom and sister for letting me talk and talk... and *talk* about this damn book. I love you guys.

To every woman who has ever doubted herself. Your words are NOT too much. Your thoughts ARE important. And yes, as long as you get your words out, even if they are beneath tears or atop of screaming, they are VALID as fuck.

# ABOUT THE AUTHOR

C.K. Hart is an author from a small town in Wyoming, but she has big dreams.

Her first book, Left by Light, was released in May 2024. From then on, she knew she wanted to become an accomplished author, and now, she is on her way.

There has always been a special place in her heart for the written word. Poetry, journaling, and now in her books. If she doesn't have a book in her hand, it is because she is hiking, cooking, painting, or petting one of her cats.

She believes there is so much more of her imagination to share with all of you, and she hopes to make that happen soon.

If I read a book and it makes my whole body so cold no fire can ever warm me, I know that is poetry. -Emily Dickenson

www.ingramcontent.com/pod-product-compliance
Lightning Source LLC
Chambersburg PA
CBHW020927260626
47169CB00006B/1608